Praise for BRENDA NOVAK's
Stillwater stories

"In the first of a compelling new series set in the small town of Stillwater, Mississippi, Novak expertly mixes her usual superior characterization with a chilling sense of evil as she pairs up a complicated heroine with a dark past with a caring, honorable man who gives her hope for the future."
—*Booklist* on *Dead Silence*

"I was held spellbound by Ms. Novak's second book in her outstanding Stillwater trilogy. This series gets better with every book. [Her] characters are extraordinary in depth and feeling. I really fell in love with Clay Montgomery. This book is a page-turner bar none!"
—*Reader to Reader Reviews* on *Dead Giveaway*

"Novak's ability to make this mystery cunning and deceptive is amazing, considering readers already know the outcome…. *Dead Giveaway* is a turbulent and brilliant romantic suspense story that is sure to bring on a case of the chills. I cannot wait to see what is revealed in the final story of this trilogy."
—*Romance Junkies.com*

"Brenda Novak has an uncanny ability to give life to her characters, even minor ones. And her work is singularly devoid of clichés….Novak also creates dynamic characters with strong emotional ties, but the threads that hold families together are sometimes tried to the breaking point. If anyone comes close to perfection, it's Clay, who stands like a wall around those he loves. This series is a must read; just be prepared for an emotional ride."
—*Romance Reviews Today* on *Dead Giveaway*

"Novak has a keen gift for combining
_____ for creating real,
_____ sterious heroes….
_____ pelling read."
_____ vs

BRENDA NOVAK

DEAD
RIGHT

MIRA®

MIRA®

ISBN-13: 978-0-7783-2439-3
ISBN-10:   0-7783-2439-7

DEAD RIGHT

www.MIRABooks.com

Printed in U.S.A.

For Joy, who left this life far too soon.
Not a day goes by that I don't think of you—
and miss you.

Dear Reader,

If you've read *Dead Silence* and/or *Dead Giveaway*, you've already met Madeline Montgomery. You know she loves the man who was her father, the man who went missing twenty years ago, and that she's absolutely determined to discover what happened to him. You also know that if she manages to find out, it'll make for a very unpleasant surprise (maybe a few surprises for you, too!). Her own family's keeping the truth from her. They have good reason, of course. Their dark secret is something she's better off not knowing. But she can't settle for that. She wants to know, and love and denial can blind her for only so long. Especially when private investigator Hunter Solozano comes to town...

As the last book in the Dead trilogy, *Dead Right* was a difficult story to write. Mostly because "the end" means I have to say goodbye to characters I've been working with for over a year—some of my favorite characters, in fact. But the sadness won't last. I'm already starting a new series that revolves around a victims-assistance charity run by three friends who have very compelling reasons to be involved in such work. The first title will be out next summer (2008).

Visit my Web site at www.brendanovak.com to view video trailers for my various novels, read excerpts and reviews, see what's coming next, enter my contests, monthly draws, etc. Also, while you're there, check out my Online Auction to Benefit Diabetes Research (my son suffers from this disease). I'd love to have you get involved so just send me an e-mail to let me know how you'd like to participate (Brenda@brendanovak.com). Together we'll do all we can.

I love to hear from readers. If you don't have Internet service, please feel free to write me at P.O. Box 3781, Citrus Heights, CA 95611.

Here's hoping you enjoy *Dead Right!*

Brenda Novak

"The first condition of human goodness is something to love; the second something to reverence."
—George Eliot (Mary Ann Evans, English novelist, 1819–1880)

1

Was his body inside?

Hunched against the freezing January rain, Madeline Barker felt her fingernails cut into her palms. Standing with her stepbrother, stepsister and stepmother, she watched the police and several volunteers attempt to pull her father's car out of the abandoned water-filled quarry. Her head pounded from lack of sleep, and her chest was so tight she almost couldn't breathe, yet she stood perfectly still…waiting. After almost twenty years, she might finally have some answers about her father's disappearance.

Toby Pontiff, Stillwater, Mississippi's, police chief, knelt at the lip of the yawning hole. "Careful, careful there, Rex," he called over the high-pitched whine of the winch attached to a massive tow truck.

Joe Vincelli and his brother, Roger, Madeline's first cousins, hovered on the other side of the quarry, their faces betraying their anticipation. They spoke animatedly to each other, but Madeline couldn't hear them above the noise. She was fairly sure she didn't want to. What they had to say would only upset her. They'd long blamed her father's disappearance on certain members of her stepfamily—Irene, Clay and Grace—

who were gathered around her now. Unfortunately, the fact that the Cadillac had been found in the quarry five miles outside of town would only convince them they'd been right all along. It'd certainly prove that her father hadn't driven off into the sunset.

The black seal-like heads of two divers who'd gone down a few minutes earlier popped up and, with a gasp, Madeline realized she could see the front grille of her dad's car through the murky water. With a sudden rush of tears, she instinctively moved closer to Clay, who remained as dark and silent as the surrounding rocks.

The car didn't break the surface. Rex hit a button that stopped the clamoring winch, halting its progress, and the silence made Madeline's ears ring.

Her stepmother, a short buxom woman with hair like Loretta Lynn's, whimpered at the sight of the barely visible car. Grace shifted to try and comfort her, but Clay didn't move. Madeline looked up at him, wondering what was going on behind his intense blue eyes.

As usual, it was difficult to tell. His expression mirrored the gray, overcast sky. Maybe he wasn't thinking. Maybe, like her, he was simply surviving the cataclysm of emotions.

It'll be over soon. No matter what happens, knowing is better than not knowing. She hoped…

"This is making me nervous," Rex complained. Short and wiry with the tattoo of a woman partly visible at his neck, he frowned as he joined Chief Pontiff. "What if we clip the rocks? The car could get hung up."

"It's not gonna get hung up," a police officer by the name of Radcliffe said.

The tow-truck driver ignored the unsolicited input, keeping his focus on the man in charge. "I don't think this is gonna work," he insisted. "I say we bring a crane in here, Toby, before someone gets hurt or we ruin my truck."

Toby, a slight blond man with a neatly trimmed mustache, had become Chief Pontiff six months earlier and was a friend of Madeline's. They'd grown up together; she'd been close to his future wife all through high school. He shot Madeline a sympathetic glance then, lowering his voice, he turned away from her.

Still, she could make out his words. "That'll take another few days. Look at that group over there. See the woman in the middle? The one who's white as a ghost? Her mother killed herself when she was ten years old. Her father went missing when she was sixteen. And she's been standing here since dawn, getting soaked. I'm not going to send her home until I get her father's car out of this damn quarry. We need to see if his remains are inside. It's already taken me a week to arrange it."

"If she's waited that long, what's another two or three days?" Rex asked.

"It's another two or three days!" Toby nearly shouted. "And she's not the only one with an interest in what's happening here, as you can tell."

Obviously, he was talking about the Vincellis, who'd been impatient with police for being unable to solve the disappearance of their beloved uncle. No doubt Pontiff didn't want them going over his head to the mayor again, as they'd done with the previous chief.

"My most prominent citizens are sitting on pins and needles," Toby said, his voice growing calmer. "I'm going to catch more grief than you can imagine if I don't put an end to it. Soon."

The man called Rex scowled and shoved his hands

in the pockets of his heavy coat. Madeline had never met him before. A distant relation of Toby's, he'd been called in from a neighboring town when their local tow truck owner said his truck wasn't capable of getting the job done. "I'm sorry," Rex said. "But with all this water and silt, combined with the weight of the car, I don't wanna risk burning out the engine of my—"

"If we wanted to wait, we would've waited," Toby interrupted. "We wouldn't be standing out here in the cold, freezing our asses off. But we called you, and you said you could do it. So can we please get this damn thing out of the water? Your truck's powerful enough to to tow a semi, for cryin' out loud!"

Madeline flinched, her nerves too raw to cope with the anxiety and frustration swirling around her. It had been an emotional seven days. A week ago, a group of teenagers had come here to party; a girl had fallen in the water and been too drunk to climb out. She'd slipped under the surface before anyone could reach her and the resulting search for her body, which police located as darkness set in almost twenty-four hours later, had turned up the Cadillac missing since Lee Barker disappeared.

As the owner, editor and primary writer of *The Stillwater Independent,* Madeline had followed the tragedy of the girl's death since the first frantic call. But she'd never dreamed it would lead to this. Had her father's car been here, so close, all this time? Since she was sixteen? That was the question she'd been asking herself for seven interminable days, while the town dealt with the immediate tragedy of losing Rachel Simmons.

Rex spat on the ground. "Toby, the divers don't know

what the hell they're doin'. With the color of this water, they can hardly see down there, even with a light. I can't be sure we won't break a tow cable and send that car crashing right back to the bottom."

Clay spoke up for the first time. "The divers said they found the windows down, right?"

Toby and Rex turned to face him. "What does that have to do with anything?" Rex asked.

"If the windows were down, they were able to get the cables through. You'll be fine. Just pull it out."

Clay was respected for his physical power and mental acuity, but he'd also endured enough suspicion where her father was concerned to give him a pretty big stake in all of this. Madeline knew the chief of police had to be thinking of that as he considered the stubborn set of Clay's jaw. She could almost read Toby's thoughts: *Are you trying to help because you don't know what's in that car? Or are you trying to cover the fact that you do?*

Madeline wanted to scream, for the millionth time, that her stepbrother didn't have anything to do with whatever had happened to her father.

"Let me handle this, Clay," Toby said, but there was no real edge to his voice, and his hazel eyes returned to the water-filled quarry before his words could be taken as any sort of challenge. Even the chief of police was careful around Clay. At six feet four inches tall and two hundred and forty pounds of lean muscle, Clay looked formidable. But it was his manner that made folks uneasy. He was so self-contained, so emotionally aloof, some people had convinced themselves he was capable of murder.

"Rex," Chief Pontiff prodded. "Let's get this done."

Rex indulged in a particularly colorful string of expletives but stalked to his truck, and the winch started again, slowly pulling the car from the water.

Madeline caught her breath. *God, this is it.*

"Watch those divers," Rex called.

Chief Pontiff had already motioned them away. "Let the winch do the work, boys," he shouted. "Stay back."

The scrape of metal against rock made Madeline shudder. It was an awful sound—almost as awful as watching the dark, dirty water seep out of the car that had belonged to her parents when she was a child. Why was the Cadillac in the quarry? Who had driven it there? And—the question that had plagued her for twenty years—what had happened to her father? Would she finally know?

As the tow truck driver had predicted, the car got caught on a large rock. "I told you!" he yelled, cursing again. But before he could shut down the winch, the rusty rear axle broke and the Cadillac continued to emerge, groaning as it climbed out of its watery grave.

Madeline's nails cut more deeply into her palms. The familiarity of that vehicle threw her back to her childhood—as if someone had yanked her up by the shoulders and deposited her in the front seat. At age five or six, she used to sit beside her mother while Eliza drove around town, visiting members of her father's congregation, bringing food and consolation to the sick and needy.

Madeline had believed, back then, that her mother was an angel.

Squeezing her eyes shut, she pressed a hand to her forehead, trying to stave off the memories. She rarely allowed herself to think about Eliza. Her mother had been a gentle soul; she'd represented everything good to Madeline. But, as Madeline's father had pointed out so often after Eliza's suicide, she was also weak and fragile. He'd had little that was positive to say about his first wife, but Madeline had never blamed him. She hadn't been able to forgive Eliza, either.

Clay's arm went around her shoulders, and she turned into his coat. She wasn't sure she could watch what was coming next.

"It's okay, Maddy," he murmured.

She took what comfort she could from his warm strength. He was capable of surviving anything. Secretly, she wished she was as tough. She also wished Kirk was here with her. They'd dated for nearly five years, but she'd broken off the relationship a few weeks ago.

"That's it." Pontiff waved the divers out of the water as Rex towed the Cadillac onto stable ground.

This time when he stopped the winch, Rex shut off the truck's engine, too. Madeline felt Clay tense, so she forced herself to look and saw her cousins hurrying to the car.

Chief Pontiff sent her an anxious glance, adjusted the hat keeping the rain out of his face and intercepted them. "Give us some room," he said, barring them from getting too close.

Madeline was glad that Irene, Clay and Grace stayed put, or she would've been standing there alone. She didn't want to move any closer to that car. She had no idea what she might see and feared it would only fuel her nightmares. Every few weeks, she dreamed that her father was knocking on her front door in the middle of the night. He was always wearing a heavy coat that parted to reveal a skeleton.

Grace, a more refined, elegant version of Clay, took

her hand and Irene edged closer. Clay stepped in front, but he seemed even more reserved than usual. No doubt he was thinking of his new wife and stepdaughter and how this might affect them. Since marrying Allie, he was happy at last. But for how long? The police were quick to point a finger at him. Last summer they'd nearly put him on trial for her father's murder—without a body, without an eyewitness, without any forensic evidence at all. Unless there was something in the car that proved Clay *wasn't* involved, this could put him at risk again.

"Door's rusted shut," Pontiff said. "Get a crowbar."

Radcliffe, who was in his early twenties, returned to one of the police cars and produced the crowbar, which he carried to his chief.

As Pontiff began to pry open the door, the car complained loudly, ratcheting up the tension that made Madeline's muscles ache. Then her heart lurched as the metal gave way and water from inside came pouring out over everyone's shoes.

Pontiff didn't seem to notice. No one did. They were all busy staring at the gush of water as if they expected parts of her father to come floating out with it.

How could this be happening? she wondered. How could she have lost her mother *and* her father—in two separate incidents?

She didn't see anything that could be connected to a human being, so she inched closer, straining her eyes for the smallest bit of clothing or—she grimaced— bone. At least, if her father's remains were in the car, she'd know he hadn't meant to leave her. She'd never been able to accept that he'd walked out on her. As the town's beloved pastor, he was a God-fearing man, always ready to help out in an emergency, always a leader. He would never abandon his flock, his farm, his family.

Which meant someone must've killed him. But who?

As the water seeped over the ground to the lip of the quarry, mixing with the runoff from the rain, Madeline clenched her jaw. Nothing macabre. Yet.

They were opening the trunk. The Cadillac's keys had been left dangling in the ignition, but the locks were corroded so they were using the crowbar again.

Bile rose in Madeline's throat as the minutes stretched on. She tried to keep her mind busy. But what did one think about at a time like this? The teenage girl they'd buried on Wednesday? The miserable weather? The years she'd lived without her father?

Pontiff lifted something with one hand. "You recognize this?"

Belatedly, Madeline realized he was speaking to her and nodded. It was the Polaroid camera she'd seen her father use on various occasions. A chill crawled down her spine. Seeing his camera made him seem so close, but it didn't *tell* her anything.

"Is that all?" she asked around the lump in her throat.

The police chief pulled out some jumper cables, a couple of quarts of oil, a sopping blanket. Familiar items that could be found in any trunk.

There'll be something that'll finally reveal the truth. Madeline was praying so hard she almost couldn't believe it when she heard him say, "That's it."

"What?" she cried. "There's nothing that tells us where he went?"

Pontiff shrugged uncomfortably. "I'm afraid not."

She didn't move—felt absolutely rooted to the spot—as Clay wiped her tears with his thumb. "I'm sorry, Maddy."

Sorry didn't have any meaning. She'd been expecting so much more. It couldn't be over. If so, she was right back where she'd been before they discovered the car. Where she'd been all along—faced with this nagging mystery and the prospect that she might never know.

"There…" Her teeth chattered from the cold. "There h-has to be…something else here," she said. "You'll… look, won't you? You'll…let the car dry out and…and go over it inch by inch?"

Chief Pontiff nodded, but she could tell he wasn't optimistic.

"Will you let Allie help?" Her sister-in-law had been a cold case detective in Chicago. Surely, she'd uncover some kind of clue.

With a grudging glance at Joe and Roger, Pontiff scowled. "You know I can't do that."

"Don't let the…the Vincellis dictate how you handle this," Madeline said. "She's the most qualified… p-person around here."

"She's also married to the man who did it!" Joe shouted.

The cleft in Joe's chin was a little too deep to be attractive. Or maybe it was his close-set eyes that gave him a shifty air. He stood six feet tall and was almost as muscular as Clay, but Madeline had never found him good-looking. "Stop it," she murmured, but he talked right over her.

"Give me a break! Will you listen to yourself? Maddy, if you want to know what happened to your father, ask that man right there!"

He pointed at Clay, but wilted when Clay pinned him with a steely gaze. Not many men could stand up to Clay, and Joe was no exception. He shuffled back, muttering, "Tell 'em, Roger."

Joe's brother was even less handsome. His teeth were straighter, but he was thinner, a full three inches shorter, and had a severely receding hairline. Although he was the older brother, he tended to stay in Joe's shadow. "It's true," he said, but weakly, as if he didn't really want to incite Clay.

Chief Pontiff ignored them both. Madeline knew he was well aware of the suspicion and accusations of the past. He'd been on the force when Clay's future wife had returned to town and begun following up on the Barker case. He'd been around when Allie's father, the former chief of police, charged Clay with murder and put him in jail last summer. He'd also been around when they let Clay go because there wasn't, and never had been, any real evidence linking him to the crime.

"This car has been submerged for more than half our lives," Pontiff said, his attention on Madeline. "Look at it. Even the metal's begun to corrode. Much as I hate to say it, the Caddy might not tell us what we want to know. You need to prepare yourself, just in case."

"No!" She hugged herself to stop the shaking. "There could be a...a tooth, or a comb stuck way down between the seats. *Some* evidence, *some* lead." She watched those forensics shows on TV religiously, recorded them if she wasn't going to be home. She'd seen dozens of cases solved with the tiniest scrap of evidence.

"We'll check, like I said, but..." His words dwindled away.

"Oh, Maddy," Grace said softly.

Madeline didn't respond to her stepsister. She wanted to calm down, for her family's sake. They didn't need the added stress of her breaking down. They'd been through a lot, too. At least no one had blamed *her* for her father's disappearance. But she couldn't seem to restrain herself. Not this time. "Don't prepare an excuse before you even try," she said. "Find s-something. I want to know what happened. I *need* to know what happened." She grabbed Chief Pontiff's arm. *"Do your job!"*

Pontiff blinked in surprise, and Clay quickly pulled her into his arms. "Maddy, stop," he murmured against her hair.

If anyone else had asked her, she wouldn't have—*couldn't* have—gained control of her wayward emotions. But regardless of the turmoil inside her, she had too much respect for Clay to ignore his wishes or embarrass him further. Burying her face in his chest, she started to cry as she hadn't cried since she was a child, with big wracking sobs that shook her whole body.

He hugged her close. "It's okay," he murmured. "It's okay."

"You're hugging the man who killed him," Joe whispered.

"Shut up, Joe," she snapped. Clay had been the one to keep their family safe through the dark years after her father was gone. At times, he'd been the only thing standing between them and destitution.

"I'm sorry," she told Clay. She didn't want to draw attention to him. She knew he simply wanted to go on with his life and forget. She wished *she* could forget. But it was impossible. She'd tried.

"You have nothing to be sorry about," he said.

With a sniff, she pulled away and dashed a hand across her cheeks. "I'm going home."

"I'll call you if we find anything," Pontiff said.

Joe and his brother were still there, but one look from Clay kept them shuffling around the perimeter of the group like jackals attracted to a carcass. They obviously wanted to come closer, to say more, but were afraid to risk the consequences.

Madeline turned to her car. The police always said they'd keep digging, keep asking questions, go back through the files, whatever. But they never found anything solid. They didn't really care about the truth. They just wanted to pin it on the Montgomerys to satisfy the Vincellis, who held political power in this town. Maybe Pontiff was a friend of sorts, but he was subject to the same political pressures as his predecessors and would probably follow in their footsteps. Nothing would change.

But Madeline couldn't accept "nothing" any longer. She had to take more aggressive action, do something that would finally provide answers.

She was pretty sure what that something had to be. But her stepfamily wouldn't like it. And there was no guarantee it'd work.

2

Madeline longed to call Kirk. She hadn't talked to him since they'd broken up. But allowing herself to do what was comfortable and convenient would only land her in the same old rut. She and Kirk had no real hope of long-term happiness together. She wanted children; he was adamantly opposed to them. He wanted to leave Stillwater, travel the world; she wanted to stay close to her family and maintain her home and business. It was better to let go and move on, better for both of them.

Maybe she was doing the right thing. But life was damn lonely in the meantime. Especially since she hadn't gone to her office today. Although she had no staff, just three people who earned a little extra money delivering papers for her once a week, the small office she leased for *The Stillwater Independent* was located on Main Street and a lot of people dropped in on her. She usually enjoyed the company—a journalist had to stay connected to the community. Today, however, she hadn't wanted to face the questions, the sympathy, the reaction that recovering the Cadillac would evoke.

Feeling guilty for hiding out, she scooped up her cat and rubbed her chin on Sophie's fur. If it hadn't been her own father who'd gone missing, she would already have produced an article on the incident at the quarry, slapped it on the front page and given it a huge headline: Reverend's Car Found. But she was too close to the story, and after the flurry of activity following the drowning of Rachel Simmons—the search, the funeral, the outpouring of sympathy for the family—she was emotionally exhausted.

She couldn't write about what she'd been through this morning. Not yet. She hadn't done much of anything today except scour the Internet for someone who might be able to help her, and pace.

Putting Sophie down, she took her mother's old quilt from the couch where she'd been curled up a few minutes earlier, wrapped it around her shoulders and crossed to the window. It was getting late. And it was still raining.

God, she was tired of the constant drizzle, tired of the cold. The steady drumming against the roof made her feel hollow. And everything looked soggy and beaten down and smelled of mold.

She glanced at her car keys, lying on the antique secretary by the door. Maybe she should go out, visit her family. But the soft chime of the clock in the hall told her it was far too late. She didn't want to go to the farm where Clay and Allie lived, anyway. She'd grown up there and wouldn't be able to return without thinking of her father.

Images of her parents' Cadillac, rusty and encrusted with dirt, once again flitted through Madeline's mind.

She pressed her palms to her eyes, but she could still see Pontiff holding up her father's camera. She also heard the squeak of the metal, the splash of the water that had poured out of the open door and the echo of Chief Pontiff's voice when he'd said, "That's it."

Heading to the small desk in her old-fashioned kitchen, she picked up the listing of private investigators she'd printed off from the Internet. She'd called several of them earlier but had been disappointed by their responses. They were too busy. They wouldn't be able to come to Stillwater to do the necessary research. They specialized in lost children or cheating husbands.

However, a few had recommended a man named Hunter Solozano. They said he could find anyone or anything and often accepted unusual jobs for the challenge. But when she'd called the number they'd given her, his voice mail had indicated there was no room for new messages.

Swallowing a sigh, she picked up the handset and tried Mr. Solozano again. It was past midnight, but she didn't care. Surely it was an office phone, which meant it wouldn't matter. Maybe she'd finally be able to leave a message so she could feel as if there was *some* hope.

She'd expected at least three rings—so she jerked upright when a deep voice answered almost immediately.

"Damn it, Antoinette, you've already got your pound of flesh!"

Madeline stiffened in surprise. "And if this isn't Antoinette?" she ventured.

There was a moment of startled silence. "That depends," he drawled, smoothly recovering. "Who are you and what do you want?"

"That also depends," she replied. "Are you Hunter Solozano?"

"Yes."

"And are you as good as they say?" she asked eagerly.

He chuckled. "Better. Particularly if you're talking about sex."

Thanks to her preoccupation, she'd walked right into that one. Embarrassed and annoyed, she cleared her throat. "I'm talking about your *professional* skills."

"So this is a business call."

"Yes."

"At ten-thirty at night."

His time. She'd wondered about the area code. Fortunately, he lived to the west of her and not the east or he'd have a lot more reason to complain. "You sound like you're awake to me," she said hesitantly, tapping a pencil on the desk.

"Thanks to you and my ex-wife." His voice dropped meaningfully. "In case you haven't guessed, that doesn't put you in very good company."

A touch of defensiveness made Madeline rub her furrowed brow. "I assumed I was calling an office number."

"That means you weren't expecting a response. Great. This can wait until morning, then."

"No!" she cried before he could disconnect.

The fact that she didn't hear a click encouraged her. "You weren't picking up earlier. And your voice mail was full."

He didn't make any excuses. Neither did he promise her she'd be able to reach him later. So she kept talking, trying to keep him on the line until she had a better chance of enlisting his help. "How was I supposed to know I'd been given your home number?"

"It's not my home number. It's my cell. If you want to talk to me, that's the *only* number. I like things simple."

"You don't have an office?"

"I have a small office, but you'll rarely catch me there."

Purring, Sophie brushed against her legs, but Madeline was too preoccupied to pay attention. "I take it you're not interested in developing new business."

"I have more business than I can handle."

That response wasn't encouraging…. "That's fortunate for you, isn't it?" she asked.

"Plumbing the depths of human frailty has its downside."

"So why don't you do something else?"

"Some people are good at building houses. I'm not one of them."

He wasn't particularly good with people, either, but she'd heard too many testimonials about him to give up now that she had him on the phone. "I have a challenge for you."

"I'm tired and I want to go bed," he said. "But thanks for the call."

"Can I leave you my number at least? Will you get back to me in the morning?"

There was a long silence.

"Hello?" she prompted.

"Why don't I refer you to a young associate of mine?"

Maybe this other person would be easier to deal with. "Is this 'young associate' any good?"

"He worked at my office for a short while doing database searches and just got his own license. He doesn't have a lot of experience, but he's hungry and he's learning."

Learning? "No! I need someone who really knows what he's doing."

"I don't know what to say, Mrs.—"

"Barker. But I've never been married. Call me Madeline."

"Ms. Barker. If I haven't made myself clear, I'm not interested. Judging by your accent, you live several states from me, anyway."

"I'm in Stillwater, Mississippi. Where're you?"

"L.A."

"It's crowded in Los Angeles," she said, hoping to point out one of the city's less appealing aspects.

"That's true, but if you've ever been here, you'd know why."

"I'll pay you. Well." She frowned at the check register lying open at her elbow. That was hardly the card she'd wanted to play. She was barely keeping herself and the paper afloat. How would she manage?

"I suggest you contact someone in your own area," he said.

Panic caused Madeline to tighten her grip on the phone. "But I haven't even told you what I want."

"Let me guess. You want me to slay the dragon that's keeping you up at night."

She glared, bleary-eyed, at the clock on the wall to her right. She was tired, and too frayed around the edges to hide it. Evidently, that wasn't working in her favor. "Isn't that the case with most of your clients?"

"These days, I typically work with people who want me to find out whether their estranged mates are hiding assets or having affairs so they can get a better divorce settlement. Or they're trying to collect on a debt. Their dragon is usually greed." There was a slight pause. "Do you fit into either of these categories, Ms. Barker?"

"No, but…" She struggled to reel in her temper at

his all-too-easy dismissal. "So you've gotten lazy? You only take on the easy stuff?"

"I take on the *convenient* stuff, the *close* stuff. Besides, I doubt you could afford me."

She finally bent down to scratch her persistent cat. "What makes you think that?"

"Maybe it's the accent."

Her jaw dropped before she could rally her response. "That's…discriminatory," she sputtered.

"You called me. Feel free to hang up anytime."

Nudging Sophie away, she stood and nearly told him to go to hell. But she was afraid she wouldn't be able to find anyone else. According to what she'd been told, she'd certainly find no one better. "I need you," she said, resorting to simple honesty. "I need your help."

He cursed but didn't hang up, so she took a bolstering breath. "You're still with me?"

"What is it you're looking for?" he asked with enough resignation to give her hope.

"A person."

"Who?"

"My father." She didn't add that he'd been missing since she was sixteen. Better to reveal the potential difficulty of the task in stages.

"Where do you think he went?"

Despite all the years that had passed, she'd clung to the dream of a reunion—until they'd found the Cadillac. "I'm pretty sure he's dead."

"Because…"

She caught her breath, letting it out a little with each word. "He hasn't been seen in…a long, long time."

"*How* long?"

"Nineteen years."

"Almost two *decades?* Aren't you a bit late in following up, Ms. Barker?"

The accusation in his tone made her throat clog with emotion. "I've done what I could," she managed to say. She'd even crossed the line a few times—breaking into Jed Fowler's auto shop, hiring Officer Hendricks to scare Allie into believing someone out there was still dangerous.

"And you've learned what?"

Very little. The mystery was beyond her own sleuthing ability, as well as that of the entire Stillwater Police Department. Mr. Solozano was right, she should've looked for an outside investigator long ago. "Not enough."

"Who stood to gain the most from his death?"

"It's not that straightforward. My stepmother inherited the farm, but she'd never hurt a soul."

"Who else is there?"

"Jed Fowler, an older man who was working on our tractor in the barn the night my father went missing. He can seem...strange. And a younger guy, Mike Metzger, who's in prison on drug-related charges. But I don't know if either one of them is responsible. That's what I want *you* to find out."

"Sounds like a murder investigation to me. You should contact the police."

She bristled at his lack of compassion. He had to know, in twenty years, she would already have tried the police. He didn't care. He didn't want to get involved. Maybe Hunter Solozano was a good investigator but he was the most insensitive jerk she'd ever met.

"Forget it. I'm sorry I bothered you. Just—" her

voice cracked "—just go back to fighting with your ex-wife. I hope she wins, by the way," she said and slammed down the phone.

Antoinette had already won. Hunter tossed his cell phone onto the side table. He deserved Madeline Barker's anger. Hell, he'd *asked* for it. He'd provoked her at every turn. After speaking with his ex-wife, and then his daughter—God, what she'd said to him—he'd been angling for a fight he could win.

But he didn't feel any better. If anything, he felt worse.

The flicker of his muted television served as the only light in the room. The darkness generally soothed him, but not tonight. Raking his fingers through his hair, he stood up, then sat down again.

Forget Maria. She didn't know what she was saying. Her mother put her up to it, as usual.

But he couldn't forget. The pain was too physical. It felt like he had an open wound in his chest, as if his daughter had reached into that wound, wrapped her little hand around his heart and squeezed with complete abandon.

Considering the Barker woman's terrible timing, it was a wonder the desperation in her voice had penetrated at all.

"*Ms.* Barker is not my problem," he said aloud. His daughter was his problem. Or, more specifically, the fact that his ex-wife had turned his daughter against him. Although he paid exorbitant amounts of child support—he'd sent Antoinette an extra two thousand dollars just this month—it was never enough to make his ex happy. He doubted his daughter was even receiving the benefits of the money he sent. The last time he'd seen Antoinette, she'd had a new nose and breast enhancements that were so large she looked like a damn porn queen. The way she was spending money and hitting the L.A. party scene, trying to keep up with the rich and famous, was humiliating even though he wasn't married to her anymore. Her behavior had to be doubly embarrassing for their daughter. How many PTA moms had tits the size of watermelons?

But Antoinette hadn't become quite so obsessive about plastic surgery, designer clothes and who was who in L.A. until after the divorce.

The guilt that fueled his self-loathing settled deeper in his gut. How had he managed to screw up so completely? If only he could go back...

But it was too late. The damage was done. And now Antoinette was using their child to extort more and more money out of him while painting him as the devil himself, the cause of all Maria's problems.

Automatically, his eyes cut to a picture of his twelve-year-old daughter. Her photograph rested on one of the empty shelves above the television, and was about the only decoration left in the beach house. Antoinette had stripped the place bare when she moved out more than a year ago.

Maria stared back at him, wearing a somber expression. He imagined the school photographer coaxing her, "Say 'cheese!'" But she seemed to be thinking, "Get real. What do I have to smile about?"

The desire for a drink slammed into him like one of the waves he could hear churning down the beach. He felt helpless, pinned beneath his craving for the smooth burn of alcohol and the resulting disconnect. He wasn't asking for a lot. Just one night of escape. Then he'd get back on the wagon. It had never been so bad before. His daughter had never said what she'd said tonight.

Please, leave us alone. You make everything worse… I don't want to be with you, okay? It's all your fault!

Wincing as the memory lashed a part of him that was already raw, he reached for his keys and his wallet, both sitting next to his phone. He'd go down to the bar on the corner. If he planned to drink, he had to go somewhere. Sober for six months, he had no alcohol in the house.

But he stopped at the door. Maria's eyes seemed to be following him, accusing him. *You're just what she says you are. A drunk.*

Clenching his jaw, he bowed his head, battling the weakness that threatened to overtake him. He'd beat the craving for booze—if only to prove Antoinette wrong.

Eventually, he forced himself to return to the couch and pick up his guitar. It was all so damned ironic, he thought, trying to gain some perspective on the phone call that had hurt so badly. Alcohol was the only thing that had made it possible to cope with the irritation and dislike he faced on a daily basis in his marriage. And alcohol had caused him to make the one mistake he'd promised himself he'd never make, the mistake that had landed him in their neighbor's bed and destroyed his marriage.

He strummed through several Nickelback songs, hoping to get lost in the music. His guitar helped him relax. But tonight nothing could release the pent-up frustration. Antoinette had promised he could take Maria to Hawaii next weekend for seven days. He'd been planning on it for two months. And then Maria had called to say she wouldn't go….

He played a few more chords, but his heart wasn't in it. His throat and eyes burned, his muscles ached with the effort of subduing his reaction.

Grasping for something, anything, to fill his mind besides the echoing rejection of his daughter, he turned his thoughts to the Southern woman who'd called. *What are you looking for...? A person... Who...? My father.*

Hunter sighed. Maria didn't want her father. They lived less than ten miles apart, but she refused to see him. Which pleased Antoinette inordinately, of course. His ex hated him—because he'd never really loved her.

Stop! Think of something else!

Madeline Barker's voice came to him again. *That's discriminatory.*

Setting his guitar aside, he frowned. Mississippi wasn't exactly high on his list of places to see. But he knew what need was. And he had nothing here, did he? He was stuck in an empty house with only his guitar for company, working night and day so he wouldn't break down and start drinking again.

His life had become too pathetic for words. He loved California, had lived in Newport Beach nearly all his life, but the steady pounding of the waves twenty yards from his house seemed to whisper, "Maria...Maria... Maria."

He'd been an idiot to lose her. And he'd been even more of an idiot to place the rope that had hanged him right inside Antoinette's beautifully manicured fingers. Now she was laughing while she watched him swing....

Maybe it was time to stop the show. He wouldn't force his daughter to see him; he couldn't bear the thought of making her any unhappier than she already was. She'd told him she'd be better off if he gave up, walked away. Maybe, for a while, he should. Lord knew he wasn't doing anyone any good sitting here going out of his mind. And he wasn't about to vacation in Hawaii by himself. He didn't need that much time on his hands. If he went, he probably wouldn't last a day before seeking out the closest pub.

"What the hell," he muttered and turned on a light so he could see the number Madeline Barker had called him from.

Madeline raised her head and blinked at the shrill ring. Could it be morning? Already?

Her body felt stiff and sore. Squinting at her watch, she realized why. It was only one o'clock. She couldn't have been asleep for more than twenty minutes, and slumping over her desk had put a crick in her neck.

The phone rang again. She almost dropped the handset but eventually brought it to her ear.

"Hello?" Her voice sounded throaty and low.

"Ms. Barker?"

"Yes?"

"It's Hunter Solozano."

She jumped up, then teetered on her feet for a moment. "What do you want, Mr. Solozano?"

"What airport should I use?"

"For… You're coming? Here?"

"Isn't that what you wanted?"

"Yes, but—" nerves made her scalp tingle "—we haven't discussed any of the logistics."

"I charge a thousand dollars a day, plus expenses."

A thousand dollars a day! She clapped a hand over her mouth. But he didn't pause.

"You said you had no worries about paying me. Is that still true?"

He cost a fortune. Even more than she'd expected. But she wasn't about to admit she had any doubts. Not after what he'd said to her before. *I think it's the accent.* Maybe she lived in the boondocks by *his* standards, but she was no uneducated, backward hick. "Sure. No problem," she lied.

"Fine. I'll need the first five thousand as a retainer."

She bit her lip. That alone would wipe out her checking account and leave her short on next month's bills. The paper was a labor of love but hardly a fabulous living. "How long do you think the…investigation will take?"

"I have no idea," he said. "How committed are you to finding your father?"

She winced at the staggering financial implications. If Mr. Solozano stayed for a month, it'd cost her upward of $20,000. And that was taking weekends off.

But she'd tried everything else. This felt like her only hope. "More committed than I've ever been to anything."

"Fine. I'll be there on Thursday."

She gulped. "So soon?"

"You're in luck. I was planning a vacation that fell through."

In luck? At one thousand dollars a day, plus expenses? "Um…just to clarify, your expenses would include what exactly? Airfare and hotel?"

"As well as a rental car, meals, any specialized tests we might need to run on the evidence I find, stuff like that."

"I see." The list could get long. And with his salary, the incidental expenses would be the least of her problems. But he sounded so confident when he mentioned evidence.

"Will you be making my hotel reservations or shall I?" he asked.

Transferring the phone from one hand to the other, Madeline wiped her palms, which had grown clammy, on her sweatpants. "I was thinking… I mean I was wondering…"

"Yes?"

She scowled at the impatience in his voice. "Is there any way we could cut corners a bit?"

"Cut corners?" he repeated suspiciously.

"I have a guesthouse. I thought maybe you could stay there. It'd be quiet," she added. "I live alone."

"And what will I drive?"

"My car."

"And you'll drive…"

"My stepbrother will let me borrow a truck from the farm. It might not look like much after hauling dirt and feed and who knows what else, but he's always got an extra."

Hunter didn't seem to mind staying in her guesthouse and driving her car, because he agreed right away. "That's fine. Does that mean you're picking me up at the airport?"

If she played chauffeur, they'd be able to talk while she drove. Then he could start his investigation the moment he reached Stillwater. Saving whatever money she could seemed prudent, especially since she wasn't sure hiring him would make any difference in the end. Would he find evidence everyone else had missed? Or would he be as ineffectual as the police?

Maybe she was bankrupting herself for nothing, for a hunger that could never be satisfied....

"Ms. Barker?"

She swallowed to ease a particularly dry mouth. "I'll pick you up. Fly into Nashville, okay?"

"It's closer than Jackson?"

"By two hours."

"Okay. I'll make my travel arrangements over the Internet and call you in the morning."

"Fine." She pretended to be as businesslike as he was. But when she hung up, she couldn't tear her eyes from the phone.

"What have I done?" she breathed.

3

"You've done *what?*" Grace asked.

Madeline held the phone to her shoulder as she rinsed her coffee cup and placed it in the dishwasher. Morning had come too soon. After a restless night, her eyes stung with fatigue. It didn't help that the coffee she'd drunk to get her going churned sourly in her otherwise empty stomach. "I hired a private investigator."

There was a momentary silence. "You're kidding."

"No."

"From where?"

"California."

"But…it's been so many years since Dad went missing, Maddy."

"I know. That's why I did it." Sophie followed her as she hurried to the bathroom. She needed to finish her hair and makeup and head over to the office. She couldn't avoid work this morning. She would sit down and write the article she should've written yesterday— and she'd finish it before the paper had to go to press. Maybe her resolve had come a little late, but she was Stillwater's only official reporter. She'd reveal the unbiased details of the Cadillac's discovery, regardless of her personal connection.

"But Allie used to be a cold case detective," Grace said. "If she couldn't find anything, aren't you afraid hiring someone else will be a waste of time and money?"

Madeline didn't want to talk about Allie—not with Grace. Once Allie had begun to feel romantic interest in Clay, she'd no longer seemed fully committed to the investigation. Had she been afraid of what she might find if she really looked? Considering what everyone else believed, probably. Madeline doubted Allie was still worried about that now that she knew Clay as well as she did. But they both seemed determined to move forward and not dwell on the past.

They *could* move forward, Madeline thought. They didn't feel the same responsibility to Lee Barker that she did. Allie's father had had his own problems before he moved away, problems that had included an affair with Irene. But Chief McCormick was still part of Allie's life. How could Allie understand what it would be like not to know where he was or even whether he was alive? And Clay had only lived with Lee for three years.

"Before she could dig too deep, her father fired her for taking Clay's side," Madeline said, trying to smooth over the issue. If she started pointing fingers at others for not doing enough, she knew Grace would feel guilty by association. And Grace had always had her own demons to deal with. It wasn't until she came home eighteen months ago that she'd had much of a relationship with her family. Before that, she'd been emotionally remote and completely immersed in her work as an assistant district attorney in Jackson.

The past had been difficult for them all.

"She would've continued to dig," Grace said. "She just didn't find anything that gave her any indication of where Dad might've gone."

"Or who might've harmed him," Madeline added.

"Or who might've harmed him," she conceded.

Madeline pulled her hair back so she could apply concealer to the dark circles that came from a week's worth of restless nights. "It's something I've got to do."

"This might not solve anything," Grace said again.

"I know, but seeing the Cadillac lifted out of the quarry made me sick." She paused, her hand on the blush she was going to apply next. "I felt as if I've let my father down by not doing more. I've let myself down, too. Even you and Clay, Grace. They almost prosecuted Clay last summer, for *murder*."

"I don't think they'll go after him again," Grace argued. "Last year, it was political pressure that caused all the trouble. The Vincellis have backed off since then."

"My aunt and uncle, maybe. Not my cousins. You saw them at the quarry."

"Joe and Roger are vultures. We're safe as long as we're still moving."

"They have a lot of powerful friends."

"But there's no solid evidence. There never has been. Clay's innocent."

Finished with the blush, Madeline smeared some brown eye shadow on her eyelids. "The car's going to stir it all up again," she said. "Don't you think it's better to get to the bottom of what happened?"

The silence stretched, and a few seconds became half a minute.

"Is something wrong?" Madeline finally asked.

"No, of course not," Grace said. "Believe me, I'd like to know what happened, too. But not at any cost."

"We're talking about dollars. What are dollars compared to peace of mind?" Dropping the eye shadow into her makeup bag, Madeline dug around for her mascara.

"Can you really afford him?" There was concern in Grace's voice.

"I'll keep him on as long as I can." Madeline heard a clock ticking somewhere in her subconscious, and it made her frantic. She only hoped Hunter found her some answers before she had a nervous breakdown or was living out on the street.

"Do you need help with his bill?"

It was a generous offer. But Madeline didn't expect her stepsister to finance an investigation she couldn't welcome. Mr. Solozano would, in all likelihood, focus on Grace and the mother and brother she loved so dearly—at least in the beginning, before he got beyond the circumstantial evidence that led everyone else to blame the Montgomerys.

"No. But thanks." She glanced at her watch. It was nearly nine. "I'd better go."

"Maybe you should discuss this with Clay," Grace said.

"I'm sure Mr. Solozano has already purchased his plane ticket."

"Where will he be staying?"

"Here, in the guest house."

"You don't even know him! Is that a good idea?"

"It'll be fine," Madeline said.

"What's wrong with having him stay at the Blue Ribbon Motel?"

"He's from L.A."

"So?"

Madeline wasn't about to stick Hunter Solozano in the aging motel located next to a trailer park of ramshackle mobile homes. Besides giving him something else to look down his nose at, it'd cost her more money, and Madeline sort of liked the idea of having her P.I. so close. Then she could be sure he was working and not watching pay-per-view at her expense. "He comes highly recommended."

"Maddy—"

"After I meet him, if I think there's any threat, I'll make some adjustments," she interrupted.

"O-kay," Grace said, but her reluctance was evident in the way she drew out the word. "And you really think this guy will make a difference?"

"I'm sure of it. Talk to you later." As Madeline disconnected, she realized that she was putting an inordinate amount of trust in Hunter. She could be setting herself up for a big disappointment. But every investigator who'd recommended him had done so in the most glowing terms. And she needed to believe he would bring her resolution at last.

It was odd, though. Even thoughts of ultimate success made Madeline nervous. She supposed, deep down, she was more terrified of the truth than she'd ever wanted to admit. Even to herself. She knew almost everyone in town, so chances were good she'd also know her father's murderer.

Clay stared out his kitchen window at the barn where it had all started. The sun peeked from behind the clouds, giving the hulking structure a long, ominous shadow that stretched across the yard, reaching almost to the chicken coop.

Unfortunately, the shadow of the man they'd buried behind it stretched even farther. Clay had been only sixteen the night everything went wrong. Yet those events continued to haunt him.

Twenty damn years... And he knew that what had happened would still bother him after *sixty* years.

Shaking his head, he let his eyes shift to the front of the barn. After his sisters had left for college and his mother had moved to town, he'd converted the stables that had once housed the reverend's mean horse and a couple of boarder horses into a large open area where he could restore antique cars. But the section that had once been Lee Barker's office sat dark and empty. Clay had no plans to use that space; he never even went in there. It evoked too many memories of the man he hated more than he'd ever hated anyone.

Clay clenched his jaw as he imagined his stepfather standing at the window of that office, watching carefully to be sure the farm chores were done to his specifications. Once Irene had married the reverend, Clay had become little more than a slave. But what Barker had done to Grace was far worse....

"You're never inside this time of day. What's wrong?"

Turning, Clay saw his wife come into the room. He'd been expecting her. She helped out at their daughter's school every Tuesday but was usually back by noon.

"Grace called," he said, his gaze lingering on her as it always did. Just looking at Allie's wide brown eyes, smooth complexion and ready smile soothed him.

Only she wasn't smiling now. He could tell by the way she put her purse on the counter and tucked her dark hair behind her ears that she was bracing for the worst. Ever since they'd heard that the Cadillac had been found, they'd been expecting bad news. "What's happening?" she asked. "Did the police turn up some piece of evidence or—"

"Not that I've heard."

Her eyebrows knitted, creasing her forehead. "Then what?"

He wished he didn't have to burden her with the worries he faced. He was used to shouldering them on his own. In some ways, he preferred it. She wasn't part of the incident that had defined so much of his life. But when he'd married her, he'd promised he wouldn't shut her out. From anything, even this. "Madeline's hired a private investigator."

She urged him into a kitchen chair where she began to massage his shoulders. "That might not be such a big deal," she said. "This case is getting so old it'd be tough for anyone to crack. And there aren't a lot of competent P.I.s out there."

Clay frowned. "This guy has quite a reputation."

"How do you know?"

"Grace did some checking. One of the attorneys she used to work with is from California and has used him in the past."

Her hands stilled. "So he has a background in criminal investigation?"

"According to what Grace learned, he was originally a cop. He moved into the private sector when he realized he could find just about anything, and that there were folks who'd pay for his skills."

"Great," she said sarcastically. "So what's his specialty? Next you're going to say men who've been missing from small towns in Mississippi for twenty years."

Clay rolled his neck. "Actually, I think he's traced more assets than people."

"So why would he come here?"

"He seems to take on anything that interests him."

She started to massage again. "We'll get through it," she murmured.

She said that about every challenge; her attitude made life easier. "I'm glad I found you," he said, kissing her hand. The past didn't intrude quite so much when Allie was around. But he knew it'd never go away entirely. That was one of the reasons he'd been so reluctant to get involved with her. It wasn't fair to bring such a dark secret into a marriage, to burden a spouse with the fear of its discovery or the task of keeping it safe.

"We were meant for each other," she said.

He closed his eyes, enjoying her ministrations despite the anxiety humming through him.

"What will you do?" she asked.

He'd been considering that ever since he'd heard the news. "I'm not sure there's anything I can do."

"You could call Maddy, talk her out of it."

"That might hold her off for a while, but her desire to know is too strong, especially since they found the Cadillac. She'd break down and hire him next month or the month after, even if I talk her out of doing it right now."

"I don't think so," Allie said. "She listens to you. You're the big brother whose shoes no one else can fill."

If his stepsister knew the truth, she wouldn't admire

him half as much. As a matter of fact, she'd never be able to forgive him. It was all so complicated. If Madeline ever learned what *really* happened, she'd lose more than her relationship with him, his mother, Grace, even their youngest sister, Molly, who lived in New York City.

"She sounds as if she's finished with Kirk," he mused, changing the subject.

"And you're disappointed."

He twisted to look up at her. "You're not?"

She gave him a wry smile. "I like Kirk, too. But we need to stay out of it. Madeline has to do what she thinks is best."

"How do you know Kirk's not what she needs? He's a good man, a hard worker."

"Just because *you* like him doesn't mean she should marry him. There's no spark there or they would've married long ago. They act more like buddies than lovers."

But Kirk had been around for so many years, he'd already found his place in the family and was unlikely to disturb the delicate equilibrium of relationships. "She needs to do something. She's thirty-six years old."

Allie chuckled. "So are you. That's hardly ancient."

"She's still talking about having a large family."

"She'll find the right man."

"Kirk's the right man," he insisted. "She should marry him, have a family and forget the past." His mood darkened as he folded his arms. "Instead, she's spending good money on a P.I.—a P.I. who could ruin her life."

"Guilt, responsibility and curiosity are all powerful motivators," Allie said. "You, of all people, should understand that."

"We're not talking about me," he grumbled.

Her smile was back. "If you only knew what a good man you are."

He shoved the hair out of his eyes. It was getting long; he could use a cut. "It's enough for me that *you* think I'm good."

"Maybe if Maddy still had her mother, the situation would be different," she said.

"Of course it would. Then my mother wouldn't have married Lee Barker. He had nothing nice to say about his first wife, but you know he never would've divorced her. That wouldn't have reflected well on him." He heard the bitter note in his own voice. "He was all about appearances."

She bent over to kiss his cheek. "You've done your best with what you were given, done your best by Maddy. You love her just as much as your other sisters."

"But it's probably not the same for her," he said. "She belongs, and yet she's the only one who doesn't really belong. That's got to be hard."

"Not as hard as it could be if she ever finds out the truth." Allie walked over to get the phone. "So call her."

"And say what? Hey, Maddy, take it from me—you don't want to know what you think you want to know?"

She tugged playfully on his hair. "*No*. Tell her the case is too old, that this P.I. won't uncover anything new, that it'll cost her a lot of money for nothing. And if that doesn't work, just let her know you don't approve."

"I can't come on too strong," he said.

"Why not?"

"Because it's a miracle folks around here haven't poisoned her against me."

"She'd never turn on you."

"She could if this P.I. comes to town."

"Which is why you have to convince her not to bring him here," she pointed out.

"I doubt that anything I say will change her mind."

"It's worth a try," Allie insisted and handed him the phone.

The phone in Madeline's office had been ringing all morning. It seemed as if everyone in Stillwater had something to say about the discovery at the quarry, which came as no surprise to her. People in this town had been talking about her father's disappearance for years, and the knowledge that his car had been found renewed public interest.

Fortunately, most were well-intentioned calls, friends and acquaintances who, after hearing the latest, wanted to give Madeline a kind word or a little encouragement. But there were a few who used this latest development to try to undermine her faith in the Montgomerys.

Madeline would rather have skipped every one of those calls in favor of some peace and quiet. It was difficult enough writing about her father without so many interruptions. But she was anxious to hear from Chief Pontiff, to learn if he or any of his deputies had managed to glean some evidence during their more thorough search of the Cadillac. She knew they must be finished by now, couldn't imagine why he hadn't contacted her. So when a call came in just as she'd settled down to work, she grabbed the receiver, despite the blinking cursor on her computer screen that seemed to mock her lack of progress.

"Hello?"

"Madeline?"

Madeline paused, confused by the *M. Ziegler* that had appeared on her caller ID. It wasn't Chief Pontiff, calling her from some remote location. If she'd guessed correctly, it was Ray Harper. Before the falling out that had left him and her father estranged, he'd been Lee's best friend. When Madeline was little, Ray had even worked for them, doing odd jobs around the farm.

"Hello, Ray. How are you?"

"Good as ever. And you?"

"Hanging in there."

"I heard about the Cadillac."

Word traveled fast in Stillwater. "Can you believe it was right there all these years?"

"Who put it there?"

"I have no idea."

"That's got to bother you."

It did. But she preferred some development to nothing at all. Besides, she and Ray had both experienced a deeper kind of pain—she'd lost her mother and, a few years later, he'd lost his sixteen-year-old daughter, both to suicide. "I'm okay."

"Did they find anything—any answers?" he asked.

"No, not yet."

"That's too bad."

"I'm not giving up hope." He didn't say anything more, so she filled the silence. "I don't see you around town much anymore, Ray. What've you been up to?"

"I've been spending half my time in Iuka. My mother fell and broke her hip and she can't live alone anymore. I'm with her now, moving her to my sister's place."

That explained the strange name on her caller ID. "I'm sorry to hear about your mother," she said.

"She'll be okay now that she's with Patti. Anyway, I should be home later in the week. Let me know if anything changes, okay? Your father and I weren't on the best of terms when he disappeared. But I think about him often."

"I appreciate that." Her telephone indicated that she had another call coming in. "Good luck with your mom," she said and switched over. But this caller wasn't Pontiff, either. According to caller ID, it was Clay. "What's up, big brother?"

"Nothing new," he replied. "Just checking in."

She finally pushed away from her computer and swiveled her chair to look glumly out the large front window of her office, which revealed an entire block of Stillwater's most prominent businesses—L & B Hardware, Town & Country Furniture, Cutshall's Funeral Home, Lambert's Auction Service and Let The Good Times Roll Billiards and Bar. A corner of the police station was visible, too. Her eyes zeroed in on it as if she could see through brick and mortar.

"I'm fine, just tired of the rain." *And growing more impatient by the minute, waiting for Pontiff to call.*

"You took yesterday pretty hard, Mad."

"He's not coming back," she said distantly. "I thought it'd be easier for me to know if he was…gone for good. But it isn't. It makes me angry. And it makes me feel guilty, as if I haven't done enough for him."

"You've published every possible lead, posted rewards to encourage people to come forward with in-formation, followed up whenever and wherever you could. You've hung on, and you haven't let anyone forget. You've done your best."

She knew her dogged persistence had created problems for Clay and his sisters and mother. They'd had to constantly defend themselves, suffer two police searches of the farm, endure the distrust of almost everyone in town and tolerate whispering behind their backs. But what else could she have done? What else could she do now but pursue whoever was responsible? Lee Barker was her *father,* the only parent who'd planned on sticking with her.

Besides, if she could get to the truth, wouldn't the Montgomerys ultimately be better off?

"I should've hired a P.I. a long time ago," she said. "Maybe it would've brought me some peace—and saved you from what happened last summer."

He didn't comment on the murder charges that'd been brought against him. Clay never made a big deal of his own difficulties. "Allie feels bad," he said. "I hope you don't think she let you down with her investigation."

"No. I'm the one who let the two of you down. I can't believe I…" She toyed with her paper-clip holder. She tended to avoid any reference to what had occurred at Allie's dad's fishing cabin the night she hired Hendricks. They all did. But she felt the need to address it today, to apologize once again. Clay could've died, and it would've been her fault. She shuddered at the thought. "I'm so sorry for what I did."

"Don't mention it. Hendricks was only supposed to rattle a doorknob or two. I know that."

"But you wouldn't have been hurt if I hadn't sent him there in the first place."

"You had no way of knowing he'd take it so far. Or that I'd even be around that night."

It was true, but she'd never be able to forgive herself for resorting to the tactics she'd used. If she hadn't allowed her hopes to soar so high when Allie returned to Stillwater and promised to look into her father's disappearance—or felt so damn helpless when Allie lost interest—maybe she would've been thinking more clearly. But her desperation and impatience had simply gotten the best of her. When she felt Allie's commitment and enthusiasm beginning to lag, she'd tried to shore it up by trying to convince her that someone out there was still a threat.

It had seemed like an innocent enough plan. But it had cost Hendricks, who'd been a member of the Stillwater Police force, his job, a year in prison and probation after that. His wife was struggling to support their family without him and, had Hendricks's aim been more accurate, Clay could've paid an even higher price. Madeline had only escaped prosecution because she hadn't intended any harm. Stealing Allie's gun—and using it—had been Hendricks's idea.

She got up and paced the room. "Sometimes I think about it and—"

"*Don't* think about it," he said. "We all make mistakes, do things we regret."

She managed a tired smile at his generosity. "You're a good brother."

He immediately moved forward with the conversation. "Grace tells me you're hiring a private investigator. Someone from California."

"That's right."

"When's he coming in?"

"This Thursday. I'm not sure what time." She stopped at the window. Why hadn't Chief Pontiff called?

If only he could come up with something that would *finally* solve this....

"That soon?" Clay said.

"Yeah." She wandered back to her desk and sank into her seat. "Grace doesn't seem to think it'll do any good."

"The odds aren't in your favor," he responded.

She began doodling on a Post-it note. "So you don't think I should do it, either."

He didn't answer right away. When he did, he surprised Madeline. She'd been expecting his customary, "You gotta do what you gotta do." He said that whenever she asked his opinion on publishing a new lead or printing a story designed to inspire renewed interest in the mystery. Instead she got, "Some things are better left as they are, Maddy."

Dropping her pen, she sat up straight. "What do you mean by that?"

"Maybe the answers will haunt you more than the questions."

She rocked back in her seat, suddenly uneasy. "What? Clay, if..." Swallowing hard, she tried to calm the butterflies fluttering around in her stomach. "If you want to tell me anything, do it now."

Could she have imagined the slight hesitation that followed? "That's all," he said.

"I don't understand. How could the answers be any worse than the questions?"

"Who knows? Maybe he was involved in something he shouldn't have been."

"That's crazy! He was a humble servant of Christ," she said, her voice rising. "You know what a good man he was. You lived with him, heard his sermons. He took religion very seriously."

Clay said nothing.

"Do you know something I don't?" she asked, her disquiet turning to panic.

"Only what I was thinking when they pulled the Cadillac from the quarry."

"Which was…"

"People don't usually murder a middle-aged man without a reason."

"He could've been robbed! Maybe whoever attacked him stole the money from his wallet," she said. "Or maybe there *was* no real motive, other than childish anger, lashing out, stupidity. There're hundreds of reasons that have nothing to do with him."

"You're thinking of Mike Metzger."

"Of course."

"Mike might be a dope hound but he's not a murderer."

"You don't know that. See? That's the problem. We all have our suspicions, but no one really knows. That's why folks keep blaming you. If Mr. Solozano uncovers the real culprit, they'll have to stop, and I'll be damn glad of it."

"It might be easier on you if you'd quit defending me," he said. "You don't have to, you know."

"Yes, I do. When folks accuse you, it hurts me, too. I'm tired of it. And I've had it with all the people who've implied that I must be an idiot to miss the obvious."

"Ignore them."

She made a face even though he couldn't see her. "I can't. You live outside town. I have to mingle with Stillwater's residents every single day."

"But this investigator can't be cheap," he argued.

He had no idea…. "He's not *that* expensive," she lied.

"You can afford him?"

She pressed her thumb and forefinger to her closed eyelids. "Of course."

"Then you're committed to this."

Hunter Solozano had asked her the same thing. "Yes. This is a gamble I have to take. Won't you be relieved to know the truth? Aren't you even a *little* curious?"

"I've put the past behind me," he said. "We have to live with what is."

She started to say she couldn't face a future of not knowing. Every time she tried, the nightmares came more often. But she hadn't told anyone about her sleepless nights. She was afraid she'd sound crazy.

"I wish I could do that," she said. "But I can't." At the sound of the door opening, Madeline turned. Irene had just walked in. "Mom's here," she told Clay. "Can I call you later?"

"Sure. In the meantime, try to relax, okay? You're worrying me."

"I'm fine," Madeline said, but she had a headache from being awake most of the night. "Fine" actually felt a long way off.

"Call me if you need anything," he said and hung up without a goodbye. He didn't waste words. She'd gotten more out of him today than she usually did, but she didn't have time to think about that. Her stepmother looked upset.

"Hi, Mom." She rounded the desk to give Irene a hug.

"Hi, honey." Irene embraced Madeline rather stiffly, proof that she was as anxious and upset as Madeline was. "Have you heard from Chief Pontiff?"

"No. You?"

An expression of disgust tugged at her stepmother's

lips. "He'd never call me. Not unless he had another search warrant. Or an arrest warrant." Although Chief Pontiff seemed less prejudiced against the Montgomerys than some people in Stillwater, he wasn't particularly friendly to them, either. In the absence of hard evidence, he was obviously making an effort to reserve judgment. But Madeline sensed that he believed what everyone else believed—that her stepfamily had caused whatever had happened to Lee Barker.

"It shouldn't be long now," she said, to herself as much as Irene.

"Do they know what they're doing? They should've asked Allie for help."

"They didn't?"

"No. She called and offered, but they turned her down."

The Vincellis had gotten to Toby, just as she'd expected. Otherwise, he would've included Allie. Allie had more experience in gathering evidence than anyone in Stillwater; she would've been the obvious choice. "I'm sure they're doing their best. Chief Pontiff is a good man."

But he was new at his job, and Madeline didn't have a lot of confidence in his ability to shrug off the political influence of people like Mayor Nibley, who happened to be a friend of the Vincellis.

"Chief McCormick was a good man, too," Irene said bitterly.

Madeline didn't respond. Her stepmother was still in love with Allie's father. That was clear. Not that she saw him anymore. The McCormicks had relocated in an attempt to save their marriage. According to Allie, they were managing, although it remained to be seen whether or not they'd ultimately succeed.

Madeline knew Irene was hoping against it. Her step-mother was so lonely she dropped in more often these days. With Clay and Grace both married, and Molly living in New York, it was natural that she'd turn to Madeline. But Madeline could've survived without today's visit. Her stepmother's angst added fuel to her own.

"Should we call him?" Madeline asked.

Irene nodded, but the phone rang before Madeline could reach it.

Bending over the desk, she pulled it toward her. Caller ID registered a blocked number, but she still hoped it was Chief Pontiff. *"Stillwater Independent,"* she said.

"Madeline?" The voice was muffled, odd, as if someone was purposely trying to disguise it.

"Yes?" she said hesitantly.

"I heard your father's car was found in the quarry."

Madeline was fairly certain it was a woman, although the caller was attempting to deepen her voice. "That's true."

"It was Clay who drove it there. I saw him," she said.

Then the phone went dead.

4

Madeline told herself that it was just another crank call. She'd gotten a lot of them, all promising information they never delivered. But there was something different about this one. The caller had seemed so nervous, so self-conscious, so...*genuine.*

Irene watched her with worried eyes. "What is it?"

"Wrong number." She conjured up what was probably a lame smile, but she couldn't manage anything more sincere. The sound of the caller's voice hung over her like the gray clouds outside. Who'd placed that call? If she'd really seen what she'd claimed, why didn't she come forward, be more specific? Madeline had a list of people who said they'd witnessed this or that. But once her father had left the church that last day, no one could say for sure where he'd gone.

Movement at the window caught Madeline's attention.

"It's Pontiff," Irene said.

Toby stepped through the door, looking very official in his police-issue raincoat.

Madeline immediately forgot about the caller. "Chief," she said expectantly.

He stood dripping on her doormat as he sent a fleeting glance at Irene, then nodded politely.

"Did you find anything?" she asked.

His eyebrows gathered over his brown eyes. "Can I speak to you, Madeline? Privately?"

Madeline hesitated. She wanted to agree, simply because it'd give her a moment to absorb what he had to say before thinking about how it might affect her stepmother. But she couldn't pull him into the tiny bathroom, and other than that her office was one big room occupied mostly by a giant printer. She wasn't about to be so rude as to huddle in a corner and whisper while Irene was at her desk. She worked too hard to make sure others treated her stepmother with respect to ever slight Irene herself. "It's okay. Anything you have to say to me can be said in front of my mother."

He looked as if he might argue, but ultimately must've decided against it. "I don't want you to get your hopes up, but we found some items this morning that could possibly turn into leads."

"Possibly?" she echoed, her pulse kicking up. "What, exactly, are we talking about?"

"Some short strands of hair, for one."

"That didn't belong to my father?"

"They're black."

She knew what he was going to say next, so she said it for him. "Like Clay's."

It was Clay who drove it there....

"Yes."

"That doesn't mean anything," Irene snapped.

The Montgomerys had been accused so many times, Madeline could scarcely blame Irene for sounding belligerent. But Madeline was afraid her stepmother's attitude wouldn't win her any points with Pontiff, so she squelched her own flicker of doubt beneath the love and respect she felt for Clay.

"Mom's right. If you look closely, you'll probably find my hair in that car, too. And Grace's. And Molly's. We took the Cadillac to church every week."

"Saying you found Clay's hair in the car is like saying you found Clay's DNA in the house!" Irene added.

Madeline recognized the dislike in Toby's eyes. As if the town didn't have enough against her stepmother, many Stillwater residents blamed Irene for the downfall of Chief McCormick. Madeline was guessing Toby was one of them. But there was nothing Madeline could do about what had happened nine months ago, nothing anyone could do. Unlike the mystery surrounding her father, the former police chief's affair with Irene was more than mere accusation; it was common knowledge.

"The hairs were stuck between the headrest and the seat," Pontiff clarified.

"So?" Irene challenged.

"On the *driver's* side."

Clay had never been allowed to drive the Cadillac. Madeline had verified that in her own statement to the police.

"Maybe he took it for a joy ride once," Irene suggested.

Pontiff's lips barely moved when he spoke. "To the quarry, perhaps?"

"What you found doesn't prove that." Irene's voice had a desperate, panicky edge that made Madeline step closer and take her hand.

"Clay might've been behind the wheel for reasons

completely unrelated to my father's disappearance," she said.

"For instance…" Pontiff prodded.

Madeline quickly came up with a plausible scenario. "To move it so he could get the tractor through."

The hair meant nothing. Like the caller today. Like all the accusations that had come before. If her stepbrother was guilty, where was the proof?

"There's something else," Pontiff said.

Madeline's stomach tensed with painful anticipation. "What?"

"A small suitcase."

"You found a *suitcase?* Where was it when we were at the quarry?"

"It's more like a small satchel. It was hidden beneath the spare tire in the trunk."

"But my father didn't take any of his clothes."

"It wasn't filled with clothes. It had some rope inside."

The anxiety grew worse. "What kind of rope?"

"Unfortunately, it's ordinary rope that you can buy at any hardware store."

"Is there anything unique about it? Anything that might help us figure out where it came from?"

"Not that I can see."

Disappointment weighed heavily. "So…do you think it was used to bind my father?" Madeline hated the vision her words evoked but refused to let fear of what her father might've experienced stop her from asking difficult questions. "That whatever happened to him was premeditated?"

Pontiff fidgeted uncomfortably. "I don't think the rope was used on your father," he said. "That wasn't the only thing in the bag."

Madeline exchanged a wary glance with Irene. "Tell us."

He lowered his voice, until she could scarcely make out the words. "There was also a…dildo."

Feeling as if he'd just tied thirty-pound weights to each of her limbs, Madeline released Irene's hand. "A *what?*"

Chief Pontiff had turned bright red. "A—a sex toy, you know, a dildo."

"What would a dildo be doing in my father's trunk?" she nearly shouted.

His blush deepened. "I have no idea. But I'm hoping we can extract some DNA from it."

Irene's hand clutched her chest. "After all this time?"

Madeline could tell Pontiff didn't like Irene enough to let her put him on the spot. But since she was present, he was trying to maintain a certain level of professionalism. "The dildo itself was inside a Ziploc bag that was sealed. If it—" he cleared his throat "—if it wasn't washed before it went into that bag, we might have a chance."

Irene turned a shade paler. "What will that tell us?"

"Maybe there's a victim out there somewhere, connected with another case—a case that might have witnesses or information that could help us. Chances are slim that we'll be able to get a sample from the…object, and even slimmer that we'll be able to tie it to someone, but we need to gather whatever we can."

Irene shook her head. "But the connection you're looking for could be clear across the country. Lee must've picked up a hitchhiker on his way home, some guy who shoved that stuff in the trunk before sinking the car."

She'd often postulated that a drifter or hitchhiker had been involved. But no one had reported seeing any strangers the day Madeline's father went missing. And strangers definitely stood out in a town where everyone knew everyone else and viewed the unfamiliar with a measure of distrust.

Pontiff studied his shoes. "We found something else in the suitcase, too," he said in a resigned manner.

It *couldn't* get worse.... Could it?

"What?" Madeline asked as Irene echoed the same question.

He lifted his gaze, and a muscle flexed in his cheek. "Three pairs of panties. They look like they came from a girl of eleven or twelve."

Suddenly, Madeline felt dizzy. The thought of a rope, a dildo and girls' panties hidden together—anywhere—made her ill. No doubt they affected Chief Pontiff the same way. He had three children—all of them daughters.

"So the man who killed my father was a pedophile?" she gasped.

"That's the way it appears."

But how did someone like that circulate among them, going so far as to murder the town's spiritual leader—and get away with it? Stillwater typically had little or no crime. There were only fifteen hundred residents—and not one convicted sex offender.

Collecting her splintered thoughts, Madeline touched Pontiff's arm. "Toby." For a moment, he wasn't the chief of police to her. He was her friend's husband, a boy she'd known her whole life, a caring adult like herself. "What if my father was counseling a man with...with unacceptable sexual compulsions. You know how confessions are supposed to be private, but some things have to be reported? Maybe my father was going to turn in this...this pathetic individual and was killed because of it."

"That's crossed my mind," he admitted.

"If it was someone he knew well, maybe even trusted and respected, think of the resulting embarrassment."

"Someone like that might go to great lengths to avoid discovery."

"Exactly. So are you planning to question all the men in my father's congregation?" This had been done before, but now they had reason to look closer.

"I might. Right now, I need the two of you to come to the station with me."

"For what?" Irene cried.

"To see if you recognize the suitcase or the panties. We need to figure out who they might've belonged to."

"You don't think they could be *mine*," Madeline said. When Irene slipped one arm around her, she realized her voice had gone shrill, but the idea of her panties, or those of anyone else she knew, being in that suitcase was too horrible to contemplate.

"I have no idea," Pontiff said. "But I'd like to find out. And it makes sense to begin with the family."

It did make sense; it was just that his discovery was so *revolting*.

"That'll be too upsetting for her," Irene said. "I'll do it."

Madeline put up a hand. "No, of course I'll come, too. We both will."

"Good."

Madeline caught his elbow. "You know what this confirms, don't you?"

He didn't seem to know at all. "What?"

"The Vincellis and everyone who's supported them are wrong." A lump rose in her throat as she spoke, surprising even her. "It wasn't Clay."

"Maddy—" he started, but she refused to let him interrupt her.

"My stepbrother might seem dark and remote to you, to lots of people, but he'd sacrifice his own life before he'd ever hurt a child."

Sympathy softened Pontiff's features. "Folks aren't always what they seem, Maddy."

Madeline wouldn't let it go. "I'd bet my *own* life that he'd never touch a child in an inappropriate manner," she said fiercely. "He's angry and he's determined and he's—" she searched for the right word to describe her stepbrother "—tough. But he's *not* sick."

"He had a hard childhood," Pontiff said gently. "That can scar a person."

It was the first time she'd heard Toby speak with any compassion for Clay. Clay was too capable, too strong to evoke sympathy from most people, despite his background.

"He has his scars," she said. "But he's always protected those who are smaller, weaker and more vulnerable than himself. Surely you've seen how much his stepdaughter adores him."

Pontiff put his hand over hers. "The fact that he has a stepdaughter means I can't take your word for what Clay is or isn't, Maddy. I have to look at the facts. You understand."

What she understood was that it was time to exonerate Clay and expose the real killer. Maybe the facts hadn't stood in his favor before. But she was more certain than ever that now they would. And if the police weren't capable of solving the case, she'd make sure Hunter Solozano did the job for them.

Madeline sat in the police station with her stepmother, waiting for Grace to arrive. The rain had finally stopped, but the cloud-darkened sky threatened more bad weather.

The heater rattled as it pumped out hot air. Officer Radcliffe, who stood at the filing cabinet in the corner, bore a sheen of sweat on his forehead—proof that the heater was working. But Madeline couldn't get warm. Not since she'd seen what the police had found in her father's trunk.

"Are you sure, Maddy?" Irene whispered.

Her tongue felt thick and unwieldy, but she forced it to work. "I'm sure."

"But *I* don't remember them. And lots of young girls wore bikini underwear."

It wasn't the fact that they were bikinis that made them identifiable; it was the picture of an island with a monkey climbing a palm tree on the back. Madeline suspected Irene recognized them, too. Her stepmother didn't want to face what it might mean, preferred to think they were dealing with some kind of coincidence or mistake. "I'm *positive.*"

She'd meant to speak gently, but she couldn't conceal her impatience. Irene was getting older and didn't have the coping skills she'd once possessed. But Madeline was so exhausted and confused, she lacked the reserves to shelter her right now.

Why were Grace's first pair of bikini underwear—the ones Madeline had bought her for Christmas—in a strange suitcase with some rope and a dildo? Grace was only thirteen when that car went missing.

"If you're sure about the…the panties, there's no need to have Grace come down here," Irene said.

"Mom, please," Madeline snapped.

Chief Pontiff looked up from his desk and met

Madeline's eyes. When she scowled and turned away, he bent over his work again, and she was grateful to him for giving her some space instead of getting up to offer her a drink or something. She knew he'd seen the instant recognition on her face as he'd carefully arranged each item for her view.

It wasn't just the panties that upset her. The dildo had been there, too, grotesque in its size.

She dropped her head in her hands. The possibility that a sexual predator had had any contact with Grace at the age she'd been when she was wearing those panties sickened Madeline.

"God help us," she whispered and began to rub her temples. Her head hurt, but not as badly as her heart. She knew Grace had problems as a teenager. Had they started because she'd been molested—or worse, raped—by some demented creep?

No. She would've said something....

But deep down Madeline knew that wasn't true. Girls who'd been molested were often too ashamed afterwards to reveal their terrible secret.

"Whoever it was better not have touched her," she muttered.

Her stepmother jumped to her feet. "I want to call Clay."

Startled, Madeline blinked. "You want him to see *this?*" She waved at the panties on the table. The giant dildo sat front and center. Not that Madeline could look at it.

"I—I need him," Irene said.

Her slightly hysterical tone made Madeline feel guilty for being so impatient a moment before. She owed her stepmother more sensitivity than she'd just shown her. Irene was the one who'd provided the love and attention Madeline had needed as a young teen. Madeline couldn't imagine what life would've been like without her.

"We're okay," she whispered, hoping to comfort her. "We can take care of this ourselves, right?"

"No." Irene shook her head adamantly.

"But you know Clay. He'll go nuts if he sees this. And we wouldn't want to humiliate Grace any more than necessary. Obviously, if something terrible happened, she chose not to share it with us. It won't be easy for her to walk in here, especially with an audience, and admit it now."

"Let's not make her come," Irene said, gripping Madeline's arm.

Chief Pontiff glanced up again, and Madeline knew, without his having to say a word that he'd insist on it. He required Grace to confirm what Madeline had, after several shocked minutes, told him. "I'm afraid it's important."

"Then I need Clay," her stepmother said. "Grace will need him, too."

"I'd rather save him this," Madeline argued, but it was too late. Irene had hurried over to one of the empty desks and helped herself to a phone.

Madeline considered asking her to hang up but was actually relieved that Clay would be joining them. At the very least, maybe he'd take care of Irene until Madeline could come to grips with all of this.

The door opened and Grace's husband, Kennedy Archer, walked in, holding her hand. He had on one of the tailored suits he wore to work, while Grace was dressed more casually in jeans, Ugg boots and an attractive sweater. A pair of sunglasses hid her eyes despite the season and the inclement weather.

She's marshalling her defenses. She knows something's up. Suddenly, Madeline was very reluctant to see what would happen next.

Kennedy said a brief hello, although his cautious manner with Grace revealed his concern. Grace nodded in their direction but said nothing.

"Kennedy, Grace. Thanks for coming down." Pontiff had walked over the second he saw them and was now shaking hands with Kennedy. He offered Grace his hand as well, but she'd caught sight of the articles on the paper-lined table and didn't respond.

"What's the problem?" Kennedy asked, his voice low and guarded.

Pontiff explained that these items had been found in the Cadillac as he motioned them closer. Grace allowed her husband to lead her, but her skin looked taut across her elegant bones.

After a moment, she swayed as if she might pass out, and Madeline stepped up to take her hand. Irene remained near the door, muttering something about Clay.

"Do you recognize any of these objects?" Chief Pontiff asked.

Kennedy went rigid. "Grace?" he murmured, and there was a world of intimacy and love in the way he said her name.

She shook her head as Pontiff pointed at the suitcase. She did the same when he indicated the dildo, the rope and the panties. But when he reached the ones with the monkey, she finally spoke. "Those were mine."

* * *

Panic crowded so close Grace could hardly breathe. She'd known this would be agonizing. But she'd had no idea how much worse it'd be with Madeline looking on. Chief Pontiff watched, too, his expression shuttered. Even Officer Radcliffe, who stood off to the side pretending to file, was taking careful note.

Their future depended on the next few minutes—and her ability to be convincing even though she was drowning in a sea of painful memories.

"Do you know how your panties came to be in the trunk of the Cadillac?" Pontiff asked.

"No." She wished she had the strength to remove her sunglasses and meet his gaze directly. She'd coached enough witnesses to know how to enhance credibility. But she couldn't do it. Kennedy's hand, holding hers tightly, reminded her that what she saw on the table was her life *then,* and he and their children were her life *now.* It was the only thing that kept her from falling apart. He was determined to get her through this. She could feel him willing her to endure and to triumph. For everyone's sake.

Don't let your stepfather win. Don't let him. He said that whenever the past began to encroach on her happiness. And, so far, it had worked.

Silently, she promised she wouldn't disappoint him and ignored the terrible stabbing sensation she remembered so clearly, along with the stench of her stepfather's breath, his eager grunts and groans, the flash of the camera when she was in the most vulnerable positions a girl could be in.

Pontiff spoke again. "No one ever used the rope or, um, the—any of these items to hurt you in any way?"

A bead of sweat rolled between her shoulder blades.

Madeline squeezed her arm as if to say it didn't matter, that nothing would change if she answered in the affirmative. But Grace knew that wasn't true. Summoning more strength—from where, she had no idea—she managed to add a scoffing tone to her voice. "Of course not."

"No one…touched you inappropriately when you were a girl?" Pontiff repeated.

She lifted her chin. "Who would do such a thing?"

"That's what we're trying to find out," he replied.

Suddenly, the door burst open and Clay charged in, his thick black hair standing up in front as if he'd shoved his hand through it so many times it would no longer lie flat.

Grace was mortified to think her brother would see what was on the table. He knew, of course, but knowing and actually seeing some of the implements of Barker's torture were two completely different things. Clay already felt guilty for the fact that he hadn't realized sooner, hadn't protected her. This would make his guilt even more intense.

He looked at each person. Then, when his gaze landed on the items arranged on the table, his jaw tightened and his blue eyes glittered with dark emotion. "What's going on?"

While Kennedy explained, Grace was afraid that Clay wouldn't be able to control his reaction. The graying pallor of his skin told her how tortured he was by the mere thought of what she'd been through, and worry for him somehow made it easier for her to cope with her own pain.

"Someone must've stolen my underwear," she said when Kennedy was through. "But I have no idea when or how. Or who might've owned these other pairs."

That last part was true. As far as she knew, she'd been her stepfather's only victim. So what did this underwear signify? That there were more?

The possibility of others having suffered as she'd suffered sent a chill down her spine. But she steeled herself against it. She'd think about that later. She couldn't add anything else to what she was feeling right now.

"I used to hang all our laundry on the clothesline," her mother volunteered from the periphery. Considering Irene's present state of mind, it was a worthy attempt at an explanation. They'd been so poor they hadn't had a dryer. But worthy or not, her mother seemed dangerously close to losing her composure. Grace feared that if Clay didn't give them away, Irene would.

Throwing back her shoulders, she pulled off her sunglasses. "Right. Which meant they were available to just about anyone. I'm guessing whoever collected these—" she motioned toward the table and fought to assume her professional persona, hoping no one could tell how badly she was quaking inside "—was in the fantasy stage."

"That was twenty years ago," Pontiff said. "So, if he's still around, he might not be in the fantasy stage anymore."

Grace focused on his neatly clipped mustache. "Have you had any complaints, Chief?"

"No, but…sometimes this type of thing goes unreported."

"That's true," she murmured as if she had as much objectivity as he did.

"Whoever it was killed Lee and ran off," Irene said.

Pontiff wore his skepticism as proudly as his badge. "But no one else has gone missing."

Irene crowded closer. "It was a drifter. It had to be a drifter. Why won't anyone believe me?"

Clay put an arm around their mother and told her to calm down while Madeline tugged Grace from the table. "Mike Metzger lived within walking distance," she said. "Do you think he might've collected these?"

Mike had long been Madeline's suspect of choice. A week before her father went missing, the reverend had caught nineteen-year-old Mike smoking pot in the bathroom of the church and turned him in to the authorities. Mike had spouted off a few threats but the circumstantial evidence pointing his way had never been solid enough for police to press charges. Now Mike was in prison for manufacturing crystal meth in his basement, and Madeline was still harassing him with regular letters.

Grace drew enough breath to speak. Before she could say anything, however, Chief Pontiff interrupted. "We can ask him. He gets home in a few days."

"A few days?" Irene echoed. "But he still has two years."

"Not anymore. He's been granted parole."

Grace felt almost sorry for Mike. He had his problems, but he wasn't a murderer. After a stint in prison, he'd be coming home to another maelstrom of questions about Barker.

She glanced at Clay, wondering if he was thinking about Mike, too, but saw him staring over their mother's head at the things on the table. From the veins standing out in his neck, she knew that what he saw bothered him as much as she'd expected. Hooking her arm through his, she rubbed her cheek against his shoulder to tell him that the past was behind them, that they couldn't allow this discovery to ruin the happiness they'd both found.

"How's Allie?" she asked to remind him of everything they had to protect.

He blinked, then let go of Irene, who was digging through her purse for a tissue.

Grace sensed him struggling to contain his emotions, but it was only when Madeline edged closer that he managed an answer. "Fine. Allie's…" His chest rose as he drew a deep breath. "Allie," he finished simply, using her name as the talisman Grace had intended it to be.

"Are you okay?" Madeline asked.

"I'm fine." He stretched his neck. "But whoever put that stuff in the trunk is one sick bastard," he said and stalked out.

Relieved, Grace watched him go. He'd been careful to say *is* one sick bastard. Not *was*. They'd handled this meeting as well as she could've hoped. With any luck, this discovery would fade into the background and they'd be able to return to their lives.

As Madeline thanked Chief Pontiff for his efforts, Grace nudged Kennedy, indicating that they should go, too. She didn't want to be in the same room with those panties, or with the other objects, either. The person she'd been was not the person she was now. "Grinding Gracie" was the one who'd been raped, repeatedly, by her stepfather, but Grinding Gracie was dead and gone. Grace wouldn't *be* her anymore, she'd reject her pain, her inadequacies, her needs.

But halfway to the door she heard Madeline say something that made her freeze.

"How long will it take?"

"Depends on the lab. Could take a few weeks. Could take months. Without a suspect, we don't have a legitimate reason to ask them to rush."

Graced turned back. "You're going to try and get a DNA sample?"

He nodded.

"From what?"

"Everything."

"But it's been nearly twenty years! Any DNA will be too degraded."

"Not necessarily. This stuff was sealed up tight."

She felt the pressure of Kennedy's hand, warning her to be careful. She was sounding panicky, but she couldn't help it. "But what good will getting a profile do?"

Pontiff's eyebrows rose. "What *good* will it do?"

"It's only helpful if you have something to match it against," she said, "and you don't even have a victim."

Wearing the same rubber gloves he'd used while laying out these objects, he started putting everything back into a brown paper sack. "True, but like I told Madeline, there might be other cases out there. Besides, you never know what we might come up with in the future, right?"

Pontiff knew her professional background, knew she should readily agree. So she did. But she was praying the whole time that the scientists at the lab wouldn't be able to develop the sample he hoped for. If they did, she knew whose DNA they might find. She also knew they might be able to match it to the panties she'd just identified as her own.

5

Irene seemed to have taken the day's events harder than anyone. Madeline helped her out to her car, then returned to the police station so she could talk with Chief Pontiff.

"I have a private investigator coming from California," she told him. "He might be able to help you decide what to do with all this—" she waved toward the box where he'd put the sacks of evidence "—stuff."

Pontiff hesitated, obviously not as pleased with this news as she'd expected him to be. "I can do my own job, Maddy," he said. "I understand you've been disappointed in the past, but I'm already planning to do everything that can be done. There's no need to bring in an outsider."

"He might see something we've missed," she argued.

"The only one missing anything is you," Radcliffe piped up, sounding exasperated. He had plenty of filing left to do—evidenced by the tall stack teetering at his elbow—but he was more interested in eavesdropping. "Didn't you see how Clay reacted? He nearly lost his composure."

"Yes, I saw!" Madeline snapped, her patience wearing thin. "He was upset. But why wouldn't he be? That was his sister's underwear lying on the table."

Pontiff sent Radcliffe a quelling glance and stepped between them. "Maddy, we've grown up together. I've seen your pain and frustration over the years, and I've felt plenty of my own when it comes to your father's case. This whole town has. The police chiefs before me couldn't get to the bottom of it, but I'm determined to be different. I plan to find the truth, okay?"

"Then what'll it hurt to have some help?" she asked.

"I don't want anyone getting in my way. This investigator is from...where did you say? California? He'll have no idea how things are done in Mississpppi."

But maybe that was good, Madeline thought. Then he wouldn't be influenced by the Vincellis, wouldn't have to worry about making the folks around her angry. "An investigation is an investigation," she said. "I hope you'll do what you can to cooperate with him."

Toby's jaw tightened, which told her he wasn't pleased with her answer. "What do you hope to achieve?"

"Resolution," she said and left.

To Madeline, the rest of the week passed with agonizing slowness. After Rachel Simmons's drowning, and the subsequent discovery of the Cadillac, it felt as if the whole town was holding its breath, waiting and watching to see what would happen next. Mothers who generally let their children run freely through Stillwater neighborhoods were keeping them closer to home. And, as she feared would be the case, Clay's name was often associated with talk that there might be a sexual predator in their midst.

Madeline couldn't believe anyone could suspect her stepbrother of being a pedophile. So what if the police had found a few dark hairs in the driver's seat of the Cadillac? It'd been the family car, for crying out loud.

But it wasn't just the hair, and she knew it. It was the fact that he didn't give a damn what others thought of him and didn't bother to hide it. They used his indifference as justification to blame him for anything they'd rather not see in someone else, even though he didn't fit the profile of a pedophile. Pedophiles liked to be around children, sought them out, worked in situations that put them in contact with possible victims. Until Grace married Kennedy eighteen months ago and brought her two stepsons into the family, and Clay's own marriage had gained him a six-year-old daughter, he was almost never around children. He'd lived on the farm alone and come to town once or twice a week for supplies or a game of pool at the billiards hall.

Besides, the things in that trunk had been put there twenty years ago, when Clay was only sixteen.

Fortunately, despite all the stress, Madeline had been able to get her paper out. And it had included the article she'd had such difficulty writing—the one on the discovery of her father's car. Next week's paper would feature an article on pedophiles and how they typically functioned. She was writing it with the hope that it would stifle all the talk about Clay. But she'd have to finish it later. Hunter Solozano would be arriving in Nashville in four hours. She had a long drive ahead of her and didn't want to be late.

Shrugging on her wool coat, Madeline turned off her computer and let herself out, into the alley that led to the gravel lot where she'd parked her car. She'd just locked the door when someone tapped her on the shoulder. Someone whose approach she hadn't heard.

Startled, she turned to see her father's only sibling, Elaine Vincelli, standing right behind her.

Her thoughts had definitely been too macabre of late, if she could be frightened so easily. But she knew it wasn't *only* her thoughts. Her dreams bothered her even more. Last night, Aunt Elaine had been chasing her around the farm with a knife, yelling, "How dare you be disloyal to your own father! How dare you side with those murderers!"

Madeline shivered as a few residual screeches echoed through her head. Reminding herself that it was just a dream, she offered her aunt a polite smile. "Hello."

"Do you have a minute?" Elaine asked.

Clenching the keys in her hand, Madeline sighed. Temperatures were dropping fast as another storm approached, bringing with it an early dark—which was why she hadn't noticed Elaine. She'd been too intent on getting off before the rain started. "Is something wrong?" she asked.

"No, of course not." Her aunt positioned herself as if she expected to be invited in. And since a light drizzle had begun, Madeline felt she should oblige.

Stifling her impatience, she reopened the office. "Would you like to sit down?" she asked, waving Elaine in ahead of her.

"No, thank you."

Her aunt had seemed tense, even a bit nervous in the alley but appeared more relaxed once the door closed behind them.

"What can I do for you?" Madeline forced a polite smile but hadn't felt quite so uncomfortable in ages. She and her aunt had never been close. Madeline remembered her real mother saying that Elaine was a difficult person to get to know—probably the worst comment her mother ever made about anyone. Madeline suspected the real truth was that Elaine hadn't liked Eliza any more than she liked Irene and Eliza knew it. Madeline's mother had been too humble and sweet, too accepting of everyone, to appeal to a "keep up or get lost" personality like Elaine's.

Madeline recalled overhearing a conversation between her father and Elaine, in which Elaine had called Eliza "pathetic" and demanded she be put in an institution where she could get professional help for her chronic depression.

Remembering her aunt's unsympathetic attitude, Madeline figured it was little wonder she'd chosen to stay with Irene after her father went missing. She didn't really know her maternal grandparents, who'd moved twice in the past year and now lived in Oklahoma. Her paternal grandparents were dead, and Irene had given her more love in the three years she'd been part of Madeline's life at that point than her aunt ever had. Even in the dark days after Eliza's death, Elaine hadn't reached out to the ten-year-old girl her sister-in-law had left behind.

So why was Elaine here now?

"Chief Pontiff came by the house last night," her aunt said.

"Did he have any news?" Madeline asked eagerly. She believed Toby would've contacted her, but she couldn't imagine any other reason for her aunt's visit.

"No, not yet. He told me you've hired a private detective." She folded her arms across her broad, solid body. The white streaks of hair at her temples contrasted sharply with the black of the rest, and the way she'd combed it back off her face reminded Madeline of Ursula, the Sea Witch in Disney's *The Little Mermaid*. "Is that true?"

Where was she going with this? "Yes. I've found someone who's supposed to be exceptionally good. Why?"

"That's my question to you," she said. "*Why?* Why bother? Chief Pontiff's looking into it again. Isn't that enough?"

"Police involvement hasn't been enough in the past," Madeline pointed out. "I know Toby's not happy about me bringing in an outsider. He told me as much. But as objective as he's trying to be, he'll most likely go down the same road as everyone else." He'd already refused to let Allie search the car, hadn't he? But Madeline didn't mention that because her aunt was probably behind it. "I'm sure you've heard about the black hairs he removed from the driver's side of the Cadillac."

"Is that why you're hiring a P.I.?" Elaine asked. "Because of the Montgomerys?"

"That's part of the reason."

"I don't think this will help. All the circumstantial evidence points at them. Any investigator worth his salt would see that." She lowered her voice. "And maybe next time Clay won't get off."

Was she *warning* Madeline? For Clay's sake? That didn't make sense. For years, Elaine and her family had been dying to see the Montgomerys in jail, especially Clay. "At the very least, an investigator from somewhere else should have a more open mind," Madeline said.

"It doesn't matter how open his mind is, the proof is the proof."

Madeline transferred her purse to her other shoulder. "There is no proof. Not so far. You said yourself that it's all circumstantial."

Her aunt began to toy with the perpetual-motion skier on Madeline's desk. It was a Christmas gift Kirk had used to invite Madeline skiing. But he'd been angry when she wouldn't leave Stillwater to take the seven-day trip. Instead of heading off together, they'd broken up.

Ironically, had they gone, she would've been out of town when the rescue workers found her father's car. Which was precisely why she wouldn't leave. She couldn't risk missing something that would finally unravel the mystery.

"You're going to force me to say it, aren't you?" Elaine murmured.

Madeline put the skier inside her drawer. Things were difficult enough these days without such a vivid reminder of Kirk and how much more comfortable her life had been with him in it. She'd thought she might get a call from him once he heard the news about her father's car. Lord knows everyone else had called. But he was obviously as determined as she was to make the split permanent. "Say what?" she replied.

"That I think you might be right about the Montgomerys."

Madeline forgot about Kirk and the skier. "In what way?"

"Maybe they aren't to blame for…whatever happened."

Last summer, when the district attorney had dropped the charges against Clay, the Vincellis hadn't hollered as loudly as Madeline had expected them to, but this was a *complete* reversal. "Are you serious?"

"Would I joke about something like that?"

Definitely not. Elaine Vincelli didn't joke about anything. "Joe and Roger still think Clay's guilty," Madeline said.

"Have they been causing trouble?"

The ominous note in her aunt's voice suggested there'd be repercussions for Joe and Roger if they had—and Elaine could definitely make good on such a threat. Although both men were in their early thirties, Roger lived at home, and Joe, divorced twice from the same woman, lived in a house near Stillwater Sand & Gravel, the business owned by his parents. Joe and Roger worked for mom and pop, too. Madeline doubted anyone else would hire them. They spent too much time drinking, gambling, fighting and chasing women.

"They were pretty adamant at the quarry," Madeline said.

"I'll talk to them," she promised. "But I, for one, hate to see you disrupt your life yet again with all this business about your father. I'm your aunt." She waved imperiously. "You should allow me to advise you. And I think it's time we all moved on."

Now? When the Cadillac had just been found? This was the first break they'd had. "What about the things in his trunk?" Madeline asked. "We can't shrug our shoulders and walk away."

"Let it go!" Elaine nearly shook a finger in Madeline's face.

"Why?" Madeline asked.

Her aunt wrapped her coat tighter around her and headed for the door. "Just listen to me, for a change."

* * *

Let it go...

Madeline tried to throw off the foreboding caused by her aunt's words as she stood at the airport in Nashville, waiting for Hunter Solozano. She was late but, fortunately, so was his plane. The storm had been responsible for a lot of delays. She was surrounded by crowds of people, many of whom shifted restlessly, shook off their wet umbrellas or held up signs designating the name of the person or party they'd come to meet.

She wished she'd taken the time to make a sign. She had no idea what Hunter looked like. From his grouchy voice, she imagined an overweight middle-aged man with a receding hairline, saggy jowls and thick, sausagelike fingers. But when Hunter's plane finally arrived and the passengers streamed into the baggage claim area, the only person she saw who even remotely resembled that mental picture was immediately approached by someone else.

As the passengers found their baggage and drifted away, Madeline began to worry that Hunter had missed his flight.

It wasn't a pleasant thought after driving three hours in the pouring rain.

She got her cell phone from her purse, checked her signal strength and punched in his number. Who needed a cardboard sign in this day and age? She'd simply call him. If he'd actually arrived, she'd tell him to meet her at the fifth carousel. And if he hadn't—

For all her aunt's dire warnings, she didn't want to even think about the fact that he might not have come. She was counting on him to put an end to the doubt and conjecture.

"I've got to catch a break eventually," she grumbled and put the phone to her ear. But then she spotted a man striding purposefully toward her from the lost luggage counter and hung up. She'd seen this guy walk past her before but... *He* couldn't be her investigator, could he?

"Hunter Solozano?" she said tentatively.

His eyes swept over her, his expression revealing little except annoyance. "That's me."

He was carrying a *guitar....* A lot of country-star wannabes came through the Nashville airport, but he didn't look anything like a cowboy. He was definitely West Coast.

"Is that all your luggage?" she asked. Other than the guitar, he had a small carry-on bag that appeared to contain a computer.

He raked his fingers through blond hair that was a bit too long and beginning to curl at the ends. "They lost the rest."

"You're kidding, right?" He *had* to be kidding— about more than his luggage. He looked like a...a *surfer.* About six feet tall, he had icy blue eyes, a lean, rugged face and a great tan. Worse, the hint of beard covering his jaw made him appear too lazy to be cunning or perceptive. And his rock-hard body indicated he spent more time swimming in the ocean than sitting behind a desk.

"No joke," he said. "But they told me they'd drive it to Stillwater as soon as they find it. Hopefully, it'll get here sometime tomorrow."

What have I done? She'd been expecting someone driven, maybe even ruthless. Someone capable of solving a mystery that had stumped Stillwater's best and brightest for twenty years. Instead, she'd hired a beach bum with a guitar—for one thousand dollars a day!

"Right." She barely managed to stifle a groan. He was wearing a long-sleeved T-shirt over another T-shirt, a pair of faded, holey jeans and…flip-flops.

Flip-flops! Frowning, she rubbed her forehead.

"I said they'd drive it out," he repeated, watching her curiously.

"I heard you."

He hiked up the computer bag he carried on one of his impressive shoulders. "So…what's the problem?"

Dropping her hand, she decided to be honest with him. "Tell me your father or your older brother is here somewhere."

One eyebrow, much darker than his sun-streaked hair, slid up. "What's that supposed to mean?"

"You're too young," she complained.

"Too young for what? I'm thirty-two. How old do I have to be?"

"Older than that. I'm thirty-six and I certainly don't feel equipped to handle this…this *mess*. Besides, you're too—" she motioned to his guitar "—God, you could pass for Keith Urban. I don't need someone who's drop-dead gorgeous. And I sure as hell don't need someone who can sing. I need a P.I. who'll take my problem seriously, who's so dedicated and tenacious that he won't give up, no matter what."

His scowl darkened. "I liked the drop-dead gorgeous part, but I'm more offended than flattered by your other remarks."

"I don't care. This isn't fun and games to me, Mr.—*Hunter*. See? Now that I've met you, I can't even call you Mr. Solozano. Mr. Solozano would be your father."

"I could go out and buy some wing-tip shoes, a magnifying glass and a trench coat. Would that help?" he asked sarcastically.

"So now you're a comedian, too."

"Should I have taken you seriously? How does my appearance preclude my ability to do my job?"

"Every available woman in Stillwater will be coming on to you, wasting your time—which is really *my* time, since I'll be paying for it." She couldn't admit that she might be tempted to come on to him herself, that he'd be a distraction she didn't need. Especially since she still wasn't over Kirk.

"It doesn't matter who comes on to me. I'm not interested."

"On the phone you mentioned an ex-wife."

"And now you know why."

When she hesitated, he said, "So where do we go from here, Ms. Barker? Can you get past your attraction to me? Or do you want to sacrifice your retainer to compensate me for my trouble and send me home?"

Both questions were so shockingly blunt, Madeline didn't know which to answer first. Money won out. "Sacrifice my retainer? Are you crazy?" she cried. "And I'm not attracted to you! I'm already involved."

"Then what's the problem?"

The fact that she'd just lied about being involved, of course. Not only was she flying solo at this point, she was beginning to miss the emotional and physical comforts a man could offer.

She swallowed hard. "You're not attracted to me, are you?" If it was all one-sided—*her* side—she should be okay. She certainly wasn't about to lose the five thousand dollars she'd given him.

It was his turn to hesitate. His gaze flicked over her

a second time but quickly returned to her face. "I told you. I'm not interested in any woman."

"Right. The ex." She took a deep breath. "That's good news."

"I'm glad you're happy." He rubbed his hands. "So…are we on?"

"Let's see how it goes this week," she replied. "If you're as good as you're supposed to be, I should be able to tell fairly soon."

"Thanks for the vote of confidence," he said dryly.

She started to lead him out, into the rain. "There's one more thing."

"I'm dying to hear it."

Putting up her umbrella, she raised her voice against the rumbling motors and the security guard telling everyone to move along. "People where I live are very…conservative. If you alienate them, we won't have a chance."

"Why would I alienate them?"

"I'm just telling you that Stillwater isn't California."

He gave her a salute. "Consider me warned. Somehow I'll keep my liberal self in check."

A minute earlier, he'd said he wasn't interested in her—or any other woman. But when she glanced back at him, she caught him checking out her behind. "I thought you weren't interested," she said.

He grinned. "Doesn't hurt to look."

6

Hunter sat in the passenger seat of Madeline Barker's economy car, watching the windshield wipers jerk across the glass and thinking that a woman driving a 1992 Toyota Corolla probably couldn't afford him. "Your windshield wipers might actually work if you'd replace the blades," he said.

She sent him an irritated look. "Thanks for the tip."

"You're welcome." Drumming his fingers on his knee, he cursed the moment he'd decided to come to the South. What was he doing here? He should be in Hawaii, sitting on the beach. But despite the rain in Tennessee and an unusual and slightly worrisome reception by his new client, Hawaii didn't sound as appealing as it should have. He'd spent most of the last month on Oahu, taking pictures of an elected public official who'd flown his children's babysitter there for a torrid affair. Without Maria, Hunter had no desire to go back so soon. What was the point? He wasn't the type to lounge on the beach all day—not unless he was doing it for a reason, as with his last job, or he had someone with whom to share the sun and sand.

Someone... He grimaced. Not only had he lost Maria's love and respect, he'd managed to estrange most of his family. He'd been too hurt and angry to be civil to anyone. And he hadn't allowed himself a romantic liaison—a romantic anything—since he'd gotten drunk two years ago and let Selena, the divorcee next door, coax him into bed.

"So…are we going to drive the whole way without speaking?" he asked, eager to interrupt his own thoughts. He berated himself over that mistake often enough without starting in well before the usual sleepless night.

"I'm thinking," she said.

"I hope you're thinking about telling me what you know of the day your father disappeared. Or is that part of the test to see if I'm any good?"

"Funny." She came up on a van, slowed, then switched lanes.

He knew they'd gotten off on the wrong foot, that he should do what he could to relieve the tension that had sprung up the moment they'd met, but he was tired and cranky after the long flight and already regretting the trip. "You know how irreverent some of us *young* Californians can be."

"At least you haven't ended any of your sentences with *dude* or *awesome*," she retorted.

His irritation level spiked. "I didn't want to come here in the first place. This was your idea."

She immediately backed off. "I know. I'm sorry. I should've listened to you. But…I was desperate."

And now she was disappointed. He could hear it in her voice.

Hunter didn't want to care—some of what she'd said made him angry—but the slump of her shoulders bothered him. Cursing silently, he dragged his eyes away from her and watched the wet pavement rush under their tires. "Don't give up on me too soon, okay?" he said. "I can't promise that I'll solve your father's murder. If it was a murder. Maybe no one can. But I'll make every attempt."

"In between working on your tan?" She'd mumbled the words, but he could still decipher them.

"You're just mad that I said I wasn't attracted to you," he snapped.

"Why should that bother me? You're not attracted to anyone, remember?"

"I remember," he said. But he had to admit she was pretty. Tall, though maybe a bit too thin, she had very distinguished features—wide green eyes that tilted up at the edges, thick dark lashes, high cheekbones and a full, sensual mouth. She had a few freckles across her nose, but the rest of her skin was as smooth and unblemished as porcelain, and she seemed confident yet vulnerable. It was an odd mix, but it definitely worked.

"I wanted someone I could take seriously," she explained.

He shook his head. "You wanted a savior, and you got a carpenter. As history suggests, they don't have to be mutually exclusive."

Her gaze slid his way. "Now you're telling me you have a Christ complex?"

He rolled his eyes. "I'm done talking to you. I hope you feel like an idiot when you're finished with this tantrum."

"*Tantrum?* I've never thrown a tantrum in my life."

Hunter told himself to ignore her until she could come to grips with her roiling emotions. He'd been where she was—pushed beyond his normal ability to cope, desperately searching for a way to avoid the pain of his situation. He'd created his own problems while, as far as he could tell, she'd done little to deserve hers. But these days his own temper lurked too close to the surface.

"What do you call *this?*" he asked. "Good old-fashioned Southern hospitality?"

"Try abject despair," she replied. "Do you know how many people think I'm foolish for bringing you to town? Only my cousins approve, which is reason enough for concern. When Clay and Grace see you—" She threw up one hand while keeping the other on the wheel.

"Maybe those who are least happy about my involvement are the very people who have something to hide," he retorted. He was taking a big leap. But he wanted to provoke her, to find or create reasons to dislike her so he wouldn't have to worry about keeping an appropriate distance between them. He'd already found one reason: he'd expected her to be grateful he'd relented and taken her on as a client. Instead, she acted as if she'd made a big mistake in hiring him.

"Whose side are you on?" she asked.

"My own," he said. "That's the way it has to be."

She didn't say anything for nearly twenty minutes, wouldn't even look at him. Finally, he broke the silence. "Is this going to continue, or are you ready to tell me what you know about how and why your father disappeared?"

She lowered the volume on the radio. "I owe you an apology," she said stiffly. "I've been trying to formulate it for the past fifteen miles, but I'm not really myself right now. And I have no explanation for my poor behavior except—there's a lot riding on this for me, you know?"

He didn't want her to apologize. Then he couldn't hold her comments against her. "Not the best apology I've ever received," he said, although it'd sounded sincere.

"So you won't forgive me?"

The entreaty in her voice made him feel something he hadn't felt in a long time—genuine compassion. She was so exhausted. He could hear it in the way she talked, see it in the way she moved. Still, he didn't want to experience *her* pain; he had enough of his own.

"Give me some background on your father," he said instead of addressing the question.

"Where should I start?"

"What was his name?"

"Lee Barker."

"What did he do for a living?"

"He was a pastor, very devout, but also popular."

"When and where was he last seen?"

Lightning flashed, illuminating the silvery glow of the rain-slicked hood as well as Madeline's classic profile. "It'll be twenty years on October fourth. He went to church to meet with a couple of ladies who were planning a youth activity, and he never came home."

He refused to consider the emotional consequences of what she'd been through. Distance—that was his first priority. Solving this case came second. "Has someone checked out these ladies?" He knew it was probably a stupid question, but he had to begin at the beginning. Being methodical kept his focus where he wanted it to be—on the facts.

"Of course. Nora Young and Rachel Cook would never hurt anyone, least of all my father. They idolized him. Imagine Aunt Bea on the *Andy Griffith Show* and you'll have some idea of what these ladies are like."

"You mentioned a stepmother on the phone. Where was your real mother when this occurred?" he asked. When one spouse went missing, the other, or an ex, was frequently to blame. Before he started investigating the stepmom, he needed to rule out the first Mrs. Barker.

But that was easier than he'd expected.

"Dead," Madeline said.

He watched her closely, trying to gauge her reaction. "I'm sorry to hear that."

She didn't respond.

"What happened?"

"She shot herself with my father's gun."

"When?"

"I was ten."

He flinched in spite of himself. "Who found her?"

Madeline's knuckles whitened on the steering wheel. "I did."

Shit... He didn't know what to say. She'd been through so much.

But sad as her story was, her pain didn't have to be his pain, he reminded himself. She didn't need him to save her. She was just a client—a beautiful client, but a client nonetheless.

"I'd come home from school and wanted to show her my report card," she went on in a monotone. "My father sent me in to wake her from a nap and—" her voice quavered "—and there she was."

Distance, remember? "Your father hadn't heard the shot?" he prompted softly. Maybe it was insensitive to ask, but he had to learn all he could about Madeline Barker and her history. It was the best way to solve her father's murder, which he intended to do as quickly as possible—before he could find too many things to like about her. Besides her looks, of course.

"No. She did it while he was out working on the farm. He saw me get off the bus and followed me to the house."

"How long after your mother's death did your father go missing?" he asked.

"Six years. We managed on our own for three. Then my father met a woman named Irene Montgomery."

"You didn't know her?"

The rain pounded harder, but Madeline didn't slow down. "No. They met at a regional singles dance. She was living in Booneville, which isn't too far from Stillwater. He was forty-three and she was only thirty-two, but she needed an older man in her life."

Was it possible she'd needed a few other things, as well? Some creature comforts she could better enjoy without him? "Why older?" he asked.

"She'd dropped out of school, pregnant at sixteen. She married the father of her baby, but after they'd had two more children, he abandoned her. She didn't have a lot of options, and was looking for some stability."

"And your father offered that."

She turned the knob for the windshield wipers until they were swishing back and forth at a frenetic pace. He guessed they were keeping time with her heart. But outwardly she remained calm. "Sure. He had the farm my stepbrother now owns, a good job, modest savings. And he was well-respected in the community."

Hunter leaned forward to see around the silky fall of her hair. "I thought your stepmother inherited the farm." He'd made a note of it when they talked on the phone the first time she'd called because the farm might've provided the stepmother with a motive for murder.

"She did. But when Molly, my youngest sister, graduated from high school, my stepmother moved to town and my brother took over."

"Is it a nice piece of property?"

The look she shot him said she'd heard the suspicion in his voice. "Don't jump to that conclusion."

"What conclusion? It's a logical question."

"I told you on the phone, my stepmother didn't kill my father."

"You were with her when your father went missing?"

Her expression grew haunted. "No, I wasn't home that night. I was staying at a friend's."

"Who was at home?"

"Grace and Molly and later, Clay. My mother was there part of the time, but she certainly wouldn't kill the one person who was putting food on the table for her children. We almost starved after my father went missing. If it wasn't for my stepbrother, we would've gone hungry—or been separated and taken into foster care."

"What'd he do to save the day?"

"Ran the farm, worked odd jobs in town, anything he had to do, really. That's why my stepmother turned the farm over to him."

"Sounds like he was the best-equipped to run it."

"He was. And five years ago, he paid each of us our portion of what it was worth at the time my father went missing," she added. "Which was very generous of him," she added. "I wasn't expecting any payment. We would've faced foreclosure without him."

"So he's done well?"

"Well enough that he could lend me a significant

amount of money last year when I needed to buy a new printing press."

Madeline's reference to a recent loan hardly put Hunter at ease. Would she be able to pay him? There were a *lot* of things about this case that were making him uneasy. Beginning with the woman behind the wheel. "So Clay's older?" he asked.

"We were both sixteen when everything fell apart."

"He took responsibility for the family at *sixteen*?"

She smiled faintly. "He's always been very capable."

Capable of murder? Sixteen was pretty young to kill, but it wouldn't be the first time a teenager had resorted to deadly violence. Madeline readily admitted that Clay's abilities had outdistanced his age. And she'd mentioned that there was a gun in the house. "How big is your brother?"

"Well over six feet. Why?"

"Just wondering."

Her lips formed a grim line.

Hunter leaned forward once again, to see her face more clearly. "What's wrong?"

"He didn't kill my father, either."

"And you know that because he has a foolproof alibi?"

"I know *him*." The loyalty and conviction in her voice sounded resolute. But the fact that she hadn't volunteered any solid proof concerned Hunter. Obviously, there was some question here.

Hunter rubbed his chin while he considered her reaction. "Where was he the night it happened?"

"Out with friends. But then he came home."

"And from that point he's only got his mother and sisters to vouch for him?"

"More or less."

Hunter's discomfort increased. Was she *really* sure about Clay—or just blind to the possibility? "What about your stepmother's first husband?"

"What about him?"

"He never called or came to visit? Never paid child support? Never sent a Christmas card?"

"Growing up, we never heard from him. Didn't even know where he was. But he showed up last summer. Turns out he's been living in Alaska all these years. He flies fishermen to remote lakes and streams, that sort of thing."

Hunter tucked that piece of information away to examine later. A boy abandoned by his father could easily harbor a deep resentment of adult males. "Tell me a little more about Irene."

"After my father met her, they got married and she brought her children to live with us. Clay and I were thirteen. Grace was ten; Molly was eight."

"Did you get along with your stepsiblings?"

"Very well."

"You never fought?" He didn't bother hiding his skepticism.

"We had the usual squabbles. But to be honest, those years were some of the best of my life. In the summer, after we finished our work, Clay would give us rides on the tractor. Sometimes Grace and I would dress up in Irene's old clothes and pretend we were getting married. Molly would beg us to put makeup on her, and we'd weave dandelion wreaths to wear in our hair."

He found the images her words created oddly appealing, like something out of a book. "What about your stepmother?"

Her turn signal clicked as Madeline passed the car in front of them. "Mom would make lemonade and bake cookies and we'd go out on the porch to read the Bible. I can still hear the creak of her rocking chair, the insects buzzing, feel the heat of late afternoon..."

"So your stepmother was as religious as your father."

The hesitation in her manner told him she wasn't as sure of her next answer. "No...he was the one who insisted on daily Bible study. But she made a party out of it. She knew how to make the most mundane tasks fun."

Hunter sensed Madeline's desire to steer his interest away from the Montgomerys. But if she wanted him to solve this disappearance—this probable murder—he had to investigate all possibilities and eliminate them one by one. "Did your father and your stepmother ever fight?"

Her teeth sank into her bottom lip and, for some reason, Hunter thought of the condom a client had recently handed him as a promotional piece for his strip joint. He'd shoved it in his wallet, but he had no plans to use it, at least in Mississippi. Fortunately, he wouldn't be tempted—not by Madeline Barker, anyway. She had a boyfriend.

"They had occasional disagreements," she was saying. "But they didn't get violent. My father never raised his voice. And my Mom—*Irene*," she clarified, "wasn't the type to fight. If Dad asked her to join the church choir, she joined the choir. If he asked her to host a funeral luncheon, she hosted a luncheon. She wanted nothing more than to be a good wife, to please him."

"She wanted *nothing* more than that? You don't think she was too servile? That she might've resented her lack of power in the relationship?"

"This is the South, remember?"

"I understand that Mississippi might not be a hotbed of feminist activism, but that doesn't mean she liked it."

"I would've known if she resented him. She didn't."

Possibly. "Did your father *expect* to be obeyed?" he asked.

"He did," she admitted without reservation. "Like I told you, it's fairly normal where I live, and was even more so twenty-five years ago."

Hunter had been raised by a strong, very opinionated mother who'd endowed him with a great deal of respect for the opposite sex. He found this take on women *very* old-fashioned, as if he'd slipped into the fifties—or earlier. "Do you fit the Southern mold?"

"I believe in equal jobs for equal pay, but I like it when a man is nice enough to open the door for me or pump my gas," she said.

His smile was slightly mocking. "The best of both worlds?"

"I don't see why those things have to be mutually exclusive. I want what's right, but I'm still a woman and I enjoy being treated like one."

"Does your boyfriend perform those little courtesies?"

She blinked at him. "What boyfriend?"

The boyfriend who meant Hunter didn't have to worry about whether or not he was attracted to her. "At the airport, you said you were involved with someone."

She looked away. "Oh, right."

He didn't think it said much for the relationship that she could forget this boyfriend so easily. But that was her problem. "Are you two planning on getting married someday?"

"I'd rather not talk about it."

What was so invasive about that question? He'd asked her much worse. But she had a point. He was wandering off topic. "Fine. If you had to name your father's greatest fault, what would it be?" he asked, forcing his attention back where it belonged.

She answered without even having to think about it. "He was too preoccupied with his work. His church and the people in it were everything to him. But he was good to us."

Hunter wondered if Irene would tell him the same thing. "Was there any life insurance?"

"My father had a small policy, but my mother's never tried to collect on it."

"Why not?"

"We were hoping he wasn't…gone forever, of course."

We… That was interesting. It'd been difficult to pay the mortgage, yet Irene hadn't tried to prove that her missing husband was dead so she could collect on his life insurance. Had she truly been hoping for his return? Or did she fear that going after the money would spark an investigation by the insurance company?

If wife number two was to blame, money wasn't the motive or she would've applied for the insurance. And he doubted she would've kept Barker's daughter.

So maybe Barker's death had been triggered by anger or jealousy…. "Any chance that either your father or Irene could've been having an affair?"

"No."

That was it. No hesitation. Only one word. "How do you know?"

"Irene turned a few heads. She still does. She tried

to be the perfect pastor's wife, but simple and demure isn't part of her personality. Wait till you meet her— you'll understand. Ever since I've known her, she's styled her hair big, worn lots of makeup, loved tight-fitting, brightly colored clothing and shown too much cleavage." She smiled affectionately. "When we were growing up, she wasn't close to anyone except us. She was new, and we lived away from town, on a farm."

"No one in particular singled her out?"

"Just the ladies who'd hoped to marry my dad. They found fault with her constantly."

"What about neighbors?" he asked. "Could your mother have had a relationship with someone who lived nearby?"

"If you'd met the neighbors you wouldn't even ask," she said with a laugh. "Besides, they mostly socialized with my father. They'd known him for years. And, as I mentioned, they didn't really approve of Irene." Madeline twisted a lock of her hair. "I don't remember her having even one close girlfriend, to be honest with you."

Even when she wasn't nibbling on her lip, something about her fascinated Hunter. But acknowledging that made him feel as if he was flirting with disaster, so he looked away. "Sounds like she was pretty isolated."

"I think she was just relieved to be able to feed and clothe her children. Chances were she would've lost them to the state if my father hadn't come along."

A thirty-two-year-old woman struggling to hold her family together would probably marry almost anyone who could provide some security. Obviously, Irene Montgomery needed Barker—but did she love him? "What about your father?" he asked.

"What about him?"

"Could he have been having an affair?"

"My father was a pastor," she replied.

"He wouldn't be the first to fall."

She shook her head. "He abhorred promiscuity, especially adultery. He called it the greatest of all sins."

Hunter felt as if she'd just pressed a hot branding iron—a large A—into his chest. He believed that marriage was sacred, too. Which was why he couldn't forgive himself. Maybe he and Antoinette wouldn't have made it, anyway. Lord knows they'd been having their share of problems. He'd moved into the guest bedroom months before The Incident. But that was no excuse for what he'd done. He should've ended his marriage first. He just hadn't recognized his own limitations.

"He taught that chastity was worth the sacrifice of all else," Madeline added.

"It had to be tough, growing up in the shadow of such a strict father."

"Why?" she asked.

"You never made a mistake? You weren't ever... tempted?"

"Sure." She shrugged. "But I managed to wait... quite a while."

Madeline's sex life had little or nothing to do with the case he was investigating, but it beat the hell out of thinking about his own. And the interior of the small car, along with the darkness and the steady pounding of the rain, created a sense of intimacy that made it all too easy to ask. "How long is quite a while?"

"Until I started dating Kirk."

"Your current boyfriend?" he asked in amazement.

"Sort of." She mumbled the words.

"So you were…what? Thirty-four when you lost your virginity?"

"Thirty-two."

"Wow." He almost couldn't believe it. Obviously, the reverend's teachings had been very effective.

"I know. I was kind of old," she admitted.

"*Kind* of?" he echoed.

"Stillwater isn't like L.A." She sounded slightly offended. "We're…conservative."

"You've mentioned that, but—" he released his breath in a soft whistle "—what made you wait *that* long?"

"I was hoping to meet the right guy."

"But you didn't?"

"No. I think I realized it even at the time. I just got tired of waiting, tried to settle."

Hunter couldn't help asking, "Did you like it?"

Her lips curved into a sexy smile. "Like what?" she asked with false innocence.

"You know what."

"What do you think?"

Her husky tone caused a strange flutter in Hunter's stomach, which surprised him. He hadn't felt anything like that since *long* before his divorce. And he didn't want to feel it now. Not for someone else's woman. "You and Kirk must be pretty serious," he said.

"Not anymore."

The flutter disappeared. "Something's changed?"

She turned down the radio, which was playing Carrie Underwood's "Jesus, Take the Wheel." Since they'd been driving, Madeline had changed the station many times, but always from one country song to another. Hunter was beginning to believe there was no other kind of music available. Being so close to Nashville, he'd expected to hear *some* country music, but he'd heard nothing else. The differences between the South and the West were even more pronounced than he'd assumed—and that included meeting a woman as beautiful as Madeline Barker who'd held onto her virginity for thirty-two years.

"We broke up six weeks ago," she said.

Hunter felt his jaw drop. That wasn't good news. He'd been counting on some other man standing between them, keeping him mindful of his boundaries. And now... "You told me you were involved. Wasn't lying on your father's list of cardinal sins?"

"I wasn't *really* lying. Kirk and I were together for five years, and it hasn't been that long that we split up."

He fiddled with the door handle. "Does that mean you're planning to get back together?"

She kept her attention on the road. "No."

Great. He'd just plunged himself into temptation. But he couldn't get too angry with her. They'd both lied. She'd said she was involved—and he'd said he wasn't interested.

Hunter wasn't happy about something. Madeline could tell. But she couldn't believe he cared that much about whether or not she'd told a white lie, especially when it had no bearing on the case. "My love life doesn't matter, though, right?" she said.

His scowl darkened. "Of course not."

"That's what I thought." She was afraid he'd question why she'd even asked. But he didn't. He shifted, sighed and seemed to make an effort to resume their conversation. "Do you think there's any chance your father might still be alive?"

She wished she could say yes, wished he'd tell her

it was possible. But he didn't know about the Cadillac yet. She hadn't provided any details the night she'd hired him and since then, they'd spoken only about the arrangements for his visit. "They've never found his body. But he wouldn't abandon me."

"I've known fathers who've done worse," he said.

She didn't acknowledge the comment. "They pulled his car out of the quarry last Monday."

"Excuse me?" There was fresh irritation in his voice. "That's an important piece of information. Don't you think?"

"That's why I'm passing it along," she said.

"Why didn't you mention it before?"

"You weren't here before."

"I've got a phone."

She rolled her eyes. "And you've been so friendly when I've contacted you in the past. Gee, I wonder why I didn't call you right up."

He didn't bother to defend himself. "Did they find anything?"

Her seat belt felt as if it was pinning her to the seat. She gave it a yank to create some slack. Then, slowing, she drove to the side of the road, let the engine idle and twisted in her seat. She wanted to see Hunter's face when she delivered this news.

"What are we doing?" he asked.

"Stopping."

"Why?"

"So we can talk."

"About the Cadillac?"

"Yes."

His eyebrows went up, but he waited for her to continue.

"They found some things in the trunk," she said. "Some very alarming things."

"Like…"

"A suitcase."

"So your father *was* planning to leave."

She shook her head. "It wasn't filled with clothes."

"I'm waiting," he said.

Summoning her nerve, she smoothed her palms over her thighs. "It contained a dildo, some rope—"

"Whoa!" He held up a hand. "Did I just hear a sexually repressed Southern woman say *dildo?*"

She wasn't in the mood for levity. "And three pairs of girls' panties," she finished.

As she'd expected, Hunter's teasing smile instantly disappeared. "Girls who would've been how old?"

"Eleven, twelve, thirteen."

"Shit!" He smacked the door. "I knew better than to get involved in this case. But instead of flying to Hawaii, I've landed right in the middle of—"

"I'm sorry to put you out," she broke in. "But I *am* paying you, if you'll recall."

Shutting his eyes, he pinched the bridge of his nose. "I don't care about the money," he said. "Take me back to the airport."

7

Ray Harper turned his bottle of beer around and around on the varnished wood of Stillwater's only bar, making wet circles. He didn't know what else to do. His hands were shaking too badly to lift the bottle to his mouth.

John Keller was seated to his right, and Walt Eastman sat beyond John. Generally, Ray liked John and Walt. They were both ten years younger than he was but when he was in town Ray spent so much time at the pool hall, he sidled up to whoever was there. Sometimes he and John would bet on a game of pool, but more often it was Walt who'd stay and help him close down the place. They usually had a damn good time.

But tonight wasn't promising to be one of their better evenings. He'd just heard Walt say something to John that made his blood run cold.

"John?" Walt prompted when John didn't respond right away.

John pulled his gaze from the basketball game playing on the television affixed to the wall. "What was that?"

Ray held his breath so he could hear Walt repeat

what he'd said a moment earlier. Maybe he'd misunderstood the first time, or the alcohol he'd had was playing tricks with his mind. But he'd only been at Let the Good Times Roll for fifteen minutes. He wasn't drunk yet.

Walt scooted his stool closer to John's. "I asked if you heard about the dildo the police found in the trunk of Reverend Barker's car."

John's mouth flattened in obvious disgust. "Yeah, I heard. Sick, huh? Who told you?"

"Radcliffe was talking about it at the café."

Ray's mouth had gone dry at "dildo." "When was this?" he asked.

"A few days ago," John replied.

Mention of the reverend wouldn't typically have alarmed Ray. He knew the Cadillac had been salvaged; he'd spoken to Madeline about it. But last he'd heard the police hadn't come up with anything important.

"Where you been, man?" John said with a nudge. "The news is all over town."

Ray had been in Iuka ever since he'd spoken to Madeline. He'd breathed a huge sigh of relief when he'd hung up with her—only to return to this?

"I heard it was huge. Where would someone get a dildo like that?" Walt asked. "Online?"

"Who knows?" John drew a dish of peanuts toward him. "It's the girls' panties that bother me."

Panties? Ray's heart nearly seized at the word. Had Barker kept a pair of Katie's underwear? Or were they Rose Lee's?

"Radcliffe told me—on the sly, you know—that one pair belonged to Grace," Walt said.

John took another pull from his beer. "Poor thing. I

like Kennedy. He's a damn good banker. Can't imagine he was happy to hear that about his wife."

Walt tossed a few peanuts into his mouth. "Question is, who owned the others?"

John started peeling the label off his Bud Light. "I don't think they know, but they're hoping to find out."

"Are they—" Ray's voice squeaked, and he coughed in an attempt to lower the pitch. "Are they actively searching, then? They're officially reopening the case?"

"I hear it's official." John proceeded to make a small pile with the curling pieces of beer label. "At least, they're doing what they can."

"It's the first real lead they've had," Walt added.

"And it's the first time they haven't immediately gone after Clay," John said. "He might be a bad son of a bitch, but he'd never hurt that sister of his. Any of 'em, for that matter."

Ray's shirt began to stick to his back even though the bar wasn't hot or crowded. He needed to calm down, think clearly. But the fear that made his pulse race had the opposite effect on his mind. "It's been twenty years now," he said. "How do they expect to find the owner of a pair of panties after so long?"

"They've been asking around," Walt said, glancing at the basketball game.

What if they asked *him?* Ray wondered. Then he'd lie and claim he didn't recognize them. No one else would be able to identify Rose Lee's underwear. He'd been raising her on his own by then.

He'd be fine, he told himself. But John's next comment inspired fresh panic.

"They're being tested for DNA."

Ray's hands tightened on his bottle. *"What?"*

Taking a napkin from a stack to his left, John wiped the counter in front of him. "Pontiff sent the panties to the state crime lab. There might be some bodily fluids on the fabric," he said.

"Could they *see* any?" Ray asked.

"Not with the naked eye. But you never know."

"If there *is* something, and they manage to solve this case, we should call the producers of one of those forensics shows," Walt said enthusiastically. "Maybe we'd see ourselves on TV."

Ray could barely hear him for the ringing in his ears. *Bodily fluids...* There'd been plenty, hadn't there? His and Barker's. "But those panties came out of the quarry. Weren't they wet? Wouldn't any b-bodily fluids be washed away?"

"Pontiff told me they were sealed in plastic," John said, tossing a few more peanuts in his mouth.

Walt waved to the bartender, trying to get another drink. "It's a wonder they didn't mildew."

"According to Radcliffe, there was some mildew," John said. "But I guess it doesn't destroy the human DNA. Pontiff thinks they can separate it."

Ray remembered the exquisite care Barker took with his victims' personal belongings. The reverend saved them, licked them, touched them, smelled them....

Sweat trickled through his hair, rolling from his temples. He must've made some noise because John suddenly looked at him a little more closely. "Somethin' wrong, Ray?"

Ray staggered to his feet and dragged some money from his pocket. "I'm n-not feeling well. M-must be the flu," he said. Then he dropped several bills onto the bar—how many, he had no idea—and stumbled out.

The instrument panel lit Madeline's right side in glowing amber. "What?" she cried.

Hunter stared straight ahead, into the darkness. "You heard me. Take me back."

"You can't be serious!"

"What did you expect?" he countered. "That I'd be happy to hear what you just told me?"

"I thought you were going to make every attempt to solve my father's murder! That's what you said!"

He focused on her. "That was before I knew there'd be children involved."

She snapped off the radio. "If you care so much about children, why not do what you can to protect them? There could be a sexual predator on the loose."

"There are a lot, believe me."

"And they have to be stopped one by one."

She had him there.

"If the good guys refuse to fight, the bad guys win, don't they?" she went on.

But he wasn't a good guy. He'd proven that with Selena. And now he had a daughter he couldn't protect from the men who came and went in Antoinette's life. Although she'd been safe so far, there was no telling who her mother might hook up with next. It worried him constantly.

This case could hit too close to home. He was looking for ways to anesthetize himself against reality, not take a cold plunge into the worst of it. "I'm not really in a position to do this."

"You came all this way. Do you have a case that needs you more?"

He couldn't say he did. Actually, he was getting tired of the emptiness with which he purposefully surrounded himself. If he didn't embrace a more meaningful cause soon, when would he? After working another twenty, thirty, forty "he's cheating on me" cases? He wasn't the only one who'd been involved in a bad marriage and paid a heavy price for his mistakes. But it wasn't just Antoinette's venom. It was the regret he felt about his own culpability. He wasn't worthy of more than he had.

"Are you going to answer me?" she pressed.

He rubbed his temples. Should he turn and run? Or stand and fight? "Were they all the same size?" he asked at length.

"No."

"Have they figured out who the underwear belonged to?"

"Only one pair."

"And?"

"They belonged to Grace."

Adrenaline shot through him. The answers to this case seemed to be very close to Madeline. "Your *stepsister?*"

"Yes."

"How do you know?"

"I recognized them, and she identified them."

"Grace is an adult now," he said. "She can tell us what happened."

Madeline didn't answer immediately.

"What?" he said.

"She says nothing happened, that she was never molested or abused."

That was more than a little surprising. "But, except for the rope, the items in that bag sound like souvenirs."

"She doesn't know how her underwear came to be in that suitcase. She says they must've been stolen while they were hanging on the line to dry."

"Seeing them didn't upset her?"

Madeline appeared to be choosing her words carefully. "She acted a bit strange, but she's always been… difficult to read. According to her, they're not necessarily indicative of a crime. She said that whoever collected those things could've been fantasizing. She was an assistant district attorney, so she knows about stuff like that."

"I don't buy it." Hunter didn't care what Grace had done for a living, he didn't believe her fantasy theory.

"Why not?"

"Think about it. That suitcase wasn't in a closet or under a bed, where someone could sit in complete privacy and fondle and fantasize. It was in a car. Plus the underwear was of varying sizes, which suggests they came from more than one source. Whoever hid those items in the trunk was an active predator. I'd put money on it." He could tell Madeline thought so, too, or she wouldn't have pulled off the road to tell him this. "Was there anything on them?" he asked.

She looked confused. "You mean a pattern or decoration?"

"I mean blood or semen."

"We haven't heard," she said, making no effort to hide her distaste. "Toby sent them to the state lab only a few days ago. He said it could take a while, possibly months."

"Who's Toby?"

"Pontiff. Stillwater's chief of police."

Hunter hated to ask this next question, but he had to. "Is there any chance those things could've belonged to your father?"

Her eyes widened in righteous indignation. "Of course not!"

"Then where'd they come from?"

"From the man who killed him! Chief Pontiff and I are speculating that whoever was carrying around that suitcase confessed to my father, and my father was going to turn him in."

"A hush murder."

"If that's what you want to call it."

Someone had gained control of the pastor's car. That person might've taken advantage of the opportunity to dispose of incriminating evidence. But sacrificing the underwear didn't seem consistent with the kind of man who'd keep souvenirs like that to begin with.

Unless the perpetrator feared someone else was on to him….

"Maybe," he said.

"I should tell you the police also found some black hairs caught in the driver's seat," she said grudgingly.

"Are they getting a DNA sample from them, as well?"

"No. Maybe they'll do that later, but there doesn't seem to be much point right now. They look like Clay's and probably are. Like the rest of us, he was in and out of that car."

"Could that suitcase have belonged to Clay?"

"No. My stepbrother would never hurt a child."

Hunter would form his own opinion on that once he'd met Clay. "What was your father and Irene's sex life like?" he asked.

The change of subject seemed to take her off guard. She blanched as if her mind had just presented her with a picture she'd rather not see. "They seemed...normal. What was *your* parents' sex life like?"

He refused to apologize for her discomfort. "I have to ask difficult questions," he said. "If you want to find the truth, there'll be a lot more of them."

"Does that mean you're taking the assignment?" She raised her chin. "Or is my father's case more than you can handle?"

She was challenging him. Obviously, she thought that would make a difference.

He'd played it safe for so long, Hunter felt like he was standing on the edge of a precipice, about to jump. By accepting this job, he was leaving the relative comfort of his own demons and surrounding himself with hers. But the possibility that there might still be little girls victimized by the owner of that suitcase made it impossible to walk away. Most pedophiles didn't stop until they were forced to.

"I'll do it," he said. "But if we're going to Stillwater, I'm driving."

She stared at him. "What?"

"When's the last time you had a good night's sleep?"

"I'm okay."

She started the car, but he covered her hand when she reached for the stick shift. "I'm taking over, or we're turning around."

"You don't know the area."

"You can give me directions."

He expected her to continue arguing. After all, they'd only met a couple hours ago and here he was demanding to take the wheel. But she must've been even more tired than he'd guessed because she nodded and opened her door.

"In another twenty miles or so, take 70 West. Turn off at 45 South and stay there for about forty miles. Then take 72 East and wake me when you get to 365. I'll help you through the rest of it."

"Will do," he said and they traded seats.

Ten minutes later, she was leaning against the door, fast asleep, and he was trying to convince himself that he didn't really find her all that attractive.

To Hunter, Mississippi had always conjured up images of pre-Civil War plantations, moss dripping from the branches of magnolia trees, the river meandering lazily through cattails and marshes. But he was in the northeast of the state near Tennessee and Alabama, hill country, and it didn't look anything like he'd imagined. Here, he saw oaks and maples and a variety of pine trees lining the road.

"Are we there yet?" Madeline murmured, rousing as he came to a crossroad with a single stop sign.

"We just passed a place called Corinth. You might want to make sure I haven't missed 365."

She pushed her thick auburn hair away from her face as she sat up and peered out the window. "Keep going, 365 is another few miles."

As Hunter gave the Corolla more gas, they passed yet another church. How many could one fairly unpopulated area support? Granted, the churches were all small, mostly one-room wooden structures with high-pitched roofs and usually a steeple, but he'd noticed several in the past ten minutes alone—Signs of Life, New Salem, Poplar Springs Free Will, Southwood, Shady Grove, North Crossroads Community and the Pleasant Grove Church of Christ.

"What was the name of your father's church?" he asked.

She covered a yawn. "Purity Church of Christ."

"Named after you, huh?"

"I'm going to regret telling you my sexual history," she muttered. "I can tell."

"Why? I'm impressed."

She eyed him warily. "You sound like it."

"I am!"

"How old were you when you lost your virginity?"

"Younger than thirty-two."

"By a decade?"

"Younger."

"Nineteen?"

"Eighteen."

"That's not *too* bad. For a Californian."

He chuckled. "I'll bet you've had more experience than I have in the last five years."

"Why? Have you been thinking of entering the priesthood?"

No, he'd been stuck in a marriage with a woman he'd come to loathe. "I'm not religious. My parents shoved it down my throat when I was young. I haven't recovered yet."

"My father would've been able to convert you," she said confidently. "You should've heard him preach."

Hunter wasn't convinced, but he didn't say so. "Who took over his congregation when he went missing?"

"Reverend Portenski."

"Was it a position Portenski particularly coveted?"

"He didn't even live here when my father disappeared. He heard about the opening and came to inquire several weeks afterward."

Portenski didn't seem to have much of a motive for murder, but Hunter wasn't crossing anyone off the list just yet.

"Turn right here," she said.

Hunter did as she told him. "Have you ever done any traveling?"

"No."

"You've never left the South?"

"Not even for college. I went to Mississippi State, which is only about three hours from here, and graduated with a degree in journalism. Now I own the only newspaper in town."

"Then you've done well."

She gave him a sheepish grin. "It's not as prestigious as it sounds. *The Stillwater Independent* comes out once a week, and I'm usually the major contributing journalist, depending on what I pull from the bigger papers, of course." She rested her head on the back of her seat and watched him from beneath her eyelashes. "What about you?"

"I went to San Diego State. But surfing came between me and a degree."

"I knew it!"

Laughing, he held up one hand. "Just kidding. Actually, I had a 4.0 all the time I was in school."

Her eyes narrowed. "No, you didn't."

He merely smiled.

"You probably surfed for as long as you could get

away with it, then went into the police academy when you realized you had to grow up."

He'd been telling the truth about his grades, but he didn't bother trying to convince her. It didn't matter if she believed he'd been a slacker. But the fact that she knew anything about his background surprised him. "Who told you I used to be a cop?"

"Grace did some research."

"Investigating the investigator, eh?"

"I guess you could say that."

"Smart. What else do you know about me?"

"That you're good."

He grinned, unable to resist the opportunity to tease her. "I told you that on the phone."

"You were talking about sex."

"Some men are good at more than one thing."

"I thought you were too jaded to be attracted to me."

"No, I'm too jaded to act on the attraction."

Despite what he'd said, the sudden silence was charged with sexual awareness. "Ours is a professional relationship," he added. But the statement sounded a little forced, and she immediately called him on it.

"Who are you trying to remind? Me—or yourself?"

He felt his mood darken. "You're not making this any easier."

"I'm not doing anything," she said innocently.

"Just tell me how to get to your house."

"Make a right at the stoplight. After about two miles you'll find a country road that goes over a hill and dead-ends at a small brick cottage with ivy on one side."

"That sounds like 'over the river and through the woods.' You can't be more specific?"

"Don't worry. You won't miss it. It's the only house on the street."

"And this *small* cottage has guest quarters?" This suddenly became a very salient point.

"It's actually a detached garage that I converted into a guestroom. Very cute."

"Will I have my own shower?"

"Yes, but no kitchen."

"Not a problem. I wasn't planning on cooking."

"I suppose that's my job?"

"We could always go out," he said with a meaningful grin. "I happen to have an expense account."

She grimaced. "Right. I'll cook."

8

The guest cottage was similar to the main house, which reminded Hunter of an old Italian farmhouse—the kind often depicted in movies—except that it had only one room with a small bathroom.

"It's a little stuffy in here after being shut up for so long because of the rain," Madeline said. She lit a vanilla-scented candle as she showed Hunter around, but as far as he was concerned, the place had smelled great from the beginning, like fresh linens and a trace of Madeline's perfume.

"Here're the clean towels." She opened a tall cupboard, made of distressed wood, standing just outside the bathroom—probably because it wouldn't fit inside—and pointed to a neatly folded stack of white and blue towels.

He nodded, thinking he wouldn't mind a hot shower—followed by a soft bed and then, hopefully, oblivion.

She walked over to the brick fireplace, which, along with some primitive-looking bookshelves, took up one whole wall. "You'll find plenty of wood in here if you'd like a fire," she said, pulling up the lid on a nearby bin.

The smell of pine and turpentine filtered into the room and made Hunter think of the time he'd taken his small family camping in Yosemite. Life with Antoinette had been difficult from the start. But Maria had made all the difference. He remembered carrying her on his shoulders as they hiked, helping her across the wet rocks of the stream where they swam. God, he missed his little girl....

When he realized Madeline was waiting for a response, he knocked on the small door at the back of the bin that indicated it could be filled from outside. "Handy."

"The fireplace should keep you warm."

The thick feather comforter on the bed would do that, too.

She tucked her hair behind her ears as she turned to face him. "I'm sorry there's no television out here. No fridge, either. But feel free to come over if you need anything. There's a key under the mat. It opens both houses."

"I'm sure a burglar would never expect to find it there," he said, with a touch of sarcasm.

"There's virtually no crime around here."

"I know of at least one man who's gone missing."

She studied him for a moment. "Take it if you don't think it's safe to leave it there. You'll need a key of your own while you're here, anyway."

"I'll do that." Hunter put his laptop on the desk beneath the room's only window, leaned his guitar case against the wall and fell back on the tall, four-poster bed. He'd be comfortable here, he decided. Madeline's guesthouse reminded him of a cottage hidden in the backwoods. Maybe it wasn't Hawaii, but it wasn't L.A., either. And for that he was surprisingly glad. He was finding it more and more difficult to lead the barren life he'd been living after the divorce, especially when he stayed in that empty house where nothing moved but him.

"There's a new toothbrush in the bathroom drawer, and there's soap, shampoo and conditioner in the shower."

"Thanks."

She gave him a tired smile. "I'm sorry about the way I acted at the airport. I should've been more polite."

"Don't worry about it," he said. He should've been more polite himself.

She paused at the door. "Do you think there's any chance I'll ever know what happened?" she asked earnestly.

"Yes." He was afraid to promise her too much. "There's a chance."

The sun slanting through the cracks of the draperies woke Hunter. He opened his eyes, expecting to see the white ceiling of the hotel he'd occupied in Hawaii but saw polished wooden rafters instead. Then the smell of damp wood and fresh linens brought everything back to him. He was in a cottage. In Mississippi. Behind the home of a woman named Madeline Barker.

For no particular reason, he reached over, retrieved his wallet from the desk and pulled out the condom that promoted his client's strip joint. It read "Bud's Babes... The hottest babes in town."

Telling himself he didn't need the temptation that condom offered, he tossed it in the trash can. But a minute later, he got up to retrieve it and shoved it back in his wallet. Then he glanced at his watch. He'd figured Madeline would come banging on his door at eight sharp. She'd said she had some of the police files on her father's case—a testament to the kind of rule-bending that was possible when one had friends in the right places. He'd been planning to get up early to read them. But it was already ten. He hadn't slept so late in ages. Not since he'd quit drinking.

After brushing his teeth, he ran a comb through his hair and pulled on the same clothes he'd worn yesterday—they were all he had until his luggage arrived. Then he went outside. The ground was still soggy, but the rain had passed.

The red brick walkway leading to Madeline's back porch meandered beneath a large willow tree, next to a small pond. The yard was covered with a patchy, swirling mist, but in the light of day he could see that it was well-tended, full of vines and plants, potted and otherwise. Obviously, Madeline spent a lot of time out here. There was even a tea table and two chairs arranged under a large oak. The Confederate flag on a pole beside it made him smile.

So where was the pretty Southerner this morning? Had she overslept, too?

He didn't have to wonder long. As soon as he located the key beneath the mat, which he pocketed when he'd opened the door, he could hear voices coming from another part of the house. *Raised* voices.

"It's not safe."

"It's none of your business."

Who was it?

Sophie, the cat he'd seen briefly the night before, got up from the rug in front of the sink, stretched and walked over to inspect him. Giving her a scratch behind the ears, Hunter considered going back to his room until Madeline's visitor was gone. But then he heard his name. And finding himself the topic of conversation made it difficult to leave.

"Hunter's an ex-cop, Kirk."

"So? You don't know if that makes him safe."

"I know you have no right to drag me out of bed and start slinging orders."

"I'm not slinging orders! I'm trying to look out for you."

"Oh, come off it. You're not here out of concern for me. You're feeling threatened because I brought someone new to town."

Hunter stiffened as he waited for Kirk's response. This was the man she'd broken up with six weeks ago. The only man she'd ever slept with.

Hunter didn't like him already.

"He's in your guesthouse," Kirk said. "That's too close."

When he'd been examining that condom, it had seemed pretty damn close to Hunter, too. But he was suddenly willing to argue the opposite.

"It's no different than having a neighbor," she retorted.

Sophie rolled onto her back so Hunter could rub her stomach.

"Yes, it is," Kirk nearly shouted. "You live alone and you've got no other neighbors. That makes it *very* different."

Hunter wondered whether he should present himself and say hello. Now might not be the best time. Without his luggage, he didn't even have a razor. But he planned to talk to everyone eventually. That was what he did, how he found what he was looking for. Sometimes people held important pieces to a puzzle without realizing it. And he didn't particularly care whether or not he impressed Kirk. The more Kirk raised his voice at Madeline, the more eager Hunter became to interrupt.

"I can look after myself," Madeline insisted, lowering her voice.

Fortunately for Kirk, he lowered his voice, too. "Maddy, it doesn't give the best impression, okay? Think what everyone at church will say."

"I don't care."

"Yes, you do. You're just not yourself right now. He can move to the motel."

"No. You've seen The Blue Ribbon. It's a dive. He thinks we're a bunch of rednecks as it is."

"Did I say that?" Hunter whispered to the cat.

"Why do you care what he thinks?" Kirk asked.

Standing, Hunter crossed the kitchen and leaned against the opening that led to the living room. From there he could see Madeline in the entryway, wearing a pair of white boxers covered with red kisses and a white tank. Her disheveled hair suggested that she'd just rolled out of bed. She was also barefoot, and she wasn't wearing a bra. Hunter noticed immediately because the thin fabric of her shirt revealed more than he'd seen of a woman in two years.

Madeline's ex-boyfriend had his back to Hunter, but he looked approximately six-two, maybe 230 pounds. He wasn't fat, but he was big, with massive shoulders and a head of fine dark hair.

Madeline was too intent on the argument to see him, and Kirk didn't turn around.

"It's easier to work together when we're close by," she was saying. "This isn't a nine-to-five proposition."

"It'd better not be a proposition at all," Kirk snapped.

"How dare you say that! You and I aren't even seeing each other anymore."

"That doesn't mean I don't care about you."

"If you still care, why didn't you call when you heard that my father's car was found?" she asked. "You had to know what that was like for me."

Hunter knew he should've broken in about five minutes ago, but he was interested to hear Kirk's answer.

"You told me not to call you again, remember?"

"That didn't stop you from marching down here the second someone told you I hired a private detective."

"I heard you'd hired a professional days ago," he said. "I didn't have a problem with it until I ran into Grace and Kennedy at breakfast this morning and they mentioned that he's staying here. They don't think it's safe, either."

"He's not some criminal. He's a P.I., for heaven's sake."

"Oh, that makes all the difference!" Kirk's voice dripped with sarcasm. "You don't know him from Adam. You could be raped or—"

At that Hunter opened his mouth to object. He wasn't going to touch Madeline. Especially without her permission. But Madeline was already responding.

"He's *not* interested in me, okay?"

"How can you be sure of that? Is he married?"

"No."

"So he's single." *I knew it,* rang through his words.

"Yes, but he's…young," she said.

"*How* young?"

"Too young—for me, anyway."

Hunter felt his eyebrows shoot up. A thirty-two-year-old man was too young for a thirty-six-year-old woman? *Why?*

She lowered her voice again. "You're making a big deal out of nothing, Kirk."

"Like hell!"

"Listen, he's recently been through a rough divorce, okay? He's not interested in me or anyone else. You've never met a person who's so closed off."

Hunter didn't want to hear any more about himself. So he coughed to make them aware of his presence and sauntered through the living room to join them in the entry.

Kirk's face darkened the moment their eyes met; Madeline's lips parted but she didn't speak. She was probably wondering how much he'd overheard about his "rough" divorce.

"*You're* a private investigator?" Kirk said.

"I seem to be getting that reaction a lot lately," Hunter replied wryly. He told himself not to look at Madeline again, but he couldn't help it. Obviously, she'd come from a warm bed, which explained why she was dressed so scantily, but it was chilly in the house. Her body was showing the effects of it and, much as he wished it wasn't so, his body had definitely noticed.

"Hunter, this is Kirk Vantassel, my *ex*-boyfriend," she said, chafing her arms to ward off the cold. "Kirk, this is Hunter Solozano."

Kirk made no secret of the fact that he wasn't feeling particularly friendly. "How long have you been in the investigative business?" he asked, sizing Hunter up.

"Long enough to know what I'm doing," Hunter responded but he smiled to soften his words and held out his hand. He wasn't trying to pick a fight. He only wanted to let Madeline's ex-boyfriend know that he wouldn't be pushed around. "Nice to meet you."

Kirk didn't respond immediately. It took a nudge from Madeline to goad him into a handshake. Even then he made the contact brief. "Nice to meet you, too," he muttered, and his eyes cut back to Madeline. "I was just telling Maddy that they have a vacancy at the motel, where you'd be within walking distance of the pool hall and the restaurants in town. You might be more comfortable there."

"*I'd* be more comfortable?" Hunter repeated. "Or *you'd* be more comfortable?"

"Madeline's grieving," he said. "She's not thinking clearly."

Madeline protested but Hunter spoke over her. "I don't have any objection to moving."

"Great," Kirk said.

"Does that mean I should send you the bill?" he asked.

The question took Kirk by surprise. "What?"

"For my expenses," Hunter clarified. "The motel won't be free."

Hunter wondered if Kirk wanted him out of Maddy's house badly enough to pay the motel bill. At first he didn't think so. It was one thing to pick up the tab on behalf of a girlfriend, another to pick up the tab on behalf of an *ex*-girlfriend.

But Kirk shrugged. "Sure, I'll pay. No problem. Get your luggage and I'll drive you over."

"No!" Madeline stepped closer and Hunter could smell the perfume he'd noticed in his room last night. "I brought Hunter to town and I'll take care of his arrangements. He's fine where he is."

Hunter wished she'd go put on a robe. His eyes were drawn to her breasts like magnets to steel. And he could tell that Kirk was having the same problem. But he knew she wouldn't risk leaving them alone, even for a few minutes. There was so much tension in the room, it felt as if they were squaring off. Hunter suspected this could get out of hand.

"It's already settled, Maddy," Kirk said.

She stubbornly held on to Hunter's arm. "No, it's not. This has nothing to do with you, Kirk. So stay out of it."

"I don't want him here!" Her ex scowled in obvious frustration. "And go put on some damn clothes!"

"Just as soon as you leave," she said.

With that, Hunter decided to give her a hand by opening the door. Kirk had made his wishes known, but it was Madeline's decision. "Maybe you should give her a call once you've cooled off," he suggested.

Hunter thought Kirk might take a swing at him—he could tell Kirk wanted to. But he didn't. He faced Hunter, nostrils flaring. Then he wrenched the door away and slammed it shut behind him.

"I'm sorry," Madeline said as the reverberation echoed through the house. "I didn't see that coming. He hasn't called me or come by since we broke up."

"Don't worry about it. Those things happen." Now that Kirk was gone, it was even harder not to let his eyes slip down to what her shirt revealed.

He knew she'd caught him when she took a step back and folded her arms over her chest.

"If you're going to walk around like that, it could be a problem," he admitted, listening to his heart pound as their eyes met.

She seemed to collect herself. "Let me put on some sweats and I'll make you breakfast."

"Sounds good." Hunter started into the kitchen but, at the last minute, he turned back to watch her climb the stairs.

Did she really think she was too old for him?

* * *

Madeline couldn't stop brooding over Kirk's visit— but that didn't surprise her. She always had trouble letting go of people, places, even things. Which was why she'd stayed with him for so long. She'd known from the beginning that they made better friends than lovers. She'd tried to tell him on a number of occasions. But he tended to accept what came easily without bothering to fight for more, so he'd never been willing to acknowledge the lack of intensity in their relationship. Ending it had been entirely her decision, not his.

Anyway, considering her own problems, she couldn't complain about *his* lack of decisive action. She had a garage, a basement and two sheds stuffed full of junk. No doubt her penchant for hanging on to everything that came into her life stemmed from losing her mother and father so early. But she *had* to overcome that compulsion. Hoarding affected too many aspects of her life. How could she be decisive about ending a relationship when she couldn't even part with simple, almost worthless items that others discarded every day—receipts, advertisements, tin foil, sacks, old yarn. She was careful to avoid the stigma that went along with being a pack rat, and stored it all out of sight, away from the main part of her house. But hiding her problem didn't solve it.

"You okay?"

Madeline glanced up from her plate to find Hunter watching her. He sat across the table, apparently finished with his meal. "I'm fine," she said. But the panic she'd managed to hold at bay since she and Kirk had broken up was rising inside her, making her heart pound and her palms sweat. Loss… Nothing frightened her more. And she cared about Kirk, loved him in many ways. They'd known each other most of their lives. What if she regretted her decision later on?

"You've only eaten a few bites."

Madeline put down the fork she'd been using to push her eggs around her plate. "I'm not hungry."

"Are you upset?"

She was having an anxiety attack. Did that count? In any case, she didn't want to explain so she shook her head.

"Maybe you should call him," he said.

"No." She was cleaning out her emotional closets. She wished Molly could do it for her, the way she'd gotten rid of old furniture and other junk by having a yard sale when she was here last. But this was something Madeline had to do for herself.

She eyed the ring Kirk had given her for her birthday a year ago. It had two small diamonds beside her birthstone. He was a good man. Should she settle for a mediocre relationship? Allow him to settle, as well? So what if he didn't want kids? Maybe she could live without becoming a mother. She was thirty-six. There wasn't much more time....

"Will you be able to concentrate on what we need to do?" Hunter asked, drawing her attention again.

His words sounded ominous. "What *we* need to do?" she repeated.

"It's time to take a stroll down memory lane."

"What do you mean?"

"I'd like you to show me your old photo albums, scrapbooks, letters, anything you might have from your parents, Irene, Clay, Grace, Molly—anyone associated with the family."

"What about the police files?" She'd thought he'd read the files and then interview people, start piecing the puzzle together that way.

"They haven't led anyone to your father's killer so far, right? Something must be missing, which might mean they've been looking in the wrong place."

"You don't even want to see the files?"

"I'll go through them eventually."

She wanted a shower. But she had a very expensive private investigator sitting in her kitchen, ready to work, and she couldn't afford to keep him waiting until she could come to grips with the upset caused by Kirk's unexpected visit. "What do you think my old photo albums will tell you?" she asked.

"They'll give me a feel of who you are, who your father was, maybe even a sense of Irene, Clay, Grace and Molly." He rested his elbows on the table. "You have a few old photo albums, don't you?"

She had more than he'd ever get through. She was the queen of memorabilia. To someone who prized tin foil, pictures were nearly sacred. "I also have my father's belongings."

When Clay had dismantled the office in the barn last summer, he'd said he'd be willing to store everything he'd packed up for her. But Clay hadn't just cleaned out the place. He'd ripped off the wall paneling, torn out the air conditioner that had filled one side of the window, even removed the carpet. If her father's personal effects couldn't be in their rightful place, waiting for him to return, then she wanted them close to her, not sitting on a concrete floor in a room she no longer recognized.

"Here, in the house?" Hunter asked.

"In the basement." She stood. "I'll get them."

"Wait till you're finished eating."

"I'm done." After depositing her plate on the counter, she headed down to the basement. She hadn't expected Hunter to follow her but he did. She got the impression that he was taking in every detail of what he saw and heard, cataloging everything in his brain.

So what would he make of the fact that she decorated with bright, primary colors? Would he decide she was basically cheerful and loved the sun?

Or that she was terrified of suffering from the kind of depression that had afflicted her mother?

She wasn't sure, but she was fairly confident that visiting the basement would give away more about her particular neurosis than she wanted. Molly always made a huge fuss about all the clutter; that was why Madeline had never admitted how difficult the yard sale had been for her. Molly probably suspected, since Madeline had ducked out midway, but they hadn't discussed it.

They all had their problems. Molly couldn't stay in town longer than a week for fear she'd never be able to leave. She said coming here was fun for the first few days, that she liked seeing her family. But any longer than that and Stillwater began to feel like quicksand, sucking at her ankles. The fact that Madeline had never escaped their hometown, never gone on to become the *Washington Post* reporter she'd once hoped to be, no doubt made Molly's phobia worse.

"I'm not getting anything that's very heavy," she said, standing in front of the basement door. "Why don't you wait in the living room?"

"Is it only one box?"

"No…" There were several and she couldn't carry them all at one time. It made more sense to let him help her. But she didn't want to see her problems through his eyes. Especially now…

She'd clean out her storage areas when she was back on stable ground. Maybe once she knew what had happened to her father, she could stop looking back. Then she'd be able to let go of everything she felt so compelled to save. She hoped. One problem at a time, right?

"Is there any need to bring them all up?" she asked.

"There're two of us. Why not bring up a couple, at least?"

Arguing would draw more attention to something that didn't really matter, she told herself. Why obsess over what Hunter might think? He was here for only one reason—to solve the mystery behind her father's disappearance. Afterward, he'd go back to California and she'd never see him again.

"Fine." Bracing herself for what he might say, she opened the door.

9

A pale light slanted into the basement, reaching only halfway down the window and not all the way to the middle of the room. Madeline pulled the chain on the bulb overhead to banish the shadows, then stiffened as Hunter whistled.

"What *is* all this stuff?" he asked.

"Just...storage." Acutely self-conscious, she began stepping over the boxes and baskets piled on the steps.

"What are you storing?" She could hear the creak of the stairs behind her. "Food and clothing for the entire town for a year?"

"There're some canned goods here." There were a lot of other things, too—things no one else would bother to store.

Hunter lagged behind as she wound through the walkways, which became progressively narrower. She knew he was inspecting the place, marveling.

Finally, she reached the area under the stairs where she kept her personal mementos, as well as her father's belongings. This seemed the safest place because it was away from the windows and the moisture that occasionally seeped in, away from the paths where she'd had to shove this or move that.

She motioned for Hunter to take the top box, and grabbed the one underneath. Carrying the boxes made getting out of the crowded basement more difficult than getting in, but Hunter led the way, using his knee to widen the paths. When they emerged into the living room, Madeline shut the door with a resounding bang.

"What's the point of all *that?*" Hunter asked, watching as she set her box on the floor by the sofa.

She pretended not to understand. "What are you talking about?"

"You have boxes and boxes and boxes of…what?"

"I told you, storage."

"What kind of storage?"

"Does it matter?"

"I'm not sure."

She could feel his gaze resting on her but refused to meet it. Shrugging, she said, "It's nothing."

He didn't press her beyond that, but only because she'd already pulled out a scrapbook.

"What do you want to see?" she asked, sitting cross-legged on the floor and staring at a photograph of herself as an infant.

He dropped down beside her. "That's your real mother holding you?"

She nodded, noting her mother's proud smile. Her father stood behind them, talking on the phone.

"She was pretty," he said.

Madeline had never thought she resembled her mother. And if she did, few people mentioned it. But she remembered her father gazing distantly at her on several occasions. When she questioned him, he'd shake his head and say, "You're the very image of her," even though she looked much more like him.

"She had…problems," Madeline said. She'd intended to say it lightly, carelessly, but there was no concealing the bitterness in her voice.

He took the scrapbook and began turning the pages. "What was she like?"

"I thought she was perfect," she told him. "She lit up whenever she saw me. She loved me. She was everything to me. Maybe that's why I feel so betrayed."

He surprised her by briefly touching her shoulder. Hunter seemed remote, indifferent, but she wondered if there wasn't a tender streak beneath that "I don't give a shit" attitude. "It's only natural to feel that way."

"I didn't know it when I was little, or understand what it meant, but she suffered from depression," Madeline said.

He examined various pages, pausing now and then to study one a bit more closely. "How did her depression manifest itself? Did she weep? Sleep? What?"

"She wept easily, but usually tried to hide it. Mostly she became quiet, subdued. And she wrote in her journal. She filled one spiral notebook after another, then tore out most of the pages and burned them up. I remember standing next to her, watching them blacken and curl."

"Did your father know she destroyed what she wrote?"

"Probably. But she always did it while he was gone. She knew it'd make him angry."

"Why would he care?"

"He was frustrated that she couldn't be satisfied with her life."

"He felt she should be?"

"He tried to give her everything she needed."

"Was there anything specific that was causing her unhappiness?"

"No. Depression runs in her family. She was just too fragile, too…weak, I guess." It hurt Madeline to say it. She didn't want to believe that about the mother she remembered so clearly, the mother who'd loved her so much.

"How did your father react when she made the decision to end her life?"

"He was disgusted."

Hunter looked up at her, clearly shocked. "Somehow that wasn't what I was expecting you to say."

"You have to understand, he'd been dealing with my mother's sickness for years and had run out of patience with it. He was disgusted with her even before she took her life."

"What about heartbroken? Did that figure into the equation at all?"

How could she explain? Hardhearted though it sounded, Madeline understood the confusion and disappointment her father had experienced. "My father admired strength and saw her as terribly flawed."

"Flawed?"

She tried again. "He was angry. He wanted his family to set the perfect example for his flock. Instead, my mother committed what he considered the unpardonable sin."

"Disgust and anger. Maybe your father was putting too much pressure on your mother. Maybe she couldn't be everything he wanted her to be and that was the only out she could find."

"I could never abandon *my* child," she said resolutely.

"Neither could I. And yet here I am," he muttered.

"What did you say?" she asked.

"Nothing." He paused at a picture taken when Madeline was eight. Leaning against the porch railing at the farmhouse, she was missing her two front teeth and smiling with abandon. Madeline was fairly certain that was the last time she'd felt so carefree. Soon afterward she'd become aware of her mother's malady and begun to worry—about everything.

"Did she leave a suicide note?"

"Yes, but it was just more of the same 'life is hopeless' kind of stuff."

"Where is it now?"

"My father burned it."

"You didn't mind?"

"What could I do? He was upset. And it seemed fitting somehow."

Hunter didn't comment on that. "How were things financially?" he asked, turning another page.

"Tight. It was that way for most people in town. But we had a roof over our heads and plenty to eat. I remember my father pointing that out to my mother again and again, telling her she should be grateful."

"Do you think she wanted more children?"

"I don't know. She had difficulty carrying me. Bonnie Ray, the neighbor across the street, told me my mother tripped and fell when she was seven months pregnant and nearly miscarried. The accident threw her into an early labor. They nearly lost me on the delivery table."

"You were two months premature?"

She nodded. "After that my parents were hesitant to try again. Which is why…" It felt almost sacrilegious to reveal what she was about to say next, but she'd avoided the subject of her mother for so long, she suddenly wanted to talk, to make sense of all the contradictions. The fact that Hunter was from out of town actually helped. He had no previous knowledge of Eliza, no prejudicial opinion one way or another.

"What?" he prompted.

"They slept in separate bedrooms."

"Every night?"

"I can't say. I only had my mother for the first ten years of my life. At the time, there didn't seem anything wrong with their not sharing a room. My mother said he snored, and that made it difficult to sleep, so they slept apart."

"And your father didn't mind?"

There was an undercurrent to this question that led Madeline to believe he had strong feelings on the matter. "Not really," she said. "What made him angry was that she let me sleep with her. He thought she was coddling me too much."

"Or maybe he wanted to visit her room occasionally, and knew he wouldn't be able to if you were there."

"She took care of him before we went to bed."

He raised his eyebrows. *"Took care of him?* God, you make it sound like she was doing chores."

"I'm just saying it wasn't like they never had sex, okay?"

"How do you know?" He leaned back on his hands.

"I know," she said, unwilling to expound on it.

"It looks to me like she preferred you to him. That might've rankled."

Madeline didn't argue. Like most children, she'd been so egocentric, she'd never questioned her mother's devotion. It was just there, like the sun and the wind and the rain. But, in retrospect, she had to agree with Hunter. She'd definitely held the number one spot in her mother's heart. *I love you more than anything,* Eliza would whisper as she pulled Madeline into the cradle of her body every night.

It'd been a long time since Madeline had thought of those words. Probably because, after her mother's suicide, they'd felt like such a lie.

She squeezed her eyes shut. Her mother's loss hurt almost as badly today as it had then….

He turned to yet another page. Her mother was holding her birthday cake, with nine candles on top. "I see a lot of pictures of you, a few of her, but not many of your father," Hunter commented.

"I told you, Dad worked too much. He was really dedicated to the church."

"He wasn't present at your birthday party?" Except for the one that included her mother with the cake, the pictures on the page depicted Madeline and a few playmates.

"To be honest, I don't remember. I know a friend's mother took that picture, so probably not."

"You didn't miss him?"

"No. I loved him, but…it was after my mother died that we grew close. She sort of—" Madeline struggled to put fragments of memory into words "—acted as a go-between, I guess."

"It doesn't sound as if your parents were all that happy together," he said.

Sophie sauntered in from the kitchen to investigate. Madeline stroked her soft fur as she answered. "Every marriage is unique. There was some tension at times, but that's normal, isn't it?"

"Do you think they'd be married today if your mother was still alive and whatever happened to your father hadn't happened?"

"Of course. Dad didn't believe in divorce."

"Under *any* circumstances?"

Sophie jumped into her lap and began to purr. "He thought it was a sin."

"Like most everything else."

"I've told you before, he was a very religious man. He felt that Mom's depression was his cross to bear, too. He even spoke of it in his sermons, many of which are in this box right here." She gently pushed the cat aside, then rummaged through the scrapbooks and photo albums until she'd located the files.

Hunter accepted the folders she handed him, but he seemed more interested in something he'd spotted in the other box. As he drew it out, Madeline realized it was one of her mother's journals—one that still had at least half the entries in it.

"Did this belong to your mother?"

She nodded. She had a few of Eliza's journals, mostly from the early years. As Madeline grew older and her mother's depression worsened, Eliza destroyed more and more of what she wrote. The notebook she'd been using at the end had barely twenty pages left in it, most of them taken up with anecdotes about "Little Maddy," and poems that were increasingly desperate-sounding and difficult to understand.

Hunter flipped slowly through the pages, perusing the contents. Madeline had separated this journal from the others several months ago because she'd been planning to read it. She thought it might bring her some peace to see the world as Eliza must've viewed it. But she'd never been able to overcome the resentment she felt over her mother's final act. Or the irrational fear that she'd somehow "catch" her mother's disorder.

It wasn't easy to see Hunter sifting through the pages of that binder. Madeline bit her cuticles as he read, fidgeting until he looked up. "It's okay," he assured her.

"What's in there?" she asked.

"Some pretty bleak poetry."

"I told you she was depressed."

He pursed his lips and didn't comment. "Mind if I cart a few of her journals to the guesthouse, along with your father's sermons? I'd like to take my time reading them."

"Why?" she asked impatiently. "My mother had nothing to do with my father's disappearance. She'd been dead for six years by then."

"People are complex beings," he said. "Sometimes the roots of an event run very deep."

"No one else has looked *this* deep."

"Maybe that's the problem." He held up the notebook, a questioning expression on his face.

"Fine. Take it," she said.

"Where are the others?"

She sorted through what was left and pulled out several more as he searched his own box. "Don't tell me this was hers, too," he said, holding up a soft plastic Disney journal with a picture of Cinderella on the front.

"Oh." Madeline's hand automatically came up to cover her mouth.

"What?" he said.

She took a shaky breath. "That was my journal. My mother bought it for me. So I could write when she did."

His voice softened. "Okay if I read it?"

"How could something I wrote as a ten-year-old possibly help you?"

"It probably won't," he admitted. "But there's always

that small chance. You might've recorded something significant without knowing it."

Madeline couldn't imagine that she'd written anything too private at such a young age. She had yet to discover boys, so there'd be no childish fantasies or girlish longing. She couldn't even remember what she might've considered important enough to warrant a few words. Miscellaneous scribblings about her parents? School? Her friends? The animals on the farm? The farm itself?

"I guess," she said. "I'm afraid you won't find it very interesting, though."

"I'm not sure about that. Meeting you as a little girl might be more interesting than you think." He tried to open the journal, but it was locked. "You got a key for this?"

"No. I can't believe I even have the book. I haven't seen it for years." She hadn't become fanatical about saving things until later, after her father had disappeared. "Go ahead and break the lock."

"You don't mind?"

She shook her head—but regretted that decision the moment the journal fell open.

Ray sat alone in his mobile home. The TV squawked in front of him, but he wasn't really watching it. There was too much going on in his mind, too many memories floating around. Memories of the keenest excitement he'd ever known—and memories of the deepest fear.

He got up and began to pace the well-worn carpet, stopping to peer through the curtains when he heard a car pull into the trailer park.

It was a beat-up truck that stopped at Ronnie Oates's place down the way.

Dropping the curtain, Ray went into his small kitchen, intending to distract himself by fixing something to eat. But there wasn't anything in his cupboards. He needed to go shopping, but he didn't dare leave his house.

They'd found the reverend's dildo! He still couldn't believe it.

Had they found the pictures, as well?

"Must not've," he mumbled for probably the millionth time. If they'd discovered the pictures, the police would've been knocking on his door long before now. Katie and Rose Lee were in a lot of them. Ray had burned the ones the reverend had given him—years ago. After it was over, he didn't like seeing what he'd done. And he wasn't stupid enough to keep any proof of his actions. But the preacher was never satisfied. His excitement fed off those pictures. Ray had sometimes wondered if he had one stuck in his Bible when he was preaching on Sundays, so he could look down and see it.

There were certainly plenty to choose from. Hell, Ray had even taken a few of them. One he'd snapped right there in the reverend's study at the church, with Katie tied spread-eagled on the floor and the reverend pretending to be some kind of porn star.

The reverend liked it when Ray made a show of it, too. So they'd watch each other, trade off, get even more creative with what they'd do to the girls. One time, Barker put a collar on Rose Lee and dragged her to the pulpit. He loved that because it showed how powerful he was. The reverend believed he could get away with anything. And Ray had started to buy into that belief. He remembered taking a picture of Barker making Katie bend over one of the pews while he rode her doggie-style, yanking back on that collar if she so much as whimpered.

That was the day Barker had demanded Ray use the dildo on his own daughter. The reverend's eyes had gleamed feverishly as he coaxed, bribed and encouraged Ray, who'd gotten so caught up in it all that he'd finally crossed the line the preacher had been begging him to cross for months and had sex with his own daughter.

Rubbing his hands nervously over his pants, Ray cursed. How was it that those memories made him hard even while they made him sick?

Because he'd do it again if he could. He'd just never had the opportunity. Without the money and cover provided by the preacher, he wouldn't have done it in the first place. He would've been too scared. Since then, he'd paid a few underage prostitutes in Jackson. And he liked the kiddie porn he viewed on the Internet so much, he knew he'd go hungry if he had to choose between his ISP and the grocery bill. He'd already stolen his mother's diamond ring and her real silver and hocked them to buy the computer equipment he wanted. But the pornography, along with his fantasies and his toys, were enough for him these days. With his surrogate devices, there was little fear of punishment. Just play; just pleasure.

It had been the damned reverend who couldn't get enough of the real thing.

And now they'd discovered the dildo and the panties….

Ray kicked over a chair, then closed his eyes and shook his head. Even if they found his semen on those panties, they wouldn't be able to trace it to him. They didn't have his DNA on record; they'd never had any reason to get a sample.

He just had to lie low and wait for it to blow over. Look at Clay Montgomery, he thought. From all indications, he'd committed murder and gotten away with it. The Stillwater Police didn't know their heads from their asses. He'd be fine.

Grabbing his truck keys, he stalked out of the trailer and headed over to the Piggly Wiggly to buy some groceries.

10

The folded piece of paper that fell out of Madeline's childhood journal made her stomach lurch. She knew instantly what it was. She'd taken that paper out of the garbage after her father had wadded it up and thrown it away. She hadn't seen it in twenty-seven years, but every word, every line, was indelibly imprinted on her memory.

When Hunter picked it up, she didn't stop him. She probably would have, except that she couldn't breathe. She watched his long fingers open the sheet, watched his light blue eyes scan the contents.

After several interminable seconds, he raised his eyes. "Your mother was going to leave your father?"

Madeline's throat burned with the difficulty of holding back her tears. She reached for the paper he held instead of trying to speak, and he relinquished it to her hands.

Dear Mom:
I can't go on this way. Each day is darker than the last. I have to leave Lee, as soon as possible. I can't explain, and I can't come to you. Not yet. I need money, though. As much as you can spare. Please. Anything…

Tears blurred Madeline's vision so she could no longer read. Blinking quickly, she pushed the note away before her emotions could completely overwhelm her. She didn't want to see her mother's beautiful script, to feel the poignant loss that settled so heavily on her shoulders. Would her mother have been any happier had she left Stillwater?

The jagged edge of guilt seemed to cut Madeline like a saw—destructive, powerful, tearing. She'd first found that note when she'd discovered a false bottom in her mother's jewelry box and had been so frightened by what she'd read that she'd started to cry. Her parents, who'd been watching TV, hurried into the bedroom. Then her mother stared with wide, desperate eyes as her father took the note and read it aloud.

He'd assured Madeline that it was just more of her mother's unbalanced writing, a side effect of her "illness," but Madeline would never forget the abject despair on her mother's face.

Hunter recovered the note and set it to one side as he moved closer. Then he held her hand. She thought he might prod her for answers she couldn't give, not right now, but he didn't. They sat in silence, their fingers interlaced.

Unwilling to look him in the eye, she focused on his short, clean nails, his darker skin. He was a beautiful man. There was no question about that. She'd also perceived him as harsh and selfish, but just now, he seemed to be neither. He was simply there, offering her support and, more importantly, hope that the mystery that had plagued her for so long would be solved at last.

"This is why you were reluctant to take on the job, isn't it?" she said.

"This?"

"The level of emotion involved."

"One of the reasons," he admitted.

Swallowing, she stated the obvious. "It's hard for you to do research when I can hardly talk about the past."

"I wasn't worried about research."

She finally met his gaze. "What then?"

"It's not important now."

Rallying, she wiped her cheeks. "I'm generally not much of a crier."

"We all have our moments," he said, and she wondered what *his* moments were like. Did they concern the woman Antoinette? What had happened to his marriage? Did he regret losing his wife?

She was curious but knew better than to ask. He'd already let her know that he kept his personal life strictly personal.

"This note…" he said.

When she refused to look at it again, his fingers curled more tightly around hers. She guessed that it was partly an apology for having to push her, and partly encouragement. He'd told her there would be difficult questions. She just hadn't expected them to revolve around her mother. That was a separate heartache—one so deep she preferred to let it lurk beneath the surface, its true dimensions unknown.

"Were there other letters like this?" he asked.

She watched Sophie find a comfortable spot on the couch. "What do you mean?"

"Other cries for help?"

The wisp of a memory encroached…her father's

voice. *She didn't mean it, Maddy. She's not going anywhere, are you, Eliza?* And her mother's response: *No, no, of course not. I'd never leave you, Maddy. Never.* "That wasn't a cry for help," she insisted.

"What was it then?" Hunter asked.

"It was…more of the same. She was depressed. She—she wrote things. There were volumes…." And yet she'd retrieved this particular letter from the garbage and saved it in her diary. That alone set it apart—and made her a liar. "She loved my father."

"How do you know?"

"Because…even though she slept with me at night, she usually went into the bedroom or bathroom with him first."

"*Every* night?"

"Most nights."

"And you think they were making love?"

"I know they were."

"How?"

"I walked in on them once. My mother was—" She cleared her throat, unable to put words to the image in her mind. "They were in an intimate position."

"Having intercourse?"

Did she have to get specific? "Does it matter?"

"It might, and it might not."

She sighed. It wasn't easy talking about such private situations with this particular man. "His pants were down, and she was kneeling in front of him."

"I see. And that means she loved him?"

She felt her cheeks burn. "She wouldn't want to be with him that often if she didn't."

"She could've felt coerced," he said.

"No. She'd offer. He'd ask if she really needed to

sleep with me again, and she'd take him by the hand and off they'd go."

When he said nothing, she felt a need to fill the silence.

"Anyway, she loved Stillwater and the people here. She wouldn't have wanted to leave. She went out all the time, visiting friends, neighbors, fellow church members."

He released her hand and leaned back, stretching out his legs. "Who, specifically?"

Her hand felt cold without his warmth. "My mother had a lot of empathy for the sick or lonely. Bonnie Ray's husband had just had a stroke. We'd go over and spell Bonnie so she could get out for a bit, or we'd bring some groceries. And Jedidiah Fowler's mother was getting old and losing her memory. My mother would take some bottled peaches and visit regularly, so Jed wouldn't worry about his mother while he had to work."

"Who's Jedidiah Fowler?"

"He's the one I mentioned to you before, the older man who was working on the tractor in the barn the night my father went missing."

"Tell me about him."

"There's not a lot to tell. He's an old bachelor who owns a small house near the elementary school. His mother used to live with him until she passed away a few years ago. He owns the car-repair shop and the only tow truck in Stillwater." She left out that she'd broken into that repair shop eighteen months ago, searching for evidence—evidence she hadn't found.

"What does he have to say about that night?"

"That he never saw or heard a thing."

"Can he corroborate Clay's alibi?"

"He can say when Clay left and when he came back. That's all."

"And he didn't see your father."

"Not that night."

"Did your father and this Jedidiah have any argument or problem with each other?"

"No. And no one, not Clay, Irene, Molly or Grace, heard any kind of argument or scuffle."

Hunter shifted the boxes around. "Maybe I'll drop by later today, talk to Mr. Fowler."

"Good luck," she muttered.

"What's that supposed to mean?" he asked.

"He doesn't say much. I'm a journalist and even I can't get anything out of him. For a long time, I was absolutely convinced he was the one who'd murdered my father."

"Because…"

"He's so different. And while there was no falling-out that I know of, he doesn't make it much of a secret that he never liked my father. Even now."

"Has he ever said why?"

"Just that this town didn't need a preacher like him. I think he found my father's brand of religion too puritanical. That's all I can guess."

Hunter went back to thumbing through her mother's journals. "Any other suspects I should know about? What about that other guy? The one in prison on drug-related charges?"

"Mike Metzger. He was manufacturing meth in his basement. But I hear he's about to get out on parole."

Hunter set the journals aside. "When did he go to prison?"

"Five years ago."

"And what's his connection to your father?"

"He and his family attended our church. A week before my father went missing, he caught Mike smoking pot in the bathroom and turned him in. Mike was only a stupid teenager at the time, but he got into a lot of trouble and made a few threats."

"Is he the type to act on those threats?"

"Hard to say. I'm sure he's more dangerous now than he was then. He's older, for one. And prison hasn't improved him. I've written to him a few times over the past year, begging, cajoling, threatening, trying to find out if he had anything to do with my father's disappearance."

"Did you ever get a response?"

"Not until a few weeks ago. Then he wrote me back, but he said something that was a little disconcerting."

"What?"

"The letter was only one line."

When she didn't volunteer the information, he waited.

"'I wish I'd killed you both,'" she muttered.

There was a weighty silence. "All because of the incident in the church bathroom?"

She gave him a tired smile. "Not entirely. I'm the one who kept badgering the police to keep an eye on him. I thought he might confess to killing my father."

"And?"

"They kept an eye on him, all right. They caught him cooking meth and sent him to prison."

"He blames *you* for that?"

"Basically. Forget that he's the one who was dealing drugs in the first place."

"Does he have an alibi for the night your father went missing?"

"He claims he was in his room, and his parents back him up."

"Are they credible?"

"Most people don't think much of Mike, but his parents are well-liked."

"Where in their house was his room? Do you know?"

"On the second story. But he could get out if he wanted."

"I'll make a note of that."

She felt slightly better. Hunter was so much more open to her suggestions, so much more interested in examining every aspect of the case than any of the police officers she'd dealt with. His attitude made her doubly aware of how difficult it had been to overcome Stillwater's prejudice against the Montgomerys. Maybe Hunter was expensive, but he seemed worth it. Surely, he'd find what the others had missed.

"Did anyone think to offer him leniency in return for information on your father's case?" he asked.

"I begged Chief McCormick, the previous police chief, to see what he could do. They approached Mike with an offer, but he basically told them to go to hell."

"And this guy's about to be released?"

"Any day."

"Will he be coming back here?"

"I doubt he has anywhere else to go."

Hunter made a clicking sound with his tongue. "I can't wait to meet him."

"Don't expect him to be cooperative." She'd finally recovered enough to smile. "He certainly won't let you read *his* journal."

He tapped the puffy plastic cover. "There's nothing in here that'll shock me, is there?"

"Save it for bedtime," she said with a chuckle. "I'm sure it will put you right to sleep."

Stacking the spiral notebooks, he added her journal and placed her mother's letter carefully on top.

"What do you want that for?" she asked.

He frowned as he got up. "I'm not sure. I'd like to take a closer look, if that's okay."

She felt strangely protective of that note. But she was paying him to ferret out the truth and needed to provide whatever he might need. "Sure. Are you ready for the police files, too?" she asked as she stood. She had to get to work, or the next issue of *The Stillwater Independent* would be nothing but a collection of articles pulled from the Associated Press. She generally used AP to fill in on the national news front, but she always included a good selection of local stories.

"Not yet. I was hoping you could take me out to the farm."

She was planning have a shower. *"Now?"*

"Why not?"

She considered letting him march up to Clay's front door on his own and immediately rejected the possibility. "Clay's not really someone you want to approach too boldly," she said.

"Why not?"

"He's had to fight for everything he has, and he's been the target of a lot of suspicion and doubt."

"So what are you trying to say? He's dangerous?"

"No! He's just not very welcoming to strangers."

"He won't talk to me?"

She contemplated the work still to be done at the paper and concluded that the next issue would be very short. "I'm saying I'd better go along."

* * *

While Madeline showered in the main house, Hunter sat at the desk in his little cottage and read her mother's journals.

Another day. Lee working over at the church, counseling someone. I don't know who. Me alone with my thoughts and my child. I look into Maddy's eyes and pray that somehow I can give her a better life than I've known. This morning, it actually seems a possibility. I grasp at such hope. If only for the money, the chance.

I'm afraid to breathe for fear I'll miss some cue. I have to get away. That's the only answer. I've known it all along, ever since *then*. But how and when? Satan will follow me. He'll come for me. I hear my name. He comes for me now.

This entry made Eliza sound almost normal. But some of the others. They were so cryptic—especially the poems and journal entries that had survived Eliza's penchant for burning. It was almost as if she was talking in riddles.

What was missing in her life? What cues was she watching for? And that part about having to leave. Was she talking about leaving the world? If not for her sub-sequent suicide, Hunter would've interpreted that line as leaving her husband. In light of the note Madeline had found in the secret compartment of her jewelry box, he still wondered.

I've known it all along, ever since then....

Since when?

He turned a few more pages.

There's a worm in my apple. More than one. Worms everywhere. Maggots. Eating the flesh, revealing the rotten core. I pray to awaken from the nightmare, but this nightmare is my life. Ironically, a life my friends envy.

On the same page, Eliza had taped a newspaper clipping of a young girl who'd lost her life in a hit-and-run accident. Madeline's mother seemed particularly distraught by this tragedy. She knew the girl, which would've made it painful. But she wrote about her for the next *two years*. Almost as if there was a personal connection, and yet the girl's name hadn't appeared in her journals before.

Katie Swanson, who'd been fifteen years old. A runaway.

"I'll do it for *her*," Eliza wrote more than once. She'd do what? And was "her" Katie or Madeline? There were times Eliza seemed to get them mixed up.

Hunter read Katie's obituary, which was taped onto the page following the article.

She'd been born in Stillwater and raised by her mother. There was no mention of any surviving siblings. The funeral had been held at the Purity Church of Christ—Madeline's father's church. Reverend Barker delivered the eulogy.

Sliding the second box toward him, Hunter began to flip through the reverend's large collection of sermons. Lee Barker seemed to admire his own work enough to save every sheet and to file each sermon meticulously by date.

Hunter was hoping he'd find the preacher's notes for

Katie's funeral. But the only reference to the girl was a brief passage in the sermon the next Sunday.

> May God strike the man or woman who took our innocent Katie from us. She was a beautiful girl, so full of life and so ready to do God's will. I don't know what I will do without her angelic service to me and this church.

The preacher had known her, too. And he'd apparently liked her. Hunter allowed himself a sardonic smile. Angelic by Barker's standards must've been good indeed.

The next week's sermon was on tithes and offerings, but Hunter saw no mention of her. It was in Eliza's journals that her name appeared again and again. Madeline's mother couldn't seem to get over the tragedy of the girl's death. She also referred to another loss—the suicide of a sixteen-year-old girl.

> Had I spoken, I could've saved her. I tried to warn them, but they wouldn't listen, wouldn't see. They thought I was crazy. That's what *he* tells everyone.

Was Barker the "he"? And how could Eliza have helped? Because she could identify with the girl's mental anguish?

According to what Hunter could piece together— there was no obituary or article that he could find— Rose Lee Harper had overdosed on sleeping pills.

"Wait…" he muttered, skimming a different section in which he spotted the girl's name. She'd been found naked on the floor of her bedroom.

Naked? That struck Hunter as odd. He didn't know of one other suicide in which the person had first stripped down. Especially not someone only sixteen years old.

The way Eliza had written the word *naked* was unusual, too. She generally wrote with a pretty, flowing script, as neat as he imagined her house would be. But *NAKED* stood out because it was printed and traced again and again until it made such a deep impression in the paper he could've read the word from the other side of the page.

He ran his finger over the engraved letters.

How well had Eliza known this girl?

He searched through the other journals but, unlike Katie, he could find no previous mention of Rose Lee.

It was possible she'd been on the pages that were missing. There were quite a few.

A knock at the door interrupted him. "You haven't showered yet?" Madeline asked when he answered.

"I got involved in reading these journals."

"What about the farm?"

"I'll go as I am, and shower when my clothes come." He glanced over his shoulder at the materials spread out on the desk. "What do you know about Rose Lee Harper?"

"Rose?" she asked. "Where did you read that name?"

"Your mother mentions her quite often."

"Oh." She straightened the strap of her purse. "I guess that doesn't surprise me. My mother was really empathetic. And what happened to Rose was so sad."

He stepped out and shut the door behind him. "It said she committed suicide."

"She did. But it was her whole life that was sad, you

know?" They rounded the truck Hunter had seen the night before, the one Madeline's brother had dropped off for her to use, and approached the car. When they reached it, she tossed him the keys.

"I'm driving?" he asked.

"It'll help you learn your way around town."

"How was Rose's life sad?" he asked as he climbed behind the wheel.

Madeline got in on the passenger side. "Her mother left her to be raised by her father when she was little and went to live in some other state with another man. And Ray Harper didn't start out as the best dad." She pulled an elastic tie from her purse as he backed out of the drive.

"What'd he do wrong?"

"He didn't have much money and—" she adjusted the rearview mirror so she could bunch her hair into a ponytail "—at first he spent what he did have on booze."

Booze… Just the word made Hunter crave a drink, but he quickly put it out of his mind. He was doing so much better since he'd left California. "Did that change?" he asked, dodging the potholes in the narrow lane that led from Madeline's house.

"He became devoutly religious. He used to bring his daughter over to the church to work for my father. She even helped out at the farm occasionally."

"Doing chores?"

Madeline put the mirror back in place and motioned for him to turn left at the stop sign. "She'd do filing and tidy up my father's office."

"It was messy?" Hunter asked. "He strikes me as the type who'd be very organized."

"He was, for the most part. He neglected the repairs and painting at the farm, but he stayed right on top of his church work. I think it was more a matter of finding something he could pay her for. They really needed the money. If it wasn't for my father, I don't know how they would've survived."

"Her own father didn't work?"

"Ray's a handyman. He was then, too. Sometimes he could get work, other times nothing."

Hunter loosened his seat belt a little. "If your father was trying to help them out, why not hire Ray to do some of the repairs around the farm?"

"He did. I remember seeing Ray once in a while. But it was mostly Rose Lee, working over at the church." She shook her head. "Emotionally, she was really messed up, a very strange girl. My father used to counsel her for hours."

"What about Katie Swanson?"

"Don't tell me my mother wrote about Katie, as well?"

Madeline had put on a little makeup, which enhanced the already vivid green of her eyes.

Hunter returned his attention to the road. "You've never read your mother's journals?"

"No. I...I couldn't. Just seeing the covers brings it all back."

He knew what "it" was—the pain. And she was lost in it now, remembering. But Hunter had to look at the whole picture, to know what had gone on before the reverend disappeared. That was necessary if he was going to figure out the possible motives of the people around him. "Madeline?"

"Katie was another of my father's 'projects,'" she said with a sigh. "She had a mother who'd sleep with anyone. No one knew who her father was. She was lonely and uncared for, and the man her mother was with at the time beat her. So my father stepped in before the state could get involved and arranged for her to live with Ray and Rose Lee."

"Why wouldn't he want the state to get involved?"

"He liked to take care of his own congregation."

They reached Stillwater, passed a Victorian that had been turned into a store, the police station, Walt Eastman's Tire Service. "Where to?" he asked.

"Keep going. The farm's on the other side of town, off the highway."

He stopped at Stillwater's only light. "Ray and Rose didn't mind having Katie with them?" he asked, resuming their discussion. "I thought they had financial problems, too."

"Having Katie there was a good thing for them. They had an extra room in their trailer, and my father paid them to let her stay."

"Where did your father get the money?"

"He collected alms for the poor every Sunday. There were specific members of the church for whom we were all praying, so it was really a joint effort. I think that's what endeared my father to so many people. He took a real interest in the less fortunate."

Hunter gave the car more gas as they cleared the busier streets and entered an open area. "Why do you think she ran away?"

"Word has it she was pregnant."

He shook his head. "At fifteen?"

"You have to remember what her mother was like. Katie probably lost her virginity at twelve or even younger. And according to the rumors, she'd been sneaking out at night, seeing Tommy Meyers, who was three years older."

"It was his baby?"

"Tommy's always denied it, but my father was sure it was. No one really knows. She died before she had the baby, so there was no paternity test."

"That *is* sad," he said.

"It really upset my father. He and Ray, who blamed himself for not watching her more closely, spent hours out in his office, trying to come to grips with it."

"By doing what?"

"Talking, of course. I could hear their voices coming through the door when I went to the barn to feed the chickens. Sometimes I'd see Ray's truck in the drive late at night. They'd tried so hard to help her, you know?"

"Did your father have any other 'projects?'" Hunter asked. Considering the luck he'd experienced with Rose Lee and Katie, Hunter hoped not.

"Not really. He continued to help Ray until my own mother…" She cleared her throat. "Well, after that, we had a couple of bad years with the farm, he had me to take care of, and people around here were struggling so he wasn't making as much at the church. It was all we could do to get by. Then he married Irene and had his hands full raising three more kids."

"Did anyone ever say anything about the fact that Rose Lee was found naked?" he asked.

Madeline's forehead creased. "She was naked?"

"That's what it said in your mother's journal."

"I don't remember that. But I was only eight or nine at the time of her funeral. It wasn't something folks talked about in front of me."

"I can't picture a young woman peeling off her clothes and then taking a bunch of sleeping pills," he said.

"Maybe she'd just been involved in a romantic encounter."

"Do you recall her having a boyfriend?"

"No. I can't really imagine her being with anyone. She was extremely shy. After Katie died, she quit working for my father, and I rarely saw her in town. When I did run into her, she wouldn't even look me in the eye. She'd stare at the ground."

"So would you say Rose Lee took Katie's death hard?"

"Harder than anyone. I doubt she ever recovered from the grief."

"Why do you say that?"

"Before Katie died, there were times she seemed almost normal. Afterward—" she shrugged "—afterward, she would barely speak."

11

The farm was bigger than Hunter had expected. "Clay runs this by himself?" he asked as they parked to one side of the long gravel drive and got out of Madeline's car.

"Yes. Can you believe it?"

He whistled under his breath. It wouldn't be an easy job to manage such a large piece of property—and yet it appeared that Clay had the place well in hand. Madeline's stepbrother obviously wasn't afraid of hard work. Hunter had to respect that. But he wondered about some of the comments Madeline had made concerning Clay. He sounded driven, protective, determined. Madeline had also implied that Clay had a very short fuse, which was an important thing to note in a possible murder investigation. The impressions of the players involved often proved more valuable than the facts. Facts could be interpreted in several ways; it was the perspective of those who'd known Reverend Barker that would finally reveal the information Hunter was after.

"So this is where you grew up?"

Madeline deposited her keys in her purse as she nodded.

It was a white two-story A-frame that sat back from

the road. It wasn't particularly large, but it wasn't small, either. Hunter guessed it to be about 2400 square feet. Behind the house, he could see a rather imposing barn. The wind carried the scent of animals and he heard some distant clucking, so there was probably a chicken coop next to the barn. A rooster strutted around the corner to confirm it.

Hunter couldn't remember the last time he'd seen a rooster. They weren't exactly a common sight on the beaches of L.A.

Madeline paused when she noticed that he'd begun walking more slowly. "Be glad that's a different bird than the rooster we had here when we were little," she said.

"Why?"

"The old one would've tried to gouge your eyes out. We were terrified of it. Especially Grace. He was very territorial."

Hunter imagined the humid days of a summer spent on the outskirts of this small Mississippi town, imagined children with denim overalls and dusty bare feet gathering at the local grocery market to slake their thirst at the Coke machine. It was a completely different world than the one he'd known growing up in Mission Viejo, one of the nicer suburbs of Los Angeles. But it held a certain appeal.

"What?" she said, and he realized he was smiling.

"I was thinking of Tom Sawyer."

"Don't be giving me any more of that west coast attitude," she said, deepening her accent.

He thought about the differences between her home and his, then decided California wasn't *better* than Mississippi, but it was different. "Just don't try to feed me any collard greens, and we'll be okay," he teased.

"Have you ever tried collard greens?"

"No, but I hate spinach."

Wind chimes tinkled as they stepped onto the wrap-around porch, which creaked slightly beneath their weight.

"Your stepbrother takes good care of the place."

"He does. It actually looks better than when my father was…er…here."

She often acted as if she didn't know whether to say "alive," and generally veered away from it. Hunter suspected that, even after twenty years and the discovery of her father's car in the nearby quarry, she couldn't believe he was really dead. That uncertainty had to be difficult for her. "How's it changed?" he asked.

She shrugged. "The house used to be an ugly, dingy green. The yard had a lot of weeds and bare spots, where our dog had dug various holes and buried this or that, usually one of our shoes."

"Your father didn't mind how it looked?"

"I don't think he paid much attention. He was a bit of a mad scientist, so interested in his work that he didn't really see anything else."

"Didn't you tell me that your father cared about setting a good example?"

"In some ways, he did. He was most severe in his punishments when we said or did something that reflected poorly on him. He felt the children of a devout preacher should be hardworking, sober-minded and well-versed in scripture."

The people in Madeline's life were beginning to seem familiar to Hunter. He'd seen a few pictures of her father, knew he'd been tall and imposing with hollowed-out cheeks, piercing black eyes and a determined jaw. Her mother had been the opposite—small, soft and gentle-looking. Madeline had obviously inherited her height and slenderness from her father's side, but her bottle-green eyes resembled her mother's. So did her smooth pale skin. Hunter wondered where the auburn-colored hair had come from—maybe a grandmother or an aunt. He had yet to see any pictures of extended family members but knew he'd probably run across them later, when he searched through the rest of her scrapbooks.

"Was there one child he singled out more than the others?" he asked.

"He was hardest on Clay. But a lot of men are tougher on their sons than their daughters."

"So you'd say they were close?"

"Not exactly." She seemed thoughtful, almost philosophical. "Clay and my father were too different to ever be very close."

Hunter wanted to talk about the ways in which her father and her stepbrother were incompatible, but she'd already knocked on the door, and a petite woman with short brown hair and brown eyes opened it before he could say more.

"Hi, Maddy." She embraced Madeline, then turned to Hunter. "This must be your private investigator."

"With a surfer-boy image," Madeline said wryly.

"Boy?" he echoed, slightly offended—especially since he'd overheard her tell Kirk he was too young for her.

She went on as if he hadn't spoken. "Allie, this is Hunter Solozano. And this," she waved a hand at the shorter woman, "is my sister-in-law. The only woman who could bring my hard-to-get brother to his knees."

"I don't think anyone's ever brought Clay to his knees," Allie said, chuckling.

"Somehow I'm not surprised to hear Clay was a challenge," Hunter said.

"He was more than a challenge," Madeline responded. "To most women around here, he was the impossible dream."

And what had made him so remote? Hunter asked himself. Was it possible that the reverend had been *too* hard on his new son?

"Whitney's the one who has him wrapped around her little finger," Allie said as she waved them in.

"Whitney is Allie's seven-year-old," Madeline explained. "She's in school right now, so you won't get to meet her today, but she's darling."

The inside of the house was as tidy as the outside. The living room smelled of fresh paint and was decorated in a rich burgundy. A wedding photograph sat on one end of the fireplace mantel; it showed a man who had to be Clay with the woman Hunter had just met and a young girl with round cheeks and long blond hair. The mantel also held a collection of candlesticks in varying shapes and sizes.

Allie was friendly enough as she offered them a seat, but there was something about her eyes that bothered Hunter. They seemed wary, a bit furtive. Considering the situation, however, he supposed that was natural. It couldn't feel good to have others suspect your husband of murder. Maybe there were even times when *she* wondered about the missing reverend and the part her husband might've played....

"We can't sit down. We won't be here very long," Madeline said. "We were just hoping to talk to Clay for a minute. Is he around?"

"He's out fixing the levee along the creek."

She didn't offer to call him in. Hunter sensed that she was reluctant to let them speak to Clay. But if Madeline felt the same thing, she ignored it and barreled on as comfortably as any journalist would. "If you don't mind, we'll walk around back and look for him."

"I'll go with you," she said, but judging by the smell emanating from the kitchen, they'd caught her with food on the stove.

"There's no need to interrupt what you're doing. We'll find him."

"We could call his cell phone," Allie said.

Madeline smiled at Hunter. "My brother's finally entering the twenty-first century. He refused to get a cell phone for the longest time. And I could understand it, I guess, since he rarely troubled himself to pick up his regular phone." She chuckled. "He was such a recluse until Allie came along."

Allie had picked up the phone next to the couch, but Madeline told her not to bother. "I want to show Hunter the farm, anyway," she said.

Clay's wife was slow hanging up. "You're sure? It could be quite a walk."

"We'll call if we don't find him." Madeline indicated that she had her own cell. "Okay if we go out the back?"

Allie's eyes ranged over Hunter in an assessing fashion. Was she merely curious?

It was difficult to say, but Hunter could tell she was no ally. She smiled with her lips, but there was a stubborn protectiveness about her that put him on edge.

He returned her smile as if he hadn't noticed, then followed Madeline into the kitchen, which was as old as hers but much larger. They walked through the back door to a deep porch that overlooked several acres of farmland. The barn he'd spotted before stood to the right, beside the chicken coop he'd already assumed was there. Some farm equipment was clustered beyond that, as well as a couple of rusted trucks that seemed to hail from the 1950s.

"My brother restores old cars and trucks," Madeline explained before he could ask. "It's his hobby."

They crossed the porch, but she didn't immediately descend the four steps. Instead, she leaned on the railing, gazing out into the distance, reminding Hunter of the picture he'd seen of her at age eight.

"Do you miss living here?" he asked.

Allie stood at the door, but Madeline didn't turn. She shaded her eyes against a pale yellow sun and stared off into the distance. "A little. Mostly it makes me sad." She waved toward the barn. "When my father wasn't over at the church, he was usually in there."

"Taking care of the animals?"

"Writing his sermons. See that window?"

Hunter nodded.

"That was his office."

"It's already been searched?"

"A few times."

"Can I see it?"

"Of course, but there's not much left. Clay gutted it a year and a half ago."

Hunter felt his eyebrows go up. "He needed the space?"

An odd expression flitted across her pretty features. "No. I guess he just decided Dad wasn't coming back."

"Which is understandable," he said for Allie's

benefit, but when he turned he found she'd gone back inside.

Madeline pushed away from the railing. "Come on, let's take a look."

The cool, dark interior made Hunter think of the barn in *Charlotte's Web*. He supposed it was because he didn't see barns very often. But there were no horses or pigs. Mostly, it was a large garage where Clay worked on cars.

"That's a 1953 Hornet convertible," Madeline said of a sky-blue car that could've been used in the making of *Grease*.

"How much is it worth?" he asked.

"A couple of hundred thousand."

Hunter coughed. There was a vehicle worth that much money sitting inside an old barn in the hills of Mississippi? "How do you know?"

"Because it's on eBay. The current bid is $160,000."

"Wow."

"He didn't start out with cars this expensive," she said. "He's been working his way up."

"Pretty soon the farm will be his hobby."

"I doubt it," she said.

"Why not?"

"He was born to work the land. He loves it."

"How did he get started with cars? His father? Your father?"

"Neither. He's just always loved them—and had the talent for doing whatever needed to be done. After my father disappeared and Clay came back from college and took over the farm, he ripped out the stalls and converted it into a garage."

"So your father had animals in here?"

"The meanest son-of-a-bitch horse you've ever met," a deep voice responded.

Hunter turned to find a man standing in the doorway. He had thick black hair falling across his forehead, blue eyes and a dark shadow of beard growth covering a very square jaw. He was tall, too. Probably three inches taller than Hunter and fifty pounds heavier.

Hunter might have felt a little intimidated, but he preferred to think of himself as light and fast—a skateboarder, surfer or skier as opposed to a football player, wrestler or one-man army.

"You must be Madeline's stepbrother."

He didn't bother to smile. "And you must be the dick from California."

Despite the situation, Hunter couldn't restrain a laugh. Clay's flat, emotionless voice suggested that he wasn't necessarily referring to Hunter's profession. "I can see you're a man who says what he means."

"Any other kind of man isn't a man."

"And if I prefer the term P.I.?"

"You're in Mississippi, son," he replied. "We don't give a damn about being politically correct around here."

Son... He was definitely pushing his advantage in age and weight. "Which makes me what?" Hunter asked. "A liberal?"

"You tell me."

"I am what I am," he said with a shrug. When he didn't act threatened or upset, Hunter recognized a positive shift in Clay's attitude. He would've relaxed—except that he suspected Allie had called Clay the second they'd stepped off the porch and that Clay didn't like them snooping around. At least not on their own.

"How old are you?" Clay asked.

Hunter cast Madeline a sidelong glance. "Did you tell him to ask me that?"

"You look young," she said with a shrug.

"I look like a certified badass," he corrected, hoping to ease the tension, and was rewarded with the low rumble of a chuckle from Clay.

"So?" Madeline said to her stepbrother.

"So what?" he responded grumpily.

"If you're finished putting Hunter on notice, we'll move ahead with the tour."

Clay held out a large hand, one that was nicked and gouged. "Be my guest. If he stays long enough, maybe we'll see what kind of dick he really is."

Hunter turned and cocked an eyebrow at Madeline's stepbrother. "I'm a damn good one," he said.

"Which means what?"

"Which means if you're involved in this mess, you should be worried."

If Clay was surprised that Hunter would stand his ground, he didn't show it. There was a slight tightening around his eyes and mouth, that was all.

"Good thing he's not involved."

Allie had joined them. She came up behind Clay and put her hand on his back in an obvious effort to calm him. That simple action let Hunter know that Allie loved and supported her husband one hundred percent. The devotion in Clay's eyes when he realized his wife was there said he felt the same way about her.

This case was going to be more difficult than Hunter had thought. The people here stood together, guarded their secrets well.

"Welcome to a small southern town," he muttered. Evidently, stereotypes were stereotypes for a reason.

"He's *not* involved," Madeline said, repeating Allie's comment.

Hunter pulled his instant camera from the pocket of his coat. "And what kind of dick would I be if I took everything I was told at face value?" he asked with a smile.

Madeline clasped her hands in front of her, so tightly he could see the veins stand out. "You're here to prove Clay innocent."

He wasn't here for any such thing. He was here to find out who'd killed her father, and at this point everyone was suspect. But he didn't say so. He wandered over to take a look at the office.

Clay's voice stopped him just as his hand curled around the doorknob. "That's locked."

He glanced back. "Because…"

"I like it that way."

"Stop it." Allie nudged her husband meaningfully. "You have to forgive Clay, Mr. Solozano. When the police couldn't figure out what happened to Madeline's father, they blamed him. It was ridiculous, of course. Clay was only sixteen at the time. But Reverend Barker was a beloved pastor, and folks in Stillwater wanted someone to pay for their loss."

"I understand," he said.

"That room is locked because we never use it," she went on. "There's just the three of us—me, Clay and my daughter, Whitney. We have plenty of space, and it gets cold in the winter. There's no heat in that room."

"I see."

"My father used to have a space heater," Madeline volunteered. "And an air-conditioning unit that sat in the window."

"It was so old Clay finally threw it away," Allie said, still trying to compensate for her surly husband.

"Is there a key?" Hunter asked pointedly.

"Somewhere," she said. "I'm not sure—"

Surprisingly, Clay interrupted. "It's in the cupboard above the fridge."

Allie hesitated long enough that Hunter knew she hadn't planned to tell them. "I'll get it," she said at last.

Hunter and Clay stared at each other while they waited; Madeline kept up a stream of nervous chatter.

"The convertible's looking good," she said. "How's the bidding going?"

"Better than I expected." Her stepbrother offered no specifics.

"When's it over?"

"Tomorrow night."

"Are you going to have trouble letting this one go?" His gaze finally strayed from Hunter's face. "Trouble?"

"Isn't this one of the rarest cars you've owned?"

"There's another one right behind it."

"You put so much work into each vehicle, I'd want to keep them all."

"The work is the part I like."

"What are you planning to do next?" she asked.

"The Chevy sitting beyond the tractor."

"Not the truck!"

"It's about time, don't you think?"

"I don't know. I'm so used to seeing that old hunk of junk, this place won't look the same without it."

No comment.

She peered into the car. "Even when you're finished, it won't be worth nearly as much as this baby, will it?"

"No."

"So why mess with it?"

"I'm ready for something different."

He didn't do it for the money. That was clear. A few other things were clear, too. Clay had a giant chip on his shoulder, and he had little, if any, interest in seeing his stepfather's murder solved.

"How do you feel about Lee Barker?" Hunter asked.

Madeline's lips parted as if she wasn't comfortable with the suddenness of this question. But Clay didn't seem startled. He looked Hunter right in the eye, stubborn, defiant. "I don't think about him anymore."

"And back then?"

"We had our differences, if that's what you're getting at."

"Just the usual stuff," Madeline added. "The kind of problems any teenager would have—"

Hunter raised a hand. "Let *him* answer, okay?"

Clay folded his arms across his chest. "I already did."

"You don't like the fact that I'm here, do you?" Hunter said.

"You thought I'd be excited about it?"

Not really. It was obvious that Clay didn't trust him. Hunter doubted Clay trusted anyone, except maybe his wife.

"Is there anything you'd like to tell me about your stepfather?" Hunter asked.

"Nope."

"Clay's been through this so many times," Madeline said and seemed relieved when Allie reappeared.

Clay gave his wife a slight nod. She walked between them and unlocked the pastor's office with one key for the door and a different one for the dead bolt. When she swung the door wide, the room's musty scent hit them full force.

Hunter tried to ignore it. "When did you put the dead bolt on here?"

"I didn't," Clay replied.

"My father kept his office locked at all times," Madeline put in.

"Why?" Hunter couldn't imagine that Lee Barker had stored anything of value in this old barn. From what he understood, Barker didn't actually *have* a whole lot of real value.

"As a pastor, he was privy to some of his parishioners' darkest thoughts and deeds," she said. "This was where he kept his notes. I'm sure he didn't want that kind of information to get out."

A pastor should be discreet, especially in such a small town, where gossip could ruin someone's life. But a simple lock wasn't enough? Who did he think was going to break in?

Hunter examined the heavy-duty bolt as Allie and Madeline entered the empty room ahead of him.

"Looks like Madeline's father was a very cautious man," he said to Clay, who hadn't moved. Again, he received no response.

"There isn't much to see in here," Allie was saying. "Clay dismantled the place a year or two ago. After eighteen years—" she turned to Madeline and her voice softened apologetically "—he figured it was time to give Maddy her father's things."

Hunter didn't make any effort to study the room. Anything that was here when Madeline's father was around had long since been removed, even the carpet.

Instead, he crossed to the window and gazed out, trying to see the farm as Barker would've seen it.

From where he stood, he had a good view of the gravel drive, the chicken coop off to the right and the back porch. This place would've been a functional home office, if not a fancy one. Because of its location, Barker would know when someone arrived, and he'd be able to keep an eye on the kids if they were out playing or doing chores.

Above him, Hunter noticed some holes in the wall that indicated there'd been blinds at one time. For privacy. Like the dead bolt.

"That was Grace's room," Madeline said, coming up behind him.

"Which one?" Hunter asked.

She pointed at the farmhouse, to the window above the porch. "The corner, near that lattice."

"She had her own room?"

"Yes, but she wasn't alone very often. I was supposed to be sharing a room with Molly. Molly was the youngest and it was my job to look after her. But Grace had two twin beds and she was always begging me to stay with her." She smiled nostalgically. "I've never known anyone more afraid of the dark. If she was up late doing homework and needed to shower for the next day, she'd wake me and ask me to go into the bathroom with her. I'd sit on the counter waiting for her."

"I was scared when I was young, too," Allie said. "But I blame my older brother. He and his friends loved to bang on the house or scratch on the wall, anything to frighten me. He thought it was hilarious."

"I was never frightened," Madeline said. "At least not of the boogeyman."

Clay hadn't entered the room, but he hadn't gone back to work, either. He leaned against the doorjamb, watching them. Hunter saw that he scowled when Madeline said what she did, as if her pain hurt him, too. Clay was angry, embittered, a loner. And yet he loved his stepsister, regardless of what might've happened to her father.

"What were you afraid of?" Hunter asked.

Madeline's chest rose, as if she'd just taken a deep breath and she met his gaze. "Becoming as unhappy as my mother."

Having a parent so miserable that she didn't want to go on would scare any child. "What about now?" Hunter asked quietly. "Are you still afraid?"

The question had nothing to do with his investigation. It was really none of his business. But there was something so achingly lonely about Madeline Barker that he couldn't help wanting to banish the haunted look that sometimes appeared in her eyes.

"No," she said. But he was fairly sure it was a lie.

Madeline hated having to bring Hunter to the farm. She knew Clay didn't like it. Her stepbrother was a man who took his privacy seriously. Yet here she was parading a private investigator around his home. The police had searched the property twice—but only after they'd produced a warrant. Even then, Clay had held them strictly to the specified areas, allowing them no extra leeway. He didn't trust the police.

She could tell he didn't trust Hunter, either—and she hated the fact that she was taking advantage of their relationship by bringing a detective here. But Hunter had to have free access to everything in order to do his job.

She stood in the center of the room, watching as he looked around. "So your father used this office to meet with people from his congregation?"

"Occasionally. He had a study at the church, but it was easier to maintain the farm if he worked out here."

"He was home a lot, then."

"Quite a bit. But he was always busy."

"Can you remember any of the people who came out here to visit him in the days immediately prior to his disappearance?"

"There's a list in the police files."

He nodded. "Good. Any chance you can show me where that guy was working on the tractor?"

"Of course."

He headed toward the entrance, but Clay blocked the doorway.

"Clay," Allie said. Hunter spoke at the same time.

"Do you have a problem with me being here, Mr. Montgomery?" he asked.

"Clay's put up with a lot," Madeline said, but Clay raised a hand.

"You don't have to make excuses for me, Maddy."

"I just want him to understand. So he doesn't jump to the wrong conclusion."

"And what conclusion would that be?" Hunter asked.

Madeline curled her nails into her palms. Hunter wasn't as intimidated by Clay as most men. Maybe he was shorter and had a smaller build, but he had a will that was every bit as strong. She hadn't expected to find that beneath his Hollywood smile and beach bum manner.

"My stepbrother's easily misunderstood," she said so he wouldn't automatically assume that Clay was guilty of any greater sin than being guarded.

Hunter thrust out his chin. It was a slight movement, but Madeline noticed it and grew more worried. "I think he's making himself pretty clear," Hunter muttered.

Allie had stepped over to the door and, as usual, tried to act as a peacemaker and go-between for Clay. Gently maneuvering Clay out of Hunter's way, she chuckled. "The testosterone levels are running a bit too high, guys. This is a friendly meeting, remember?"

Hunter ignored her. "You're not interested in helping me find out what happened to your stepfather," he said as he moved into the larger part of the barn.

"Not particularly," Clay admitted.

Hunter's eyes narrowed slightly. "I'd be interested to hear why."

Clay glanced at Madeline, and she sent him a pleading look. "It's not going to change the fact that he's gone. Far as I'm concerned, you're just more trouble."

"It'd bring Madeline some peace if she knew," Hunter said.

"Says you," Clay retorted. "But you don't know her or care about her the way we do, so don't talk to me about what would or wouldn't be good for my sister."

"She's the one who brought me."

"That's the only reason you're still standing here."

Hunter didn't back down. He stood his ground, returning Clay's glare. And despite herself, Madeline was impressed. Clay was so intense that, at times, he made even those who were close to him a little nervous.

"Where did the police search when they came?" Hunter asked. He was still addressing Clay, refusing to give in, as most other men would've done. But it was Allie who answered. Madeline guessed she was just as eager to defuse the tension between the two men as Madeline was.

"The first time, they searched the house and the barn."

"They searched more than once?" This finally pulled Hunter's attention away from Clay.

Allie nodded. "Eighteen months ago, they took a backhoe to the yard. They didn't find anything, of course."

"Why would they do that after so long?" he asked.

"Because of Joe Vincelli," Madeline explained. "He followed Grace over here one night, decided she was about to exhume my father's body and move it to a better hiding place."

"Did she have a shovel?"

"Yes."

"What was she doing?"

"She'd come here to dig, like he said, but only to prove that all the rumors were false," Madeline told him.

Hunter seemed skeptical. "Then why not do it during the day?"

"Because she knew I'd never let her," Clay responded, chiming in for the first time since the standoff between them.

"Why not?" Hunter asked.

Clay smiled humorlessly. "Because I'm not stupid."

"They've been hoping to pin this on Clay for a long time," Allie said. "He couldn't take the chance that they might stumble upon something they could misinterpret, something that might appear to give him more of a motive or whatever. People see what they want to see, you know? I was a police officer for ten years, spent five of those as a cold case detective. I've watched it happen before."

"So you approve of your husband's refusal to cooperate?" he asked.

Her smile disappeared and she stepped closer to Clay. "Completely."

Hunter nodded at Madeline. "I'm finished here."

"You don't want to see where Jed was working on the tractor?" she asked, surprised by his abrupt change.

Hunter had already started moving. "You can show me when we leave."

But he barely looked when she pointed out the back part of the barn. And he didn't speak until they reached the car. Then he got in, slammed the door and said, "Your stepbrother's hiding something."

12

Madeline refused to look over at Hunter while she drove, for fear he'd see the uncertainty she worked so hard to deny, the uncertainty she often concealed in vociferous protestations of Clay's innocence.

"You're making the same mistake as everyone else," she said flatly.

When he didn't respond, she finally glanced over and found him staring sadly at her.

"I'm sorry," he said. "But if the truth's going to be too hard for you to take, then we need to quit right now."

"Stop it." She waved an impatient hand. "Clay doesn't make the best first impression, that's all. He's the kind of man you have to get to know."

"And you know him."

"Of course."

"He doesn't let anyone know him."

She shook her head. Maybe Clay had his secrets. But those secrets didn't include murder. "If you knew what life used to be like for him, you'd have a better understanding of who he is."

"Tell me about him," he said.

She pictured the proud, long-legged boy Clay had been at sixteen, the boy who'd proven himself as tough as any man. She'd already mentioned that it was her stepbrother who'd kept the family together, but it was the smaller details that really defined his character. "He wore the same clothes to school over and over so Grace and Molly and me could have an occasional new dress. He gave up his friends, because he no longer had time to play. He went from being one of the most popular kids in school to being an absolute loner, a boy too old for his years. He skipped lunch more days than he ate so we could eat, and he pretended he wasn't hungry, so we wouldn't have to feel guilty about it. He worked like a dog at sixteen, seventeen, eighteen years old, long hours for low pay, to keep a roof over our heads. And he was willing to come to blows with anyone who threatened or mistreated us." She glanced away from the road long enough to peer into Hunter's face, to be sure she'd made her point. "I don't know of another person who could've done what he did at such a young age. My whole family owes him. *I* owe him. He was our protector—our *father,* in a way, although he was my own age."

The passion in her voice must've convinced him, because Hunter's expression grew more thoughtful. "What about Irene?"

"As time went by, even she leaned on him as if he were the parent and she the child. He did what needed to be done regardless of the sacrifice involved. And he never complained about the price he paid."

"No wonder you admire him," he said softly.

"He's earned it."

He seemed to weigh her answer, to mull it over and examine every angle. "I appreciate what he's done for you, Maddy."

It was the first time he'd used her nickname. She liked the sound of it on his lips, and that worried her. But she shrugged it off. After the breakup of her closest relationship, she was looking for the warmth and security she'd lost. Hunter was confident almost to the point of being cocky, coolheaded, always in control. She found everything about him attractive. It'd be almost too easy to want to get involved.

Easy for now but dangerous for later. He couldn't stay forever. She didn't even know what kind of life he led in California....

"I appreciate what he's done for Grace and Molly and your mother, too," he was saying.

As sincere as he seemed, he was holding something back. She could tell. "But it still doesn't change your mind about Clay."

His light eyes bored into her as if he could see right through her. "It tells me you have a decision to make."

She knew what he was about to say. She'd faced the same decision for nineteen years. Did she question certain events, conversations—pursue the truth despite her loyalty to the Montgomerys? Or did she play it safe and cling to what her heart told her *had* to be true? So far she'd done a little of both, but she didn't know how long she could go on doing that.

"They're my family," she said. "The only family I have left."

He touched her shoulder, his fingers warm through her blouse. "Then maybe it'd be better if I went home."

She shrugged off his hand because she found it so confusing, so mystifyingly *welcome,* and raked her fingers through her hair. She didn't want him to leave, although there were moments she was absolutely terrified—like back at the farm, when Clay was glaring at Hunter and she was seeing her stepbrother through Hunter's eyes. Or when she remembered the strained silence that had permeated the house as she'd walked in the morning after her father hadn't come home. Or the tense, wan face of her stepmother in the days that followed. Or the complete absence of emotion with which Clay and especially Grace had talked about her father in the years afterward.

But that was craziness, wasn't it? Focusing on those little curiosities was simply allowing herself to succumb to the power of suggestion. The Montgomerys had a rational explanation for each and every behavior. Clay didn't see any value in opening up to Hunter or anyone else. Why would he? He couldn't risk coming under attack again, particularly now that he had a family. And of course Irene would be under a great deal of stress and the house would feel odd the morning after her father hadn't returned. They were all waiting to see what would happen next, to receive some word of him. And Grace had become increasingly secretive and unreachable—and not just when they were talking about her father. Madeline suspected that what they'd found in the trunk of the Cadillac might've had something to do with it, but even if Grace was telling the truth about not knowing how her underwear had ended up in that suitcase, teenagers were notoriously moody.

How could Madeline let the suspicion evoked by those tiny details erode her confidence in her family? She knew the Montgomerys were good people. They'd been there for her, proven themselves over and over. That was a greater testament to their innocence than any strained look could be proof of their guilt. Wasn't it?

It was Irene who'd sat at her graduation ceremony, Irene who'd held her when she cried over the breakup with her first boyfriend, Irene who'd helped her move into her cottage and was there any time she needed a sympathetic ear. Clay still came by to patch her roof, fix a leaky faucet, paint her office or keep her old printer going. She and Grace had grown apart for a few years, but since Grace had returned to town, they'd become close again. And Madeline had always adored and mothered Molly. Because Irene had been so busy helping Clay earn a living and save the farm, and Grace had been so remote, Madeline had taken care of the youngest Montgomery. They often talked on the phone, and when Molly came to visit, she stayed as many days at Madeline's house when she came to visit as she did with anyone else.

They were nearing Stillwater's main intersection. Madeline stopped at the light, but when it turned green, she didn't accelerate.

The person behind her honked.

"What's it going to be?" Hunter asked.

She rubbed her face as the driver of the pickup behind her, frustrated with her lack of response, honked a second time and gave her a dirty look as he sped around her.

Slowly, she started to drive again. She'd already made her decision, hadn't she? Or she wouldn't have brought Hunter to town. "I have to know what happened to my father."

Her words had come out as a mere whisper, but she knew he'd understood her when he said, "You could be making a terrible mistake."

Tears gathered in her eyes. The stress, the worry and the sleepless nights were catching up with her. "They didn't do it," she said.

Hunter watched tears spill over Madeline's lashes and roll down her cheeks as she drove. He wasn't sure he'd ever had a more tortured client. Or one who was probably in for a more unpleasant surprise. He wished she could be satisfied letting the past drift farther and farther away from her.

But he couldn't blame her for her inability to do so. If he were in her shoes, he'd seek the truth, too. Some people couldn't stop themselves from rushing toward the one thing that could destroy them.

He thought of the alcohol that had taken the edge off his own disappointment and, for a moment, was tempted to tell her he wouldn't be an accomplice in her fate. He'd sensed something dark lurking inside Clay, some secret pain or scar, and feared that Madeline's stepbrother was indeed involved in her father's disappearance. But there was only one way to find out. And that was to move forward with the investigation.

Maybe, if they were lucky, they'd reach a dead end before the big crash. If he couldn't go any further, Madeline would have to accept that she might never know. Or hire someone else. Then, if she did find out, he wouldn't have to be a party to it.

Locating a napkin in the glove compartment, he handed it to her to wipe her tears. "Take me to meet the rest of your family," he said.

* * *

Elaine Vincelli was nearly a hundred pounds over-weight. But she carried it well. With shoulders broader than those of most men, she looked solid. Compact. And her get-to-the-point-and-make-it-quick manner suggested she possessed a keen mind.

"What do you want?" she asked as soon as Madeline had introduced him. They were standing on her doorstep, but she didn't bother to invite them in.

"I want to know who killed your brother," Hunter replied.

"And you think I can tell you?"

"I'm hoping you can help."

"If I knew, I'd be demanding the police put him in jail," she told him.

She'd once insisted the police arrest Clay, hadn't she? What about that? Wasn't that the excuse Madeline had given him for Clay's behavior—that he'd been through a lot and was afraid of being blamed again?

Hunter assumed a casual pose. He wanted to convince her he wasn't a threat, so she'd relax and say more than she otherwise would. It was an act he'd per-fected over the years, a way to make the most of a face that was too pretty to look very dangerous. "Madeline says you think it's Clay Montgomery," he said.

Elaine shot an irritated glance at her niece. "I've had my doubts about him in the past."

He lifted one eyebrow. "Not anymore?"

Her mood seemed to darken. "I wasn't there that night. I don't know what happened."

"I'm only asking for your opinion."

He'd used just the right inflection to imply that she

could trust him, but she wasn't so easily fooled. "Shouldn't you be more interested in the facts? What good is an opinion?"

"You strike me as an excellent judge of character," he said. "Sometimes it's as important to know *who* to ask as it is to know *what* to ask."

She was tempted by the flattery. He could almost see the locks snapping open in her mind. "I *am* a good judge of character."

"Which is what makes me wonder about Clay."

He'd set the stage for her to tell him every vile thing she'd ever seen or heard about Madeline's stepbrother. So he was surprised when she broke eye contact and muttered, "I'm not sure he would've been capable of cold-blooded murder. Not at sixteen."

"So you think it was 'cold-blooded' murder?" he asked.

"Is there any other kind?" she replied.

He shrugged. "It could've been an accident."

Her lips formed a thin colorless line. "It could've been a lot of things."

He ran a thumb over the whiskers on his chin. Why wasn't she going after Clay as he'd expected, as he'd been told she'd done in the past? "So…if it wasn't Clay, who was it?"

"How should I know? Maybe it was a vagrant, like Irene Montgomery's always claimed."

From the corner of his eye, Hunter caught the startled rounding of Madeline's mouth. But he didn't turn or acknowledge her reaction and was grateful she didn't break into the conversation. "I don't think so," he said. This was only his first day in town and already he was willing to bet that whoever killed Barker had known the man well. This whole case suggested hidden actions and emotions.

"Regardless of what you think, this is a peaceful community," she snapped. "No one who lives here would commit murder. I'm afraid you're wasting your time."

She'd gone from blaming Clay to blaming no one. Interesting. "Do you remember Katie Swanson?" he asked.

"Katie?" she repeated. But he doubted it was because she didn't recognize the name. She just didn't know how to react to it.

"The fifteen-year-old girl who was killed in a hit-and-run accident twenty-seven years ago."

Elaine frowned at Madeline. "Why are you asking about her?"

"I was just wondering how well you knew her."

"Hardly at all."

"She was at the church quite a bit, wasn't she?"

"No—I...I don't remember that."

"From what I understand, she used to work for your brother."

"I never saw them together," she said.

"Your brother never mentioned her?"

She stepped back, out of the path of the door. She was longing to close it; he could tell. "Why would he?" she asked.

"He seemed to care about her a great deal. And what was the other girl's name? The one who killed herself?"

She half closed the door, so that only eight or so inches remained through which he could see her. "I wouldn't know."

"You don't remember her, either?"

"It's been too long," she said, but in such a small community, she'd recall something *that* sensational. Rose Lee's suicide had occurred six months after the hit-and-run and only a year before Madeline's mother ended her life.

"How long have you lived here?" he asked.

"I don't see why I should continue answering questions about people who weren't even part of my life. I'm afraid I can't help you."

Hunter grabbed the door before she could shut it. All the people who might know something about the past didn't want to talk, and he was damned curious about that. "Just one more thing."

She hesitated, and he went on. "You and your brother were close—isn't that right?"

Obviously taken off guard by the change in subject, she stared at him. "I—I guess you could say that."

I guess? A lukewarm answer if Hunter had ever heard one. "So—" he kept one hand on the door and used the other to scratch his head in exaggerated puzzlement "—if there was anything strange going on in his life, he probably would've told you about it."

"We both had families of our own when he went missing," she said, resuming her customary authority. "We didn't spend much time together. But thanks for coming by."

He stopped the door again. "Did you attend his church?"

"Every Sunday."

"So you were proud of him?"

"Who wouldn't be proud of a preacher?" she said. "The whole town loved him."

He hadn't asked about the whole town. He'd been trying to establish how much *she* loved him. "Then that suitcase they found in the Cadillac. That couldn't have belonged to him?"

Shoving his hand out of the way, she slammed the door.

"I can't believe you asked her that!" Madeline said as soon as they were in the Corolla and she was angling away from the curb. "What are you trying to do?"

"What you're paying me to do," he said.

Her cheeks were flushed with anger. "You're insulting someone who isn't even here to defend himself. You're insulting my *father!*"

"I'm searching for the truth, Maddy."

"Don't call me that!"

"Why not?" he asked. "That's what everyone else calls you."

"You don't know me. You don't know my father. You don't belong here. I—I've made a mistake."

"Madeline…"

She wouldn't look at him. He could see her grinding her teeth, wanting to say more, trying to hold the words back, along with her tears.

"Listen to me." He reached out to touch her. "We have to figure out what happened *before* your father went missing. That'll lead us to the person who might've killed him."

"So you insult my father and accuse my brother?"

"I didn't accuse your brother."

"You said he's hiding something. But he's not! He didn't kill my father."

"Maybe he didn't. But I'm not going to find out who did unless I press a few buttons, stir things up around here."

"And hurt those who are closest to me?"

"You want me to pull a freakin' rabbit out of my hat!" he shouted. "I can't deliver the perfect villain. It's going to be someone you know, and probably someone you love. You're aware of that, even if you don't want to admit it!"

She didn't answer. They'd left the expensive, antebellum house of her aunt behind and were now surrounded by farmland.

"Pull over, so you can look at me," he said. "I want to be sure I'm getting through to you."

At first, he thought she was going to ignore the request. He opened his mouth to tell her they needed to talk, but before he could get the words out, she suddenly jerked the wheel to the right and nearly ran them into a ditch. Shoving the gearshift into park, she left the car running, got out and started to walk.

Where the hell did she think she was going?

"Maddy, get back here!" he called. Turning off the engine, he went after her. "You said you were committed to the investigation, remember? You knew the risks, but you said you wanted the truth."

She didn't even turn. "Take the car and go back."

"Listen, this is an investigation," he argued. "I have to run it objectively. You're paying me a lot of money. I can't handicap myself by questioning only the people you wouldn't mind seeing in jail. If that's what you expect, I'm wasting my time—just like your aunt said."

She kept moving, her back straight and rigid as she marched away from him.

"I only know one way to do this and that's to question everything and everyone," he yelled after her.

Finally, she faced him. "So I should let you destroy my father's reputation with questions that have nothing to do with how he went missing or who might've killed him? Don't you understand that his good name is all I have left? That I've had to endure doubt about every single person I love, except him? And now you come here and try to make him out to be some sort of—" her words snagged on a sob "—some sort of pervert? Suggest he might've molested my own *sister?*"

He shoved a hand through his hair. What he'd read in her mother's journal this morning had him worried. There was more going on with the reverend's disappearance than a simple mugging gone awry or a wife hoping to claim some life insurance money.

"What about that dildo?" he asked. "It had to come from somewhere, didn't it? It was found in the trunk of *your* father's car. Along with your *stepsister's* underwear. Do you know what that tells me?"

"I don't want to hear," she cried, the tears coming faster.

"It tells me it probably belonged to him. What are the chances that some unknown assailant molested your sister and planted the evidence in your father's vehicle?"

"You don't know *anything,* Hunter! It's possible."

"Why do you think Grace said she wasn't molested? For her own sake? Or for yours!"

"You're fired!" she screamed. "Go to the airport and leave my car in long-term parking. I'll pick it up later. Use the rest of the money to buy a ticket. I don't care. I just want you gone!"

She started running. But he caught up with her and, grasping her arm, turned her around. "So I'm the bad guy now?" he asked in frustration. "Or is it easier to blame me than deal with the truth?"

"You don't know the truth!"

"I know your father might've been a pedophile!"

She lifted her hand as if to strike him, but he grabbed her wrist. Then the fight drained out of her and she dropped her arm to her side. "I can't take it anymore." She stared up at him, her expression tortured. "I just want—" Her hand rose again, but with a completely different intent. Touching his cheek, she slid her fingers over the line of his jaw, his lips, his chin, as if seeking some kind of solace.

Hunter told himself not to react. The hunger in him was too strong, and she was confused and distraught. But when she raised her eyelids, he could see tears glistening on her lashes. "Tell me it isn't true."

He couldn't. But he wanted to erase the pain, to ease her burdens for a little while. Meeting her mouth lightly with his own, he whispered, "It's okay, Maddy. You're going to be okay."

He'd meant to let it go at that, with a sweet, comforting kiss. But she parted her lips and pressed them to his so quickly and greedily that he was soon cradling her head in his palm as he met the thrusts of her tongue. She responded eagerly, frantically, compelling him to take the kiss even deeper until they were so out of breath they broke apart panting.

"This isn't wise," he managed to say. "You're not thinking rationally. Hell, *I'm* not thinking rationally. Kissing you like that is making me want…too much."

She didn't seem to hear the first part, only the second. Taking his hand, she began to run for the shelter of some trees, pulling him with her.

Ray pushed his shopping cart up one aisle and down the next. He didn't have much money for groceries. Work was scarce during the winter months, and he liked saving most of his change for the porn sites and the pool hall. But now that he was out and about, he actually felt safer, less trapped. Maybe he should move away, find a new place to live. He'd often wondered if it would come to this.

But where would he go? And what about money? He was barely surviving as it was. He leased his trailer, had nothing but the broken down furniture inside it and his old truck. And he couldn't sell his truck or he wouldn't be able to work. Besides, he liked Stillwater. He knew everyone and could only imagine how strange and lonely it'd be anywhere else. Lord knows he couldn't live any closer to his mother and sister. It'd been difficult enough spending so much time with them the last few weeks. They henpecked him so badly he'd want to kill them inside of twenty-four hours.

No, leaving wasn't the answer. If he wasn't here to guard his secrets, the truth might come out. Then the police would come after him no matter where he was. And his mother, sister and friends—*everyone*—would despise him. Worse, his ex-wife would crow to the world that she'd been right about him all along and he'd live as a hunted man. Or he'd go to prison.

He shuddered. He couldn't go to prison.

If he was careful, he wouldn't have to, he told himself.

He was getting worked up again, that was all. He just had to lie low, like he'd decided back at the house.

But then he overheard Beth Ann Cole, who worked in the bakery section, talking to Mona Larsen while she bagged a few donuts.

"He's *cute,* isn't he?"

"Gorgeous! But who is he?"

"Hunter something or other."

"What's he doing here?"

"He's that P.I. from California. The one Madeline hired."

P.I.? Ray had been pushing his cart toward the dairy section, but at this he paused and pretended to consider a box of cookies. A P.I. *A private investigator.*

Shit!

"God, even his job sounds sexy," Mona was saying with an excited laugh. "How long do you think he'll be in town?"

"Until he solves the case, I guess."

"Well, then, he could be here for quite a while. Maybe we should introduce ourselves."

"Why not?"

"Who've you been seeing lately?" Mona asked, and the conversation veered off the subject that interested Ray, so he moved on. But Beth Ann and Mona weren't the only ones talking about recent developments. When he went through the checkout, Lizzie brought up the investigation.

"Did you see the flyer?" She motioned with her head to indicate a blue sheet of paper taped above her register.

Ray's eyes weren't what they used to be. He leaned closer so he could read the small print.

Please stop by the police station to view pictures
of two pairs of girls' panties found in my father's
Cadillac this past week. I'm offering a $500 re-
ward to anyone who might be able to identify
who they belonged to or offer any other information on their origin. Let's finally discover what
happened to my father—and your pastor, friend
and neighbor. Thanks for your help. Madeline
Barker.

Five hundred dollars? That would have everyone in
town traipsing down to try their luck.

Anger and panic swirled together, creating a dead-
lock inside him. Damn Madeline Barker. Ray had
wanted to include her in the fun he and Barker had had
with Rose Lee and Katie, but the preacher wouldn't
hear of it. As far as he was concerned, Madeline was
too pure to be defiled. But she deserved the same treatment, and this was proof. Barker had used Ray's
daughter easily enough.

The anger coalesced, curling through his veins like
smoke.... Anger that Barker could protect his own
daughter while using his. Anger that Madeline, of all
people, would be a threat to him.

"Are you going to go over and take a look?" Lizzie
asked.

Ray nodded. As frightened as he was, he had to
appear to do his part. Then he had to stop Madeline
from pushing the investigation any farther.

Even if it meant staging another accident.

Madeline didn't care that she'd left her car on the
highway. She didn't care that she'd slept with only one

other man in her life. Or that she'd known Hunter Solozano for only a couple of days. She was hurting so badly, she had to end the pain. And when he touched her, it was gone.

Ducking behind some large oaks, where they'd be shielded from the road, she grabbed his shirt and pulled him to her again, desperate for his kiss.

"Maddy." She could tell by the way he'd spoken her name that he was trying to persuade her to slow down. He obviously hoped to discourage her, to talk her out of what she wanted to do. But it wouldn't work.

"Don't ruin it," she said. "Just kiss me and keep kissing me—"

Burying his hands in her hair, he backed her up against the tree as his mouth met hers. She reveled in its warmth, the solidity of his larger body, the pressure of his erection, his need answering hers. His arms around her felt so satisfying, she couldn't think about anything else. Except the craving to feel him inside her, to let him carry her away from all thought and memory.

She began fumbling with his pants.

"Maddy, wait."

"Don't talk," she whispered.

"But you're going to make it too difficult to stop. It's been a long time for me. Do you understand?"

"I don't want to stop." She silenced him with another kiss, the kind that promised him she wouldn't refuse at the last minute.

She felt the change in him when he gave up his struggle to resist. He lifted her skirt and his fingers grazed her bare thighs.

She shivered, almost too sensitive to withstand even

such light contact. But she kept kissing him. She was afraid if she stopped, he would, too. Then they might reconsider.

"Is this what you want?" he asked.

"Yes." She moaned when he touched her.

"Last chance to change your mind," he whispered as they fumbled with their clothing. But his voice sounded ragged, desperate—as desperate as she was—and she wasn't about to stop him. Not now. He'd already taken a condom from his wallet. While he opened it, she felt the velvety softness of him in her palm and experienced a thrill of satisfaction as his muscles jumped in response.

"God, I hope you don't regret this," he said.

"Just make the pain go away," she begged. Then she slid her panties to one side and stared into his eyes, eyes that were stormy and intense as he lifted her up and buried himself inside her.

13

It was over almost as quickly as it had begun. Despite the cool, overcast weather, Hunter could feel the quiver in his muscles from bearing her weight, the sweat on his back, her chest rising and falling against his own as they recovered from the physical strain and the emotional intensity.

"You okay?" he murmured.

She nodded, but she wouldn't meet his eyes. She was busy adjusting her clothes. "My office is on the way home. We'll stop there and check for outbound flights. If we can get you on a plane today, we'll go home and grab your guitar and your computer." She hesitated. "Or...maybe we should wait for your luggage."

"You can send it on when it arrives," he said, as eager to leave Mississippi as she was to see him go. They couldn't continue on as if nothing had happened. If he stayed, he'd remember the feel of her every time he looked at her. And he'd want her again.

"I'll do that." She seemed relieved that he'd let her off so easily.

He fastened his pants. "I'll return your money before I leave."

"No, I—this was my fault. You deserve the week's pay."

"That's okay." He hadn't really done anything yet.

If he couldn't help Madeline resolve the questions that were tormenting her, he at least wanted to leave her no worse off than he'd found her. It was bad enough that he'd just broken one of his cardinal rules and had sex with a client. "I don't need it. I'll write you a check."

She didn't answer. Careful not to even brush hands for fear the passion that had ignited between them would start up again, they walked back to the car. But there was a truck parked behind the Corolla. And a man was peering into it.

A moment later, he came toward them.

"Oh, God," Madeline said, her step faltering.

"What?" Hunter murmured.

"I recognize that walk."

"Who is it?"

"Mike Metzger. He's back."

Madeline was so shaken from the frenzy that had just occurred, she wasn't sure she could face Mike. It'd been five years since she'd seen him, even longer since she'd become convinced he was her father's killer.

When he spotted them crossing the field to the highway, he shaded his eyes. She hoped that when he recognized her, he'd get right back in his vehicle and drive away. But he didn't. He met them about fifteen feet from the road.

Guilt over her brazen behavior, and embarrassment at being caught with her hair mussed and her clothes wrinkled, roiled through her. She felt as if anyone looking on would be able to tell exactly what she and Hunter had been doing behind those oak trees and didn't relish the idea of her greatest enemy being privy to that knowledge. But guilt and embarrassment were only a small part of what she felt. A chilling apprehension crawled through her, inspired by Mike's hateful glare and made worse by the fact that he no longer resembled the seemingly harmless, straggly haired stoner he'd once been. Judging by the ropy muscles bulging beneath his clothes, he'd spent much of the past five years weight-training. He had several white supremacy tattoos to go along with the added weight.

"What are you doing in Stillwater?" she asked, refusing to show her fear.

"I live in Stillwater, no thanks to you."

"Why'd you stop here?"

"When I saw your car, I thought someone was broken down." A muscle twitched in his cheek. "If I'd known it was you, I wouldn't have bothered."

"No one's keeping you from leaving."

His dark eyes flicked Hunter's way. "Who's this?"

Hunter stood close enough that she could smell the aftershave she'd breathed in when she'd buried her nose in his neck—and that brought back the very recent and vivid memories of what they'd done. "He's a—" she fought to steady her voice "—a private detective from California."

"A *P.I.?*" There was no mistaking the panicky edge in Mike's voice. "God, you don't give up, do you?"

"I want the truth, Mike."

"That's fine, as long as your so-called truth has nothing to do with me. I didn't touch your lousy self-righteous hypocritical father!"

"And you'd tell me if you did touch him?" she challenged.

"Just leave me the hell alone. Do you hear? I won't

go back to prison. I'll kill myself first." He lowered his voice. "And I'll take you with me."

"That's enough." Hunter stepped between them. "Get back in your truck and keep driving."

Although Mike was about the same height as Hunter, his arms were so big they didn't lie flat against his sides anymore, and his hands had curled into fists. But Hunter didn't seem intimidated. He even took a step forward. "I suggest you go *now*."

"Or what?" Mike asked, chuckling softly.

"Or you'll be asking for trouble you don't need."

Madeline caught her breath. Mike was obviously bigger, and she didn't trust him not to fight dirty. She could see him weighing his desire to lash out against his awareness of the possible consequences. Fortunately, another car drove by right then. When the driver, Minnie Hall, honked and waved at Madeline, Mike immediately backed off.

"Don't you dare try to pin it on me," he muttered and strode to his truck.

Madeline drew a deep, steadying breath as she watched him peel out, narrowly missing the left rear panel of her car. "See what I mean?" she said to Hunter.

His expression revealed little of his thoughts. "It's not my case anymore," he said, but she got the impression he wasn't talking to her. He was trying to remind himself.

Madeline's office was a small retail establishment that smelled like ink and had old-fashioned gold lettering on the wide front window. *The Stillwater Independent. Established 1898.*

Hunter walked around, trying to keep his mind

busy while Madeline sat at the computer. He didn't want to think about the malevolence he'd seen in Mike's gaze when he looked at Madeline, or the things found in the car, or the oddity of two young girls and a woman, all of them closely connected to the reverend, dying within eighteen months of each other. There could be a good explanation for all of it. There *were* good explanations—a hit-and-run and two suicides, right? No one else seemed to question those incidents.

But that was because no one else had ever doubted Lee Barker, Hunter thought. Barker had been friend, uncle, brother, father to these people. He'd been their spiritual leader.

Hunter circled the gigantic printer that took up half the room. Accusing someone like Barker required an outsider, someone who was willing to examine *all* the possibilities. Someone like him. But if Barker had a dark side, especially one as dark as he was beginning to suspect, Hunter would rather not be the one to tell Madeline.

Better to leave while he had the chance. Better to leave before he could get caught up in anything that would threaten his carefully constructed post-Antoinette world. "Are there any flights out of Nashville?" he asked.

She sighed. "Not so far. But I'm still checking."

Besides the giant printer, the room was mostly utilitarian. A school lunchroom type of floor, white walls, plain blinds. Except for the corkboard above Madeline's desk, the office could belong to a man, Hunter decided.

He eyed the pictures she'd tacked up. There was one of her and Kirk, laughing at a dinner table; one of her and Kirk in a swimming pool with Madeline hugging him from behind and resting her chin on his shoulder; one of Kirk sitting on Madeline's sofa, drinking a beer. Then there was Kirk standing in a doorway without a shirt.

Kirk, Kirk, Kirk.

Scowling, Hunter turned away, feeling a strong dislike for the man he'd met that morning. He tried to blame it on Kirk's autocratic behavior, but he knew it stemmed from something far more primitive.

"How much did this cost?" he asked, using the old printer as a much-needed diversion.

She was still clicking her mouse. "A lot."

"So you print your newspaper right here?"

"Um-hm."

"Do other small papers do the same thing?" He'd never really considered how someone might run a business like Madeline's.

"Not really." She didn't look up. She was avoiding making eye contact with him, and he was sort of grateful. If their eyes were to meet, he might see the same naked desire staring back at him that he felt himself. And if that happened, he knew they'd put a much more satisfying finish on what they'd begun out in that field.

"These days, most of them contract with printing houses," she added.

"Why don't you do that?"

"I might have to resort to it eventually, but there isn't one nearby. And it's tough to get a house to take on a paper like mine. They prefer bigger jobs."

"Because of the money?"

"Money and logistics. I only print 2500 papers a week."

"If you could find an outside company, wouldn't it be cheaper?"

She glanced over her shoulder but her attention was fleeting and perfunctory. "I was fortunate. I found that printer at a government auction in Jackson."

"How'd you know it worked?"

"I didn't. But I knew Clay could fix just about anything."

The depth of her admiration for her brother annoyed Hunter, too, although it made no sense. He'd never been particularly possessive.

What was the matter with him?

He wandered to the back corner of the office, where she had a counter with a sink, a microwave and a mini-fridge. "Can I have a drink?" he asked.

"There should be some bottled water."

He opened the refrigerator and helped himself.

"It looks like your first available flight is tomorrow morning," she called.

Was that disappointment in her voice? He twisted off the cap. "That's fine. I'll stay at the motel tonight." He had to remove himself from her house....

"Okay," she said. With him gone, she could go back to believing Clay wasn't involved in her father's disappearance, that there was no chance her father had owned the suitcase in the Cadillac. And maybe she could forget what had just occurred in the field.

No doubt she found all that denial very appealing. Hunter found it appealing, too, because he couldn't bear the thought that she might feel guilty and miserable over what they'd done.

He came up behind her as she stood. "You're going to be okay, right?"

She tensed, as if uneasy with his close proximity. "I don't know."

"It happened. It's over. Please don't worry about it."

"I still can't believe I did that," she murmured.

"It was understandable under the circumstances. Forget it."

Her eyes rose to meet his, then dropped to his mouth. "I'm not sure I can forget."

His heart started to pound again. "What's that supposed to mean?"

"All I want to do is remember."

He tilted up her chin with one finger. "What are you doing to me?" he asked and bent his head to kiss her, but the bell over the door jingled before their lips could touch. Letting his hand fall, he looked up to see Kirk standing at the entrance.

Madeline made no startled gasp, but Hunter could sense her distress. "Kirk," she said. "I—I wasn't expecting you."

Her ex-boyfriend regarded her with utter contempt. "Sorry. Didn't mean to interrupt."

"No, I—" she self-consciously smoothed the skirt Hunter had lifted less than an hour earlier "—wh-what do you need?"

"I just came by to tell you to listen to your damn messages," he said and stalked out.

Madeline covered her face as the door banged shut and the jingling died away. "The whole world's gone insane," he heard her whisper.

He didn't know what to say. He didn't want to be the cause of any more anguish. And yet they couldn't seem to stop, or even slow, whatever was going on between them.

"What should I do?" she asked, finally lowering her hands.

He wasn't sure if she was talking about him or the case. He couldn't tell her what to do about the powerful attraction between them. He didn't know himself. But he knew what he'd do about the past. "I think you have only one good option," he said.

"What's that?"

He resisted the urge to take her in his arms. "Gut it out."

"You said I should let it go." Her words were barely a whisper.

"I was wrong. You've already come too far, Maddy. You've got to see it through or the doubt will eat you alive. It'll destroy the relationships you're trying so hard to protect."

She nodded. But when she looked up, her eyes glittered with challenge. "Does that mean you'll stay? Are you willing to see it through with me?"

Was he? Every time he thought of his ex-wife he felt such intense anger he could scarcely function. Alcohol was the only thing that deadened the sensation, and he couldn't have it. He spent his life in a constant tug-of-war between the anger and the craving. And yet, somehow, a third craving had managed to distract him. Was it another mistake?

"If we do it on my terms," he said at last.

"What're your terms?"

"I stay at the motel."

"That won't help as much as you think it will. We'll still be together a lot. You'll have to work fast." She didn't wait for him to question that comment or respond.

Turning away, she hit the play button on her answering machine.

"Madeline, little Brittany's going to be starring in *The Wizard of Oz* at the school. Any chance you might like to do a story on her big debut? Give me a call…."

"Is that what the news is like here?" he asked, putting some distance between them.

She smiled nostalgically as she jotted down the number. "Yes. That's what I've always loved about this town."

The next message began. "Madeline, this is Mom. Why aren't you answering your cell? I've been trying to reach you all day. Please tell me you're not parading that private investigator all over town. Clay and Grace have been through enough. I couldn't take it if Clay was put back in jail…"

Gut it out. With a visible wince, Madeline hit the fast-forward button, then straightened.

"Madeline," a deep voice rasped.

Hunter froze. "Who's that?"

She shook her head in apparent confusion.

"Mad-*dy?*" the voice went on. "It's your dad-*dy.*"

"It's a crank call," Hunter said. But the blood had already drained from Madeline's face, and the message held them both riveted.

"I'm coming back, baby. I'm finally coming back. How did you like my pantie collection? Grace's always smelled the best." He groaned in sexual rapture. "She was so tight. But they all are at that age. That's why I love 'em. They're hot and tight and know how to obey—especially when they wear a collar." There was a pause. "Spread your legs for me, okay, baby? You're the one I wanted all along."

There was a click as the caller hung up. Hunter stopped the playback, but before he could say or do anything more, Madeline ran for the bathroom. After the door slammed shut, he heard her retch.

"What's he like?"

Before Clay could answer his mother, Allie turned from the kitchen sink where she was doing dishes and angled her head toward the living room. "You'd better check on Whitney, don't you think?" she said softly.

Nodding, he walked to the entrance of the living room to find his stepdaughter fully absorbed in the Disney movie he'd rented for her—and was relieved to know she wasn't listening to their conversation. Irene had shown up shortly after lunch, as frantic as she always seemed to be these days. But this time Clay couldn't blame her. He was feeling more than a little nervous himself. He'd endured a lot in the past two decades, but he'd always been able to count on Madeline's unwavering support. As long as Barker's own daughter insisted Clay was innocent, he had a fighting chance of beating any charges the police brought against him.

But it was possible that this private detective could change her mind. Beneath Hunter's tanned face and movie-star smile, he had a keen intellect and plenty of confidence. Clay knew he was no longer dealing with a small-time police force that was completely inexperienced when it came to a murder investigation.

"She okay?" Allie asked as he walked back into the kitchen.

"She's fine."

"Clay?" his mother said, growing impatient.

"Solozano's nothing to worry about," he lied.

Irene's fearful eyes fastened on his. "Are you sure?"

She *wanted* to believe him. If only he could convince her. "I'm sure."

"But he could expose everything."

"He won't." They had to get his mother to settle down—before she aroused even more suspicion and curiosity than normal. She was the weak link. If Hunter was as good as Clay suspected, it wouldn't take him long to figure that out and exploit it.

"How do you know?" Irene cried.

Clay pulled out a chair and slouched into it. In the beginning, his mother had been determined, smart and strong. But the years and the stress had taken a toll. He didn't like seeing how she'd changed, how what had happened had worn her out, weakened her. A person could run scared for only so long.

But she couldn't unravel now. They'd taken their stand and had to persevere.

"Mom, Madeline came to me for a loan a little over a year ago," he said, leaning an elbow on the table.

"What does that have to do with anything?"

"It means she doesn't have a lot of money. And this guy Solozano can't be cheap."

"So?"

"So she'll have to send him packing before he's had time to do anything." He'd poured more confidence into those words than he actually felt. If Madeline was as certain of Hunter's ability as Clay was, she'd be loath to let him go. But he wasn't about to admit that to his mother.

"She hasn't returned my calls in the past few days," Irene wailed. "Why? She's never done that before. Do you think she suspects?"

Allie warned her to keep her voice down, and Clay checked on Whitney again.

This time his stepdaughter turned when she heard the creak of the floorboards and smiled brightly at him. "Hi, Daddy. Want to watch the rest of *Madagascar* with me?"

"After Grandma leaves, okay?" he said.

She nodded and immediately returned her attention to the television while he walked back into the kitchen. "Madeline feels guilty for bringing him here in the first place," he said, his voice a low murmur. "That's why she hasn't called."

"She *should* feel guilty. Think what this could do to us!"

Exchanging a concerned glance with his wife, he sat down and took her hands. "Mom, you have to listen to me."

"What?"

"Calm down, okay? You're too worked up. We'll get through this the way we've gotten through everything else—by keeping our wits about us."

"But it won't end," she said. "It just goes on and on and on."

"Daddy?" Whitney called.

Clay sat up straight. "What, baby?"

"Is Grandma *crying?*"

"No, honey. She's just worried about—"

"The eye guy?" Whitney broke in.

"The eye guy?" he repeated to Allie.

Allie frowned. "P.*I.*?"

With a sigh, he pinched the bridge of his nose. Whitney had heard about the discovery of the Cadillac at school and had already asked him about the man the other kids were saying he "killed." He'd convinced her it was all untrue. But if this got away from him, she might see her new stepfather go to jail....

"Grandma's been hearing some of the rumors you were told at school, that's all," he said.

"Oh. Don't worry, Grandma," she called. "Daddy wouldn't hurt anybody."

Clay exchanged another look with Allie, then lowered his voice even more. "You can't come over here again when you're this upset, okay?" he said to his mother. "If you need to talk, call me."

"No one's willing to listen," his mother said as tears filled her eyes.

"Pull yourself together!"

At the steel in his voice, his mother stood.

"Where are you going?" he asked.

"Home."

"Don't do anything stupid," he warned. "Don't do anything at all."

"But I can't take it anymore!" she burst out.

"You have to." Clay took her by the shoulders and forced her to focus on him. "We don't have any choice."

Madeline sat on the visitor's side of her own desk. Hunter leaned against the wall closest to her. And Kirk stood at the window, staring moodily out at the street. Pontiff had called him as soon as Madeline said he'd told her to listen to her messages. The police chief wanted to know why Kirk had been so interested.

Madeline was pretty sure her ex-boyfriend had nothing to do with the message. Still, it was difficult having Hunter and Kirk in the same room. And she couldn't stomach the constant repetition of those grating words on her answering machine. Chief Pontiff was playing the sickening message over and over again in hopes of recognizing the voice or isolating some irregularity of speech that might give the caller away.

"Maybe you should go home," Hunter said to her, his manner gentle. "I'll deal with this and have Chief Pontiff drop me by your place later."

"*You'll* deal with this?" Kirk cried. "Who the hell do you think you are?"

Hunter shoved off from the wall to face him. "Can't you see what this is doing to her?"

Madeline squeezed her eyes shut. "Stop it! I'm not going anywhere." She felt weak and clammy, but she wanted to know who'd left that message. And she kept thinking that maybe, if she listened *one* more time, she'd be able to compensate for the voice distortion and come up with a name.

"So you have no idea who this is?" Pontiff finally stopped the recorder and pinned Kirk with a meaningful stare.

"Of course I don't!" Kirk nearly shouted. "Toby, you know me. Why would I be behind something like this?"

"We've all heard about the break-up, Kirk. Maybe you're angry and looking for a target."

"I wouldn't hurt her," he said. "I'd never hurt her."

"So why'd you tell her to listen to her messages?"

"*Not* because I knew about this." He threw up an impatient hand. "Her mother had just called me and said she hadn't been able to reach Maddy all day. I saw the car parked out front, so I stopped by to let her know. That's all."

Madeline believed he'd also stopped by hoping

they'd have a chance to talk after their confrontation that morning. They'd been friends for years, so the animosity between them felt unnatural. But then he'd found Hunter about to kiss her....

"Why aren't you asking *him* who it is?" Kirk asked, motioning to Hunter. "He's the one who's supposed to be solving the mystery, right?"

Hunter didn't bother to respond. He merely folded his arms and regarded Kirk dispassionately.

"I don't need him," Pontiff said. "I can handle my own work."

The chief didn't seem to be handling it very well. According to what he'd said when he first arrived, he still didn't know whose panties had been found in the trunk, despite Madeline's offer of a reward.

But *someone* had to know where they came from and how they got where they were....

"I'm taking this tape," Pontiff announced, acting more self-important than he would have if Hunter hadn't been in the room. "It's worth keeping, just in case."

"Just in case," Madeline repeated, chuckling bitterly.

"What?" he said.

She didn't respond. He wouldn't like what she had to say. The answer—the resolution for which she hoped and prayed—never came to pass. All she did was wait. She'd been waiting for almost twenty years.

Hunter, seeming to understand her frame of mind, interceded. "Give us a call if you find anything," he said, showing Pontiff to the door.

Once Toby had left, they were alone with Kirk. He eyed Hunter, then looked at her and made a startling announcement. "I'm taking that ski trip, Maddy."

Madeline gaped at him. "By yourself?"

"Why not? It isn't like you're going to change your mind about going with me. And I'm not planning to stick around to watch what I saw earlier."

She couldn't deal with this. Not now. "I'm sorry, Kirk. I never meant to hurt you. You know that, don't you?"

She thought anger and jealousy might tempt him to contradict her or blame her but, after a moment, he seemed to become once again the man she'd always known. "Yeah. It's just…too bad it didn't work out."

It *was* too bad. Her life would've been so much simpler if she could've thrown her whole heart into their relationship. But she'd always felt torn about Kirk and not completely committed. "You've been good to me," she said sadly.

He jammed a hand through his hair. "Hearing you say that hurts worst of all."

She frowned. "Why?"

He started toward the door. "Because that tells me it's really over." Pausing at the exit, he added, "But you're a fool if you get involved with him."

If? Madeline was already involved with Hunter.

When she didn't answer, couldn't answer, Kirk walked out.

She sat perfectly still, waiting for the customary panic to set in. She was really letting him go. After five years, this was it. The end.

But she didn't feel the urge to run after him. And that was scariest of all. Because there could be only one reason.

Hunter Solozano.

14

Madeline sat with Hunter in a corner booth at Two Sisters, with her back to the door. Two Sisters did more breakfast and lunch business than dinner, but this was Friday and at six-thirty it was fairly crowded.

Madeline kept her face averted from the people sitting at the other booths and tables. They'd just finished a meal of meat loaf and mashed potatoes and were settling in for coffee and pie. But she didn't want to see anyone she knew. She was still reeling from the events of the day. Stillwater had always seemed so safe. And yet suddenly, everyone and everything looked different.

As a result, she felt jumpy, defensive, even a little lost. Hunter was forcing her to question everything she'd once believed.

"You're sure you want me to stay?" he asked.

Was she? She was caught in the middle of some dark mystery that seemed to have no solution. If he continued to search for the truth, she'd have to accept whatever he uncovered—good or bad. And she already knew what he thought might've happened.

But if he left, would she be able to pretend that nothing had changed?

"Are you going to answer me?"

She still longed to feel his hands on her. What they'd shared earlier wasn't nearly enough.

"I don't know what to do," she admitted, running a finger back and forth over the smooth handle of her coffee cup. Where was her confidence? Her faith in those she loved? She remembered her father sitting her down at the kitchen table to tell her that her body was a temple, that she should never let anyone defile it.

Those were not the words of a pedophile.

"Do you trust me?" Hunter asked softly.

She stirred a spoonful of sugar into her coffee. "I don't even know you."

"Is that what you think?"

No. She hadn't known him long and wasn't familiar with the details of his personal life, but she trusted him instinctively. Or she wouldn't have done what she'd done with him out in that field. Maybe it was because they'd skipped the usual small talk of strangers and jumped right into subjects that affected them on the deepest levels. Maybe that was why their relationship had progressed at such lightning speed. But she knew he was smart, he was a leader, he'd do a thorough job, and he wouldn't hurt her if he could help it.

That was a reasonable start, wasn't it?

"I'd like you to stay," she said.

"Then I should move to the motel."

"Because…"

He met her gaze, and it was almost as if she could watch every detail of their earlier encounter played out in the reflection of his eyes. "Because you know what'll happen if I don't."

She was fighting so many battles at once, part of her

felt it wouldn't be so bad to concede that one. What was one torrid affair in thirty-six years?

But the saner part of her knew she might not be capable of making the best decisions right now.

You're a fool if you get involved with him...

What if her infatuation with Hunter grew? What if it turned into something more? Where would that leave her when he went home?

"Okay."

The waitress came to refill their coffee. Madeline mustered a smile because she recognized the woman from church.

"So...after hearing that message a hundred times, do you think it was Mike?" Hunter asked.

"I don't know. He couldn't have gotten home and left that message before we reached the office. But he could've left it earlier, I suppose."

"I'll drop by tomorrow, see what he has to say about it."

She'd made the right choice, she decided. She needed Hunter here. But, God, it was terrifying to consider what he might find....

"We should call Clay, too," he said. "Tell him about the message."

The old defensiveness instantly reared up again. "Clay would never do that to me."

Hunter reached across the table to squeeze her elbow. "I was just thinking he might have some ideas about who did. He certainly knows more than we do about what happened twenty years ago. Of course, whether or not he'll tell us is another story. But he might talk if it meant keeping you safe."

Until today, Madeline had never felt personally

threatened. "Can we talk about something else for a while?" she asked, using her fork to make little peaks in the whipped cream on her pie. She couldn't think about her own situation anymore. If she didn't figure it out soon, she'd be as depressed as her mother. And the mere thought of that terrified her. Never did she want to find herself so desperate.

Hunter stretched one arm across the back of the booth. "Like what?"

She put down her fork and pushed the rest of her pie away. "Like you."

He hesitated briefly, then shrugged. "What about me?"

"How long have you been divorced?"

"Thirteen months."

She'd guessed it had been recent. "So you were married for what, five or six years?"

He pulled her pie toward him and started to finish it. His own was already gone. "Twelve."

That was unexpectedly high. "You got married young."

"I was nineteen."

"I thought you surfed through college."

He paused to take a sip of coffee, then laughed dryly. "Only in my dreams."

"Really?"

"There was no time. Besides, I didn't even have a board."

"You were working?"

His cup clinked against the saucer. "At night. During the day I went to school. I was working toward a business degree until I had to drop out."

"What went wrong?"

"I had to get a second job."

She remembered teasing him about spending his days at the beach and felt like an idiot for making such a snap judgment. It didn't sound as if his life had been as easy as she'd envisioned. "Is that when you became a cop?"

"No, that's when I became a bartender. It was another two years before I decided to join the force."

"Did you like police work?"

"I did. But this is better. In many ways, I do basically the same work, but I set my own hours, pick my own clients and make more money."

"Can't beat that," she said.

"Exactly."

"Did you meet your wife in college, then?"

"Sort of. She wasn't in school. I ran into her at an off-campus party."

She added cream to her coffee. "If you were married nearly twelve years and you've been divorced for one, you must've been a sophomore?"

"A freshman."

She whistled under her breath, feeling more like her old self. The change of subject seemed to make a difference. "Was it love at first sight?"

He chuckled. "That depends on what you mean by love. It was definitely my first crush."

"What attracted you to her?"

"She was the entertainment at the party. I'd never seen anything like it before. I was completely captivated."

She stirred her coffee. "She was a dancer of some sort, then?"

He laughed again. "Of some sort. She was a stripper."

She held her cup halfway to her mouth. "I take it your father didn't have *Playboy* lying around the house."

"Absolutely not. I come from a religious family with very strict parents who sent me to an all-boys' school."

She took a sip, then set her cup down again. "Did you mind?"

"Not really. When I was in high school, I was more concerned with sports than girls."

She liked that he was revealing more about himself. She suspected he was only doing it because he could see the distraction was helping her cope with her own problems, but she was interested all the same. "And?"

"And then I went away to college. Suddenly Dad wasn't there to keep a bridle on me. It was my first brush with real freedom and I was off and running for broke." He finished her pie and stacked the two plates on the edge of the table. "Those first few months were a lot of fun. But I was naïve and made some really stupid mistakes."

"Like getting involved with a stripper?"

"Antoinette was…" He frowned and shook his head. "Have you ever seen *Risky Business?*"

"Several times."

"What we had was like Tom Cruise and Rebecca DeMornay's relationship in that movie. She was the first girl I'd ever slept with, but she was five years older and a *lot* more experienced."

"Was she going to school, too?" Madeline asked in surprise.

"She said she was taking a few classes at the community college, but I soon found out it wasn't true. She just gravitated toward the preppy crowd, liked the attention and the money she made dancing."

"And you liked her."

His eyes took on a faraway look. "Yes. I was so crazy about her I was actually stupid enough to bring her home to meet my folks."

The waitress came around with the coffeepot. She collected the empty plates, but Madeline put up her hand to indicate she'd had plenty of coffee and Hunter did the same. "How did they like her?" Madeline asked.

A bitter smile curved his lips. "About as much as you'd expect."

"They weren't impressed."

"No. They told me she was trash. That I needed to get rid of her."

"Seems like a harsh judgment for your parents to make after just one meeting. Maybe she didn't have a good family and had resorted to stripping because it was the only way she could earn a living."

"They didn't know she was stripping. I wasn't about to tell them *that*. They didn't like her because…" He tapped a finger against the rim of his cup as if he hadn't decided whether or not to go on.

"What?" she prompted. "Lord knows you're already familiar with all my dirty secrets."

"That you waited until you were thirty-two to make love isn't exactly a dirty secret," he said.

She felt her cheeks warm. "And now there's that…incident behind the trees."

His smile was crooked. "I realize you don't really want to face what happened. But can I say one thing?"

She wasn't sure she wanted to hear it. "What?" she said tentatively.

"*That* was amazing. *You're* amazing."

"Stop it." She laughed for the first time that day. "We were talking about *you* for a change."

"I was there, too."

She wasn't likely to forget. She could hardly breathe just remembering. But remembering wasn't going to make it any easier to leave him at the motel tonight.

"Why didn't your parents like Antoinette if they didn't even know she was a stripper?" she asked.

He sobered reluctantly. "She stole a piece of my mother's jewelry. My mother called me once I returned to school, terribly upset and full of accusations. I got angry that she could even *think* Antoinette would do such a thing. I was sure my mother was looking for any excuse to split us up, and I said so." His smile revealed more chagrin than anything else. "But in the end, my folks were right. I found my mother's diamond necklace in Antoinette's lingerie drawer three months later."

Madeline tucked her hair behind her ears. "That's horrible. You must've felt awful."

"I did."

"And yet you married her. Didn't the fact that she'd stolen from your mother make you doubt her character?"

"By the time the truth came out, I'd grown up enough to understand that sex isn't the same as love."

With Kirk she'd had the opposite experience. They had friendship and respect, but no sexual chemistry. Not like she'd experienced with Hunter. "So did you break up for a while?"

"I was going to break up for good. But it was the week of finals when I finally decided I was through, and I didn't want to say anything to Antoinette until my exams were over."

"Because you needed to focus on studying?"

"No, we were living together and I wanted to finish the semester before she went crazy on me. When I tried to break up one other time, she flipped out—threatened to harm herself."

"I bet your parents were relieved you'd soon be rid of her."

"I didn't tell them. My relationship with my parents had grown worse and worse, mostly because I was still with Antoinette. But I was stubborn enough to insist that I was an adult and should be able to see whoever I wanted."

"Typical male."

"Thanks for your support," he said sarcastically.

"No problem." She smiled. "So how did you wind up marrying her? You were about to break up."

He cradled his cup in his hands. "I was, that very next weekend. But—" his own smile disappeared "—that was when she told me she was pregnant."

What a blow that must've been. "And marriage was your solution?" she breathed.

"I thought it was the right thing to do."

"Because of your folks?"

"No. They agreed with my decision, but I'm the one who made it."

She leaned closer. "Did they really think that kind of marriage would work? Did *you?*"

"It was my responsibility to make it work—for the sake of my daughter."

"For the sake of your daughter…" She toyed with her spoon. "Were you ever happy together? You and Antoinette?"

He fell silent for a few seconds. She could tell by the

sudden tightness around his mouth that he wasn't interested in talking about it anymore. But she was curious.

"Hunter?" she said when it became apparent that she'd lost him to his thoughts.

"Maria was worth any sacrifice," he said with a shrug.

"Maria's your daughter?"

He nodded.

"Where is she now?"

Abruptly, he stood and grabbed the check the waitress had left. "Let's go," he said. "Now that we know I'm staying, it's time for me to meet Grace."

Madeline wasn't any happier about taking Hunter to see Grace than she'd been about going to the farm. Especially after what he'd said at Aunt Elaine's and at Clay's. She was afraid he'd soon alienate her from everyone she'd always loved, and yet her feet were now set on a path from which she couldn't deviate. There was nothing to do but march forward, and pray that her search wouldn't cost her as much as she feared.

Since their meeting at the police station, relations between her and Grace were already a little awkward, which didn't make this visit any easier. Madeline had called Grace the day after they'd identified those panties, hoping to offer her love, support, condolences—anything Grace might need. But Grace had insisted she was fine, that the presence of her panties in that bag meant nothing to her.

Nothing… Yet she'd gone stark white at the police station. *And* she hadn't called Madeline since, although they usually talked several times a week.

"This is quite a place," Hunter said, gazing up at Grace and Kennedy's historic mansion.

Madeline's eyes moved over the sweeping lawns and immaculate gardens, which looked even more perfect beneath the glow of a full moon. The lights shining warmly through the windows created an appealing effect, like the front of a Christmas card. Yet Madeline was afraid to approach. What more lay in store for her this day?

"It's just as pretty inside," she said and turned off the engine. That Grace had come from one of the poorest families in town and married into one of the richest made her and Kennedy's love affair a sort of Cinderella story. This was Grace's castle, the nicest home in Stillwater.

But Madeline was beginning to wonder if Grace's childhood had been worse than anyone, including her, had ever guessed.

"What are we waiting for?" Hunter prompted when she didn't get out right away.

"Nothing." Buttoning her coat against what was becoming a blustery night, she climbed out.

When she came around the car, Hunter stood at the end of the walkway. "Is Grace as tough as her brother?" he asked wryly.

"In some ways." Grace wasn't as intimidating as Clay or Madeline's aunt, but she could be every bit as aloof. And because Hunter would no doubt be perceived as a threat to Clay, Grace would never trust him. "Not quite so direct."

"But just as stubborn." He'd obviously picked up on the cautious note in her voice.

"Grace hides her feelings behind a cool, courteous manner."

"You mean she protects herself from others by remaining detached."

Madeline couldn't help appreciating his perception. But that perception, that intellect she'd begun to respect, frightened her. Because respecting his opinions meant that if he came to her with the worst possible news, she'd have to believe him. "Yes. It's a survival tactic she learned early on. Probably the result of all the judgment and censure she had to endure once my father disappeared."

"Is she close to Clay?"

"She is now. Before, she wasn't that close to any of us."

They didn't have time to discuss Grace further because movement in an upstairs window told Madeline they'd been spotted.

"Come on." She stepped onto the wide veranda, where brown wicker furniture with green cushions waited for spring.

The porch light went on only seconds before Grace met them at the door, holding her seven-month-old baby girl wrapped in a fuzzy blanket. She greeted Madeline with a hug, but her body felt stiff and unnatural, and her expression held more than a hint of wariness as her eyes darted to Hunter. "I wasn't expecting you," she said, returning her attention to Madeline. "What a nice surprise."

Madeline tried to bury her own apprehension—and the memory of that voice on her answering machine—in the positive feelings evoked by Isabelle. Taking the baby, she made the child laugh with a few sloppy kisses under the chin. "How's my girl?" she asked, thinking this was as simple as life should be—for everyone. A comfortable home, a beloved sister, a laughing baby.

"She's doing great," Grace replied.

Isabelle seemed to agree. She cooed and jammed a

chubby finger in her mouth while giving Madeline a drool-laden grin.

Madeline kissed the child's downy head, breathing deeply, trying to reassure herself that in the end all would be well. "No more cough?"

"Not even a sniffle."

"That's good." Propping Isabelle on her hip, she steeled her nerves and jerked her head toward Hunter. "I'd like you to meet Mr. Solozano."

He held out his hand. "Call me Hunter."

Grace didn't immediately accept it. So far, no one had been all that welcoming.

"Hunter is your birth name—or a nickname you acquired because of your work?" Grace asked, finally offering him her hand.

"It's my birth name."

"Interesting. You don't hear it very often."

He backed away from her to lean against the pillar of the porch. Madeline noticed that his actions were very casual and unthreatening, a far different Hunter than the one who'd visited the farm. "No, you don't."

Grace waited in silence, leaving the burden of the conversation to them. So Madeline jumped into the gap, hoping to ease the tension. "Can you believe the airline lost his luggage?"

Grace gave them a bland smile. "No."

"It should be here tomorrow," he said.

"I hope it arrives safely."

Silence fell again. "Hunter's been reading my mother's journals," Madeline blurted out. She wasn't sure why she'd brought up that particular detail. She supposed it was because she felt nervous and was hoping to show Grace that she hadn't brought him to

Stillwater because she doubted Clay or Irene. Hunter's interest in the journals, something removed from them, meant that the investigation was all-inclusive—even more than Madeline had expected.

But, oddly enough, the mention of her mother's journals didn't seem to relax Grace. If anything, she held herself more rigidly than before. "I thought your mother had burned most of her journals," she said.

"Not all of them."

Grace turned her blue, enigmatic eyes on Hunter. "And what did you learn from those journals, Mr. Solozano?"

"Not much," he said. "Madeline's mother refers to a couple of people I'm interested in learning more about, though."

Grace didn't ask who. Now that Hunter had Madeline doubting everything and everyone, she wondered if that was because Grace already knew.

Stop it! I don't want to think like that....

"Do you remember anyone by the name of Rose Lee Harper?" Hunter asked.

"Rose died before I moved to Stillwater," Grace replied. "I know her father, but only as a slight acquaintance."

"He still lives in town?"

"In the Shady Glen Trailer Park off Digby Road," Madeline murmured. "He's a handyman."

The shadows deepened as clouds scuttled across the moon, obscuring the finer details of Hunter's face. But he still looked handsome—and a little mysterious. "Didn't Mr. Harper come to the farm often?"

"Not when I lived there," Grace said.

"Ray and my father had a falling out before Dad remarried," Madeline told him.

"Were you aware of that?" he asked Grace.

"Madeline might've mentioned it."

Hunter shoved his hands in his pockets. "Do you know what it was over?"

Several lines appeared on Grace's normally smooth forehead. "No, but...like I said, I wasn't around at the time."

"I think my father got tired of paying Ray's rent," Madeline volunteered. "I once heard them arguing about money."

"Do you remember what was said?"

"Ray wanted more. My father refused."

"When was that?"

"A few weeks before my mother died."

"So it was after Katie and Rose Lee were gone."

"Yes. I don't think my father felt quite so sympathetic toward Ray's financial needs when he no longer had children to support."

"Do you have any interaction with Ray Harper now?"

"No," Madeline said. "None. Why?"

The brief flicker of Hunter's smile curved his lips. "Just curious."

"That's an interesting response, coming from an investigator," Grace commented.

His smile widened—Madeline could tell by the glint of his teeth—but he didn't explain himself. He proceeded to ask Grace what she knew about Katie Swanson.

"Almost nothing," Grace said. "Again, I wasn't around when Katie was alive."

The wind was picking up. Madeline wrapped the baby's blanket more tightly around her, and Hunter turned up the collar of his coat. "Do you recall the reverend ever talking about either of these girls, Grace?"

She stepped out to wipe some drool from her baby's chin. With Grace only inches away, Madeline could see, even in the dim porch light, the dark smudges under her eyes. Grace didn't look as if she was getting enough sleep—and this after positively glowing with happiness since her marriage. Was the baby suddenly fussy at night and keeping her up?

Or was it because of the panties she'd seen at the police station? The past resurrected, like the old Cadillac...

"No," Grace said indifferently. "Any reason you're asking?"

He shrugged. "I'm not a big fan of coincidences."

If they weren't coincidences, what were they? Madeline wondered. But confronting that question made her heart beat so hard she was afraid she might drop the baby. So she sat on the nearby wicker loveseat and pretended to be engrossed in playing with her niece.

Please let this end soon. Let Grace give all the right answers....

"I'm not sure I see any alarming coincidences," Grace said.

Hunter moved away from the pillar. "The girls were both helping Madeline's father. Both names show up in his wife's journal. They were both living with Ray Harper. They were only a year apart in age. And they died within six months of each other, just a year before Madeline's mother. Three deaths within an eighteen-month period. That's a lot of tragedies in so short a time, wouldn't you say? Especially for a place like this?"

"Accidents happen," she countered. "We lost a teenage girl out at the quarry just last weekend."

"How many others have you lost in the past twenty years?" he asked.

Grace didn't answer. But Madeline knew that from Rose Lee to Rachel, they hadn't had any other unusual deaths.

"There's nothing to connect their deaths," Madeline said, speaking up in spite of herself.

"Isn't there?" Hunter asked. "Did the police ever catch the driver of the vehicle that struck Katie?"

His words raised goose bumps on Madeline's arms. "No."

Grace suddenly glanced at her watch. "I'm sorry, but I've got to go. Kennedy's got a late meeting, and I promised the boys I'd pick them up from their Grandma Archer's by eight."

Hunter held his finger up to Isabelle, who grabbed hold of it. "Sure. We won't keep you."

Madeline blinked, taken aback by his response. He'd asked about Rose Lee and Katie, which had nothing to do with anything, as far as she knew. And he *hadn't* asked about the night her father went missing or the panties that were found in his trunk.

Grace smiled politely. "Thanks for stopping by."

"Thanks for giving us a few minutes of your time," Hunter said.

Madeline kissed Isabelle, handed her to Grace and pivoted to head back to the car—only to bump into her private detective, who was standing on the walkway, gazing up at the house. "You have a lovely home, Mrs. Archer."

"We like it," she said. Then she waved and disappeared inside the house.

Hunter remained where he was, studying the grounds.

But Madeline got in the car. By the time he joined her, Grace emerged from the detached garage behind the house and began backing down her long drive.

"Nice Lexus," Hunter said.

Madeline fastened her seat belt. "Why didn't you ask her about the night my father went missing?" she asked. She knew it hadn't been an oversight. Hunter was too good for that.

"Two reasons."

She started the engine. "The first?"

"I'm sure she was prepared for that. She must've answered similar questions a hundred times."

"And the second reason?" Madeline pulled away from the curb. *Please don't tell me she's hiding something, too.*

"Haven't you ever played with a potato bug?" he asked.

Madeline shot him a look that said he was making no sense. "A what?"

"A potato bug. If you poke them, they curl into a protective ball."

"You're saying that's what Grace would do."

"Exactly. And what do we have to gain from that?"

Madeline drove in silence until they reached the outskirts of town and saw the lighted Vacancy sign at the Blue Ribbon Motel. Then she asked the biggest question of all. "So...does she know more than she's saying?"

"Yes."

Foreboding curled through Madeline's whole body. "How could the conversation you just had tell you that?"

"It didn't," he said.

She looked over at him.

"I'm sorry, Maddy. But the odds aren't in her favor."

* * *

Grace's hand shook as she called Clay on her cell phone from inside her car.

"Helló?" He'd answered on the first ring.

"We've got problems," she said. "It's Madeline's private investigator."

"What about him?"

"He's even better than we thought."

15

Hunter's luggage had finally arrived. He sat on the cheap, rickety bed at the Blue Ribbon, staring at his black suitcase while strumming thoughtfully on his guitar. He needed to get some sleep so he could hit the Barker case early in the morning. But something was bothering him. He wasn't sure what it was. Most likely, it was more than one thing. That message on Madeline's answering machine. Their encounter with Mike.

The fact that he wanted to be in bed with her now...

He was tempted to call her—and if not her, Maria. He wanted to go back home as soon as he finished this job and fight for custody of his daughter even if she wouldn't speak to him. But he knew that would make her life miserable, that she'd hate him more because of it. Antoinette wasn't the best mother in the world, but she wasn't the worst, either. He couldn't really justify such a fight. He could enforce the visitation agreement, but Maria didn't want that. Not right now, anyway. Having no good options made him long for a drink.

The pool hall was only a block away. He could walk there.

He imagined the music, the crowd, the dim lighting. If it was like most bars, a man could hang around the dark edges of the room and be almost anonymous. Even in Stillwater.

Focus on something else. Work.

He'd piled the police files Madeline had provided on the floor. He frowned at the sheer volume of reading material—one entire box with another two behind it—and figured he'd better get started. There was Madeline's childhood diary to read, too.

Setting his guitar aside, he hung up the damp towel he'd just used for his shower, flung his wet hair out of his eyes and pulled out a statement by Bonnie Ray Simpson—the neighbor across from the farm—that said she was "fairly certain" she saw the "headlights" of Barker's car turn into his drive the night he disappeared.

Unfortunately, "fairly certain" didn't help him. Neither did "headlights," considering every car had a pair.

He put Bonnie Ray's statement back in the file and moved on to a document signed by Nora Young and Rachel Cook.

After we finished planning the Children for Christ Youth Group Day, we said goodbye to Reverend Barker in the parking lot of the church around 8:15 p.m. We assumed he was going home. He didn't mention another destination, and he didn't appear to have any luggage with him. He turned left, and that was the last we saw of him.

"Not much there, either," he muttered. Flipping through pages and skimming headings, he found a

document with Clay's name at the top. It was the transcript of a police interview taken, according to the date,
three days after Reverend Barker had gone missing.

Officer Grimsman: Did you see your stepfather the night of October 4th?

Montgomery: No.

Officer Grimsman: He wasn't there when you
came home from school?

Montgomery: No.

Officer Grimsman: Was he usually there when
you arrived in the afternoon?

Montgomery: Sometimes. Not always.

Officer Grimsman: What did he do when he
was home? Work on the farm?

Montgomery: He gave me chores and watched
at the window to make sure I got started on them
right away.

Officer Grimsman: Did he give the girls
chores?

Montgomery: Here and there.

Officer Grimsman: Not as many as he gave
you?

Montgomery: What does that have to do with
anything?

Chief Grimsman: Just answer the question.

Montgomery: No, but it didn't bother me.

Officer Grimsman: Right. You're different
from most other kids, then.

Montgomery: Who knows? Maybe I am. Like
I said, it didn't bother me.

Officer Grimsman: Did you find it odd that
your father wasn't home last Thursday?

Montgomery: You mean my stepfather? No. He'd left a list for me. And my mother said he was at the church. Why would that send me into a panic?

Officer Grimsman: I suggest you quit being smart with me, boy.

Montgomery: It was a normal day, okay?·

Officer Grimsman: Did your mother tell you she had plans to go out?

Montgomery: Go out?

Officer Grimsman: Didn't she leave before you did?

Montgomery: Yes, but you're making it sound as if she went dancing or…or drinking.

Officer Grimsman: Why don't you tell me what she was really doing?

Montgomery: She left dinner in the oven for Barker—

Officer Grimsman: *Barker?*

Montgomery: Reverend Barker.

Officer Grimsman: (to Chief Jenkins) Now that's gratitude and respect. A man takes in a woman and her three kids, puts food in their bellies and—

Montgomery: (interrupting) Does this have anything to do with my stepfather's disappearance?

Officer Grimsman: That's what I'm trying to find out, smart-ass!

Montgomery: And this is leading there *how?*

Officer Grimsman: Your attitude is a big part of this, buddy. Trust me.

Montgomery: I don't trust you worth shit.

You're questioning me without an adult present. I figure there has to be a reason.

Chief Jenkins: I don't want your mother to hear what you say, *that's* the reason.

Officer Grimsman: If you can work, party, play pool and please the ladies like a man, you can sure as hell talk like one.

Montgomery: My reputation precedes me.

Officer Grimsman: You might not be so smug when this is all over.

Montgomery: If you have your way, I'll be in jail.

Officer Grimsman: Isn't that where you belong?

Montgomery: Not unless it's illegal to hang out with my friends. That's all I did.

Chief Jenkins: (to Officer Grimsman) Get back to the point, Roger.

Officer Grimsman: Fine. Where did your mother go that night?

Montgomery: You already know where she went.

Chief Jenkins: State it for the record.

Montgomery: For the record, she went to choir practice. No secret there. It's easy enough to check.

Chief Jenkins: But she didn't normally attend. That makes it an unusual day, doesn't it?

Montgomery: If that's all it takes to be unusual. Barker called and told her he wanted her there.

Chief Jenkins: Did that make her unhappy?

Montgomery: Why don't you ask her?

Chief Jenkins: I'm asking *you*. Did his call start a fight? Did they argue?

Montgomery: No.

Officer Grimsman: What kind of mood was your mother in after your stepfather asked her to go to choir practice?

Montgomery: How the hell should I know?

Chief Jenkins: I suggest you quit being such a pain in the ass and answer the question.

Montgomery: She seemed fine. She asked me to watch the girls for her and hurried out so she wouldn't be late.

Officer Grimsman: Did your stepfather call to make sure she went?

Montgomery. Not that I know of, but I wasn't paying much attention.

Chief Jenkins: You never talked to him that evening?

Montgomery: No.

Officer Grimsman: According to Grace, you got a call.

Montgomery: It was a friend.

Officer Grimsman: Who?

Montgomery: Jeremy Jordan.

Officer Grimsman: What did he want?

Montgomery: He wanted me to go with him to Corinne Rasmussen's.

Officer Grimsman: And you agreed?

Montgomery: Yes.

Officer Grimsman: So you left your little sisters alone.

Montgomery: They're eleven and thirteen. I thought they'd be fine.

Officer Grimsman: Were they?

Montgomery: (stares off into space)

Officer Grimsman: Mr. Montgomery, I asked you a question.

Montgomery: What time is it?

Officer Grimsman: 2:00 a.m.

Montgomery: (rubs hand over eyes)

Officer Grimsman: Tired, Mr. Montgomery?

Montgomery: I'm sixteen. I think you can call me Clay. Or does *Mr. Montgomery* make you feel justified in grilling me for hours without my mother in the room?

Chief Jenkins: The sooner you answer our questions, the sooner you can go home. Your mother has her own questions to answer.

Montgomery: You only want me to say what you want to hear. (growing more upset) Listen, my mother needs me. Her husband's just gone missing.

Officer Grimsman: Your mother will be fine. Irene Barker always lands on her feet, eh?

Montgomery: Screw you! (restrained by Chief Jenkins)

Chief Jenkins: Are we going to have to cuff you, boy?

There was some other writing, but it had been blacked out. From the flow of the conversation, Hunter almost wondered if the chief, or possibly Officer Grimsman had struck Clay, then had the incident removed from the records.

Officer Grimsman: You ready to talk now?

Montgomery: (hunched over)

Hunter read that line a second time. Hunched over? Whoever had created this record was meticulous in noting every nuance. Hunter was willing to bet it wasn't the same person who'd changed it.

Chief Jenkins: You need more convincing, huh, Clay?
Montgomery: (no answer)

Hunter frowned as he came across more lines that had been blacked out—and doubted those changes had anything to do with correcting a mistake.

Officer Grimsman: Where did you go that night?
Montgomery: (breathing hard—no answer)
Officer Grimsman: I'm talking to you, *Clay*, and I can promise you it's going to get real ugly if you don't start cooperatin'. Do you hear me? *Real* ugly. And not just for you. For your mom and your younger sisters.
Montgomery: Leave them alone!
Officer Grimsman: Where did you go?
Montgomery: Corinne's house.
Officer Grimsman: What?
Montgomery: (louder) Corinne Rasmussen's house.
Officer Grimsman: What happened while you were there?
Montgomery: Nothing. We just hung out. Ask Corinne or Jeremy. They'll tell you the same thing.
Officer Grimsman: When did you return?

Montgomery: About nine o'clock.

Officer Grimsman: That early?

Montgomery: It was a school night. And I was hoping to beat my mother home.

Officer Grimsman: Did you?

Montgomery: No.

Officer Grimsman: She was there when you arrived?

Montgomery: Yes.

Officer Grimsman: Was she angry with you?

Montgomery: What do you think?

Chief Jenkins: (holding subject's arms back)

So Montgomery couldn't strike was written in the margin, but Hunter suspected Clay wasn't the one swinging his fists.

Chief Jenkins: Officer Grimsman is not the person answering questions here.

Montgomery: (head hanging down) Of course she was angry with me. I'd disobeyed her.

Officer Grimsman: Were you punished?

Montgomery: She said I'd be punished when my stepfather got home.

Officer Grimsman: But he wasn't home yet.

Montgomery: How many times do I have to say it?

Several lines had been blacked out right below that.

Officer Grimsman: Wasn't anyone beginning to worry about him?

Montgomery: (answer difficult to decipher)

Officer Grimsman: Clay?

Montgomery: No. We figured…he got hung up at the church. He sometimes…had meetings that…ran late. (shakes off Chief Jenkins)

Hunter frowned while shuffling through the papers. So the chief had restrained Clay that whole time? Or had he been holding Clay for Grimsman to *convince?*

Whatever had happened, the next line didn't follow.

Chief Jenkins: What about you?

Montgomery: I don't have any secrets.

Officer Grimsman: Did he punish you when he got home? Is that what happened, Clay? Did things get a little out of hand? You can tell us, you know. It would be better for you, for your mother, too, if you'd tell us.

Montgomery: He never came home.

Chief Jenkins: Yet you didn't call the police.

Montgomery: Why would we call you ass-holes?

Another dark line made Hunter suspect some more information had been cut from the transcript. Disgusted to think they'd beaten a sixteen-year-old boy, Hunter shook his head.

Chief Jenkins: This time with respect.

Montgomery: We went to bed, thinking he'd come in eventually.

Chief Jenkins: Your mother didn't wait up for him?

Montgomery: I don't think so.

Officer Grimsman: What did she do?

Montgomery: Far as I know, she put his dinner in the fridge and went to bed.

Chief Jenkins: That sounds pretty indifferent, considering he was later than she expected.

Montgomery: Was she was supposed to cry that his dinner was getting cold?

Officer Grimsman: It doesn't bother you that he could be dead, son?

Montgomery: It bothers me that I've been here for eight hours.

Officer Grimsman: Sorry to put you out, but a man's life could be in jeopardy. Or is that man already dead?

Montgomery: How should I know? He's probably fine. Nothing ever happens here in Happy Valley, right? And he's a preacher. Who would hurt a preacher?

Chief Jenkins: That's what we'd like to know.

Montgomery: I'm guessing he's tired of this piece-of-shit town and—

More black marks.

Officer Grimsman: Didn't your mother get worried, try to reach him?

Montgomery: Don't know.

Officer Grimsman: You went to bed?

Montgomery: That's what I said. Mrs. Lederman is taking it all down right over there. If you're confused, just have her read it back to you.

Officer Grimsman: You son of a—

More black marks.

Chief Jenkins: Did you go right to sleep?

Montgomery: (nods once)

Officer Grimsman: You weren't agitated or upset about your impending punishment?

Montgomery: I wasn't in any hurry to meet up with it.

Officer Grimsman: What type of punishment were you expecting?

Montgomery: To be grounded.

Really? Hunter wondered. Somehow Clay's answer didn't ring true.

Officer Grimsman: Had he grounded you before?

Montgomery: Yes.

Officer Grimsman: For what?

Montgomery: The usual.

Officer Grimsman: Spell it out.

Montgomery: He caught me behind the barn with my hand up a girl's shirt—

Officer Grimsman: Whose?

Montgomery: I won't say.

Officer Grimsman: It better not be *my* daughter.

Montgomery: You'll never know.

Officer Grimsman: You little prick—

More document tampering. Hunter was positive of it. The marks on the paper, the cadence and timing of the questions… It all hinted at physical interference. If Hunter had his guess, Clay had sustained quite a beating that night. But Clay didn't break down and promise Grimsman it hadn't been his daughter he'd been feeling up. Hunter had to smile about that.

The phone rang. Lowering the document he was reading, Hunter rocked back and reached for the receiver.

Unable to sleep and not wanting to disturb Allie, Clay slipped quietly out of bed and went to his study, where he hoped to get caught up on paperwork. He preferred to spend his time outdoors or in the barn, restoring his antique cars, so he sometimes let the office work languish. But he couldn't put it off any longer. He had bills to pay and bookkeeping to do in preparation for tax time.

He picked up the day's mail, which Whitney had placed on his desk. She loved running out to visit the mailbox, felt important carrying in the parcels and letters that arrived. She usually collected all the junk mail she could, which she liked to play with. But it didn't appear that she'd scavenged anything today. There were a couple of credit card offers and a catalog from an office supply store that she would normally have taken. Allie must not have gone through the mail, either, he decided. Nothing had been opened.

As Clay glanced through the envelopes, he tossed the credit card offers in the trash—he didn't believe in doing anything on credit except, perhaps, purchasing land or a house—and added the bills to the pile he planned to pay. A letter at the very bottom bore his name and looked as if it had been addressed on an old typewriter instead of a computer.

He nearly threw it in the trash. Over the years, he'd received his share of anonymous letters. Some called him to repentance. Others told him he'd burn in hell for what he'd done to the reverend. He didn't need to hear any more of that. The actions he regretted weren't the ones they condemned him for. Even now, when he revisited The Night in his mind, he knew he'd make the same decisions he'd made then.

His hand hovered over the trash can. *Screw them and their scorn,* he thought. They had no idea what he'd been through, the battles he still fought. Why give his critics an audience?

But then he noticed that this letter hadn't come through the USPS. It didn't have a stamp.

Curious as to why someone would hand-deliver him a message, he tore it open and pulled out a piece of lined paper.

The same typewriter had been used on the letter as on the envelope, but there was still no indication of who'd sent it. There were only five words:

Stop her or I will.

"Hello?" Hunter held the phone to his ear with his shoulder so he could continue to turn through the transcripts of Clay's interview.

"You comfortable?"

It was Madeline. "I'm fine. Just familiarizing myself with the files."

He lowered the volume of the TV. "How'd you get these, anyway?"

"I borrowed them last fall, made a copy."

"Most police departments won't turn something like this over to a private citizen, even on loan. That's taking all kinds of risks."

"I'm the owner of the paper, the closest thing they have to an investigative reporter. And after last year when they let Clay go, no one seemed particularly concerned about the files. Allie had already been through them and found nothing. Everyone else seemed to be giving up. So I asked Allie's dad to let me take a look. He'd just been fired and was moving to Florida, so he didn't have anything to lose, and he knew I'd return them right away."

"Does Pontiff know you've got a copy?"

"I'm not sure if he remembers, but he was there when I returned the originals." He heard fresh tension enter her voice. "So was all the time I spent at the copy machine worth the effort? Have you found anything promising?"

"I wouldn't categorize it as promising yet," he said cautiously, "but I'm finding Clay's first interview with the police interesting. I'm guessing they were none too gentle with him."

"They were insistent."

"I mean physically."

There was a slight hesitation, which gave him the impression that she'd been trying to avoid addressing that issue. "Yes. That, too."

"What'd he look like when he got home?"

"He was pretty banged up."

"Did anything come of it?"

"No. Chief Jenkins claimed Clay started swinging while they were questioning him. They forced him back into a chair, but the chair fell over and he went down, hitting his face on the corner of the table."

Hunter stared at the evidence of the changes that had been made to the records. "What'd Clay have to say about that story?"

"He didn't contradict it."

"Probably because he felt powerless to do anything about it."

"I've asked him since, but he always says none of this matters."

"Chances are good that it doesn't have any bearing on the case. It just makes me angry."

"Me, too." She moved quickly to a new subject, as if Clay's being hurt was too difficult to think about. "Anything else stand out?"

He eyed her childhood journal. "Not yet."

"Okay. It's getting late." Her words came through a yawn. "You'd better get some sleep."

"I will," he said, but when he hung up, he went back to his reading.

Chief Jenkins: Did your stepfather spend much time with you on the farm?

Montgomery: No more than he had to.

Officer Grimsman: Then what'd he do every day?

Montgomery: Jacked off in his office, I guess. Can I go? I've been sitting here for hours. And I already told you I don't know anything. There was no fight. He didn't come home.

Officer Grimsman: Would you rather sit in a jail cell until you can speak with a civil tongue?

Montgomery: Where's my mother?

Officer Grimsman: We're taking care of her.

Montgomery: If you're taking care of her the way you're taking care of me, so help me—

Chief Jenkins: Don't you threaten me, boy.

More blacked-out lines.

Officer Grimsman: If there was no fight, how do you explain the bruises on your face?

Montgomery: The ones I got *before* I came in here?

Chief Jenkins: Before the accident with the chair.

"Accident, my ass," Hunter muttered.

Montgomery: I told you, I hit a tree.

Officer Grimsman: You weren't driving that night. According to your friends—

Montgomery: (interrupting) We went to Corinne's house in Rhys Franklin's truck. But once I got home, I remembered I'd left my coat out in the south forty where I'd been working earlier. I knew I'd catch hell if anything happened to it. So I jumped into the old Ford and went after it.

Officer Grimsman: I thought you weren't allowed to drive your stepfather's vehicles.

Montgomery: I couldn't take them off the farm.

Officer Grimsman: Tell us about the accident.

Montgomery: I was afraid to turn on my headlights in case my stepfather got home and realized I wasn't in the house. I was going too fast. On the way back, my right tire hit the soft lip of the irrigation ditch, I overcorrected and rammed into a tree.

Officer Grimsman: What happened to your face when you hit the tree?

Montgomery: What do you think? It went into the damn steering wheel!

Chief Jenkins: That's enough profanity.

Montgomery: (no response)

Chief Jenkins: Getting back to this accident. You didn't call for help?

Montgomery: No. I was scared my stepfather would get home any minute and I wanted to be in bed.

Officer Grimsman: Wouldn't he see the damage to the truck?

Montgomery: It was already so old and beat up, I was hoping he wouldn't notice.

Officer Grimsman: You thought he might not notice the damage to your face, either?

Montgomery: I was leaving for school early the next morning.

Officer Grimsman: And if he saw you?

Montgomery: I'd tell him I got into a fight or something.

Officer Grimsman: So you're admitting you're a liar.

Montgomery: I'm telling you the accident didn't do any major damage to the truck, and I didn't want to get in more trouble than I already was.

So, according to Clay's own words, his face had been banged up *before* he went into the police station.

Whatever injuries he sustained there were in addition to the truck accident or, as the police implied, a fight with Barker.

Hunter pulled out a manila folder marked *Photos*. Inside, he found several pictures of Clay with dates written on back. One read October 5th, the day after the Reverend went missing but before the police interview. It showed him with a black eye, a swollen lip and a cut on his cheek.

A steering wheel could've done that damage. But it looked more like a fight....

Picking up the phone, Hunter called Madeline.

"Hello?" she said, sounding groggy.

"Were you asleep?"

"Not quite. What's up?"

"Can you remember what Clay looked like *after* his police interview?"

"Not good. When he hit the table, he broke his nose."

Hunter put the photos away and set the file aside so he could lean back on the bed. "Is Mrs. Lederman, the woman who typed the transcript, still around?"

"Yes. But she's in assisted care. She's got Alzheimer's. Why do you ask?"

"I'm trying to piece everything together, wondering if I find the police version plausible."

"Which incident do you doubt?"

"The table incident, for sure. Maybe even the truck wreck."

"The police had a problem with the wreck, too," she said. "My mother, when she was questioned separately, said Clay hurt his face when she accidentally elbowed him while reaching into a cupboard."

"Why the discrepancy?"

"I think my mother didn't know about the accident and was afraid the bruises on Clay's face would make him look guilty."

"You know what that proves, don't you?"

"It proves they were scared and were afraid they'd get blamed for something they didn't do," she said, a little too quickly.

"It also proves she'd lie for him."

Madeline didn't respond. Hunter could understand why. This was one of those details she'd rather not acknowledge.

"Was there any damage to the vehicle?" he asked.

"A dent, right where it should be," she said triumphantly, obviously much more awake.

He stared at the ceiling. "I don't suppose that truck is still around."

"No. It was old then. We sold it for scrap metal shortly after. We sold everything we didn't need, so we could eat."

"Did your father ever beat Clay?" he asked.

"*Beat* him? No. Not in the sense you mean it."

"In *any* sense?"

"My dad believed in corporal punishment, Hunter. It was how he was brought up, how he'd been taught kids should be raised. 'Spare the rod, spoil the child' and all that. But he wasn't excessive, and it happened only when we misbehaved."

Hunter reached over and turned off the light to rest his eyes. "How often did Clay misbehave?"

"Once in a while. But it really wasn't a problem."

Or so she thought. Did she know everything? Clay was out on the farm quite a lot, out of their sight. And from what Hunter had gathered so far, he didn't seem particularly eager to involve his sisters and mother in his problems. Clay's first instinct, even then, was to protect them.

"I'll let you get some sleep," he said.

"What about you?"

"I can't relax right now. Maybe in a couple of hours."

"What's wrong?"

He pressed a thumb and forefinger to his closed eyelids. "I keep picturing how you looked in that shirt and those boxers you had on this morning."

Her voice lowered seductively. "You liked it?"

"God, yes," he said and hung up.

16

After she'd spoken to Hunter for the second time, Madeline couldn't go back to sleep. She got up and rambled around the house, trying to make sense of the inexplicable attraction between them. She'd never felt so sexually aware of a man and found herself creating fantasies the likes of which she'd never entertained before.

It was exciting, risky; it was also inconvenient and confusing.

Did she like him so much because he was different from the other men she'd known, with his west coast accent, athlete's body and beautiful tan? Or was it some kind of hero-worship, because he seemed capable of giving her the answers nobody else could? Or maybe she was merely looking for a quick replacement for Kirk, so she wouldn't have to feel the pain of separation.

She couldn't name the specific reason with any certainty. She only knew it was all she could do not to drive over to the motel.

When she entered the kitchen, mumbling to herself that she had to be crazy to feel as strongly as she did, Sophie yawned and gazed up at her.

"You're not concerned," she said. "And I shouldn't be, either. These things happen to people sometimes, right?"

But never to her. She'd known the same men her whole life....

The telephone rang. Thinking it was Hunter, she felt a tingle of anticipation as she crossed to the opposite counter to answer it.

"Hello?"

"Is he still there?"

Kirk. The arousal humming through her died instantly, followed by a heavy dose of guilt. "I thought you were going out of town," she said.

"I am. In the morning."

"When will you be back?"

"In a few weeks. Maybe."

Maybe... She took a deep breath. "So this is it? This is where you move like you've been talking about for months?"

"This is it."

She knew he was hoping she'd talk him out of it. She didn't want him to go, and yet she felt a strange measure of relief at the idea of his absence. If he left, they wouldn't wind up marrying each other someday by default and living without any real passion, the kind she now knew existed.

"You don't have anything to say?" he said.

"I don't know what to say."

"Because he's there?"

"No, he's at the motel."

"Why?"

She flinched at the reason that came to mind: *Because we'd be in bed together if he wasn't.* "He just is."

There was a long silence, during which Madeline felt more self-conscious than ever. Her natural defensiveness over what she'd done earlier had led her to say more than she should have. The fact that Hunter was now staying at the motel revealed more about how she was feeling toward him than if he'd still been in her guesthouse. She and Kirk had argued over his lodging arrangements that very morning.

Fortunately, Kirk didn't force her to defend herself on that point. Maybe he didn't want to face what Hunter's relocation signified.

"He won't find anything, Maddy," he said. "Allie was a forensics specialist and she came up with squat."

So let him go, not just to the motel, but back to California. Wasn't that what Kirk was really saying? But unlike Allie and the others, Hunter could be completely objective. That was why she'd brought him in, and that was what she liked about his investigation. He had dark suspicions about everyone she loved, but he had no vested interest in swaying her opinions one way or another, and would never act without proof—because he had no personal stake in anyone's downfall. The hope of finally reaching the truth, no matter how painful it might be, kept her hanging on, despite the fear that she wouldn't like what Hunter found.

She remembered him telling her that Clay was hiding something. Allie would never have told her that. Madeline had denied it, even to herself, for a long time, but in her heart she knew it was true.

"I'm going to give him the week," she said. "And then…"

"And then?" Kirk echoed hopefully.

"And then I'll decide what to do next."

Silence. At last he said, "I'm going to miss you, Mad."

More guilt washed over her, for whatever it was—attraction? lust? the cravings of a lonely soul?—that had made her do what she'd done with Hunter earlier that day. She and Kirk hadn't even been apart six weeks. How could she already desire someone else?

"I'll miss you, too," she said. And it was true. She didn't want to be lovers, but she couldn't wait until they were friends again.

"Be careful," he said.

She opened her mouth to respond, but he'd hung up. *Be careful?* Of what? The truth? Having her heart broken? Both?

As she set the phone back in its cradle, she tried to sort through her conflicting thoughts and emotions. But she couldn't come to any resolution. She was frightened of the doubt she felt about Clay, but she still felt it. She was frightened of the attraction she felt to Hunter, but she still felt it. And the list went on from there.

With a muttered curse, she stopped trying to understand her own behavior and phoned Molly, who answered on the first ring.

"Hello?"

At the sound of her youngest stepsister's voice, Madeline felt strangely tongue-tied. Was she betraying her family by getting involved with Hunter? The fact that she'd had sex with him had already forged a bond that pulled her a little farther away from them. Could she honestly say, if he pointed his finger at Clay or Irene, that she wouldn't believe him?

"Maddy?"

At the concern in Molly's voice, Madeline forced out a few words. "What're you doing?"

"I'm about to watch a video with friends."

"Oh, bad timing. I'll let you go."

"I don't mind missing the first few minutes," Molly said. "Are you okay?"

Madeline considered the cracks that were beginning to weaken the dam of loyalty she'd built to protect her stepfamily. She wanted to ask Molly to level with her, tell her if there was any way Clay could be hiding something about The Night. While talking to Molly, Madeline often discussed her efforts to find her father, her latest theory on what might've happened to him. But Molly generally didn't add much. And Madeline had never really *asked,* not in earnest.

She attempted to do so now—but couldn't go through with it. She couldn't bear the thought of Molly knowing that she'd begun to lose faith in spite of everything Clay and the rest of the family had done for her.

"Mike's home," Madeline said instead.

"Mike?"

"Metzger."

"Oh boy. Why isn't he in prison?"

"He's out on parole."

"You're sure?"

Madeline could hear others talking in the background. "I saw him this afternoon."

There was a long pause. "Does he scare you, Maddy?"

He hadn't scared her until today. He'd seemed so far removed when he was in prison. But the malevolence in his eyes was difficult to forget. Whoever had made that call to the office, claiming to be her father, had to hate her. Was it Mike?

She shivered. "Maybe a little."

"You should go to the police."

"And tell them what?"

"Show them the letter he sent you."

"He sent it from prison so that means someone in authority read it, Mol. They must not have deemed it a direct threat. And it probably isn't. Saying you wish you'd done something isn't the same as saying you're *going* to do it."

"It made the hair on the back of my neck stand up when you read it to me."

What he'd written—*I wish I'd killed you both*—had the same effect on Madeline. But even she wasn't completely convinced he'd ever act on the threat. "No one in this town will take me seriously. They think Mike's a burnout, a waste—a danger only to himself. Clay's the one they believe is capable of violence, remember?"

"But your friend's husband is the chief of police. He'll listen to you, won't he?"

A noise in the back yard brought Madeline to the window. She'd let Hunter take her car. Had he returned for some reason?

"Toby? He might." She peered out, but the guesthouse was dark. "I'll give him a call tomorrow."

"Let me know how it goes."

"I will. Enjoy the movie." She disconnected. Then she made sure the doors were locked and spent another few minutes gazing out at the yard. Was someone out there?

Mad-dy...it's dad-dy...

The first part of that message had been even crueler than the last, because that was the part she longed to believe—that he'd suddenly call her or appear after all these years.

She moved from window to window, imagining what it'd be like to see her father again. Maybe they were wrong, all of them, and he was out there somewhere. Maybe someone had hit him over the head and stolen his wallet, and he'd awakened with amnesia....

It wasn't likely. But it was possible. And sometimes *possible* was enough to cling to, wasn't it? Then Irene, Clay, Grace and Molly would be cleared. Madeline would have them in her life, without the doubts. And she'd have her father, too. The driving need to reclaim what she'd lost would then be satisfied.

But it wasn't realistic to hope for such an ending. She had a feeling she had a visitor, but she knew better than to believe it was her father.

Clay was tempted to ignore the ringing phone. He had Allie in his arms and was trying desperately to reassure himself that he'd *always* have Allie—even though there was a body buried in his cellar. But after the letter he'd received earlier, he didn't dare ignore a late-night summons. Anyone who tried to reach him at midnight had to be calling for a reason.

He just hoped it wasn't his mother, with more histrionics.

"Not now," Allie groaned.

He kissed the delicate spot beneath her ear and reluctantly pulled away from the soft warmth of her body. "Sorry." Throwing back the covers, he grabbed the phone. "Hello?"

"It's Hunter Solozano."

"I'm busy," he said, already missing his wife. They wanted a baby, but now Clay was almost afraid to make one. If he went to prison, he didn't want to do it knowing Allie was pregnant with a child he'd never get to help her raise. Losing Whitney would destroy him as it was.

"We need to meet."

Clay froze, his senses on full alert. "Why?"

"You'll see."

"Where?"

"I'm at the motel."

"Do you have a car?"

"I have Madeline's."

"Then meet me at the pool hall in twenty minutes. If I'm going out, I'm having a drink," he said and hung up.

Allie ran a hand over his chest as he turned back to her. "You have to go?"

Clay hated to leave her, although he no longer felt like making love. Why would Madeline's P.I. want to talk to him?

He had no idea. But he couldn't refuse. Hunter was a wild card.

Hunter could change everything.

A bang woke Madeline from a deep sleep. She sat up and blinked at the papers she'd wrinkled by slumping onto the desk in her small office.

What time was it? How long had she been sleeping?

Pulling the clock toward her, she rubbed her bleary eyes, then realized she was looking at the date and not the time and switched modes. It was just after midnight. She couldn't have been sleeping for more than half an hour.

She was exhausted. So what had disturbed her? Sophie? No. The cat was sleeping at her feet. Cocking her head, she listened carefully for several minutes but heard no sound.

She'd probably had another bad dream. She could even remember part of it. She'd heard a car pull up out front, the purr of an engine, followed by silence. Then she'd turned around, and her father was standing in her living room, smiling and holding out his arms as if she was still the little girl he'd left behind.

She didn't get a chance to ask him where he'd been, though. The dream ended before he could speak.

The comfort of her bed beckoned. She wasn't sure what had awakened her, but earlier she'd thought there was a noise—and it had turned out to be nothing. She was nervous, jumpy. She'd tried to channel her unease into work, but hadn't gotten very far.

With a sigh, she got up and walked toward the kitchen to get a glass of water, but a rustle in the next room made her heart leap into her throat. This noise wasn't coming from outside. And it wasn't Sophie. Sophie was at her heels but she hadn't made a sound.

Was it Hunter? Had he come back?

She waited, expecting him to call her name. But he didn't.

"Hunter?" she said. "Is that you?"

No answer. What was going on? Someone was in the house. She was sure of it. If it wasn't Hunter... was it Mike?

Thrusting a hand through her tousled hair, she peered cautiously around the corner. She could see part of the kitchen and living room, as well as a portion of the entry. But she couldn't see whoever had made the noise. Because she'd been so nervous before, she'd left the lights on for comfort, but now she felt exposed. Vulnerable. Whoever it was might have been looking inside the house, seen her sleeping.

Heart thumping loudly in her ears, she reached for the closest light switch.

The thud of heavy footsteps nearly made her knees give out. The intruder had been near the front entry. But now he was in the living room; she could tell by the movement.

Sophie darted back into the study, but Madeline couldn't let him catch her there. She'd be trapped.

Ducking, she ran out and caught a glimpse of someone's shadow flitting toward the kitchen. She wished she had her cell phone, but she'd left it on the counter earlier—in the kitchen, where her uninvited visitor was now. Grabbing one of the antique colored bottles that lined a shelf on the wall, she turned off the light switch for the living room, plunging it into darkness, too. Then she pressed herself to the wall and tried to peek around the corner.

Whoever it was had moved again. She couldn't see anyone. He was most likely against the same wall she was, but she felt too afraid to come farther into the doorway. Why give him an advantage? She'd be smarter to draw him toward her—and her only weapon. "Who are you and what do you want?" she cried.

Again, nothing. Panting with fear, she broke the bottle by smashing it on the wall, and held it in front of her. *This can't be happening,* she thought. But her earlier conversation with Molly kept echoing in her brain. *Are you scared of him?*

She was scared, all right. She'd never been more scared in her life.

"Mike, unless you want to go back to prison, I

suggest you get the hell out of my house," she said. "Why do you think so many lights were on? I'm waiting up for the man you saw earlier, the private investigator. He just went out for a drink and should be back any minute. He's staying with me, you know."

Her mouth was so dry she could hardly form the words. But her lie seemed effective. Indecision suddenly turned into action. Feet pounded across the kitchen; then the door slammed shut.

She raced around the corner, flipped off the light and stared out the window, hoping to see who it was. But all she caught was a flash of something white—a man's head or arm—and then he was gone.

Shaking, she set the broken bottle aside and reached for the phone. The dial tone hummed warm and comforting in her ear.

Calm down. Take a deep breath.

She fumbled through 9-1-1 and finally got the police. Then she tried to call Hunter on his cell phone and at the motel. But he didn't pick up.

"Where are you?" she muttered. Taking him to the motel had been a mistake.

Waiting for the siren that would tell her help was on its way, she slid down the side of the cupboards—only to sit in something wet. Confused, she got up and turned the lights back on. Then she covered her mouth.

It was blood. On the floor. Smeared by her own feet.

Spotting Madeline's hulk of a brother in the far corner, Hunter started toward him, trying not to smell the alcohol that seemed to say "welcome home." Instead, he focused on the cigarette smoke that hung thickly in the air, burning his lungs and nostrils. California had outlawed smoking in most public buildings years ago. Evidently, Mississippi was as far behind in public safety as it was in everything else, including fashion.

Most of the men around him were wearing Wranglers—so tight Hunter didn't know how they could still father children—wool, button-up shirts with T-shirts underneath and cowboy hats. Except for two old men at the bar, dressed in overalls, Clay seemed to be the exception. He had on a pair of worn, faded jeans with a fashionable rip in the knee. Funny thing was, Hunter suspected his rip had actually come from wear.

"So you got me out of bed. Now what?" Clay said gruffly.

Hunter took the seat opposite him and didn't respond because a waitress was already approaching.

"Can I get you boys somethin' to drink?" she asked.

"I'll have a Sam Adams," Clay said.

Hunter wanted a beer, too. There might be cigarette smoke in the bar, and maybe they were playing country-western music—two things that set this place apart from the trendy pubs he used to frequent in California. But a bar was a bar. Hunter's conditioned response to the atmosphere, from nearly a decade of visiting such places, was to order a real drink, then another…and eventually sink into oblivion.

But this was his first time inside a bar since he'd given up alcohol. He wasn't going to blow it.

"Club soda."

They sat without speaking until the waitress returned. Then Hunter tried not to watch Clay take his first drink. Averting his eyes, he stared out over the dance floor, where a bunch of women were laughing drunkenly while trying to do the Macarena.

Apparently that song was still popular in some parts of the country.

"You ready to tell me why we're here?" Clay asked.

"I've found something," he said.

Clay's arm froze momentarily before carrying the bottle to his mouth. After another long swig, he set his drink back on the table. "What?"

Hunter took Madeline's puffy journal from his coat pocket and slid it across the table.

"You found a child's journal?" he said without picking it up. He slouched lower in his chair but watched Hunter closely.

"It's Madeline's," he explained. "From when she was eight and nine years old."

"We were living in Booneville then," he said with a shrug. "Whatever's in it couldn't refer to me. Or any of my family."

"I realize that, of course."

Clay lifted his half-empty bottle with two fingers and swung it from side to side. "Then why are you showing me her journal?"

"Have you ever read it?"

One lazy eyebrow arched up. "Aren't journals supposed to be private?"

"She gave it to me." Hunter took it back again, opened it and began to read aloud.

"Katie has another sore on her neck. She won't tell me how she got it. But Daddy said someone must have grabbed hold of her necklace or something. Why would that be such a big secret?"

Clay regarded him with half-closed, heavy-lidded eyes. "So Katie was teasing her about some minor injury. What's that supposed to prove?"

Hunter flipped through a few more pages and read another entry.

"I'm so mad at Mom. Daddy wanted me to go to Jacksonville with him to see his cousin. We were going to stay two whole days. But she wouldn't let me go. And when I started to cry, she shook me hard."

"What do you have to say about *that?*" Hunter asked.

"From what I hear, Madeline's mother wasn't right in the head." Clay spoke in a monotone. "Committed suicide. It was a real tragedy."

"I think it might've been her father who was sick," Hunter said meaningfully. "And now I'm wondering just *how* sick."

Clay broke eye contact and gazed at the candle flickering in a red votive glass at the edge of the table. "I should warn you that won't be a popular opinion around here."

"Fortunately, I'm not running for office."

Clay said nothing.

"When did you find out about it?" Hunter asked.

"Find out about what?"

"What he was doing to your sister."

Clay appeared relaxed, but Hunter suspected that illusion was created only at the expense of great effort, "He didn't do anything to my sister. Ask Chief Pontiff. She told him as much last week."

"Why don't I ask *her?*" Hunter countered softly.

"Because you'd have to go through me first," Clay said.

Hunter didn't respond to the comment. He had no intention of approaching Grace; he was sure she'd suffered enough. That was why he'd called Clay instead.

He'd wanted to witness Clay's reaction—which had turned out to be exactly as he'd expected.

Locating one more entry in the journal, Hunter cleared his throat and read again.

"I saw a naked lady in a magazine in my dad's drawer. She had a man on her!"

Clay's lips curved into a smile, but it seemed more nostalgic than anything else.

"Interesting that she'd find pornography in her father's desk, don't you think?" Hunter said, "Someone who preached so energetically against sins of the flesh?"

"When we were kids, Madeline told us she'd found that magazine." Clay's odd smile lingered. "She said it was *gross.*"

"To a nine-year-old, I'm sure it was." Hunter used his straw to stir the ice in his glass. "But when she was older, didn't it make her question her father's adherence to his own standards?"

"Why would it?" Clay said. "The minute he found out she'd seen that magazine, he told her he'd confiscated it from one of his parishioners, who was a 'vile sinner on the surest road to hell.' He burned it in front of her, said he'd planned to do that all along."

"Bummer he had to dispose of it before he was finished with it," Hunter said sarcastically.

"He didn't need it. He had other things to entertain him."

Hunter's stomach muscles tensed. "Like…"

Clay shrugged and wouldn't volunteer any more. So Hunter asked him directly. "Who do the other panties belong to?"

Madeline's stepbrother used his index finger to circle

the top of his beer. "How much is she paying you?" he asked instead of answering.

Hunter shoved his club soda away. "Why? Are you going to try and buy me off?"

Clay's gaze never wavered. "Would it work if I did?"

"No. It's not about the money." Returning Madeline's five thousand was the only way Hunter could ease his guilt over what had happened between them earlier. He'd decided to send her a check the minute he got back to L.A.

"What's it about then?" Clay asked.

"I want to help her."

"If that's true, you'll go home tomorrow," he said and walked out, leaving the rest of his beer on the table.

Ray swore as he tried to stanch the blood from the cut on his right arm. The glass had sliced him so smoothly he hadn't realized how deep the injury was. He was pretty sure he needed stitches. But he couldn't go to a doctor. He'd seen the shows on TV, knew they'd trace the break-in at Madeline's place back to him. It wasn't as if he lived in a big city. He was probably the only person who'd cut himself tonight.

Holding his arm close to his body, he fumbled with the gauze from the old first aid kit he'd found under his bathroom sink. He wanted to bandage the wound, but it was awkward with just his left hand. The damn thing wouldn't stop bleeding. Maybe if he applied a little more pressure…

A knock on his front door made him go rigid with fear. *Had Madeline seen him?* Had she sent the police? The bitch wasn't even supposed to be home. When he found her car gone, he'd thought he was safe.

He glanced up at the tiny window above the shower.

It was too small and too high to climb out of. But he could get to the back bedroom, crawl through that window and sneak out via the woods, heading toward the highway, where he could flag down a trucker. He was just trying to calculate how much of a lead that would afford him when the second knock came. It was more insistent than the first, but the voice that accompanied it left Ray sagging in relief.

"Hey, Ray. You in there? It's me, Bubba."

Bubba lived next door and was always trying to bum cigarettes off him. But it was after midnight. He'd thought he was safe. "Don't have any smokes," Ray yelled.

"That's not why I'm here. The light in your car is on, man. Wouldn't want to let your battery run down, ya know?"

Ray had been planning to go back out and clean up the car. He couldn't leave the blood on his seat and steering wheel. "Don't worry about it," he called. "I'll take care of it in a minute."

There was a long silence, during which Ray hoped Bubba was lumbering back to his own damn trailer. At nearly five hundred pounds, Bubba was on state assistance because he couldn't work. But he managed to get around pretty damn well if he wanted something.

"I saw you bringin' in some groceries earlier. You don't happen to have a beer, do ya?"

Son of a bitch. Ray gritted his teeth. Bubba was still there. And he'd obviously seen the six-pack Ray had carried in earlier. Which meant he wouldn't leave until he had a cold beer in his fat hand.

Hastily wrapping the gauze around his cut and taping it as well as he could, Ray changed his clothes, being careful as he slipped the sleeve of his shirt over his injury. Then he shoved the box he'd taken from Madeline's house into the back bedroom, where it couldn't be seen. He wanted to go through it right away, make sure he had what he thought he had. But with Bubba nosing around, it'd have to wait.

"Hey, Ray?" Bubba's voice again.

Ray felt a muscle twitch below his left eye. Bubba was annoying on a *good* day. And this was *not* a good day.

Hauling in a calming breath, he said, "Yeah?"

"You okay in there?"

He was just closing the door of the back room, but the hesitancy in Bubba's voice gave him pause. "Sure. Why?"

"The *blood,* man. I tried to turn off the light for you and found blood all over the inside of your car. Are you hurt?"

Fuck! That was it. Clearing his mind, Ray began walking very deliberately toward the living room. Bubba was no problem. A man that obese could die at any moment.

Too bad it'd have to be tonight.

17

If that's true, you'll go home to California tomorrow....

Hunter sat at the table he'd shared with Clay more than an hour earlier, mulling over that statement while nursing another watered-down soda. He had half a mind to take Clay's advice, to get out of town while he could.

But it was already too late. When he'd read Madeline's childhood diary, the mention of Katie's neck injury had jumped right off the page. He'd immediately connected it to the word *collar* used by whoever had called Madeline's office and left that raspy message.

Or was he grasping for something that wasn't there?

He didn't think so. Someone knew what had happened and was nervous about its coming out. But he felt surprisingly confident that it wasn't Clay who'd called. Clay wouldn't have left that message on Maddy's answering machine. He loved her, for one thing. And the Montgomerys' position was that Grace had never been molested. Understandably, he wanted to distance his family from such a strong motive for murder.

And that meant someone else was involved. Hunter wanted to figure out who it was. But there was so much else to consider—including the memory of making love to Madeline against that tree and the desire to be with her again. He wasn't ready for a relationship. Falling in love would be the ultimate betrayal of his daughter. He couldn't love Antoinette, but could he love someone else? Find happiness elsewhere?

Besides, if Clay had killed Reverend Barker, the evidence he was finding suggested Barker deserved it. How could Hunter pursue a case like that? Maybe it wasn't right for Clay to take the law into his own hands, but being sixteen and pitted against a man as powerful as Barker, he might not have had much choice. Given the circumstances, Hunter—*anyone*—might've done the same thing.

Hunter didn't want to see Madeline's stepbrother go to prison for trying to protect his family. And he didn't want to get emotionally involved with Madeline. Two powerful reasons to turn back. And yet, the existence of those other panties suggested Barker had hurt more than Grace. Should the reverend be exposed for what he'd done to these women?

If there were others, why hadn't any of them come forward?

A chilling thought stole over Hunter: *Maybe they were all dead....*

Katie was a hit-and-run. Rose Lee was a suicide. They'd both been close to the reverend, and they were both gone. So was the reverend's first wife, who'd become obsessed with "protecting" Madeline. What if the girls had been molested, and Eliza had found out? Then the three of them would know. Which made it damned convenient for Barker that they'd all met tragedies that would silence them forever.

Hunter thumbed through the journal again. *Katie has another sore on her neck... I found a naked lady in a magazine in my dad's drawer... My mother wouldn't let me go...*

Madeline resented her mother and idolized her father. But what if her mother *hadn't* taken her own life? Or did it because of the helplessness she felt?

He remembered the letter Madeline had discovered in that secret compartment of Eliza's jewelry box. She'd been begging for help, which seemed to fit. Maybe Eliza was afraid for her life, afraid for Madeline, and was trying to get away. If so, didn't she deserve to be remembered differently?

And what about Katie's mother and Rose Lee's father? They probably had no idea that the man they'd trusted to help them had likely molested, maybe raped, their daughters—repeatedly. It was even possible that Mr. Harper blamed himself for Rose Lee's suicide and had lived in hell for the past twenty-some years.

Who else was out there suffering because of the reverend's actions?

"I'm sorry, but you're going to have to leave."

Hunter blinked as the booming voice penetrated his concentration. It was the bartender. Hunter was almost the last person in the place.

"It's closing time," the man explained. "Do you need me to find you a ride home?"

Hunter chuckled dryly. "No." For once he'd closed down a bar stone-cold sober. "I'm fine."

After the initial fifteen or twenty minutes, he hadn't even craved a drink. But maybe that was because he was fighting something else; he craved the feel of Madeline's body. Craved it more than the booze. That was why he hadn't left the bar. He didn't want to go back to the motel.

* * *

The blood was immediately apparent. There was a spotty trail, smeared with a few pawprints from before Madeline had locked Sophie in an upstairs bedroom. Someone had obviously cut a hand or an arm reaching through the window to open the door. From there, the trail led to the middle of the room, then disappeared as if the intruder had wrapped something around his or her injury.

Hunter could hear the low murmur of Chief Pontiff and Officer Radcliffe, questioning Madeline in the other room. They'd already photographed the kitchen and taken a sample of the blood. By the time he'd returned to his motel and found the message the night manager had tacked to his door, the police had been at Madeline's for almost an hour.

If he'd followed his first instinct and gone back to the cottage, this might never have happened....

Stepping over the blood, he started toward the living room. He was planning to join the others, but as he passed the door to the basement, he noticed that it stood slightly ajar.

"It had to be Mike," Madeline was saying. "Maybe he just wanted to scare me. But I don't know anyone else who'd break in. Nothing was stolen."

Hunter opened the basement door a little wider and flipped on the light. "Madeline?" he called.

"What?"

"Has anyone been in the basement tonight?"

There was a few seconds of surprised silence. "No. Why?"

"The door was open."

Chief Pontiff appeared in the living room doorway. "So? Maybe she went down there earlier and left it that way."

"No, I didn't." Madeline came out, with Radcliffe a step behind. "I thought I heard someone outside before I fell asleep, so I went around to check the windows and doors. I passed the basement. I would've noticed because I don't like Sophie going down there."

Hunter squinted at a few dark spots toward the bottom of the stairs—and on the railing. "Does that look like blood to you?" he asked, pointing.

"I'll be damned," Radcliff muttered and they all followed him into the basement.

"There you go," Chief Pontiff said, crouching beside one speck. "That *is* blood."

"What's it doing down here?" Madeline asked.

Hunter turned in a circle, trying to see into the dark recesses. "Anyone have a flashlight?"

"I do," Radcliffe piped up. But he handed it to Pontiff, who slowly swung the beam around the perimeter of the concrete room. When he reached the area behind the stairs, Madeline clutched Hunter's arm.

"What is it?" he asked.

"My father's things!"

That section looked as if it had been ransacked, but they'd been rummaging through boxes there earlier, and it hadn't been all that neat to begin with. "What about them?"

She reached out and held the flashlight steady, directing the beam more carefully between the gaps in the wooden stairs. "The big box on top, the one we didn't bring up yesterday is gone."

* * *

"Why would anyone want to steal your father's belongings, Maddy?" Pontiff asked.

Madeline sat on the couch, holding the cup of hot tea Hunter had thrust into her hands. He stood at the window, presumably watching the sunrise as he listened to them talk.

"I have no idea," she said.

"Are you sure something's actually been taken?" Radcliffe sat across from her. "With all the stuff you've got in that basement, it could be difficult to tell. Maybe you shoved a few boxes off to the side and don't remember doing it."

She felt embarrassed to have had these men tramping through her private neurosis. Embarrassed and *exposed*. It was a bit like having a car accident in holey underwear. Such an exposure was a minor consideration; she realized that. But still, it wasn't a pleasant experience. "I know exactly what was where. Hunter and I were just down there yesterday morning. There was a heavy box filled with stuff from my father's office."

"You haven't had a chance to search everything carefully," Pontiff argued. "If his stuff is shoved off to the side somewhere, maybe buried under something else, we'd be connecting this break-in to your father's case when it might be completely unrelated."

"Finding the Cadillac's probably made you nervous, Maddy," Radcliffe added. "Maybe you're jumping at shadows."

Frowning, Hunter turned and folded his arms across his chest. "Shadows don't drip blood on the floor."

Both policemen looked up, obviously not pleased

that he—the hotshot from out of town—would presume to contradict them. "I'm not talking to you," Radcliffe snapped, clearly irritated.

"I don't care," Hunter said. "Like Maddy just told you, I was down there with her yesterday morning. I saw the box she's talking about."

"Other than Maddy, who would see any value in her father's personal artifacts?" Pontiff challenged, getting quickly to his feet.

"Someone who was afraid I might go through them?" Hunter said.

Pontiff exchanged a glance with Radcliffe. "If there was anything incriminating in those boxes, why haven't they gone missing before?"

"Maybe whoever's responsible for Madeline's father's murder wasn't concerned until now."

"And you're the one who has them running scared?"

Hunter ignored Pontiff's verbal jab. "Things have changed," he said. "Beginning with the discovery of the Cadillac and what was in it. This case is heating up again and it's making someone very nervous."

"That someone has got to be Clay," Radcliffe said.

"My stepbrother's the one who gave me those boxes in the first place," Madeline retorted. "Why would he steal them back?"

"Maybe he's just remembered there was something in one of 'em."

"Not likely," Hunter said.

"Don't you think it's odd that this 'intruder' knew right where to go?" Radcliffe asked.

That detail bothered Madeline, too. She didn't show her basement to very many people. Only Hunter, Kirk, her family and Ray Harper, whom she'd hired to build some shelves a few months ago, had been down there.

"It's not Clay," Hunter insisted. "If there was something potentially incriminating in those boxes, he would've removed it long ago. Besides, he was with me last night."

Madeline glanced up at him. Had she heard right? "What'd you say?"

"We met for a drink," he explained, his attention still on Pontiff. "The waitress at Let the Good Times Roll can vouch for us."

"What time did you leave?" Toby asked.

"Just before I came here."

"And Clay?" he persisted.

Madeline sensed that Hunter wasn't particularly eager to answer this question. "About an hour and a half before me."

"That would put him in town and out on the streets *alone* right around the time of the burglary," Pontiff said smugly.

Hunter circled the small table separating them. "I'm telling you, it wasn't Clay."

Dislike and impatience made deep grooves on Radcliffe's forehead. "Maybe whatever was in there was only incriminating together with the evidence from the Cadillac—evidence he thought we'd never find."

"No." Hunter shook his head.

"How can you be so sure?" Radcliffe asked.

"Because Clay would have easier ways of getting to those boxes than breaking Madeline's window in the middle of the night."

"How do you know so much?" Pontiff asked. "You've been here, what, two days?"

"A lot can happen in two days." Hunter's light eyes flicked Madeline's way, and she knew he was referring to what had already occurred between them.

"Besides," Hunter added, "Clay wouldn't risk scaring Maddy—or getting caught."

"To my mind, that would depend on how much he wanted that box," Radcliffe said. "Like most criminals, he cares more about himself than anyone else."

"You're *that* sure he's guilty?" Hunter asked.

Radcliffe glared at him. "The whole town *knows* he's guilty."

A muscle twitched in Hunter's cheek. "Is that why the police tried to beat him into a confession?"

"I don't know what you're talking about," Pontiff said.

"Read the reports," Hunter responded.

"I've read them. There's nothing to indicate he was struck even once."

"Then you're not reading very closely. You should pay special attention to the deleted parts."

Pontiff's face grew mottled. "Who the hell do you think you are?" he shouted. "You can't come down here, slinging around accusations designed to make my force look bad. Not without proof—and I'm guessing you don't have any."

"We could always ask Clay," Hunter said.

"As if we could trust him." Radcliffe jammed a finger in Hunter's chest. "Without proof, you haven't got anything!"

Hunter knocked the other man's hand away and immediately blocked the fist he threw.

"Radcliffe!" Pontiff barked.

Madeline nearly spilled her tea trying to set it down so she could move between them.

"That's enough," she said. "Why fight about it here? Why not go see if Clay's been cut? If he has, come back and let us know. If not, quit making allegations against him until you have some proof!"

Pontiff gripped her elbow. "Listen to me, Maddy. You're paying this guy a lot of money to have him tell you what you want to hear. You love Clay, so he says it's not Clay. But that doesn't make him right. You're paying for nothing," he spat out.

"Kiss my ass!" Hunter said, finally goaded into losing his temper. "You don't know what you're talking about!"

Pontiff ignored him in favor of appealing to Madeline. "Get rid of him. I'll find your father's murderer *and* whoever broke in last night, and it won't cost you a dime. I'm a public servant, remember? Not a bloodsucking leech."

"Hey, Barney Fife, maybe this is news to you but, so far, you haven't done anything except defend your department—men who used their power to abuse a sixteen-year-old boy."

Despite all the confusion and emotional upheaval, Madeline found Hunter far too appealing. Especially when he was sticking up for Clay.

"He's full of shit, Maddy," Radcliffe added, mistaking her silence for indecision and piling on. "Clay wasn't beaten up."

"I've read the reports," she said. "Maybe Clay's never made any accusations, but I think Hunter's right."

"What?" Radcliffe cried.

She raised both hands, indicating her desire for silence. "It makes too much sense—and it's further proof that I need someone with a different perspective than our own. Someone like Hunter."

"He's a troublemaker, Maddy," Pontiff said. "Send him packing. He doesn't belong here."

Maddy *was* tempted to let Hunter go. But not because she agreed with anything Pontiff or Radcliffe had to say. Her reasons were purely those of self-preservation. She was beginning to fall in love with him—in a headlong tumble she'd never dreamed possible. And he was the one person most likely to destroy everything she'd ever believed about her father and her family.

"Hunter stays," she said.

Pontiff's fingers tightened on her hand. "Why?"

"Because it's time to face the truth."

Hunter stood, gazing down at Madeline, who was still asleep. He'd made it all the way to morning without touching her. He was proud of that, especially since it hadn't been easy. He'd wanted to comfort her, but he knew where any break in his resistance would lead and refused to take advantage of her vulnerability. So he'd wrestled with himself until they'd both fallen asleep, with her on the couch and him in the recliner. And now he was hoping to leave before she woke up. There were people he needed to talk to, and he preferred not to take her with him.

Careful to move quietly, he gave Sophie a quick pat and walked outside, but as soon as he reached the porch he pulled his cell phone from his pocket. Flipping it open, he studied Maria's picture, although he'd already memorized every detail.

He wanted to speak to his daughter. Maybe that would help him remember why he couldn't afford the kinds of emotions he was starting to feel for Madeline—

tenderness and compassion, the instinct to protect, sexual desire.

With one kind word from Maria, he could give up any hope of a relationship with Madeline. He could make the sacrifice. If his daughter agreed to see him, he'd leave for California tomorrow. He was afraid they'd miss so much. She was only twelve years old. What about all the places they'd never visit? The prom dates he'd never meet? The pictures he'd never take?

He sighed. How did it get to this point? He hadn't been a bad husband or father, at least not until the final year of his marriage, when he and Antoinette had grown so estranged that he could hardly make it through the day without pickling his brain in alcohol. Before that last year, he'd actually been a decent husband, especially in the beginning, when his resolve was fresh and he believed the love he felt for his daughter could compensate for the love he didn't feel for his wife.

His fingers caressed the phone button that would automatically dial his little girl. But if he tried to call her, chances were she'd rebuff him again. Antoinette made sure Maria heard, on a daily basis, a litany of his faults and shortcomings—how he was a womanizer, even though he'd only slept with two, now three, women in his life; how he was an alcoholic, even though she drank heavily herself and used cocaine and other drugs when she partied; how he'd stolen her best years even though he hadn't wanted them in the first place.

He knew what Antoinette said. Maria had told him in the past, when she'd craved reassurance. Unfortunately, she didn't come to him with her concerns anymore. She'd finally succumbed to the poison of her mother's words.

He wasn't sure he could take hearing his daughter repeat what she'd said during their last conversation. So he started to put his phone away. But then he changed his mind and sent the call.

It rang several times before someone picked up.

"Hunter, have you mailed my check yet?"

It was Antoinette. Obviously, her caller ID was in good working order.

He didn't answer. He was too busy searching for the right words. The ones that would make peace, patch things up, turn the situation around.

The ones he never seemed to find.

"If you think you're going to get out of paying your child support this month just because you gave me a little extra last month, you're wrong," she said. "Maria's the one who didn't want to go to Hawaii. You can't blame me. I had nothing to do with it."

He could blame her, and did. The only way Antoinette could hurt him was through Maria, so she turned their daughter into a weapon at every opportunity. The woman who'd claimed she loved him more than her own life—who'd been so obsessed with him that she'd once hired a private detective to trail him, who'd gone so far in her paranoid delusions that she'd bugged their home phone—now hated him in equal measure.

"Is she there?" He stared out over Madeline's front lawn without really seeing anything.

"She's here, but she doesn't want to talk to you."

He drew a steadying breath. "Will you ask her?"

There was a long pause. "Hang on," she snapped as if she'd rather not be bothered.

She was gone for precisely eighty-nine heartbeats.

"She wants to know why you're calling," she said when she returned. "And she told me to remind you of your promise."

"My promise?"

"To leave her alone."

"I only promised because she asked me to."

I can't stand the tug-of-war any longer, she'd said. *Please, give up. Let me go.*

"Then keep your word," Antoinette said simply. "She's fine, you know. We've grown very close."

"That's it, then?"

She seemed unsure of his attitude. Knowing her, she was trying to figure out how to work his current mood to her advantage. It probably alarmed her that he seemed resigned to the situation; she didn't have any power if he gave up. If she'd held anything else over his head, he would've sacrificed it a long time ago just to be rid of her. But this was his *daughter,* for God's sake.

"She might change her mind, but not if you don't send that damn check," Antoinette was saying. "Or are you spending all your money on *Selena* these days?"

She knew better. He hadn't been with their neighbor since that night two years ago, when he'd been too drunk to stop himself from accepting the kindness Selena had offered him. It was just that he didn't appear to be in enough agony right now, so Antoinette was revising her tactics.

Why couldn't she see that the animosity between them was hurting Maria more than anything that had or hadn't happened in the past? Why did it have to be this way? They could let bygones be bygones for Maria's sake, couldn't they?

He'd asked her to do that, again and again. But it was no use. Antoinette refused to cooperate—and now he didn't have any influence with Maria, either.

"Hunter?" she said when he didn't take the bait.

He hung up because there was nothing more to say.

18

Hunter knew Irene Montgomery was home—he'd heard movement when he rang the bell, felt the scrutiny of someone on the other side of the peephole—but he had to knock several times before she answered. She finally opened the door, but only an inch or two.

"What do you want?" she asked, staring out at him.

Hunter summoned his most engaging smile. "I'm Hunter Solozano."

"I know who you are." She looked him up and down. "Why are you here?"

Rain dripped down the back of his neck. He wanted to move closer, so he'd be sheltered by the eaves. But he was trying not to crowd Irene; Madeline's stepmother was nervous enough already. "I was in the neighborhood."

"Where's Madeline?"

"At her own place. She had a little…incident last night."

"Incident?" she echoed suspiciously.

"Yes. That's partly why I want to talk to you. Someone broke into her house."

The door suddenly flew open. "What? Is she okay?"

"She's upset and confused, but physically she's fine."

"Come in." Stepping back, she waved him past her.

He had to turn sideways in order to fit through the cluster of furnishings. The place was spotless, but stuffed with knickknacks, decorations and furniture. Beyond the usual couch, chair, television and coffee table, Hunter saw a velvet chaise, a cabinet full of collectibles, a stool that sported fringe all the way around, an old-fashioned teacart with hand-blown glass and delicate china, several inlaid accent tables and two Victorian lamps. All in one small living room. And the upholstery was a sort of dusky pink.

"Nice," he said vaguely, because he couldn't find anything specific to admire. It was just that the moment seemed to call for a polite remark and he didn't know what else to say when confronted with so much pink and gold.

Irene's tastes definitely ran toward the ornate and feminine, even in her personal appearance. Dressed in a tailored turquoise blouse with turquoise jewelry, a pair of skin-tight jeans that had sequins down the front, and high heels that matched her shirt, she still had a good figure. Like Grace, she also had pretty blue eyes and dark hair, which she'd piled on top of her head, leaving a few tendrils curling around her face.

He couldn't imagine anyone like Madeline's stepmother marrying a conservative preacher, especially one who seemed as strict in his beliefs as Barker—his ostensible beliefs, anyway. She had "sex kitten" written all over her.

"Was it Mike?" she asked.

Now that the door was shut, he could scarcely breathe for the strength of her perfume. Evidently, she applied scent as liberally as she did makeup. "We don't know. Whoever it was got away."

"What happened?"

"Madeline heard someone in the house. When she called out to him, he ran out."

The color had drained from beneath the heavy powder on Irene's face. "Did he take anything?"

"A box of your husband's things."

She steadied herself with a hand on the back of the sofa. "But why?"

"That's what I was hoping you could tell me."

"If they were the ones Clay packed up when he dismantled the office, there was nothing in them but sermons and personal effects, none of which had value to anyone but Madeline. Other daughters would probably have tossed some of it. But not Madeline. She saves everything."

She waved at the living room. "I have too much stuff myself. But none of it's old. I want to purge. She wants to save."

"Maybe it's because so much in her life has slipped away from her."

"And I can't rid myself of the past no matter how hard I try," she muttered.

He couldn't help liking Irene. She seemed nice, almost childlike. "Speaking of the past, I want to ask a few questions about your husband, if you don't mind."

The wariness instantly reappeared. "I've already answered every conceivable question."

"I might have some new ones."

"I wouldn't bet on it." She glanced at the window.

"Are you expecting someone?" he asked.

She ignored this and moved toward the kitchen. "Can I make you a cup of coffee?"

"No, thanks. This'll only take a minute. I—"

"Madeline's not returning my calls," she interrupted, stopping her retreat.

He would've thought she was dodging him, but the concern in her eyes was real.

For Madeline's sake, he tried to reassure her. "She hasn't had a chance. She's been busy since I came to town."

"Too busy to call her mother?"

"She's struggling with the fact that you don't want me here, and that she's the one who brought me."

The frankness of his response begged equal candor. And she didn't disappoint him. "How can she expect me to be happy about it?"

"She doesn't. She's just in a tough spot, caught between the love and loyalty she feels for you and the love and loyalty she feels for her father."

"We're all in a tough spot," Irene said. "And life never seems to get any easier. Believe me, I've seen it all."

Was she talking about the heartbreak of having a husband abandon her? The fear of nearly losing her children to the state? The dubious reception she'd received when she moved to Stillwater? The lack of acceptance, and the judgment and skepticism that had followed her ever since? Or the murder of a man she'd found out was molesting her daughter?

She wanted to talk, Hunter could tell. She seemed weary, desperate, as if looking for a safe haven she'd never been able to find. He had to pity her, she seemed harmless in so many ways. And yet he recognized the opportunity she afforded him. "Maybe it's time to finally sort it all out," he said.

She straightened abruptly. "There's nothing to sort out.

I—I want you to leave. I can't deal with the past anymore. It's over, do you hear me? It's over. I only did what I—"

"You did what?" he asked. Like Clay, she knew more about Barker's disappearance than she was telling.

Her eyes rounded in fear. "Nothing! I did nothing!"

She was growing agitated, panicky. To calm her, he turned the conversation in a different direction. If he could keep her talking, he might eventually learn what she wanted to reveal yet was so desperate to hide. "Did Lee ever talk about his first wife?"

Her mouth parted as if this question surprised her. She seemed to examine it, looking for traps, then answered hesitantly. "He talked about her occasionally."

"Did he seem to miss her?"

"No. He never had anything good to say about her, although I begged him not to malign her in front of Madeline. No child should hear such things about her mother."

"What 'things'?" he asked.

"He hated Eliza, pure and simple."

Hunter had sensed as much from what Eliza had recorded in her journals and even in the sermons Barker had given. Often focused on self-denial, self-reliance and strength through adversity, each sermon seemed to tout a virtue Barker did not believe his wife possessed. One sermon actually went so far as to say that anyone who suffered from depression was afflicted by God for the sin of ingratitude.

Eliza didn't come across as a particularly strong individual. But she'd always managed to care for her daughter, which was unusual for someone so consumed by despair. He had to respect that. And she was fiercely determined to protect Madeline. Hunter thought he knew from what—but he needed more than his own conjecture if he wanted to convince anyone else.

"Hate is a pretty strong word," he said.

"There's no other way to describe it," she responded. "He said she let him down in the worst possible way. That she was stupid and weak. The only time I ever heard him curse was when I tried to get him to tell me some of her better qualities. He couldn't come up with one. Instead, he called her a…" She lifted a hand that sported several large, sparkling rings, probably as fake as the gilt around her mirrors. "Well, I'm sure you can guess."

He took a stab at it. "Bitch?"

"Worse. Much worse."

"Can you give me a hint?"

She shuddered as if it was too abhorrent to contemplate. "It doesn't matter. You get the idea."

Irene couldn't even say the word, and yet her preacher husband had used such terms to describe his first wife, who was the mother of his child?

Hunter was pragmatic when it came to people. He put no one on a pedestal, realized that preachers had the same appetites, desires and weaknesses as everyone else. But after reading Barker's fiery sermons and knowing what kind of hell Madeline's father preached about, Hunter could hardly imagine him speaking in terms much more vulgar than bitch. But if Barker was so hypocritical in this regard, it followed that there'd be other inconsistencies, as well.

"Wasn't he afraid you'd repeat what he said?"

"Who'd believe me?" she said with a laugh.

"What made you approach him about his ex-wife in the first place?" he asked.

Irene fingered the necklace at her throat. "I did it for Madeline, of course. I wanted her to have something positive to identify with. The poor girl was struggling to figure out if her mother was the loving person she remembered or this monstrous figure Lee made her out to be."

"He couldn't see that he was making the situation even harder on Maddy?"

"He didn't care. The less she loved her mother, the more completely he could replace Eliza in his little girl's esteem."

That sounded like Antoinette. "How selfish," he murmured.

"I'll be the first to admit that Eliza Barker had problems," Irene said. "You only have to read one of her poems to see that. But no one's all good or all bad. There are so many people in this town who worshipped her. They must've had some reason." Her voice turned wry. "Lord knows it's not that easy to impress folks around here."

He felt the deep loneliness in that statement. "You would know."

"Yes," she said sadly.

"Why do you think he was so ungenerous with Eliza?" he asked. "Because of the hurt he felt over her suicide?"

"The hurt?" she scoffed. "He wasn't hurt. If anything, he was relieved to have her gone."

The vehemence in her last phrase surprised Hunter. It surprised Irene, too, judging by the frightened look that suddenly claimed her pretty features. "But we never argued over Eliza," she said. "We never had any real problems."

She'd been grilled about her own complicity in

Barker's death so often that she was afraid to make any negative comment, especially one spoken with such passion. "I understand that," he told her.

At his response, she seemed to calm down, so he ventured another question. "Did he keep any pictures of her?"

"No. He destroyed any he came across. But I managed to save a few, and let Madeline keep one between her mattresses. She pretended she didn't care if she had it or not, but I know she did. She felt angry and lost, that was all."

"At least she had her father," he said, just to see how Irene might react.

She glanced at the window again. "You'd better go."

"I have just a couple more questions—"

"I've got to be at work by noon. And all of this happened a long time ago. Sometimes it's better to leave the past alone."

"Even if there's a chance Barker killed his first wife?"

She swayed as though the shock of what he'd just said had hit her like a physical blow. "I—I...*what?*" she stammered.

"You heard me."

"It was a suicide."

"It *appeared* to be a suicide," he conceded. "But I don't think Eliza would've left Madeline. She was too determined to protect her."

"She was depressed."

"She loved her daughter more than anything, was absolutely consumed with taking care of her. Why would she suddenly abandon her?"

Irene's throat worked as she struggled to swallow.

"It can't be. There…there was a note. From what I heard, it was written in her own hand."

Hunter realized he was probably going too far by suggesting what he had. Now that he'd said the words aloud, they'd spread. And he didn't want this to get back to Madeline. But he'd never know more than he knew now if he didn't follow his instincts. And the shocking question had definitely caused Irene to lower her defenses.

"Was it a note or was it another journal entry?" he asked.

"Good Lord." Squeezing her eyes shut, she brought a quivering hand to her mouth.

"Irene?" He gently touched her arm.

She gazed up at him, her eyes filled with torment.

"Was he capable of murder? Were you afraid of him?"

She started to shake her head, but he tightened his grip. "Tell me the truth."

"The truth?" she said bitterly. "I'm not sure I know what the truth is anymore."

"Were you afraid of him?"

She stared into space.

"Were you frightened of him?" He'd spoken more loudly, more insistently, and this time she answered.

"Yes," she said. "He was one of the most vile men I've ever known."

Hunter's heart tripped over itself at this admission. "Was he a pedophile?" he asked. "Did he molest Grace?"

Before she could respond, the sound of a motor intruded. They both turned to the window as a large, black truck whipped into the drive.

It was Clay. Irene must've called him the moment Hunter knocked. And he didn't look happy.

"Get out," he said as soon as he reached the doorway. "And don't come back unless you're with the police or you have a subpoena."

Hunter didn't argue. Clay was well within his rights. But as he got in Madeline's car, he knew he'd never forget the tears running silently down Irene's cheeks as she stood there shaking.

Clay answered the door to find Pontiff standing on his front porch. "What is it?" he asked, instantly concerned. There was a purposeful, determined air about the police chief that set off alarms in his head.

Pontiff rocked up on the balls of his feet, as if he was conscious of his height, which was a mere five-ten. "Did you do it?"

Narrowing his gaze, Clay stepped outside so that his wife wouldn't hear the conversation. Fortunately, Whitney was upstairs playing with her Barbies, so he didn't have to worry about her. His mother had told him that someone had broken into Madeline's house. Until now, he'd chosen to think of it as some kind of prank, just as he'd told himself the "she" in that note could be anyone. *Stop her or I will?* Who would've written that about Madeline? Everyone in Stillwater loved her, except maybe Mike Metzger. She believed Mike killed her father and had pressed him a little too hard because of it. But no one knew better than Clay that wasn't true. "Do what?"

"Steal that box?"

"I don't know what you're talking about."

The door opened behind him and Allie stepped out. Clay immediately recognized the stubborn glint in her eye that told him she'd heard their voices and wasn't about to be left out of this. But she didn't speak. She slipped her hand inside his and turned her attention expectantly to Pontiff.

"Someone broke into Madeline's house last night," Pontiff explained.

"I know." Allie's grip tightened on his hand. "But that has nothing to do with my husband. He's as upset by it as anyone."

Pontiff didn't respond. He was too busy glaring at Clay, looking as if this was the last straw, as if this was where he finally brought Clay down.

But it wasn't Pontiff who scared Clay. It was Hunter Solozano. Hunter hadn't taken his advice about leaving town. He'd shown up at Irene's first thing this morning, asking if Barker might've been responsible for killing Eliza! That was something Clay had never considered—none of them had—but Clay wouldn't put it past Barker.

Somehow Hunter already knew more about the bastard than anyone in Stillwater. To top it off, Irene had admitted that Madeline's father was the vilest creature she'd ever known, which they'd all sworn never to do.

"That remains to be seen." Pontiff finally deigned to speak. "Who else would care about that box?"

The wind smelled like snow. Clay noticed it, and noticed the feel of his wife's slim fingers intertwined with his—because he didn't know how long he'd be free to enjoy such simple pleasures. "I have no idea what box you're talking about."

"The reverend's things. One of the boxes you packed up when you dismantled the office in your barn."

Clay made a noise of impatience. "You're not making a damn bit of sense, Toby. Why would I break into a house for which I have a key to take what I gave freely in the first place?"

At this a flicker of doubt passed over Pontiff's face, but he spread his feet and propped his fists on his hips, near his gun. "Just show me your hands. And pull up your sleeves past your elbows."

Clay nearly refused. This was bullshit. He'd die before he'd ever hurt or threaten Madeline. But Allie squeezed his hand again, silently pleading with him to make it easy for a change.

"I'll do you one better," he said and Pontiff backed up as he stepped forward and stripped off his whole shirt, as well as the T-shirt beneath. "You see anything here that concerns you?" Clay challenged, turning around. "You want to take pictures? Allie, go get a camera. We'll send Chief Pontiff on his way with a bunch of time-stamped digital pictures for his files."

"No." Pontiff shook his head, looking bewildered. "No, there's...there's no need."

Clay tossed his shirts on the chair of the porch. It was only forty degrees outside, but he didn't care. He was going to make a statement, guarantee that Pontiff saw all he wanted. "What were you hoping to find, Toby?"

"The—the perpetrator cut himself pretty bad. There was blood everywhere. It led from the window that was broken through the kitchen and down into the basement."

The mention of blood caused fear to uncoil in the pit of Clay's stomach. Who'd want to break into Madeline's house badly enough to stick around once he'd been injured? And who, besides Maddy, would give a damn about Barker's belongings?

Stop her or I will... Stop her from what? Digging for the truth?

It wasn't logical that anyone else would feel threatened by Madeline's persistence. Clay had Barker's body buried in his own cellar, which was why he could never leave this place. It was his secret, his problem. No one else's. So why the note?

"That's all I needed," Pontiff muttered, then started for his car.

Their interview was over. Pontiff seemed satisfied. But something strange was going on, and Clay had no confidence in the local police department's ability to solve it.

That left Hunter.

Clay couldn't believe he was even considering it but he knew what he had to do. For Madeline's sake, he was going to turn that note over to the man who could destroy him.

The trailer was cold. As if the door had been left hanging open for hours. Or the windows. A woman sat crying on the tattered couch, her face buried in her hands.

Madeline recognized her as Bubba Turk's sister, Helen, because she'd occasionally seen them together, along with the woman's teenage daughter, who was with her now, trying to comfort her. Chief Pontiff and Norman Jones, a recent hire, were also in the threadbare living room, as was the county coroner, Ramona Butler. Pontiff and Ramona were bent over Bubba Turk, who was lying on his back on the floor, his massive body taking up all but a small perimeter in which they were trying to work.

"Hi, Maddy," Norm said. The pallor of his skin had a noticeable green tinge, and he stayed as far from the body as possible.

"Hi, Norm. Where're the emergency personnel?"

"Wasn't any need to make 'em drive all the way

over here. It was—" he cleared his throat "—obviously too late by the time we arrived."

At this exchange, Toby, still kneeling on the floor next to the body, glanced over his shoulder. "Who called *you?*" he asked.

"Your *wife,*" Madeline replied. "We happen to be friends, remember?"

He stared at her for a second, then sighed. "I shouldn't have told her," he grumbled. "It's already too crowded in here."

The past few days certainly hadn't strengthened their relationship. Toby himself had called her when they found Rachel Simmons' body; she'd joined them at the quarry at his invitation. Now, only two weeks later, he seemed to have an aversion to her presence.

Her life was changing. Opposing people she'd known for years and hiring Hunter was costing her everything that had once meant so much to her. Family. Friends. And even, indirectly, Kirk. Who knew how many times they would've reconciled and split again if Hunter hadn't come along? Despite her growing resolve, their breakup wouldn't have lasted, not in the face of all this pressure. It was the incident behind the tree that told Madeline it was *really* over.

"I have a right to be notified," she said, her tone no kinder than his. "I'm the press, remember?"

"There's nothing here to report."

"The loss of a fellow citizen is important to me," she told him tartly and tried not to wrinkle her nose at the smell, some of which came from the trailer itself and not Bubba. "What happened?"

Ramona Butler, the county coroner, was a small, bony woman who raised horses outside of Iuka. "I'm betting it was a heart attack," she said, leaning back on her haunches. "I imagine he clutched his chest, then stumbled and hit the corner of the counter. There's quite a lot of blood, so his heart was still beating when he hit it. Maybe that's what actually killed him."

Pontiff looked at the counter she'd indicated, but Madeline couldn't bear the sight. The bloody gash she'd glimpsed on Bubba's forehead upset her. *Death* upset her. Bubba's lifeless body brought back images of her mother. Opening the door to her bedroom. Finding the dark figure, barely visible because of the tightly drawn shades, lying on the floor like a discarded garment. Rushing forward and crying out, "Mama! Mama, what's wrong?" as she touched her shoulder. Then bending close to see why her mother wouldn't answer and, as her eyes finally adjusted to the dim light, finding a hole in the side of her head.

Madeline suddenly felt claustrophobic in the tiny room. She wanted to run outside and drag big gulps of air into her lungs. But Helen, weeping on the couch, reminded her that she wasn't the one suffering here. Refusing to do anything that would draw undue attention her way, she edged closer to Norm. "Don't tell me Helen found him," she whispered.

He nodded. "They were supposed to go grocery shopping. When he didn't answer the door, she came in and—" he wiped beads of sweat from his forehead "—and then she called us."

"He never locked his door, not while he was home," Helen said, interrupting their hushed conversation. "Why would he lock it now?" she demanded of the room at large. "I couldn't find the key he gave me, couldn't *help* him."

Norm grew a shade paler as his eyes fastened on the bloated body, and more sweat popped out on his forehead. He was too rattled to help the crying sister, so Madeline slipped past him and knelt in front of her. "Did you know something was wrong, Helen?"

"I was worried."

"Why?"

"Because I kept calling him this morning, and he didn't answer. I even called Ray next door and asked him to go over, but Ray couldn't get an answer, either."

"You think Bubba might've been alive when you got here?"

"Stop beating yourself up," Ramona said. "That definitely wasn't the case." She'd answered with less tact than Madeline might've hoped for, but that was Ramona. She wasn't highly empathetic or patient. She was merely efficient, with a cool, detached air that was probably necessary to her emotional well-being, considering the gruesome nature of her work. "Judging by the temperature of the body, he's been dead for hours. At least eight."

Madeline took Helen's hands while Ramona made the notations on her clipboard. "Are you going to be okay?" she murmured.

"Why'd he lock the door?" she asked again.

Madeline just shook her head.

"He never did, you know," Helen said again. "Not when he was home."

Pontiff rose to his feet. "How'd you get in?"

"I finally located the key he gave me a long time ago, in case he ever lost his. He'd lock up when I came over to take him places so the deadbeats around here wouldn't steal his beer. That's all he had. A few bottles of beer." She dissolved into tears, and her daughter put an arm around her, crooning, "It'll be okay, Mama. It'll be okay."

"I can't believe he's gone," she moaned.

Ramona's pen scratched on the sketch she was creating to show Bubba's head wound. "This much weight would kill anyone."

"I told him that." Helen nodded, still sniffling. "I told him he had to get a couple hundred pounds off. But he wouldn't listen to me. I said, 'Bubba, that weight's gonna kill you someday.'"

"And it did," Ramona said. "You want to have the funeral here in town, Helen? At Cutshall's?"

Helen nodded again. "Of course."

"I'll give them a call so they can pick up the body," she told Pontiff.

Madeline heard Ramona request a hearse and tried to distract Helen. "I'll write a nice obituary for the paper, okay?" she said. "If there's anything in particular you'd like me to say, you just let me know."

Helen pulled away long enough to wipe her eyes. "I—I'm not much of a writer. But he was a good brother. Say that he was a good brother."

"I'll do that," Madeline promised.

"You sure we shouldn't do an autopsy?" Toby asked Ramona as she hung up.

"I don't see any reason to go to the added trouble or expense," she said. "Do you?"

When he seemed uncertain, she went on, "At his weight, he either died of a heart attack, or that bump on his head when he fell. Nothing mysterious about that."

Toby turned to Helen. "What do you think, Helen? You want to hold off on the funeral for a few days so we can drive the body over to the hospital in Corinth and have a pathologist take a look?"

Helen pulled a fresh tissue out of her purse. "What good would that do?"

"It might give you some peace of mind to know the exact cause of death," he said.

But Helen hid her face again and spoke through her hands. "There's no need. It won't bring him back. It was his heart. It finally gave out on him, just like I told him it would."

19

Madeline stayed with Helen until Cutshall's had removed the body, even though she had a glass company coming out to repair her window and a lot to do at the office. Thanks to the revelations of the past week, she'd had trouble concentrating and had fallen behind in her work. Now that Hunter was here, the situation was getting worse. To make sure it didn't become a problem, she'd hired Bea Davis just this morning to help her. Bea used to write for a bigger paper—before she and her husband moved to Stillwater and started a dog grooming business—and was going to do a short piece on Brittany Wiseman's debut in the school play, as well as an article on teenagers and alcoholism, in response to the Rachel Simmons drowning. Bea had also asked Madeline if she could do a story on Hunter. Everyone was "so curious" about him, she said. Madeline had refused at first, then relented because she felt she needed to toss the citizens of Stillwater some kind of bone to compensate for her preoccupation.

Besides those stories, Madeline was planning a follow-up on the panties that had been found in the Cadillac so she could thank the people who'd come by to view the pictures and mention the reward again. She thought she might add something about how DNA was helping to solve so many old cases these days. And now, of course, she had Bubba's obituary to write, which she'd print with his viewing and funeral information.

"What are we going to do with this trailer? And all his stuff?" Helen asked, obviously overwhelmed at the prospect of what lay ahead.

"Just take it one day at a time." Madeline stood beside her at the door as Toby, Ramona and Norm followed the hearse out of the park. Helen and her daughter were supposed to head over to Cutshall's to make the funeral arrangements. They walked to their car, but Helen suddenly turned back.

"Wait. What about Sarge?"

"Sarge?" Madeline asked.

"His cat. Someone's got to take care of the cat."

Madeline hadn't realized Bubba had a cat, but now that Helen mentioned it she could identify one of the smells that had nearly overpowered her inside. "Of course."

"He must be sleeping in the back room."

"I'll get him." Helen's daughter slipped past Madeline, but when she came back, she was carrying a small aquarium instead of a cat. "Sarge isn't in there. But I should bring Uncle Bubba's tarantula, shouldn't I, Mama?"

Helen nearly twisted an ankle as she scrambled to put some distance between herself and the spider. "No! Get that thing away from me. It's not coming in my car!"

Madeline wasn't any more thrilled with spiders than Helen was, especially big, hairy, poisonous ones, but they couldn't leave it in the empty trailer. There was no telling when Helen would get around to sorting through Bubba's belongings. It could take a week, maybe two, and Madeline had no idea when the spider had last been fed, what it needed to eat or when it should eat again.

Her own phobia precluded really looking at it, but she reached for the container. "Here, give it to me. I'll see if one of the neighbors might be willing to adopt it. And I'll search for the cat at the same time. What's his name again?"

"Sarge," the daughter informed her. "He's big and white and fluffy."

"Got it." Madeline tried not to think about the eight-legged creature behind the glass that was now pressed against her arm. "Okay. You two go ahead. They're waiting for you at Cutshall's."

Helen was still eyeing the spider, keeping a safe distance, but Madeline noted the sincerity and relief in her thank-you and was glad she'd offered to help.

"It's no trouble," she said. "It'll give me a chance to get some statements from the neighbors that we can include in the obituary."

"That would be nice," Helen said, eagerly reaching for the door handle to her car as if she couldn't escape fast enough. "These people were his only friends, you know."

Madeline adjusted the aquarium so she could wave. Then, when Helen turned out of the park and her tail-lights disappeared, she held the tarantula as far away from her as she could and tried to decide which neighbor might be most receptive to an arachnid adoption.

That was when a flicker of movement told her Ray was watching from his window. He was probably wondering what all the fuss was about, she realized, and walked over, careful not to jiggle the aquarium.

"Here, give it to me," she muttered sarcastically, but she felt so sorry for Helen she couldn't really begrudge doing her such a small favor.

As she approached Ray's trailer, she expected him to come to the door. She knew he'd seen her. But he didn't.

Finally, she knocked—nearly dropping the glass container in the process. "Ray?"

When he appeared, he looked rumpled and unshaven. But she knew he typically stayed out late and had a drinking problem.

"Hey, Maddy." He peered at her through bloodshot eyes, smiling as congenially as ever. "How are you?"

"Fine, I guess." She once again adjusted the awkward aquarium.

His bushy eyebrows, brown tinged with gray, were far too long. They drew together as he studied the object she held. "What you got there?"

"Bubba's spider."

"Is Bubba okay?" he asked. "I saw the cop cars."

He must've missed the hearse. "I'm sorry to tell you this, Ray. I know you and Bubba were friends, but…" A lump suddenly rose in Madeline's throat. She'd gotten through the whole morning without crying. And now that the pressure was off… "Bubba's dead," she managed to say.

His jaw dropped, and he rubbed his whiskers for several seconds before responding. "That's terrible. What happened?"

"Heart attack, I think."

"He was far too heavy," he said. "Wasn't healthy."

She nodded, blinking back tears. Granted, this latest tragedy didn't affect her as personally as the other events of the past few weeks. But she'd liked Bubba, had seen him almost every week at church. He was jovial and kind and quick to call her with a hot lead. He even fancied himself a journalist of sorts and had written a few pieces for the paper—*had* fancied himself a journalist. It was so hard to think of him in the past tense. He wasn't the best writer, he didn't have much of an education. But he had a lot of enthusiasm, and he'd been part of the fabric of this town.

And now he was gone.

"His sister's frightened of spiders—" she couldn't completely quell the shudder that went through her as her eyes flicked involuntarily toward the tarantula "—and she's looking for a good home for his…pet."

Ray stared at her. "You want *me* to take Terrence Trent?"

"Is that his name?"

"Yeah. Bubba and I were best friends, you know. But I'm not really a pet sort of guy."

"I'm not sure, but I think tarantulas are pretty easy."

"Well…" His hand rasped over his whiskers again. "I guess I could give it a try."

Relief swept through Madeline as he took the aquarium from her. "I can't thank you enough."

He smiled. "It's the least I can do."

She drew a deep breath. Now her first mission had been accomplished, and she needed to find that darn cat…. "You haven't seen Sarge, have you?"

"Isn't he over there?"

"No."

"Seems like he's been around. I'm sure he'll turn up. I'll keep an eye out for him, okay?"

"Will you call me when you find him?"

"Of course." He hesitated. "You know, you don't look too well. Would you like to come in and sit down? Maybe have a cup of coffee?"

Madeline glanced at the spider again. "As long as you keep that thing across the room," she muttered.

"Hey, come on. Terrence Trent is as harmless as I am."

"He gives me the creeps. But I'll come in rather than force you to stand there with your door open in this cold. I was hoping you could tell me a little more about Bubba, anyway. I'll be writing his obituary, and you knew him better than I did."

"Sure, I'd be happy to. Bubba was a great guy." He stood back and held the door for her. "Get in here, out of the cold."

His smile widened until it showed the tobacco stains on his teeth. And his trailer smelled almost as bad as Bubba's. But Madeline wasn't planning on staying long.

"What do you like in your coffee?" he asked.

There were plates with moldy food cluttering the counters, dishes heaped in the sink and a puddle of something sticky fanning out from under the fridge. "No coffee for me, thanks. The way I'm feeling right now, caffeine would make me too jittery."

"Tea, then?"

"Actually, I don't need anything. I'm fine." She paused in front of a picture of Rose Lee that was hanging in a cheap frame on the wall. Hunter's questions about her father's relationship with the girl made her stomach ache with anxiety. Her father simply wasn't capable of the behavior Hunter was willing to attribute to him. She prayed he'd soon learn that for himself.

"Do you still miss her?" she asked, suddenly very conscious of how much Ray must've suffered over his only daughter's death. Maybe he hadn't always been the best father, but he and Rose Lee had been closer than most parents and children. The last time Madeline had seen her, Rose Lee had been in the passenger seat of Ray's pickup.

"You bet I do."

Madeline started as he reached over her shoulder to straighten the picture. She hadn't realized he was so close.

"Nothing's been the same without her," he said.

"It wasn't me," Mike said.

"You expect me to take your word for it? You threatened Madeline right in front of me, remember?" Hunter leaned against the bumper of Madeline's car. He knew Mike's mother was watching them from the house. She'd answered the door, then reluctantly called her son out of his bedroom. And because Hunter could sense her weary concern, he'd pulled Mike away, out of earshot. Hunter didn't want to send Mike's parents into a fresh panic, assuming that Mike was in trouble again. Not if Mike didn't have any injuries consistent with the blood found in Madeline's house.

"I'm not going back to prison," he said stubbornly.

"Where were you last night?"

"Here. My parents will kick me out if I leave the house after dark. Ask them. They're terrified you're going to blame Barker's death on me, that the past'll come back to bite us again."

"I'm not here to blame anyone," Hunter said. "I'm only interested in the truth."

Mike pulled out a pack of cigarettes and lit one up. "No one's interested in the truth," he countered. "Only their own version."

Ice covered a shallow puddle at Hunter's feet. He broke the surface of it with his foot as he spoke. "What's *your* version?"

Mike took a long drag, letting the smoke curl slowly into the air. "You wouldn't believe me, even if I told you. My own parents don't believe me."

"Try me."

Squinting toward the large piles of manure, now covered with black plastic, that would fertilize his parents' fields once spring arrived, Mike took another drag on his cigarette. "Barker wasn't the saint everyone thought he was."

Hunter kept his expression passive. "Because he turned you in for smoking pot?"

"No, because he was having an affair."

"Who with?"

"I don't know. But I heard them. In his office. And it wasn't Irene. She was canning peaches for the poor that day at Velma Lowe's. I know because my mom was there, too."

"What'd you hear? Voices?"

"Moaning."

Rose Lee and Katie had both "helped" Barker at the church. But they would've been dead at this point. Was it Grace Mike had heard? "How do you know he wasn't groaning with…indigestion, for instance?"

Mike mimicked the panting and release that often accompanied sex, then scowled at him. "If you heard *that* behind my office door, would you think I had indigestion?" he said belligerently. "I knew what was going on, even back then."

"Maybe he was alone, caught up in a particularly arousing daydream."

"No." He shook his head resolutely. "I heard a female voice, too, begging him to stop." Mike flicked his ashes onto the frozen earth. "I think they were playing some kind of domination game."

There wasn't any more ice to break so Hunter crossed his legs in front of him and looked up. "Do you know who the woman was?"

"I already told you, no." He left the cigarette dangling in his mouth so that it bobbed as he spoke. "I tried to go around to the window, to climb up that tree outside his office. I didn't want to miss what was going on in there. My hormones were pumping just hearing it. And I knew it'd be the sweetest revenge I could find—to catch the reverend doing something even worse than I'd done."

Out of the corner of his eye, Hunter saw a curtain move in one of the windows at the house. It was obviously Mrs. Metzger. She didn't like that he was talking to Mike, but that wasn't going to stop him. Especially now. "So that's why you were at the church during the middle of the day? You were angling for revenge?"

"I was supposed to scrub down the bathroom as part of my penance for smoking pot, something suggested by my dear parents," he added bitterly. "Barker wasn't expecting me for another two hours. But I'd been invited to a friend's house. He had a bag of weed—" he grinned, clearly unrepentant "—and I wanted to get the work done first. So I dropped by early. I saw the reverend's car in the lot, but the church was locked up and I was afraid to knock in case he was praying. I didn't need to piss him off any more, you know? He was a harsh old bastard."

"So how'd you get in?"

"The window in the bathroom was broken and didn't close all the way. I wrenched it open and crawled through. Then I went to see if I could find the reverend. If he was cleaning or writing a sermon or on the phone, I figured I'd tell him I knocked but he didn't hear me. If he was praying, I'd slip back out."

"But then you noticed the moaning."

"Damn right." He flicked his ashes again.

"Did you see anything when you climbed the tree?"

"Someone was on their hands and knees behind the desk. All I could see was a bare thigh. But he was naked and riding whoever it was."

"You're sure it was a woman?"

He considered Hunter for a moment. "I know a woman's thigh when I see one."

"Is that all you remember?" Hunter asked.

"What are you looking for?"

"Another vehicle in the area? An article of clothing that only one person in town ever wore? A driver's license?" he added jokingly.

Mike didn't laugh. He finished his cigarette and ground it out with his foot. "There was one more thing."

Hunter felt his muscles tense at Mike's somber tone. "What's that?"

"The person on bottom was wearing a collar."

Hunter felt the hair on his arms prickle. "How do you know?"

"Barker had hold of the chain, was jerking back on it."

"What happened then?"

Mike paused, studied him for a moment. "You don't seem surprised."

"I didn't know the Reverend Barker."

Mike felt for the pack of cigarettes in his front pocket and pulled out a second one. "He spotted me almost as soon as my head rose above the windowsill. Our eyes met and I fell out of that damn tree. Nearly broke my neck in the process, but I got up and ran like hell."

"Did he catch you?"

"Didn't need to." He lit up again. "He knew it was me."

"Did you tell anyone what you saw?"

"Hell, no."

The wind ruffled Hunter's hair, which flopped into his eyes. He shoved it out. "Why not?"

"They'd say I was making it up because he got me in trouble the week before. And I couldn't identify the woman. Didn't have any proof. I wasn't stupid enough to think I could say he was an adulterer without pointing at someone who might agree. Folks around here would've hung me for less."

"Did you tell your parents?"

His jaw clenched. "Yes."

"And what did they say?"

Mike let the smoke from his cigarette come out his nose. "My dad gave me a beating the likes of which I've never received before or since."

"And now what do they say?"

"I figure the cops finding that stuff in the Cadillac must have them wondering if I was telling the truth all along, but they say it doesn't matter. That was then. This is now. My dad just wants me to straighten out my life."

Hunter shoved the hair out of his eyes again. "Are you going to be able to do that?"

"Are you going to let me?" he countered belligerently.

"That depends," Hunter replied.

"On what?"

"Roll up your sleeves and let me take a look at your hands."

"What?" He spoke with the cigarette still in his mouth.

"You heard me."

His eyes narrowed. "And if I won't?"

"You don't want to know," Hunter said.

Tossing his second cigarette away, Mike unbuttoned his sleeves, which he pushed back to reveal well-muscled forearms. There were plenty of snake and eagle tattoos. Ink covered almost every inch of skin. But there wasn't so much as a recent scratch.

"Tell your parents you have nothing to fear from me," Hunter said and started toward the driver's side of his car.

"Damn! You do believe me, don't you?" Mike said incredulously.

When Hunter didn't answer, Mike followed him and caught his door before he could shut it. "You believe I'm telling the truth about the reverend."

Oh, yes, Hunter believed him. But that was no woman Barker had in his office. A woman was too much of a risk. If Hunter had his bet, it was a girl. Probably Grace.

But he wasn't happy to learn that his instincts had been right.

"He was worse than an adulterer," he said. Then he pulled the door out of Mike's grasp, closed it and drove away.

Ray could feel the Viagra and ecstasy he'd taken juicing him up like a rechargeable battery, and he felt invincible. He was rock-hard, if Madeline cared to look. It was titillating to think she might. For a man of fifty-five, he was impressive, he told himself. And if she wanted him even bigger, he had an extender.

He had anything she could want.

But her eyes never wandered south. She was too absorbed in taking notes for that obituary she planned to write for Bubba. And weeping.

How dare she! It was her fault Bubba was dead. If she could just leave the past alone instead of digging, digging, always digging. And now she'd brought that private detective to town, that guy who was causing so much trouble, asking too many questions about Rose Lee. Ray had heard something about it last night, when he'd stopped by the bar for a few drinks while building up the nerve to visit Madeline's house.

That bastard detective had better keep his mouth shut about Rose Lee....

"I guess that's it." Madeline closed her notebook. "Thanks for your help."

"It's the least I can do." He adjusted his sleeve to make sure it hid the Band-Aid covering the gash on his arm. "I'm shocked by what happened. But you seem... extra distraught."

"I know. I'm not handling this very well. Bubba and I weren't even close, but—" she sniffed "—it seems like I'm taking everything harder than I ordinarily would."

"You've been under a lot of stress," he said sympathetically.

She stood and moved toward the door, avoiding the table where he'd put the tarantula, and he had the sudden impulse to stop her. He could do it. If she went missing, there'd be no one to pay the investigator, so he'd have to go home, right? Of course, the police would search for Madeline, but he'd hide her body so well no one would ever find it.

Maybe they'd blame the Montgomerys for Madeline's disappearance, too.

Ray wanted to laugh at the thought. But killing wasn't as easy as he'd expected. Last night, he and Bubba had gotten into a scuffle, during which Ray had bruised his leg on the corner of the coffee table. Then the cat, frightened by the violence, had pounced and scratched him, and he'd thrown it against the wall. If Bubba hadn't tripped when he saw that, if he'd reached the phone he'd been hoping to grab, Ray didn't know how it would've ended. Even after the big man fell and lay unconscious, and Ray had pressed that pillow over his nose and mouth, it seemed to take him forever to die.

Bubba Turk had a stronger heart than everyone believed, that was for damn sure.

But Ray had won.

Then he'd burned the pillow out back in the woods and stood in his shower for twenty minutes at least, whimpering and crying as he washed off the blood. He'd been terrified that someone had heard the ruckus and called the cops, so terrified that he hadn't returned to bury the cat he'd dumped in the shed. And now it was too late. They'd already found Bubba. He didn't want to go back there. He wanted to stay as far away as possible.

So far, no cops had knocked on his door to take him into police custody. So far no one seemed to have seen or heard anything. And so far, in the wake of Bubba's death, no one acted too concerned about the darn cat. He wanted to keep it that way.

To celebrate his victory—and take the edge off his fear—Ray had popped some ecstasy and gone on a porno binge. The image he found the most erotic, a woman who looked a great deal like Madeline being raped by three men, was still on his computer in the other room. It'd shock her to see it, he knew, make her gasp in horror.

Longing to watch the blood drain from her face as recognition dawned, he blocked the door. He needed something more visceral than he'd had in the past twenty-eight years. Pornography was no longer as satisfying as it had been only a week ago.

He imagined tying her up and letting Bubba's tarantula crawl over her bare body as he tightened the garrote—and found it strangely compelling that he'd violate Barker's daughter the way Barker had violated his. To Barker, Rose Lee had been expendable. But not Madeline. Madeline was too good.

Well, not anymore.

When he didn't move, Madeline frowned in confusion. "Excuse me."

He smiled. "Don't go yet. I have something to show you."

She hiked her purse up higher. "What's that?"

"It's a surprise." He pointed over her head, down the hall. "Check out what's in that first bedroom."

A hint of suspicion entered her lovely green eyes. She could tell something wasn't quite right with him. But years of knowing him, of seeing him in church and around town and experiencing no fear—that, and her innate friendliness—were working against her.

Still, she was hesitant. "It's getting late," she said, "and I've got to get back to the office. I'm meeting someone there."

He tried to act casual. "Your private investigator?"

"Yes."

"How's that going? Is he finding anything new?"

"Not yet." She waited for him to move out of her way, but he couldn't let her go. He was sure no one had seen her walk into his place. Ivy, the neighbor on his left, was gone. And he'd watched Madeline for a long time, seen Helen and her horse-faced daughter drive away first, leaving her alone.

"That's too bad," he said. "Your father and I didn't end on the best of terms, as you know, but in some ways, no one could speak to my inner self like he could." Ray envisioned the tarantula crawling between Madeline's bare breasts. She wasn't a little girl anymore. She'd be harder to handle. But she was still Barker's child. He found that intensely erotic.

"I appreciate your saying so," she said, tearing up again. "He was a good preacher, wasn't he?"

"The best. He was good at a lot of other things, too. That's what I want to show you," he added. "Something your father gave me."

This caught her attention. He saw her pause, glance over her shoulder toward the hall.

"I got it out last night so it's kind of a coincidence

that you're here. It reveals the, uh, real Lee Barker like nothing else."

She was puzzled now. And too curious to insist on leaving.

Turning, she started toward the room where she'd find the sex toys he'd already used. He wanted her so badly he almost lunged at her right there and forced her to the floor.

But it'd be better to wait, he promised himself. More shocking. More electrifying. And more private, as he'd taped thick black paper over the window in that room.

She was nearly at the door. When he was finished with her, he'd have to figure out how to dispose of her body. But night would come and there'd be plenty of time for that. Maybe he'd even keep her alive for a while as a sex slave. He had the credit card and cash he'd taken from Bubba's pockets. Surprisingly, the cash amounted to more than he'd expected Bubba to have—he must've just cashed his welfare check. If he wanted, he could rent a cabin in the Tennessee mountains online, using Bubba's credit card, then bind and gag Madeline and take her there. He'd strip her down and tie her to the bedposts, where she'd be ready for him at all times.

The thrill of arousal rushed through him as he imagined slipping the garrote around Madeline's neck. He'd have to act quickly to subdue her before she could scream. But then her cell phone rang, and she opened it before he could stop her.

"Hello?… Hunter! Where've you been?…Ray Harper's… Oh, they're coming to repair the window this afternoon. Have you heard about Bubba?"

Ray clenched his hands at his sides. He should've

sprung the trap early. Now that she'd mentioned his name, there was nothing he could do.

Catching her arm, he stopped her just before she could turn the corner and see everything. What shitty luck. He'd been so...damn...close.

She looked at him expectantly.

"Let me clean up the room a bit," he whispered, acting slightly embarrassed as he edged past her.

She remained where she was, and he listened to her tell her P.I. about Bubba while he shut down the computer and shoved the dildo, the lotion, the Chinese herbs, the garrote and the bikini underwear he sometimes wore under the bed. The place smelled strongly of sex and sweat, so he sprayed some of the cheap cologne he kept on the dresser.

"Ray?"

He froze. She'd hung up already. "Yes?"

"Are you ready for me?"

He was more than ready. Thanks to the Viagra, he'd had an erection for nearly three hours and felt like he could perform for another three. His revenge on her and her father would be delayed—but it would come.

He took a last sweeping glance around, satisfied that he hadn't left out anything that could give him away. Maybe he'd make Madeline service him for months, years. Until he tired of her. Wouldn't *that* make Barker roll over in his grave?

"It's not exactly clean," he said with enough uncertainty to sound sincere. "But...come in."

She stepped over the threshold. For a few seconds, her beauty held him spellbound. He couldn't wait to touch her. That it wouldn't be today made his whole body throb and ache in disappointment.

"What is it?" she asked, her eyes circling the room.

"This." He retrieved a picture from the dresser and brought it over to her. It was a photograph of Rose Lee standing next to Barker, wearing her Sunday best.

"How nice," she said, her expression pained as though she missed him terribly.

Ray smiled. She had no idea that Barker had his hand up the back of Rose's dress even as he smiled so benignly for the camera.

"Your father sure loved her," he said as if they were sharing a deep, touching moment. But what he really meant was that her father loved his own power more than anything else.

Even Madeline.

20

Madeline called Hunter back as soon as she left Ray's trailer. She'd told him about Bubba, but she'd felt awkward standing in Ray's hall, waiting for some mysterious surprise, and had wanted to get out of there. Ray didn't seem himself. He watched her a little too closely. Or maybe he'd just had a bad night. She'd never seen anyone with eyes as bloodshot as his.

"I'm in the car, so I can talk now," she said.

"How are you?" he asked.

She could tell by his tone that it was more than the typical formality. He really wanted to know. "Shaken," she told him. So much had happened; so much had been lost. First Rachel Simmons. Then learning that evil had touched Grace when she was little more than a child. All of that was heartbreaking enough. Add Mike's return, the crude message on her answering machine, the break-in last night, Bubba's death—and she was overwhelmed. Even Kirk's leaving town upset her. It wasn't that she wanted them to be together romantically. She just wanted everything to be okay.

And yet, suddenly, even the things that used to be okay weren't.

"I'm sorry about your friend," he said.

She swallowed around the tears that rose in her throat, the tears she'd been fighting all morning. "Please don't show me any sympathy right now."

"Why not?"

"Because it'll make me cry."

"Poor Maddy," he murmured. "What can I do to make it better?"

She tried not to think of what they'd done behind the tree. But nothing had made her feel better than those few minutes—not in a long, long time. "Tell me something good."

"It wasn't Clay who broke in last night."

"How do you know?" she asked, sitting up straighter.

"I called Pontiff. He said there were no cuts anywhere on Clay's upper body."

"I *knew* it wasn't him, but—" she smiled tearily, feeling vindicated "—I'm glad Pontiff and Radcliffe know, too."

"Problem is…"

She automatically tensed. "What?"

"It wasn't Mike Metzger, either, Maddy."

Slowing for a stop sign, she sat there without giving the car any gas. "You're sure?"

"I'm sure."

She rubbed her tired eyes. Who else could it be? And why would someone else want her father's books and sermons and cuff links?

There were always more questions than answers.

"What's it like in California this time of year?" she asked simply because it had nothing to do with what she was experiencing, and because she needed to remind herself that Hunter belonged in a place that was miles away.

"Nice."

"How nice?"

"Meet me at Two Sisters, and I'll tell you. Have you had any lunch?"

It was almost three o'clock, but she hadn't even had breakfast. "No. My day got crazy." She thought of the close confines of Bubba's trailer, the terrible smell. "But an empty stomach turned out to be a good thing today."

"I can imagine. I'll see you there, okay?"

"Actually, I have to meet the window company first. Do you have something you can do for an hour?"

"I'd like to swing by the bar, ask if anyone came in acting unusual last night. I've called two area hospitals, but I'd like to try a few more to see if anyone showed up at the emergency room with a deep cut on his hands or arm."

"Sounds good." Until she saw him again, she needed something to hang on to, a positive image. "Meanwhile, what's the best thing you can think of?" she asked.

His voice grew deeper, rougher, sexier. "Are you sure you want me to answer that question?"

"What do you mean?"

"The best thing I can think of is you."

Lunch didn't turn out to be as relaxing as Madeline had hoped. Hunter seemed rather pensive, even guarded, and he didn't flirt with her like he had on the phone. He sat on the opposite side of the booth and didn't even touch her hand when he set their menus on the edge of the table so the waitress would know they were ready to order.

"Are you going to tell me where you've been all day?" she asked after the waitress had gone.

"Out and about, doing interviews, checking details."

She considered his answer. "Are you being purposely vague?"

He wiped the condensation from his glass. "Maybe. How'd it go with the glass company?"

"Fine. It's repaired."

"Good."

"So, where were you when I got up this morning?"

"We were going to talk about California, remember?" he said.

Folding her arms, she sat back. "But you've barely said a word since we arrived—about the case *or* California."

"Somehow my home doesn't seem like a much better subject," he muttered.

"Because…"

"Because that's real life, Maddy," he said intently.

"And this is…what, Hunter? Make-believe?"

"Maybe. In any event, it's a…short detour."

"Right."

"I'm just here to do my job," he reiterated.

"What do you want me to say?" she asked in a quiet voice. "That yesterday meant nothing to me? That I would've done the same with any other man?"

His forehead rumpled in consternation. "No, I don't want to hear that, even if it's true."

"It's not true."

"What happened was probably just the result of all the upset and stress and—"

"No. It wasn't that, either."

His eyes filled with some unnamed emotion, and she

lowered her voice. "Maybe it was the stress that caused me to act on what I felt. But I wanted *you*, okay? I think I wanted you from the first moment I saw you."

"Maddy, stop. You know what that does to me?"

"I do. It makes you want to run."

"No. It makes me want to drag you home and up to your bedroom. You don't understand what you're asking for by getting involved with me. You don't need any more complications in your life. And neither do I."

She didn't speak for several long seconds. "Okay."

"Okay, what?"

"I get it."

"Then explain it to me!"

"You prefer not to form any emotional attachments to me or this place or anything else."

"Yes." He seemed relieved. "I can't, okay? I have to go home. I'm here for a reason, and I need to stay focused on it."

"Fine. You've put me on notice. What happened yesterday won't happen again. Satisfied?"

She could tell that he wasn't, but she went on anyway. Because she knew he was right. What did they have in common? What did they expect would happen if they continued to act on the desire they felt?

"So, *Mr. Solozano,* give me an update. Where have you been all day?"

"Out and about," he said.

"You mentioned that already."

"Just trust me."

"Trust would violate our no-emotion rule. Give me the hard facts."

His scowl darkened. "Maddy, stop. You're…"

"What?"

"You're driving me crazy."

She refused to soften that easily. "If I hired someone else, I'd get a report."

"You've been through enough for one day. You don't need to hear what I have to say. Not right now."

"Someone else wouldn't care what I've been through, so neither should you."

"But I do care, damn it!" The people in the next booth turned to stare, and he lowered his voice. "And I don't have any proof."

Visions of yesterday flew through her head. His eagerness to touch her. His lips on her neck. His arms bearing her weight.

Shutting her eyes, she struggled to forget. "Tell me what it is."

The ice in his glass clinked as he took a sip of water. Madeline had the impression that he was stalling, so she cleared her throat. "I'm waiting."

"I don't think it was Clay who killed your father."

She didn't respond immediately. She was so distracted by desire and by fear, it took her a moment to absorb those words—and to realize that this was actually good news. Maybe.

"Why?" she asked tentatively. "Because he was so young?"

"No. He was and still is the most physically capable—the biggest, the strongest, the oldest," he said gruffly, giving it to her straight and hard now as she'd demanded. "And statistically most murders are committed by men."

"I thought this was where you told me why Clay *didn't* do it," she said.

"It is."

"So why do you think it wasn't him?"

His gaze fell to her lips, and she could tell he was feeling the same awareness that was humming through her. It was there, just beneath the surface, every time they were together. Their encounter yesterday only made it more intense.

"We were talking about Clay," she reminded him, trying to squelch the fluttering in her stomach.

He swallowed. "Clay isn't the type to depend on his family to protect him with their silence," he went on. "I can't see him killing your father, then orchestrating a big cover-up on his own behalf. He'd run first, separate himself from his family as quickly as possible, so that whatever happened to him wouldn't hurt them, too."

She licked her lips, drawing his eyes back to her mouth. "So if it's not Clay, who is it?"

"Someone he'd protect. Someone he loves."

Hunter already understood Clay better than almost anyone in Stillwater, which frightened Madeline, because she could so easily grasp his logic. For the first time, she had reason to believe that someone with the right kind of knowledge was taking an unbiased look at what had gone on twenty years ago.

But Hunter was still pointing a finger at her family.

"Irene knows what happened, and she's starting to crack."

Suddenly the fear Madeline was feeling overtook the desire. "How do you know?"

"I talked to her."

"You talked to my mother?"

"You haven't," he retorted.

She stared into her lap. "I'm not sure what to say to her."

"You should return her calls. She's worried about you."

"She shouldn't be. Last night's break-in was no big deal. I've been thinking about it and I figure it was probably a prank, meant to send our investigation off-track, you know? No one's particularly happy that I brought you here, even my aunt, and I thought *she'd* be thrilled."

"I don't believe it was a prank," he said.

"It could've been," she persisted.

He shook his head. "Irene didn't seem to think so, either."

"You're citing my stepmother as a credible source? You think she's in league with Grace and Clay!"

"They're all in on it. I just don't know which one actually did it."

Their waitress brought their salads, but Madeline couldn't eat. "So how do we find out?" she asked at length.

He stretched his arm casually across the back of the booth. "Let's leave it for now, okay?"

"Until…"

"Until I have some sort of proof. Before that, what I think doesn't really mean anything."

But it *did* mean something. He seemed so damn sure of everything. "Molly was only eleven years old at the time. Grace was thirteen. Surely you don't think it was one of them!"

He gave a little shrug. "I've heard of more unbelievable things."

She set her fork on the table and pushed her plate away.

"Eat," he said.

"No."

"You need a good meal."

"Would you stop? You don't give a damn about me, remember? All you care about is in California!"

He said nothing.

"Maybe you should just go back."

She felt his hand touch hers, felt him tuck her fingers into the warmth of his palm. "Not until I know you're safe."

Don't care. Do care. Feel. Don't feel. It's the Montgomerys. It's not the Montgomerys. Grace was molested. Grace wasn't molested. Madeline couldn't seem to get her emotional bearings.

"We'll figure it out," he said.

She stared at their joined hands. "I knew them at that age," she whispered. "They couldn't have done it. They were so…gentle and sweet."

"You're probably right," he agreed.

Pulling away, she took a deep breath. "If Clay had killed him, he would've run and didn't, so that only leaves my mother."

When he didn't speak, she knew he thought it was Irene. *She's beginning to crack…* What did that mean? Would her stepmother go to jail? Would Clay and Grace and Molly join her?

It was *unthinkable.* Especially because…

"And you suspect she did it because my father was molesting Grace," she added quietly.

He looked as if he'd reach out to her again, but he didn't. "I'm sorry."

Too numb to even cry, Madeline averted her face as the waitress came to collect their salad plates.

"How was it?" she heard the woman ask Hunter.

"Fine," he responded. When she was gone, he leaned forward. "Knowing Irene, and Clay, it'd have to be a strong motive. And what could be stronger?"

"*If* that was happening—and that's a very big *if*—there were other options besides cold-blooded murder."

"Maybe it wasn't planned, Maddy. This is an emotional issue, an explosive issue. Maybe there was an argument and it spiraled out of control."

Was it possible? Madeline had been at a friend's house that night. She had no idea what'd gone on at home. But Jed Fowler had been there. If there'd been a fight, he would've heard it. And there was another problem with the accident theory.

"If it was an accident, why didn't she come forward?"

Hunter leaned even closer. "Maybe they kept it quiet for your sake."

"*My* sake?"

"You'd already lost your mother, Maddy. Learning that your father was...what we think he might have been would be worse than losing him to death. Have you thought of that?"

"No." She hadn't. She refused to. "My father was a preacher, not a predator. Irene didn't kill him because she wouldn't have had any reason to!"

The pity in his eyes made the pain worse. She'd been hoping he'd argue with her, give her a reason to fight for what she so desperately needed to believe. But he didn't.

The bell jingled over the door. When Hunter's eyes

went to the entrance and stayed focused there, Madeline turned to see what he was staring at.

Clay was crossing the restaurant, coming toward them. Her stepbrother nodded a greeting to her, then sat down in the booth beside her and slid a piece of paper toward Hunter.

"What's this?" Hunter asked, obviously startled that Clay was addressing him instead of her.

"Someone put this in my mailbox last night."

"Someone?"

"Read it."

"'Stop her or I will,'" he said, then glanced up.

"I think this is talking about Madeline." Clay slumped back against the seat, large and powerful and forever watchful.

Was it true, what Hunter believed? Madeline wondered. Was Clay protecting Irene? Had he been lying to her all these years, pretending to love her and to commiserate with her when he knew all along that he'd buried her father with his own shovel?

Madeline didn't have those answers but she agreed that this note probably referred to her. She reached out to take the slip of paper.

"You have no idea who this came from?" Hunter asked Clay.

"I wouldn't be here if I did," her stepbrother said pointedly. "I wouldn't need to be—because they'd no longer be capable of hurting her."

"Why are you sharing this with me?" Hunter rested both elbows on the table and studied Clay intently.

"I have a family now." Clay's gaze softened as it landed on her, and Madeline's heart twisted. *God, how*

I love my big brother. Please, let Hunter be wrong. "I need you to help me keep her safe."

"What about the police? Have you gone to them?"

He gave Hunter a disbelieving look. "Why would I go to *them?*" Standing, he bent swiftly and kissed Madeline's temple, but she shrank away from him.

His eyes—shockingly blue and far older than his years—met hers, showing hurt and surprise, but she glanced down. She didn't know who to trust anymore.

Madeline couldn't sleep—even though Hunter was spending the night in the room beside her own. Her arms and legs felt heavy, as did her heart, but her mind was overrun with chaos. Accusations that had proven empty. Sympathetic excuses for Irene, Clay, Grace—even her father. Snatches of memory that supported one view or another. Images of where her father might be buried at the farm. A churning fear that Hunter was completely credible in what he'd surmised so far. Brief flashes of hope that he was wrong...

She couldn't relax and the harder she tried, the more uncomfortable she became. Even Sophie had given up on trying to sleep beside her.

The tension was bringing on a headache. She needed aspirin, but when she sat up to get it, she didn't move right away. There was a picture of her and Grace and Molly on her dresser that caught her attention. It was from way back, when they were girls.

"Grace," she murmured, wishing she could simply talk to her sister, be reassured and go on with her life. But it was too late for that. Staring down her doubts had made them grow. Now she was even beginning to question her father. That suitcase had to come from somewhere. Was it really feasible that some drifter had put in there and sunk the car? Or that Mike had done it? He'd never molested anyone else. And he wasn't the one who'd broken in last night.

With a frustrated groan, she flopped back onto the bed. Even if Grace knew the real story, she'd never tell. She'd stand by Clay. So would Irene and Molly. How could Madeline expect anything else? They were all related by blood. True sisters united with a true brother.

She, on the other hand, had no one. And she'd never felt that more deeply than now. She had no mother, no father, no stepfamily—not anymore.

Burying her head beneath the pillow, she squeezed her eyes shut, willing away the tears that were burning her throat. As terrifying as it was to confront her doubts and fears, to allow herself to question the love, loyalty and honesty of those closest to her, now that she'd started she couldn't seem to stop.

If only her mother had lived. Eliza's presence would've changed everything.

She was driving herself crazy. Kicking off the covers, she got out of bed. She didn't care about the consequences; this was one night she wouldn't spend alone.

Hunter heard the creak in the hall. He'd been lying awake, listening to the night sounds and straining to distinguish any noise that might not belong—a car in the drive or movement downstairs. For hours, everything had been quiet, still, peaceful. Except for the woman in the room next door. Even before Madeline got up, he could sense her restless tossing and had nearly gone to her a hundred times. After what they'd said in the restaurant, he'd been trying to keep his mind where it should be—

on the case. But he couldn't. Just as he couldn't choose the guilty party in what had happened twenty years ago.

Some situations were unfortunate all the way around. Hunter was fairly sure this was one of them. Until a few hours ago, Clay had wanted him to go home, had been determined to eliminate the threat he posed. Yet, for Madeline's sake, he'd appeared at the restaurant and all but asked Hunter to stay. That reversal was just one more indication of how much Madeline's stepbrother cared about her. Clay hadn't admitted the truth; he was still guarding his secrets. But what other choice did he have?

Madeline stood in the open doorway. Hunter could see her womanly shape in the moonlight drifting through the window. He'd left both the door and the draperies open, wanting to be more aware of everything that went on around him.

But he didn't need to be more aware of her. That came without any help.

"You okay?" he asked, even though he knew she had to be feeling lost and alone and was probably seeking comfort. He liked the idea of having her even closer than the next room—as close as she could get.

But she was so emotionally vulnerable right now. And he was so far from being able to offer her a committed relationship. Maybe he could protect her from an intruder—but who was going to protect her from him?

"No," she said. "I don't think I've ever been worse."

Tell her that it'll look better in the morning. Send her back to her own room, his conscience demanded. The picture of Maria he kept on his cell phone was on the nightstand right next to him, reminding him that he had no business wanting Madeline.

But he couldn't say the words. He longed to kiss her, to reassure her that everything would be all right.

He'd be careful, wouldn't let it escalate, he told himself. But he was only wearing boxer briefs. And the memory of yesterday, of how eager they'd been to touch and taste and feel each other—how eager they still were—told him that they wouldn't be able to stop.

He hesitated. But when she took his lack of response as rejection and started to leave, he knew he couldn't let her go.

Reaching over, he put his cell phone in the drawer where he wouldn't be able to see it anymore. "Come here," he told her and as he lifted the covers, she slipped in beside him.

The warmth that suddenly enveloped her felt like a cocoon—a cocoon from which she didn't want to emerge. Especially when Hunter's arms went around her and drew her up against his muscular chest.

"You're freezing," he murmured.

"Not anymore." Every place he touched felt like it was on fire.

"You're going to be fine, Maddy," he whispered. She didn't believe him for a minute. Because it wasn't only her body that was on fire. Her whole world seemed to be burning in one massive conflagration.

"Don't talk about tomorrow," she said.

His hands slid under the fabric of her shirt, massaging her back, then climbed up to her shoulder blades, drawing her closer. "Are you sure you want this?"

She was sure. It was the only thing powerful enough to block the pain. But she didn't say so. She pressed her mouth to his in answer, then parted her lips and licked him in invitation.

With a groan, he rolled her beneath him, pinning her hands above her head as he kissed her deeply, occasionally using his teeth to nip at her bottom lip before meeting her tongue again. Madeline didn't think she'd ever been so thoroughly kissed. The way he used his teeth made her lips tingle and her stomach muscles tighten with anticipation.

"That's good," she said with a sigh. She couldn't wait to tear away the clothing that separated them, to feel him push inside her—filling her, stretching her tight—like he had behind the tree. But he wouldn't let her hurry him.

"Not this time," he murmured. "I want to draw it out, Maddy. Every whimper and moan. Every shudder."

He leaned back and slid her shirt up over her breasts. "Look at you," he whispered. "You're the most beautiful woman I've ever seen."

He didn't immediately touch her. His eyes swept over her, taking her in. Then, lightly, his fingers caressed the skin of her stomach before cupping the fullness of one breast. He held it, studying it for a moment in the silver moonlight, then lowered his head to take it in his mouth.

Madeline gasped as his tongue moved over her. Pleasure pooled hot and low in her belly. Closing her eyes, she buried her face in his neck, luxuriating in the masculine scent of his skin and hair. Then he lifted his head to watch her as he slipped his hand beneath the elastic waistband of her boxers.

She jumped when he touched her, and she saw him smile in satisfaction before he kissed her neck, her ear.

"Tell me you've got birth control," he said into her hair, his voice ragged.

She could hardly talk for what he was doing with his hands. "In my room," she said between panting breaths.

He peeled off the rest of her clothes and gazed at her for a moment. Then he carried her across the hall.

Madeline had never made love four times in one night. But there was an urgency between her and Hunter that hadn't existed between her and Kirk. It was as if they had to take it all in this one night. Just in case there wouldn't be another chance.

Now or never…

"You hungry?" she murmured shortly after one o'clock.

"Hungry for you," he said, sounding half-asleep.

"What?" She laughed. "You're exhausted."

"Give me fifteen minutes."

"Sleep," she said, threading her fingers through his hair, which felt so foreign on her bare shoulder. "We're out of condoms, anyway."

"I'll go to the store."

"It's the middle of the night."

"I don't care."

"You'd have to drive for an hour."

She felt the rasp of his whiskers against her skin as he spoke. "The piggy iggy or whatever isn't open?"

"That's Piggly Wiggly. And the answer is no."

"Then I'll make the drive."

"It might be raining."

"Mmm, you're worth it."

Smiling, she raised herself onto her elbows. "You're insatiable!"

He grinned but didn't open his eyes. "I guess I'm making up for lost time," he muttered sleepily.

"What lost time?" she said. "We made love practically the first day we met!"

"But then we wasted last night and this morning. That was stupid."

Or this was. Madeline wasn't willing to gauge which was worse. Reality would descend soon enough.

She glanced at the clock on her nightstand, dreading the next morning.

"You should call your mom tomorrow," he said.

"I will."

He noticed the lack of commitment in her voice right away. "That sounds more like a maybe."

"It was," she admitted. She already knew that her mother would plead with her to send Hunter back to California. And she couldn't do that. Earlier she hadn't known who to trust.

Now she knew she trusted him.

It felt as if she'd barely closed her eyes when the telephone rang.

Madeline lifted her head from Hunter's shoulder to squint at the clock and realized she hadn't been asleep long. No more than thirty minutes. Who could be calling her at one-fifteen in the morning?

"I'd offer to get it," Hunter muttered, "but I'm sure you don't want me answering your phone this late at night. Especially when I sound so satisfied."

She would've laughed, if not for the unease that had settled in the pit of her stomach. Calls that came in the middle of the night were rarely good news. "Probably not a smart idea," she agreed. "I'll get it." She extricated herself from his body and the blankets that were wrapped around them both. "Hello?"

"Maddy? It's Joe."

She pushed her tousled hair out of her eyes. "Joe who?"

"Your cousin! Remember me?"

Oh. That Joe. She rubbed her face. "What is it? What do you want?"

"I've got a package that belongs to you." His words were thick and slurred. He'd been drinking. But that wasn't surprising. He drank every weekend.

She stiffened, and Hunter immediately understood that something was wrong. He sat up and leaned close, so they could both hear.

"*What* package?" she asked, confused.

"The one I found by the front door of the paper on my way home from Good Times."

She didn't want to wake up for this. "I don't know what you're talking about, Joe. It's late. Call me in the morning."

"Whoa, wait a sec…" There was a long pause, followed by a guttural chuckle.

"What?" she said, now fully awake and so nervous she was jittery.

"I just opened it."

She glanced at Hunter, felt his hand curl more tightly around hers on the phone. "What is it?" she asked.

"You'd better get over here," he replied and hung up.

21

Madeline's hands shook from the adrenaline rushing through her body as she and Hunter dressed. It was nearly two in the morning. She didn't want to see anyone. Especially her cousin, who was as unpredictable as he was uncouth. But something had happened. Joe would not have expected her to show up at his insistence, immediately and without question, unless what he had was good.

And *good* to him was probably not *good* to her.

Banging her hip on the corner of the dresser in her hurry to leave, she cursed at the pain but started for the stairs.

Hunter pulled her back, holding her by the shoulders as he gazed intently down at her. "Hey," he said. "Calm down, okay?"

She couldn't. No matter how much stuff she shoved in her basement, she was losing everything that counted in her life.

He lifted her chin. "You're going to make it through this."

She forced a smile and nodded briskly before pulling away.

He trailed her downstairs and grabbed her keys from the kitchen counter.

She almost snatched them back. Joe had something that would shock her or he wouldn't be so happy. Was this when she learned whether or not Hunter was right about the Montgomerys? The moment she'd have to face irrefutable facts?

If that was the case, she wanted to brave the next few minutes on her own, wasn't sure she could tolerate a witness like Hunter, who would understand so clearly the depth of her pain.

But it wasn't safe to go out alone.

Ducking her head, she followed him to the door. Who said "ignorance is bliss"? If they'd lived *her* life, they would've said "ignorance is only slightly less painful than the probable truth."

Probable truth… God, she was losing all confidence.

Joe wouldn't answer. Madeline rang the bell, knocked and rang the bell again. Then she called him using her cell.

"Are you going to let me in or not?" she snapped, moving to the porch railing and staring out at the cold, misty night. She'd talked Hunter into letting her go to the door alone, just in case Joe wouldn't deal with her otherwise. Moody and quick to anger, her cousin was not an easy guy to get along with. She never knew what to expect from him—except an undying jealousy of Clay and an undying hatred of Grace.

"Sorry, I was busy," he said.

He still sounded happy. *Too* happy. "Doing what?"

He chuckled. "Describing what was in your package."

What the heck did that mean?

A lone car passed on the highway fronting the

property. Not many people in Stillwater were out this late. "Who were you talking to?" she asked.

"Cindy."

His ex. "Why?"

"She likes it when I talk dirty to her."

Madeline eyed her car, which was sitting in the drive, the engine ticking as it cooled. Hunter was there, in the driver's seat, but she couldn't see him. The light streaming through the windows of Joe's house made it too bright where she was and too dark where he was. "What're you talking about, Joe?"

Her cousin didn't answer. He'd already hung up. But he opened the door almost immediately afterward. "You gotta see this to fully appreciate it," he said beckoning her in.

Hunter had told her not to go inside. "Just turn on the porch light," she said.

"It's burned out."

"That's okay. You can give me the package here, especially since you had no right to take it in the first place."

"We only need a minute," he said with a scowl. "And it's not like I'm going to hurt you. Jeez, Maddy. What's up with you? We're *family*."

Considering her opinion of his character, she wasn't pleased to be reminded of the connection. But she couldn't think of one reason he'd want to hurt her. For the first time, they were on the same side. She was going after the truth about her father—his uncle—regardless of the risk it posed to the Montgomerys. He'd wanted her to force the issue for years.

"Are you coming in?" he asked.

She told herself to quit being silly and go inside. She

was just skittish because of that note Clay had brought to the restaurant....

"Fine." She turned in the direction of the car and shrugged, then stepped across the threshold. "Where's my package?"

"Right here." He kicked an open box sitting beside him.

"It's empty."

"I've got the contents in my office." He waggled his eyebrows. "I wanted to show Cindy on my webcam."

"I thought you and Cindy hated each other." Madeline spoke mostly to distract herself from the smell of alcohol on his breath.

"She's good for an occasional lay," he said with an indifferent shrug.

"You disgust me," was on the tip of Madeline's tongue, but she held it back. "Just tell me what it is," she said instead.

But he didn't have to tell her. They'd already reached his computer alcove; she could see it lying on the desk.

It was a dildo, grotesque in its enormous size but life-like in its shape and imitation flesh—exactly like the one found in the trunk of the family car.

"Cool, huh?" Joe said.

Madeline broke out in a cold sweat as the caller's voice again echoed in her head: *Spread your legs for me, okay, baby?*

Distantly, she heard the front door open and close. Then Joe said, "Hey, who the hell are you? And what makes you think you can just walk into my house?"

But she couldn't turn away. Not until she felt Hunter's hand on the small of her back, urging her to move. "Go to the car," he said gently. "I'll bring it with me."

* * *

The next morning, Hunter watched the sun begin to peek through the blinds in Madeline's bedroom. She was warm and pliant and gloriously naked, but he hadn't made love to her since they'd come home. The menace of what that package contained had been too dark. He'd simply held her for the rest of the night, and now that she was finally sleeping, he didn't want to wake her.

Getting carefully out of bed, he dressed as silently as possible and went downstairs, where he found the keys to the car and let himself out. The break-in. The dildo. If Barker had been molesting girls, as Hunter now believed, he'd been killed because of it, so whoever was tormenting Madeline couldn't be him. If Irene had killed Barker and then enlisted her family's help in covering it up, it couldn't be the Montgomerys. Otherwise, this would expose their motive, which threatened to expose their culpability. So who else was there?

He was missing something, something important and potentially dangerous to Madeline. And he knew only one person who could tell him what that might be.

Ray sat in the far corner of the diner. He'd come to town early so he could drive by Madeline's office. He was eager to see if the package he'd left her last night was still out front. He could hardly wait for her to get it—and had felt a definite thrill when he'd found it gone. Deciding to celebrate by enjoying some eggs and ham at Two Sisters, he'd been smiling to himself ever since, relishing what she must've thought and felt when she pulled out that gigantic dildo and realized it was the same as the one in Barker's Caddy.

Ray was staring at his plate, trying not to chuckle out loud, when Walt Eastman slid into the booth opposite him.

"You okay, buddy?" his friend asked in concern.

Ray's levity evaporated. Glancing up, he held his fork halfway to his mouth. "I'm fine," he said cautiously. "Why?"

"I know you were close to Bubba."

"Oh, right," he mumbled. "It was a real tragedy." In his preoccupation with Madeline, Ray had almost forgotten about Bubba. It wasn't a memory he cherished. Maybe Barker could kill without compunction—Ray knew the reverend had run Katie down; he could remember Barker telling him with absolute certainty that she'd never talk and that was well before there'd been any news of the accident. But Ray didn't have the stomach for murder. In order to get what he wanted from Madeline, he knew he'd have to resort to it eventually. But that was later. Hopefully, much later. If a guy was smart, he could keep a captive in the mountains for a long time, couldn't he? He'd make it so she could never get away. And who'd hear her scream? She'd get used to having him visit, get used to the games he wanted to play. Soon she'd perform for him just like a little girl.

And when he had to kill her, it'd be easier up there. He'd have plenty of privacy and lots of forest....

"And then to have this private investigator going around asking questions about Rose Lee," Walt said, shaking his head. "If you ask me, he's going too far, implying there might be something strange about her death."

Ray set down his fork. "What's he saying about Rose?"

Walt leaned closer and lowered his voice. "You haven't heard?"

Ray waited instead of answering, and Walt started in, as Ray knew he would. No one loved gossip as much as Walt. "Word has it he thinks Barker was a pedophile. Can you believe it? The *reverend?* The Vincellis are going to flip when they hear this. Elaine considers herself a pillar of the community. She's always been proud of her brother's reputation."

"Who told you?" Ray's heart thumped in his chest.

"Mike Metzger was at the bar last night, claiming he knew Barker was twisted all along. Said this Hunter fella agrees, that he believes Barker was worse than an adulterer."

"What's worse than an adulterer?"

"A rapist? A pedophile? He must think that suitcase in the Cadillac belonged to *him.*"

"He isn't suggesting Barker molested Rose?" The fear was back, the same cloying panic that had driven him to kill Bubba. If the police found out about Barker and Rose, they'd start asking questions about *him.* Then he might say the wrong thing, fail a lie detector test, unwittingly give away some damning detail. Or, if they really started searching for evidence, the police might be able to prove he was as guilty as Barker, that he'd essentially sold his daughter for rent and groceries— and then participated.

God, there'd been pictures of him abusing Katie in the worst possible ways, even a signed confession. Barker had demanded it, or he wouldn't let Ray continue with their sessions. He'd said Ray had to write everything down. That way, if Ray ever told a soul about their private indulgences, Barker would take the confession to the police and blame the whole thing on him.

Ray had been too addicted to deny him. And now he had no idea where that confession was. It wasn't among the crap he'd stolen from Madeline's basement. That was for darn sure. He'd scanned every piece of paper, torn the binding out of every book.

"That's my guess," Eastman was saying. "He's been asking how much time they spent together. Whether or not you were around. What happened to your relationship with Barker there at the end."

"He wouldn't pay me enough for my work, that's what," Ray said indignantly. And it was partially true. Barker wanted to use Rose Lee, but he didn't want to pay for her anymore. He'd been doing it too long, had begun to feel entitled. Then Eliza had found some of the magazines Ray had gotten for Barker, and the reverend knew she was watching him closely, so he went back to being the perfect pastor. For a while. But soon after that she shot herself, or Barker shot her—Ray didn't know which—then he married Irene, and the opportunity presented itself again.

"He expected it to be free," Ray complained. "Just because he was my pastor. But a man's got to eat."

"You'll have to explain that to Madeline's P.I.," Walt said. "But it doesn't seem fair that you should have to talk about it at all. This is supposed to be about Barker's disappearance, and we know who was behind *that.*"

It was true. The Montgomerys must've murdered him. Clay was the kind of guy who'd kill any man who hurt his sisters, right? And Barker had raped Grace. Ray knew it. He'd tried to get in on the action, but Barker was different with Clay's sister. He wouldn't share.

He'd been absolutely obsessed with her, *in love* with her, if Ray had his guess. And because she was so reserved, so remote, Barker had probably been especially cruel. Although Barker hadn't allowed Ray to watch, to be a part of it at all, he'd once made a strange comment. He'd said that Grace wasn't common like Rose Lee and Katie, that she'd let him kill her before she'd pretend to like what he did.

Ray supposed it was her stubborn resistance that fascinated Barker. But it was her budding beauty that had fascinated Ray. Particularly the budding part.

"I'm not going to say anything to anyone," he said. "Barker was a fine man. And Rose Lee was well taken care of. That's all there is to it."

"Walt!" Clancy Jones, a partner in Walt's tire store, stood in the doorway. He'd been working a toothpick through his teeth while waiting for Walt. But now he was growing impatient.

"Coming." Walt got up. "See ya later."

Ray lifted a hand in a halfhearted farewell. He had to stop that P.I., which meant he had to stop Madeline.

And he had to do it fast.

Clay was busy digging a posthole for a new stretch of fence along the back of his property when he saw Hunter cutting through his fields, coming toward him. He knew something was up. But he didn't pause in his work.

"No one answered at the house," Hunter said as he drew closer.

"Allie and Whitney left for Jackson half an hour ago." He shoved the posthole digger into the earth, squeezing and lifting in a rhythmic fashion. "Her mother flew up from Florida so Allie and Whitney could help celebrate her birthday."

Hunter found a clump of grass to wipe the mud on the bottom of his shoes, which looked like heavy-duty sandals no one from Mississippi would ever wear. "Why didn't you go with them?"

Clay slammed the posthole digger deep into the ground and wiped the sweat from his brow. "Why do you think?"

The fabric of Hunter's parka rustled as he folded his arms. Maybe it wasn't brand-new but, except for skiing, this was probably the only time Golden Boy had ever worn it, Clay thought wryly.

"Why don't you explain it to me," Hunter suggested.

"I can't leave town when someone just broke into my sister's house."

"You were going to trust me to take care of her, remember?"

"I don't trust anyone that much."

"I might be able to do more if you'd level with me, Clay."

Clay started digging again. The memory of Madeline cringing when he touched her yesterday was all too present in his mind. The only way to ease his pain and guilt was through the kind of hard physical work that left him too exhausted to feel anything else.

"Will you talk to me?" Hunter persisted.

Here they come, the same questions I've been asked for the past twenty years. Only now, for Madeline's sake, he felt obliged to answer them truthfully.

"That depends on what you ask," he said, but Hunter's next words weren't a question at all.

"Something happened last night," he said.

Those words sounded even more ominous than the searching queries Clay had expected. "She'd better be okay," he said, straightening.

"She's fine. For now. But there's trouble lurking, and I need your help to figure out where and why."

"Trouble?"

"Someone sent Madeline a package."

"To her house?"

"According to Joe, it was outside her office. He saw it and picked it up on his way home from the bar."

"What was in it?"

Hunter raked his fingers through his hair. "A gigantic dildo."

Clay tossed his shovel to the ground. "A *what?*"

"You heard me. Just like the one in the trunk of the Cadillac."

Clay had been hoping that whoever was harassing Madeline would quit after stealing that box from her basement. He couldn't believe there was anything valuable or potentially damaging in it. Unless someone knew about the pictures Barker had taken and was hoping to find them before Madeline's P.I. could.

"Who put that suitcase in the trunk, Clay?" Hunter asked. "Barker?"

Clay didn't answer. "The package," he said a moment later. "Was there any message with it?"

"I think that was message enough, don't you?"

"But from whom?" Clay whispered to himself. Who would do this? Barker's sister, Elaine, was aware of the existence of the pictures; Allie had shown her copies last summer. That was what had finally brought the Vincelli family and his to a truce of sorts. But Elaine wouldn't want to upset the delicate equilibrium that protected her from the humiliation those pictures would bring if they were ever made public. Besides, Elaine knew Madeline didn't have them. Madeline had no idea they even existed. So why would Elaine send someone over to break into Madeline's house?

"Who stands to gain the most from what's going on?" Hunter pressed.

"No one," Clay said. That was the confusing part. As far as Clay knew, he and his family were the only ones who had something to hide.

"If you want to help Madeline, you need to be honest with me." Hunter was growing more insistent. "What happened the night Barker died?"

Clay knew he should fend off the questions, play the usual games: *Died? How do you know he's dead?* But he couldn't. He cared too much about Madeline.

Taking a deep breath, he said what he'd never dreamed he'd say. "There were other girls."

If Hunter was surprised, he masked it well. "Girls who what?"

"Who were molested by Barker."

"When?"

"Before we ever moved here."

"Who were they?"

"Rose Lee Harper and Katie Swanson."

Hunter's frown became more pronounced. "How do you know?"

Clay wiped his forehead with his sleeve. "We found pictures. I destroyed all the ones I found, but Allie came across some more last summer."

"Will you get them for me?"

Again Clay searched for a way out and couldn't see one. This was the beginning of the end. And he was the one pulling the plug. But he didn't have any other choice. He wouldn't allow another member of his family to be hurt. "Yes. Just be prepared."

"For what?" Hunter asked.

"The worst."

Madeline heard the heavy knock and knew immediately what it meant. Jumping out of bed, she flew down the stairs. It was her father. She could hear him calling her.

"Maddy? Where's my girl?"

She could see his shape through the cloudy glass inset and couldn't wait to throw her arms around him. Putting her hand on the knob, she started to turn it, then paused, feeling oddly reluctant. Something was wrong.

"Maddy? Why won't you answer me?"

She tried to respond with the welcome he expected, but she was no longer excited. A bone-deep dread settled in as she watched him force the door open from the other side.

Finding her voice, she spoke over the racket of her racing heart. "Wait! Don't come in, Daddy. I'm not dressed."

She'd used a lie, an easy excuse, but suddenly it was true. She *was* naked. She could feel her own skin, her bare breasts. But that didn't stop her father. He stepped inside and closed the door behind him, leering at her while he slowly revealed something hidden under his coat—something flesh colored.

The dildo!

Madeline screamed as she sat up. She was in such a hurry to get away, to escape the degradation and pain of what she saw and felt that she'd scrambled out of bed before realizing she wasn't in the entryway at all. She was really naked, but she was in her bedroom, alone.

Gasping for breath, she looked wildly around. She could smell a hint of Hunter's cologne, but even he was gone.

Calm down. It was just another nightmare.

Only this one was worse—far worse. And then she realized, dimly, that the telephone was ringing. Its jangling was probably what had drawn her from the clutches of that terrible dream.

Anxious to hear another human voice, she grabbed the handset. "Hello?" she said eagerly, trying to slow her heart and regain control. But when her stepmother answered, she knew she should've taken the time to check caller ID. She'd wanted to hear another human voice, but she didn't want it to be this one.

"There you are. Madeline, I've been so worried about you. Are you okay?"

She didn't think so. Her reality—her nightmares, too—was getting worse. But she couldn't admit it. Irene hadn't wanted her to bring Hunter to Stillwater in the first place. In a way, all of this was her own fault, wasn't it? She was the one ripping off the scab that had for so long covered the wound of her father's disappearance; she was the one drawing fresh blood.

"I—I'm fine," she managed to say.

There was a short pause. "Why haven't you been returning my calls?"

Madeline blanched at the hurt and accusation in Irene's voice. "I've been…busy," she said. "*Really* busy." The excuse sounded every bit as lame as it was. But what was she supposed to say? That she was beginning to believe Irene had killed her father? That she was terrified her father might've deserved it?

"That private investigator came by," Irene said. "He…he has some odd notions. I hope you're not listening to him, Maddy. I hope you know that—"

"What?" she countered, unable to avoid it anymore.

Her mother seemed startled by her almost vehement response. "That—that he's wrong, of course."

"Is he, Mom?" she asked.

Irene shrank from the challenge. "Well, that depends on what he's saying, of course, but—"

Normally, Madeline would've let her talk, would've accepted what she had to say because the thought of any truth except the one she wanted most was unbearable. But the questions in her soul had grown just as unbearable. "He's saying Dad molested Grace," she blurted out. "He's saying you killed him because of it and that Clay's been covering for you all these years."

There was shocked silence.

"Is it true?" she demanded.

"No! Madeline, listen. Your father was a—a reverend. He—he didn't come home that night, and—and there was a—a transient and—"

She was babbling and crying—and *lying*. It had never been more apparent than it was at that moment.

Slowly, Madeline sank to the floor. Dropping her head onto her knees, she began to cry, too. "How do you know he molested Grace?" she interrupted. "Maybe it was someone else, someone he was counseling. Maybe you killed him for nothing!"

"Maddy, stay right there. I—I'm coming over. Clay's coming, too, okay? Did you hear me, Maddy? I'm calling Clay."

"To keep it all together for you, Mom? To help you convince me of your lies?"

Madeline hung up. She couldn't stay on the phone any longer, didn't want to hear the panic in her stepmother's voice. She had to get out of the house before Irene arrived, before Grace and Clay showed up, too. They'd all come so they could convince her that she was wrong....

Without even bothering to comb her hair, she yanked on some clothes, ran down the stairs, ignoring Sophie who looked up from her food dish, and scooped up the keys to Clay's old truck. She grabbed her purse, too, and left immediately. She couldn't deal with the Montgomerys right now; she needed time to think. But her cell phone kept ringing and ringing.

"Leave me alone!" she cried and swerved around the next corner, nearly crashing into Ray Harper, who was coming the other way.

Hunter wondered how he could show a man the pictures he had in his possession and ask, "Is this your daughter?" He couldn't imagine the pain of recognizing his own child in such a photograph. Or maybe he *could* imagine it. That was why he was having trouble approaching the door, why he was holding back.

But he had to talk to Ray, didn't he? He had to figure out the role these girls played in what had happened.

Maybe Ray already knew what Barker had done to his daughter. It was possible that Rose Lee had gone to her father for help. That might've been what caused the falling out between Ray and Barker. It was even possible that Ray, and not Irene, had killed Barker.

For Madeline's sake he hoped it was true. Hoped he

was wrong about the Montgomerys. That the whole town had been wrong.

Unzipping his parka, Hunter took a deep breath and finally climbed the four rickety steps to Ray's door, where he knocked loudly.

No response.

He banged on the cheap metal panel once again.

An old Buick was parked in the narrow carport beside the trailer. The sight of it had led him to believe Ray might be home, but when Hunter gave up knocking and went over to the vehicle, he could see that the front left side was up on blocks.

Just as he was about to get back in Madeline's car to search elsewhere for Ray Harper, the neighbor, a tall thin woman with a cigarette dangling from her mouth, came out wearing a robe and slippers and carrying a bag of trash.

"Hey," he called. "You haven't seen Ray this morning have you?"

"No." She paused to remove her cigarette. "He usually sleeps in."

From the look of the woman's mussed hair, she'd just rolled out of bed herself. "What does he drive?"

She hesitated, studying him. "You're the investigator fella."

"That's right."

Her face lit with interest. "You findin' anything?"

"Apparently not this morning. Can you tell me what Ray drives?" he asked again.

She seemed a little crestfallen that he wasn't more forthcoming, but she answered him. "A Dodge truck. If it's not in Bubba's carport, he's probably gone to church."

"*Bubba's* carport?"

"Bubba Turk." She motioned with the hand that held the cigarette. "Lives on the other side. Least he did. Poor guy had a heart attack and died this weekend."

Madeline had mentioned Bubba's death. It had really upset her. "Why would Ray be using Bubba's carport?" he asked.

She tilted her chin toward the broken-down Buick. "Until he gets rid of that piece of junk, he has no place else to park. The streets are already so crowded in here he finally arranged it so I'd quit complaining. But he *still* pulls up front half the time," she said in disgust.

"Didn't Bubba have his own car?"

Her lips twisted into a pained grimace. "You've never met Bubba, have you?"

He shook his head.

"Bubba weighed over 500 pounds and couldn't fit behind the wheel. He didn't even have a driver's license."

Five hundred pounds? No wonder he'd had a heart attack. "Did he live alone?"

"Except for his cat and his spider. But his sister came around once or twice a week to see if he needed anything."

"You don't happen to have her contact information, do you?"

"Sorry. She lives in Iuka, though. I know that much. You could see if she's listed."

"What's her name?"

"Helen Salazar."

"Thanks," Hunter said with a wave. "Appreciate it."

A row of trees shielded his view of Bubba Turk's carport. He started to walk toward it, but the neighbor who'd helped him called out before he'd gotten very far.

"Don't go too close," she warned.

"Why not?"

"Smells awful. Who would've thought the stench would linger like that?" She grimaced as she shoved her garbage into the large outdoor container, then went back inside her mobile home.

It did smell bad, Hunter noticed as he reached the trailer. He'd been under the impression that they'd found the body fairly soon after Bubba's death and transported it to the funeral home. But he was beginning to wonder if the hearse had yet to show up. Only death smelled like this.

The carport was empty, which meant Ray was gone.

Hunter tried to open Bubba's mobile home to see what was causing the cloying stench, but the door was locked. It didn't seem to be coming from inside the house, anyway. It seemed to be coming from—he walked around the place, trying to narrow it down—a small shed behind the carport.

Holding his breath, Hunter opened the flimsy shed door. There were no windows, and it was too dark to see. But he was fairly sure he'd discovered the source of the stench, especially when he had to take a breath and the next inhalation nearly caused his stomach to revolt.

What had happened here?

Pulling the chain on the bulb overhead, he leaned in and looked around. There, behind the door, was a black garbage bag. With the handle of a broom, he nudged the opening wide enough to see inside.

It was a dead cat.

22

"Is Madeline with you?"

It was Clay. Hunter held his cell phone with his right hand while carrying the garbage bag with his left. He'd knotted the top, but that didn't help much. The cat's remains had begun to liquefy and it was all he could do not to gag.

"No. I haven't seen her since this morning." Since he'd left her bed. But he wasn't about to share that detail with a protective older brother. Hunter felt guilty enough about their involvement. Despite what she'd done to instigate their physical encounters, he knew Madeline wasn't the type to take intimacy lightly. "Why?"

"She knows."

Hunter lifted the lid of Bubba's garbage can. It was empty, so there was plenty of room. But what if no one remembered to put it out on garbage day? Then the smell would get worse. And he didn't want Bubba's relatives to be faced with something as nasty as this when they came back to clean out his trailer. Losing a loved one was bad enough.

"Knows what?" he asked, changing direction and heading for Ray's garbage can instead.

"Everything."

The gravity in Clay's voice made Hunter stop, despite what he was holding.

"You mean she knows who killed her father?"

There was a long pause, but Clay finally answered. "Yes."

Hunter could hardly believe the secret was out. After twenty years... "What makes you think so?"

"She confronted my mother, then hung up. We're at her house now, but she's gone."

Hunter set the cat on the ground and turned his face downwind. "What about her cell phone?"

"She doesn't answer."

"I'll check the office."

"Grace has already been there. It's locked up."

"Where else would she go?"

"Kirk's."

A jab of hostility almost made Hunter say, "She wouldn't go there." But he bit his tongue. "Has anyone looked?"

"He's out of town. No one's home."

"What about the quarry?"

"Why would she drive to the quarry?"

"If she's upset, who knows? That's where her father's car was found, right?"

Clay sighed heavily. "I'll ask Kennedy to go up there, just in case."

In even more of a hurry to finish his distasteful chore, Hunter grabbed the garbage bag again. He imagined Madeline coming to the painful realization she'd been trying to avoid for years, and he knew what it'd do to her. "I'll drive through town, ask around, see if I can spot her."

"Sounds good."

"Let me know what you find."

"You do the same." Clay hung up as Hunter opened Ray's can. He was eager to be rid of the poor cat, but the can was too full. He started to shove down the rest of the garbage to make room—and then he saw something that stole his breath.

Inside were stacks of typewritten pages that looked exactly like the ones he'd been reading himself. Single-spaced. Faded ink. A raised letter or two every few words. As if they'd been typed on the same typewriter.

Setting the cat on the ground once again, Hunter reached in, removed several sheets and began to read.

They were Reverend Barker's sermons.

The farm seemed to be deserted. Allie's car was gone; Clay's truck was missing, too. Madeline supposed they were all out searching for her, rushing around trying to cover their tracks. They were good at that, weren't they? They'd done it for twenty years.

She swiped at the tears rolling down her cheeks as she turned into the long drive. She'd been so stupid, so blind. Everyone in Stillwater had been able to see what she couldn't. She'd searched high and low, pointed her finger at Jed Fowler or Mike Metzger, anyone but the people who were really to blame, while everyone else, including her aunt and uncle and cousins, watched in frustration, craving justice and receiving none.

How, exactly, had the Montgomerys managed it? Had Irene and Clay called a family meeting whenever she left the house to discuss how they were going to handle her? Did they take note of what she'd said or done that might expose them? Suggest ideas on how to counteract it?

White-hot anger, and the pain that went with deep betrayal, slashed through her, making the lump in her throat grow so large it hurt to swallow. Was the love they'd offered her a lie, too? More pretense to keep her from suspecting?

God, she'd been a fool! Not only had she trusted everything they said, she'd hotly defended them against the rest of the town. *Her father's town.* He'd brought them here. He'd provided for them. He'd owned *this* farm.

And they'd killed him....

It was almost too incredible to believe. Yet she did believe. Now. Hunter was right. Clay was good at protecting, at shielding. He'd protected his mother from prosecution all these years, would've gone to jail himself rather than reveal the truth. But there was no need to protect Grace from Lee Barker. No, she couldn't accept that. She *knew* her father. Clay must've planted that stuff in his trunk. Maybe Grace even gave him a pair of her panties to include, in case the car was ever found. Her father would *never* harm a child. She would've known, would've sensed that something was wrong with him. The things in that suitcase had to be more lies, part of the coverup.

Parking behind the house so the truck Clay had lent her couldn't be spotted from the road, she got out. She wasn't sure what she was doing here—still searching for her father, she supposed. This was the place where she'd been born and had spent the first eighteen years of her life. This was the last place she'd seen him. And she suspected he was still here, that he had never actually left.

What, exactly, had happened the night she went to

Hanna Smith's house for a slumber party? And what had gone on beneath the tranquil surface of those hot summer days right before? How did it—how could it—have come to murder?

Or had Irene planned her father's death from the very beginning?

Madeline had no idea. She'd been so starved for attention that she'd readily and eagerly embraced them all. She hadn't been looking for hidden motivations or evil intent. She'd admired Clay, befriended Grace, helped raise Molly and nearly worshipped the beautiful Irene, who was so much happier than her own mother had been. And she'd done it all with a sense of gratitude for the love she wouldn't have had otherwise.

Her boots crunched in the gravel as she crossed to the barn. The wide, sliding doors were locked, as usual. Clay was so cautious....

She grimaced bitterly at the thought, then stood at the window, staring into her father's empty office—at the stripped walls, the concrete floor.

Her soul felt just as bare.

"How did she do it?" she muttered as if Clay was present. "And where did you hide the body, big brother?"

The memory of Grace showing up here with a shovel eighteen months ago entered Madeline's mind. When she was caught, Grace had said she'd been planning to see for herself if the accusations against Clay had any merit, but she already knew. Like Joe said, it was probably an attempt to move the body. Why not? Joe had been right about everything else.

But the police had searched. They'd dug up the entire backyard and found nothing.

"What did you do with him?" she whispered. Her

father was here somewhere. He had to be. But where? Was he buried out near the creek? Beneath the cypress trees? In the barn?

She turned to face the house. Or was he in the cellar? Taking a shovel from the shed behind the chicken coop, she started for the back door. She didn't bother to see if it was locked. Clay secured everything, trusted no one, and now she knew the real reason.

Using the handle of the shovel, she broke a window, then cleared away the glass. "I'll find him," she promised. But as she was about to hoist herself through the opening, she heard the creak of footsteps on the porch behind her.

Was Clay home already? She whipped around, expecting to confront him. Instead she confronted the metal end of the shovel she'd just used to break the window. The last thing she noticed before she fell was the ringing in her left ear and the satisfaction on Ray Harper's face.

Using a crowbar from Bubba's shed, Hunter pried open Ray's back door. It was broad daylight, and the neighbor was out again, obviously perturbed that he hadn't moved on, but he didn't care.

"Hey? What do you think you're doing?" she cried when the door gave way. "You can't do that!"

"I just did," he said and tossed the crowbar aside.

She followed him when he went in, but hovered at the door. "I'm going to call the police!"

"Please do," he responded. "Tell them to pick up Ray Harper as soon as possible."

The shrill edge left her voice. "Why? What'd he do?"

"Just tell them I said he's the one we've been looking for."

He did no more than glance at her, but he saw her eyes go wide as she popped her gum. "Who killed the reverend?"

"Who broke into Madeline's house!" he said impatiently.

"Oh. I heard about that."

He motioned to the phone. "Hurry!"

She came in and dialed as he searched the kitchen and living room, then headed down the hall. In the bathroom, he found a smear of blood on the vanity and bloody bandages in the trash can. In the bedroom across the hall, he found a bottle of Viagra on the nightstand. Someone had shoved a bunch of sex toys under the bed and left a photograph of Madeline as a young girl on the dresser. Like the sermons in the trash outside, Hunter suspected that picture had come from the boxes in Madeline's basement.

Her gap-toothed smile made him feel things he really didn't want to feel—tenderness and concern...

"They want to talk to you," the neighbor said, standing in the doorway.

"I'll call them from my cell phone." He was too busy now. He needed to fire up Ray's computer, check his files and e-mail. But the picture that confronted him as soon as he opened Ray's "recent folder" caused the neighbor to gasp and nearly made Hunter sick.

It was a picture of Madeline's head, which had been scanned in from the photograph he was holding, on some other woman's body who was being raped by three men. Below the picture were the words, "Make her beg."

Ray dropped the shovel, then dragged Madeline's unconscious body to the end of the porch. He had to hurry in case Clay returned. If Clay was as guilty of the reverend's murder as everyone believed, he couldn't want Madeline poking around in the past any more than Ray did. But Clay was unpredictable and possibly dangerous, and that was all there was to it.

"They'll search for you," he said over the scrape of her boots against the wooden planks. "But they won't find a trace." He grunted as he heaved her over one shoulder. "I doubt anyone'll look for too long. Maybe that big bad brother of yours seems protective, but let's face it. You're not his real sister. And, frankly, his life would be easier without you."

Using some rope he'd brought from home, Ray bound Madeline's hands and feet. Then he gagged her with a bandanna and tied her into the bed of his truck, so that even if she awoke, there wouldn't be enough slack to allow her to sit up. Finally, he threw an old blanket over her.

That's good for now. Glancing nervously around, he jumped into the driver's seat and drove away from the farm as slowly and comfortably as if he'd just stopped by for a visit. But once he was several miles down the road, with nothing but rolling hills on either side, he pulled over and took the time to arrange a tarp on top of her, in case it rained. They had a long drive ahead of them, and it was cold. It'd be even colder in the hills of Tennessee. He didn't want her to freeze before they could reach the cabin he'd rented.

He pulled out the money he'd stolen from Bubba and counted it again. He'd have enough to buy supplies for at least a week.

He couldn't wait to start the fun. It would be even better than those afternoon and late-night sessions with

the reverend, Katie and Rose Lee. That was before
anyone had invented Viagra.

Maybe he'd invite one of the buddies with whom he
traded pornography on the Internet to join him. He
wasn't sure if anyone lived close, since it was such a
clandestine group—for their own safety it had to be.
But Madeline would be worth the drive. And when the
week was up, maybe he'd rent her to someone else for
a while, like the folks who made money on the cabin.
She'd be an investment!

He chuckled at his own thoughts, even waved cheerfully as he passed a woman whose fence he'd mended
last summer. They could take pictures, too, and sell
them on the Internet. Some guys made a lot doing that.
Of course, Madeline wasn't a child, so the pictures
wouldn't go for a premium, but they could chain her up
and get some good rape and torture stuff. And when
they grew bored—he drummed his fingers on the
steering wheel as a rush of nervous excitement ran
through him—maybe they could make a snuff film.
That would have to bring in the big bucks, a beautiful
woman killed right on camera.

With such big plans, Ray began to worry that he
might've hit Madeline too hard with that shovel. "Come
on, Maddy, come back to me," he muttered, frequently
turning to look through the back window at the tarp that
covered her. "Don't ruin it."

After another fifteen minutes, he nearly stopped to
check for a pulse. But just as he slowed down, he saw
the lump beneath the tarp begin to move.

The gag cutting the corners of her mouth made it difficult to breathe. Closing her eyes, Madeline tried to calm

her racing heart, tried to control the panic that edged closer with every second. Where was she? What'd happened?

She'd been at her house. No, she'd been at the farm. She'd broken a window and then…

Her memory finally cooperated, and she saw Ray holding the shovel, swinging it at her head. But why had he done that? She'd known Ray her whole life!

Slowly, her faculties returned, accompanied by more pain. She was in a—a trunk or…the hard bed of a pickup truck, under a musty-smelling blanket. Her head and jaw ached, her hands and feet burned unmercifully, and a knot dug into her hip. She shifted as much as she could, hoping to relieve that discomfort if no other, but it only made the shoulder that bore most of her weight complain more loudly.

The black void of unconsciousness edged close and rolled back, edged close and rolled back, like lapping water on the shore of a lake. Madeline's body screamed at her to dive in, to simply drift away with the tide.

But there was something inside her that warned against succumbing….

Wake up… Move… Fight… Save yourself!

The truck swerved around a sharp turn, putting even more pressure on her shoulder. She moaned, and reached eagerly for oblivion, anything to block out the misery. But then, just before it descended, she recognized a new smell. Pine trees. Not only was she hurt, bound and gagged, she wasn't in Stillwater anymore.

When Hunter barged into the police station, a stout woman behind a small desk glanced up and tried to intercept him, but he sidestepped her. "Why aren't you doing more?" he demanded, confronting Chief Pontiff at the water cooler.

"You're not the one calling the shots around here," Pontiff retorted and drank from his partially filled paper cup.

"So what? You saw those pictures on Ray's computer. We've got to find Madeline!"

Pontiff crushed the cup and threw it in the garbage. "We're trying, damn it!" The quaver in his voice would've given away his anxiety—if the tremor in his hand hadn't done so first. "I've called his sister's house and talked to her and his mother. They haven't seen or heard from him. I've canvassed the trailer park, talked to all the neighbors. No one knows where he might've gone. I've called in my new rookie. He and Radcliffe have driven up and down every street in this town. Right now they're searching the barns at some of the outlying farms. What more can I do?" he asked miserably.

"Organize a civilian search party," Hunter said. "Ask the town for help."

Pontiff stared at him for several seconds. Hunter guessed pride tempted him to refuse. He didn't like having someone else take charge, especially an outsider. But, ultimately, he nodded. "I'll call Pastor Portenski, see what he can do."

"Thanks," Hunter said and meant it. Planning to head out so he could search again, he hesitated when his cell phone rang. It was Clay.

"Tell me you've found her," he said, answering immediately.

"No. But I've located the truck she was driving. It's here at the farm. We missed it earlier because it's parked way in the back. And there's a broken window at the house."

Hunter's grip tightened on his phone. "She's not inside?"

"No. Bonnie Ray across the road says she saw Ray's old Dodge pull out of the drive over an hour ago. But she doesn't remember seeing Maddy."

"Did she notice which direction he went?"

"He turned east, away from town."

"Son of a bitch," Hunter muttered. What were they going to do now? If Ray Harper had Madeline and had left town more than an hour ago, she could be anywhere within a sixty- to eighty-mile radius.

Every bump caused Madeline more agony. Her head, shoulder, hip and jaw throbbed; her hands and feet had stopped burning but she could no longer feel them. She needed to move, get her circulation going. She craved a change of position more than she'd ever dreamed she could crave something so simple. But it was no use. She'd already struggled with the ropes until she'd rubbed her wrists raw.

She couldn't get loose. And it was noticeably colder. She was beginning to shake violently—from the cold and the pain.

"Hunter," she whispered, wishing he could hear her. She remembered how he'd cradled her body against his last night, the comfort he'd offered and tried to imagine she was with him now, safe and warm.

But other visions intruded. Like the message on her answering machine. *Spread your legs.* The blood on her kitchen floor. The giant dildo. It had to be Ray. *But why?* She didn't understand.

The truck slowed, its shocks squeaking as it bounced and swayed from side to side. They obviously weren't on a paved road anymore.

That realization terrified Madeline. There had to be a million little turnoffs between Stillwater and wherever Ray was taking her. How would anyone ever find her?

She blinked hard, trying not to give in to the despair that was bringing tears to her eyes. She'd think of something. This couldn't be real. This didn't happen to people like her. This kind of thing always happened to someone else.

Briefly, she prayed it was just another one of her nightmares, that she'd wake up in a few minutes.

But when the truck came to a stop and the driver's door creaked opened, then slammed shut, she knew with absolute certainty that she was already awake.

"We're here," Ray announced cheerfully.

She wanted to ask him where "here" was. She wanted to ask him so many questions. But even if he removed the gag, her mouth was too dry to speak. The gag was so tight she hadn't been able to close her lips or even swallow properly since he'd put it on.

"Let me check it out, and I'll be back for you, okay?" he said.

When she made no sound, didn't move, he suddenly pulled the blanket off her, and their eyes met. "Scared me for a minute," he said, chuckling.

His boots thudded against the earth as he walked away from her. Then she heard the jingle of keys. She couldn't figure out where they were, but it was so damn cold. Colder than Stillwater. And higher in elevation. The smell of pine was stronger than ever—pine and wood and moist earth.

"No bathroom," he said when he came back. "But what can you expect for thirty-five bucks a night?" He untied her from the bed of the truck. Then, using the rope to jerk her into a sitting position, he almost broke her arms.

When she groaned, he laughed. "Sorry about that. You're a tall woman, and I'm not as young as I used to be."

He rolled her toward the tailgate, then shoved her again and let her fall to the ground. Pine needles poked her cheek and nearly went in one eye. She tried to turn her face away, but in her effort to get enough air she breathed in some dirt, then hacked helplessly because she couldn't cough.

Ray didn't seem to care. He'd gone back to the cab of the truck. "I've got everything we're going to need right here, but—" she heard him rummaging around "—damn it! I gave you the dildo. Am I an idiot, or what? I wasn't even there to see you open it, and now we don't have one of my favorite toys. If you fail to plan you plan to fail," he said, chastising himself.

She tried to ask, "What do you want from me?" but her words came out as helpless grunts.

"Just be patient," he said. "I'll get you fixed up." He pulled her into a sitting position. Then he picked her up and carried her into a small cabin. There was some very plain, inexpensive furniture in the living room, but no television and, from what Madeline could see, no phone.

"It's pretty basic," he said as he put her on the couch. "But that's okay. We won't get bored. If we do, I brought some good reading material." He took some magazines out of the bag he'd carried in and showed them to her.

They were all hard-core pornography. Turning to the first page, he began to read aloud, but it was so revolting Madeline squeezed her eyes shut and repeated, "This isn't real…this isn't real," over and over inside her head.

"We'll get back to that," he said, tossing the magazine aside. "I wouldn't want to get ahead of myself. The anticipation is half the fun."

We'll get back to that? The lust in his voice made the cold knot of fear in her stomach grow bigger. Did he intend to rape her? She couldn't believe it. This man had been part of her father's congregation. He still attended church almost every week.

"Ray." His name was unintelligible when she said it, but he looked up.

"Please. The gag."

"Hmm…I guess there's no harm in it," he said. "Just remember not to say anything I don't like, or it could go back on again. There might be other consequences, too. Especially if you don't remember to call me Master. 'Yes, Master.' 'No, Master.' Okay?"

He was crazy. How could she have missed it? The hard, ugly edge to his weathered face, the gleam in his dark eyes. He'd gone over the edge.

He must've noticed the defiance in her attitude because he purposely smashed her mouth into his crotch as he untied the gag. Madeline told herself not to absorb this detail, but she shuddered anyway.

"For what I got for you, you'll have to wait till later," he said. But the gag was off. She tried to be grateful for that as she stretched her swollen lips, wet her dry tongue and tried to ease the pain in her jaw.

"So what do you say?" he prompted.

She didn't know what he meant. When she didn't respond, he grabbed her hair so she couldn't move her head and brought his nose right up against hers. "I asked you a question."

"Why are you doing this?" she croaked.

The blow surprised her, rocked her head back. As the sting radiated through her entire body, she blinked up at him in shock. "Why—" She couldn't get the rest out.

He smiled, obviously enjoying the violence. "That was the wrong thing to say, 'Thank you, Master,' would be correct. Would you like to try again?"

The lift in his voice was deceiving, and she knew it. He wanted her to refuse. And she longed to do so. But in order to escape, she needed to stay as able-bodied as possible.

"Thank you, Master," she murmured from between gritted teeth.

"That's better. See? You'll learn. Pretty soon you'll be begging me for all kinds of favors. If you're a good little girl, I might even unchain you now and then."

Unchain her? Fighting tears of shock, anger and disbelief, she watched him bend over his bag. "Ah, here it is," he said and pulled out a spiked collar. "No sex slave is complete without one."

23

"He doesn't have an address book," Clay called impatiently.

Hunter knew Madeline's stepbrother wanted to be out, actively searching for her. Taking the time to go through Ray's mobile home heightened his anxiety. And Hunter could understand why. With each passing minute, Ray could be taking Madeline farther away from them. But they couldn't drive aimlessly. They had to track him. It was their only hope.

"Then dig around for scraps of paper, anything with a name or a number on it," he said. "Classified ads. Receipts."

"Did he pack?" Clay asked. "Are his clothes gone?"

It was difficult to tell. To Hunter, it looked as if Ray had left in such a rush that he hadn't taken much with him.

"There's a receipt on the kitchen floor," Clay said a moment later. "It's from the hardware store."

"What's the date?"

"Today."

There was nothing in the master bedroom to indicate where Ray might've gone, so Hunter went into the room with the computer. Maybe he hadn't looked carefully enough when he was here before. It was possible that Ray had exchanged e-mails with someone or visited a site that would tell him something. "What'd he buy?" he asked as he clicked through Ray's "sent" folder.

"A chain and a spike."

Containment objects. Hunter paused long enough to rub a hand over his face. Ray was likely seeking privacy, someplace he could take Madeline and—

He wouldn't even think of the possibilities. But he knew what they were. The screen saver—and the porn sites on his computer—told him exactly what Ray wanted.

The apathy that had overwhelmed Hunter after his divorce had evaporated, leaving him in a world of feeling, a world of hurt. He was desperate to think more quickly, be smarter, work faster.

As he'd noticed earlier, Ray's e-mail contained mostly spam. There were a few personal e-mails from other men, offering to sell lewd pictures. But Hunter ignored it all, remaining intent on only one thing— finding any information that might lead him to Madeline.

Where had Ray taken her? There had to be some-place he thought it would be safe....

"Anything?" Clay asked.

"No." Panic and disappointment collided. Hunter had nowhere else to look. They had to find *some* clue to Ray's destination. But Ray's computer told him nothing. The pervert had visited a long list of porn sites. That was all. No—

And then he saw it. What he'd been searching for all along.

www.TNcabins.com

* * *

What to do…what to do… Ray rapped his knuckles nervously on the wobbly kitchen table. He'd put the collar on Madeline, just to show her what she was in for. He liked the fear that entered her eyes when he pulled it so tight she could hardly breathe. It made her close her eyes and concentrate on *living*. Made her realize just how tenuous the line between life and death really was—and that he was the one who'd decide if and when she crossed it.

That was power. It made him feel invincible…and a little out of control. She was completely vulnerable to him. As vulnerable as Rose Lee had been. He actually felt more excited than he had before, because now *he* was in charge. Not the reverend.

How would Barker have liked his darling Maddy wearing that collar?

Ray grinned. He would've hated it, of course. Hated that what he'd started had eventually consumed Maddy, too. And yet there was a part of the sick bastard that would've loved it. Loved it as much as Ray did. Maybe he would even have joined the fun.

Ray imagined Madeline's breasts naked to his view as she writhed on the bed, struggling to breathe. Their first experience would be beautiful. Perfect. He'd do whatever he wanted to her while she whimpered beneath him.

But…that would have to wait. It was getting dark, and he had no groceries or candles for light. He hadn't gotten that far before he'd run across her. He'd already collected what he needed from home and was driving to her cottage to stake out the place, to decide how and when he'd grab her—and to break a basement window if he found her house empty so he could get in. He'd planned to return after dark, when he was completely ready. To take her so quietly that Hunter Solozano, if he was there, wouldn't even know she was gone.

But then she'd pulled out of her street and driven right past him. And she'd been alone.

So he followed her.

When she stopped at the farm and he realized everyone was gone, it was simply too good an opportunity to pass up. Which meant he'd had to alter his plans and come straight to the cabin. He couldn't stop along the way once he had her in the back of his truck. It was too risky. Someone might've seen the tarp move or heard her groan.

He'd done the right thing, he told himself. He had the rope and tarp and the collar. And he could go shopping now, before the stores in this remote area closed. He didn't want to leave her, but if he didn't, they'd both go hungry until morning—and his stomach was already complaining.

Might as well get comfortable before starting his binge, he decided. He wanted to buy a Polaroid camera, anyway, and some Presto logs and lighter fluid— enough for several days. Then he could give Madeline his full attention. And he could record their best moments on film for his new Internet business.

The chair squeaked on the wooden floor as he got up and went to his bag. There, he found the bottle of sleeping pills he'd taken from his medicine cabinet. They'd insure she'd be here when he got back. But how many should he give her? He only wanted to knock her out for a few hours, not incapacitate her for the rest of the night. That would be a real tragedy. Because he had big plans—plans for which he wanted her very much aware.

Clay knew the area better than Hunter did, so Hunter didn't argue when he said he'd drive. They'd called the Sevier County Sheriff's Department, who'd agreed to send a deputy to the Misty Mountain Cabins. But they'd been told the cabins were rarely used this late in winter, that they were very spread out and that it'd take a while to visit them all.

So Hunter couldn't relax. He was afraid the deputy wouldn't arrive in time, afraid of what the deputy might find. What were they really dealing with?

Obviously, Barker had been a pedophile. He was in some of the pictures Clay had given him. But how did Ray figure into that? Hunter might've assumed Ray had killed Barker for molesting Katie and Rose Lee, but Barker had been around for seven years after Rose Lee's death, which didn't suggest the instantaneous reaction of a father who'd just learned that his preacher was molesting his daughter. And the pornography on Ray's computer clearly indicated that Ray was a sexual sadist himself.

The more he tried to piece the puzzle together, the more questions went through Hunter's head. What had Ray done? And what was he capable of doing?

"Stop here," Hunter said when he spotted the drugstore.

Clay looked up in surprise. "What?"

"I need to buy something."

"We don't have time. The cabins are seven hours away."

They had no hope of saving Madeline. Ray had too much of a lead. Her fate depended on the deputy. But

Hunter didn't want to face that truth, let alone state it. "The deputy we called should be there any minute. And this'll only take a second."

Scowling, Clay hesitated. But then he pulled into the parking lot. "Make it quick," he said, waiting in the truck while Hunter ran inside.

Ray strolled through the aisles of the mom and pop grocer with his duffle bag on his shoulder, studying the shelves, trying to calculate what he might be able to steal and what he'd have to buy. He had Bubba's money, but he knew it'd be smart to make it last.

"Can I help you find something?"

A plump woman with curly red hair and a piggy nose smiled at him from where she sat on a stool behind the register. A small television squawked on the counter in front of her, but he could hear the loud jingle of a commercial, which was probably why she'd turned her attention to him.

He considered lowering his voice and telling her what he really wanted. But he figured she wouldn't react well if he asked for sex toys. And he couldn't raise any suspicions.

"No, uh, these cucumbers will do," he said and returned her smile as he selected the biggest one on the produce table and put it in his basket.

"You just passing through?" she asked conversationally.

"No, I'm planning to stay for a few days." He didn't want to say any more than he had to, but she'd be able to tell by his purchases that this was more than a pit stop.

"Where ya comin' from?"

"Nashville," he lied.

"That's a fun place."

He pretended not to hear her as he moved to the small dairy section, where he saw a tube of frozen cookie dough that was even thicker than the cucumber, and decided he might be able to make good use of it, too.

"That sweet stuff's addicting," she said.

He grinned. She had no idea.

The program she'd been watching came back on the TV. "Let me know if you need anything."

He nodded, and she became absorbed in her show again.

He continued through the aisles as someone else entered the store, someone the woman knew, and they began to talk about a new bar going in next door. The woman didn't want the bar anywhere close to her store and became so engrossed in telling her friend exactly why that she seemed to forget about him, which allowed him to slip several items into his pockets.

"I don't want to arrive to broken beer bottles in my parking lot every morning," she was saying as he stepped up to the register.

"I hear ya." Her friend shook her head in sympathy and moved politely out of his way.

The woman told Ray his total. He paid and started to walk out, but then he saw something that caught his interest. There were several pairs of gold stud earrings hanging on a small rack in the corner.

"How much are these?" he asked, holding a pair out to her.

"Six ninety-nine," she said.

He remembered his mother piercing his sister's ears

using an ice cube and a needle. That method would work for more exciting body parts as well, right?

He couldn't see why not.

Putting them on the counter, he got out a ten-dollar bill. "I'll take some sewing needles, too."

*

The knocking reached Madeline through a deep haze. She was in a coffin, buried alive. Buried next to her father. Her mind seemed to float freely, to see them both from some vantage point above, lying side by side. She, chalk-white but perfectly whole; her father, a macabre skeleton with only a few tufts of hair and bits of decaying skin. He looked gruesome, as gruesome as he'd ever looked in her nightmares. But now he didn't frighten her. There was nothing she could do to get away from him, anyway. She couldn't move. Her body remained immobile. Dead. As immobile as Bubba, lying prostrate on his living room floor....

But Madeline didn't care. The pain was gone. So was the fear. There was no Ray, no threat, no motion or movement.

Just that persistent knocking. Where was it coming from?

"Hello? Brian Shulman here. I'm with the property management company and I'm with someone from the Sevier County Sheriff's Department. Anyone home?"

The voice filtered through Madeline's head, sounding distorted and surreal and evoking an odd flutter of expectation in her stomach. Sheriff's Department. That was good, wasn't it? Something told her she should respond to it, but she couldn't find her voice, wasn't even sure why she needed to.

Besides, what if it was a trick? What if it was really Ray? He'd said that if she tried to escape, he'd punish her severely.

She was better off staying where she was, hidden in the dark…hidden in the closet.

Closet? A memory surfaced—Ray forcing her to swallow some pills, moving her into the bedroom closet and piling blankets on top of her before shutting the door—and she realized she wasn't in a safe place at all. She wasn't dead, either. She was in danger because he was coming back. He'd promised he would. And he'd tighten the collar when he did.

Madeline could feel the weight of the leather around her neck. He'd moved it one notch, so she wouldn't suffocate while he was gone, but it still cut into her skin. That was why she'd swallowed the pills, which had left such a terrible, bitter taste in her mouth. She'd been trying not to, but she could hardly breathe, had already been on the verge of blacking out.

She tried to remember what'd happened in those last few seconds. Where had Ray gone? When would he be back? And what should she do now?

She couldn't think straight. She felt numb, groggy.

"Sheriff's Department," a different voice said. "Hello? Anyone here?"

Me! She tried to scream that one simple word but no sound came out. She could hear someone moving around, opening doors, striding down the hall—and imagined whoever it was directing a flashlight around each room.

"Mr. Harper? Anyone here?"

The man who possessed that voice opened the door to her room. Madeline told herself to move, to hit her head against the wall, to shift, to kick—*anything* to let him know where she was. But she was completely paralyzed. There wasn't a muscle in her body that would respond to her brain's command, despite the intensity of her efforts.

She tried again to speak, but the gag was back. She hadn't felt it a moment before but now the cotton fabric cut across her mouth, making it impossible to move her jaw. It must've been there the whole time.

Groan! Scream! Anything!

The door to the closet slid open. Madeline prayed that some part of her was showing, that Ray had left a strange object behind, something that would make the sheriff or whoever had come from his department search more thoroughly. But the door shut almost immediately.

"Find anything?" someone else called from the doorway.

The floored creaked as the man who'd opened the closet walked away. "An empty bed and a bunch of bedding."

No! Madeline was hyperventilating now and sweating profusely. She'd never felt more helpless or vulnerable in her life. She couldn't move or speak. She could only hear. And getting upset wasn't helping. Her panic brought unconsciousness drifting toward her again. The harder she tried to move or speak, the closer it came.

The last thing she remembered was a man saying, "Someone's been here recently, but everything looks fine. No kidnap victim." He repeated those words into a radio that hissed and sputtered.

Then a single tear rolled down Madeline's cheek and the darkness swallowed her whole.

* * *

Hunter sat in the passenger seat of Clay's truck and tore the package off the magnifying glass he'd just bought.

"What's that for?" Clay had been mostly silent ever since they'd left Harper's trailer. Determined to make the seven-hour drive to the string of cabins in about half that time, he was speeding and weaving in and out of traffic, but Hunter didn't mind. The more he thought about Ray, the more frightened for Madeline he became. He was even becoming suspicious of Bubba Turk's death. It was one thing for Bubba to die of a heart attack. But who killed the cat?

How bad was this guy? He wouldn't *kill* Madeline, would he? It was Barker who'd probably killed Katie, Barker who might've killed Eliza, too. He'd had so much to lose if the truth ever came out.

But what about Rose Lee? She'd committed suicide in *Ray's* trailer. And she'd been naked when she was found, which hadn't made sense to Hunter from the beginning.

Now he was afraid he knew why....

"Are you going to answer me?" Clay asked, impatient when Hunter didn't respond.

Hunter retrieved the pictures from his coat pocket. "I want to take a closer look at these."

Clay switched lanes. "What're you looking for?"

"I don't know yet. Anything that might tell me more about what was going on and who was involved."

"I can tell you where most of them were taken."

"Where?"

"My stepfather's office at the farm, or his office at the church."

"And the rest?"

"They don't show the background. They're too close to the subject."

That was true. The distortion in those photos suggested that Barker had held the camera out and snapped the pictures of himself. Others he'd stood back and taken of each girl or both of them together—all in various compromising positions. The pictures made Hunter so angry he found he couldn't blame Irene or Clay if they'd done something to stop Barker. He couldn't even ask Clay what had happened because he suddenly didn't want to know the details, didn't want the burden of telling Madeline the truth, if she asked him, or the burden of deciding whether or not he should go to the police with the whole sordid tale.

"Have you known Ray since you moved here?" He tried not to imagine where all of this could end, with Maddy terribly hurt or even dead, and the Montgomerys in prison. No one had forced Clay to come forward with these pictures. Revealing them risked everything he'd been trying to hide, and yet he'd done it right away, for Madeline's sake. Without them, Hunter would never have gone to Ray's trailer, found the cat, found the pages from Barker's sermons or known where to search for clues about where Madeline might be. Madeline would just have disappeared and no one would've known where to look.

That redeemed Clay in Hunter's mind. He'd sacrificed himself for his stepsister. But there were those who might not view the past so kindly….

"I know him. But obviously not well enough," Clay said. "Otherwise…"

He let his voice trail off, leaving Hunter to wonder what he meant. Otherwise he would've been able to protect Madeline? Or otherwise he would've made sure Ray could never hurt anyone again?

Here he was, with someone he was almost positive had been involved in a murder, and yet he considered Clay one of the most ethical people he'd ever met.

It was more than a little ironic. But he didn't have time to consider all the nuances. He needed to concentrate, despite his fear and the various questions running through his head. The photograph he was examining showed the edge of a window cooler. It'd probably been taken in the office at the farm. Madeline had mentioned an air-conditioning unit being in the window at one time. Since Hunter had visited that very room, he could easily picture the setting. But that was it. There was no visible object to tell him anything more than he already knew, so he switched to another picture. "What's Ray like?"

They passed a car and slipped in between two more. "Pretty nondescript," Clay replied. "Always minded his own business before. Or so I thought. I felt sorry for him because of his daughter." Clay shook his head as if he blamed himself for missing signs that no one else had seen. "I never expected him to be dangerous."

"I don't think anyone did." Hunter pulled out another picture. This one had been taken elsewhere. He could see part of a desk in the background. "Where's this?"

He handed it over, and Clay glanced at it while he drove. "At the church."

"God, was there no end to his hypocrisy?" Hunter asked in disgust.

"No," Clay said simply.

Hunter began to examine the third picture. It looked like it had been taken at the church, too. There was the same desk. But in this photo, Katie was performing a sex act on Rose Lee and Barker wasn't in the picture at all. Hunter almost set it aside when he saw something near the edge that made him pause.

"Son of a bitch," he muttered.

"What?" Clay said.

Disbelieving, Hunter shook his head. "Your stepfather wasn't alone when he tortured those girls." He glanced over at Clay, but Clay didn't return his look. The muscle that flexed in his cheek was his only reaction.

"What are you talking about?"

"I can see part of him in the corner of this picture."

"Part of him?"

"His knee or something."

"How do you know?"

"If you look closely, you'll see that he's wearing the same pants he had on in the other picture."

"I saw a lot of skin, but no pants," Clay said bitterly.

"They were on the bottom edge of that photo of him and Katie—down around his ankles."

A scowl etched deep lines in Clay's face; Hunter guessed it wasn't easy for him to talk about these pictures. It'd be impossible not to think about what'd happened to his own sister—and what had probably occurred as a result. There was no telling how horrifying that must've been for a sixteen-year-old boy. "He's in a lot of those pictures," Clay said.

"I know, but in this one, he's not close enough to be holding the camera since he's in the picture—or his pant leg is, anyway. Someone else had to be taking it."

Clay's eyes, hard and glittering, were finally riveted on Hunter's. "You think Ray would do that to his own daughter?"

Hunter set the magnifying glass aside. *Mad-dy, it's your dad-dy. Spread your legs for me, okay, baby? You're the one I wanted all along.*

The idea of incest excited Ray Harper.

"Yes." Staring straight ahead, Hunter watched the little dash lines in the center of the road. They flew past in a blur, but not fast enough. What was Ray doing to Maddy?

He could only hope the deputies from the sheriff's department had already found them. He'd called to check, but a woman with a nasal voice had said, "We're looking into it."

24

When Madeline regained consciousness, the cabin was completely silent. She sat still for several seconds, listening—and praying that the officers from the sheriff's department hadn't left. She was feeling slightly more clearheaded, could even move a little. But they were gone. As far as she could tell, she was alone.

How long had she been unconscious? The thought of Ray returning sent a spurt of fear-induced adrenaline through her blood. If he wasn't here now, he'd be coming soon. Surely, he hadn't planned to be gone very long. Which meant she had to get out of the closet, out of the cabin and somewhere safe. Right away.

But how? Ray had retied her hands and feet. Although he hadn't connected the rope between them, forcing her into a crouched position as he had before, her hands were behind her, where they weren't much use. And she was so terribly weak....

Fighting the effects of whatever drug he'd given her, she managed to wriggle into an upright position. The blankets on top of her felt like a thousand pounds of wet sand, weighing her down, burying her. They were so heavy she almost couldn't move. But she had no choice. If she didn't take action now, she might not get out alive.

She used her head to push the bedding from side to side until she could feel the cold air of the cabin on her skin. Then she took a few seconds to suck fresh air into her lungs, trying to clear her mind and bolster her strength.

The collar and gag made it difficult to breathe, and she had to mentally override a constant sense of panic. But the sudden chill after the heat of her own breath against the blankets helped.

Freedom. She had a chance. If she hurried. But it was so dark she couldn't see anything. Even after she slid open the warped closet door with her shoulder, she couldn't distinguish even the general shape of the furniture.

She'd have to be very careful to keep her bearings. This far from the lights of the city, the night was far blacker than any she'd ever known. She needed to make her way as unerringly as possible straight to the front door. Then, maybe she could find a neighboring cabin or a road where someone might drive by and see her. She wouldn't last long out in the cold, but she preferred to take her chances there rather than face what awaited her here.

Fortunately, she recalled the basic layout of the cabin. She thought about trying to stand, but knew she'd never be able to remain upright. Ray had tied the ropes so tightly she could no longer feel her feet. They were so numb and swollen that, had they not started hurting again, they wouldn't have felt like part of her body anymore.

Come on. She couldn't get up and she couldn't crawl. Her only option was to use her head, shoulder and left hip to scoot across the floor. But she didn't make it far before she banged into the closed door of the bedroom.

With a silent groan, she rested her head on the floor and concentrated on breathing. The exertion made it that much more difficult. And now this. Why couldn't the sheriff's men have left the door open?

Don't cry. Don't get upset. She needed her energy, and her air, for more constructive endeavors. Maybe the police hadn't even come. Maybe it had all been a dream. She'd originally thought she'd been entombed with her father, hadn't she? There were so many echoes in her head right now she couldn't decide what she'd heard and what she hadn't. But, either way, the door was closed—that was real enough—and she didn't know how to open it.

The only way was to get to her feet and to stay there long enough, with her back to the door, and use those thick, unwieldy things currently tied behind her back. Those things she'd once called hands...

Taking as much of a breath as her gag and collar would allow, she slid up the wall. The pain in her feet made her head swim. She fell twice. But, determined, she eventually succeeded in standing.

"I did it," she breathed, but it came out as a low, guttural moan. She couldn't form words with that gag in her mouth. She'd managed the first step toward escape. That was good. She had to think in terms of small victories, couldn't consider the whole situation at once, or she'd give up before she got anywhere.

Now for Step Two. She closed her eyes, trying to remind herself what it was. For a few seconds, she lost touch with reality, seemed to float through the air, to dip and twirl.

Think. Focus. She needed to open the door. That was it. But she had a problem. She was leaning against it and didn't want to fall again or she'd lose the progress she'd gained.

You won't fall. Not if you're careful. Slide over. Inch by inch. That's it.

She edged to the left until she could feel the doorjamb against the ridge of her spine. The handle was where she could reach it with her bound hands, but she knew she'd probably fall when she opened it. There wasn't enough room for her on the left side of the door because of some bureau she wasn't strong enough to move, and she couldn't slide back to the right or she'd be in the path of the door again. To get any momentum at all, she'd have to hop out away from the wall after she turned the knob—yet she still couldn't support her own weight. Even if her feet were free, she doubted she'd have the balance. The drug Ray had given her had left her nauseous and dizzy.

She had to try.

Be careful. You only have one chance, she told herself and turned the knob.

Now! Hopping forward, she tried to fling the door open with her wrist while she fell. The metal of the bed frame scratched her back as she crumpled to the floor, but she was pretty sure she'd managed to stayed out of the door's path. It didn't slam against the opposite wall but, judging by the ascending pitch of the noise, it drifted open.

A sudden creak terrified Madeline. Was Ray there, sleeping on the couch? If so, he would've heard all the bumping and scraping. And she couldn't think of anything more frightening than what would happen if he caught her trying to escape.

The house remained dark and quiet.

He's gone. I'm okay.

Okay had never seemed a more relative concept than when she scooted into the wooden hallway on her left. Moving like this was a painstaking process, but she couldn't risk hopping around the cabin in the dark. She needed to chart her way carefully, to do everything she could to keep her head clear. Too much hurry, too much panic, could get her hurt—or worse.

The kitchen seemed a mile away. Hoping there might be other people, possibly in a neighboring cabin or driving along a nearby road, Madeline strained to hear every noise. There was nothing but the wind, whipping under the eaves.

A little more. Not far now. You're doing fine. You can do it.

God, she couldn't even breathe. She had to pause every few seconds just to recover. But it was the only way she could keep going. Whatever he'd given her made her feel as if she weighed three times her normal weight, and she was so restricted that any movement required great effort and concentration.

Frustration threatened to immobilize her. But fear, the cold underlying fear of knowing her life depended on what she did in the next few minutes, kept her moving.

That's it. There you go.

The kitchen had linoleum on the floor. Madeline felt the difference in textures the moment she reached it and nearly cried in relief. She spent considerable time—too much time—feeling her way around, searching the drawers and cupboards for a knife or a pair of scissors. But the kitchen wasn't stocked. There were no implements at all.

Hot tears rolled down her cheeks as she sagged onto the floor and gasped for breath. If only she could move. If only she could *run*.

But she couldn't. She was completely helpless. And then she heard it. The sound of a car engine, coming toward the cabin.

Clay's cell phone rang just before he went out of range. He knew he wouldn't have reception much longer. They were entering the Great Smoky Mountains.

"Have you found her?" Allie asked as soon as he answered.

He'd tried to call her, had left a message when she didn't pick up. Grace must've filled her in. "Not yet."

"What do you think's going on?"

"I don't know." He wasn't a superstitious man, but acknowledging what he thought could be happening seemed to increase the chances that it actually was. And his heart rebelled at the images bombarding his mind—images like the ones he'd seen of Katie and Rose Lee in those pictures with Barker. Madeline was his sister just as much as Grace or Molly. When he learned what Barker had been doing to Grace, he'd promised himself it'd never happen again, that he'd protect them all.

Yet here he was….

"You'll get there in time," she said. But he knew that probably wasn't true. No drive had ever seemed so long.

"Have you heard anything from Pontiff?" he asked hopefully. "Did the Sevier County Sheriff's Department get back to him?"

"Haven't you called the sheriff yourself?" she asked.

"Hunter's tried to, more than once. They won't put us through to him, won't tell us anything. They say it's a police matter. That they're looking into it. No one on the Stillwater force will tell us anything, either."

"Why not?" she asked indignantly.

"Pontiff's angry that we searched Ray's cabin illegally."

"You didn't have time to get a warrant! You did him a favor!"

"He feels we've overstepped our bounds, that we're trying to do his job."

"How can he care about his precious ego at a time like this?" she cried.

"He's not about to let Hunter take charge."

"I'll bet Elaine knows what's going on. I'll check with her and get back to you," she said. But when she called again, Clay's cell phone coverage was so spotty her voice cut in and out.

"What did you learn?" he asked.

"Two—ties...the c—"

He eased off the gas, hoping he wouldn't lose her. *"What?"*

"I said, two deputies vis—ted the cab—"

That he could decipher. "And?"

"It was empty. Some—thinks—sp—"

"Say that again."

"Some guy thinks he spotted Ray's truck going south toward Tupelo, and Pontiff's all over it."

To Iuka perhaps? *Shit!* They were heading in the wrong direction. No wonder Pontiff was playing it so smug.

Slamming on the brakes, Clay skidded to a halt on the side of the road. "Allie?"

She was gone.

"What is it?" Hunter asked. "Why are we turning around?"

Clay cursed again. "Madeline's not at the cabins."

When the headlights of Ray's truck swung over the extra set of tire tracks in the snow, his heart began to thud. Someone had been at the cabin. Not only were there tire tracks, there were footprints everywhere.

For a moment, he was tempted to run. To get the hell out while he still could. But the cabin was dark. Whoever had come by wasn't there now. If he was busted, the police would've already cut him off, pulled their guns, *something*.

Leaving the engine running, he waited for several minutes, trying to determine whether or not it was safe to get out. When nothing happened, nothing stirred, he took the flashlight and the knife he kept in his truck and approached the front door. There were other cabins in the area, but they were miles away. It wasn't as if someone would've come here by mistake, was it?

No. His flashlight had just passed over something small and white. A business card. Wedged in the door.

Taking it, Ray held it in the light so he could read. It belonged to a Mr. Brian Shulman, an employee of the property management company from which he'd rented the cabin. Turning it over, he saw a brief note.

Enjoy your stay and don't forget to put the key in the lock box when you go.

Had this Mr. Shulman gone inside?

Probably not. Why would he?

Still, panic poured through Ray at the possibilities. Unlocking the front door, he went straight to Madeline's room.

The door that he'd closed when he left was now standing open. So was the closet.

His gut tightened as he set his flashlight on the bed and dug through the blankets. She was gone.

Whirling, he checked the rest of the room and under the bed. Nothing. The place was empty. Where was she? Had someone taken her? No. That didn't make sense. Mr. Shulman wouldn't have bothered to leave his card if he'd found Madeline.

She must've gotten away by herself. How the hell had she done it?

Regardless, he couldn't lose her. She was his. A replacement for his own daughter. It was Barker's fault that Rose Lee had tried to pass that note to Eliza. Nothing would've happened if Barker hadn't insisted on having Ray bring Rose to church every Sunday. Then she wouldn't have passed that note and Ray wouldn't have had to punish her with his belt. And she might not have overdosed afterward.

"Madeline?" he called softly.

There was no response. But she couldn't have gotten far. He saw no rope piled on the ground, no gag. And he'd drugged her. Chances were she was stumbling around in the snow, staggering through the trees, maybe even going in circles.

But the dead bolt on the front door had been set when he arrived. How could she have gotten out?

A muted noise drew him across the hall. He hurried, anxious but relieved, thinking he'd found her. But it was only the soft clank of the blind stirred by the wind. The wind? The window was open, and there was a chair underneath it.

She'd managed to get outside. *Shit!* A white-hot rage built inside him. He'd find her. He'd find her before anyone else could.

And God help her when he did.

Madeline could hardly hear above the racket her heart was making as she listened to Ray move around the cabin. He'd gone to the room where he'd left her, as she'd expected. Then he'd crossed the hall to the window she'd opened by biting the latch with her teeth and using her chin. If she was lucky, he'd rush outside, and start looking for her in the forest—because she didn't have much of a chance if he started searching the cabin. She was only three feet from him when he came back into the hall, hiding behind the door of the third and last bedroom. She hadn't had time to think of—or get to—a better place. It had been all she could do to open that damn window.

"She'll pay for this," he muttered. Then he went out the front door, and turned off the truck's engine.

She'd hoped he would be in too much of a hurry to think about his truck. If he'd gone directly to the back, she might've been able to slip out the front and drive away, even with her hands and feet still tied. The sound of his engine had given her hope and helped cover her movements. She'd opened a window, so she could move a gear lever and manage a steering wheel well enough to drive a mile or two, someplace she could find help. That was why she'd opened the window in the back room—to draw him away from the road.

But he was too smart, too cautious. For all she knew, he was standing on the porch waiting for her to come out the front door. What if there was snow on the ground? If it remained undisturbed beneath the window where she would've had to land, he'd know it was a trick.

She'll pay for this....

Was he waiting for her to make a move? To reveal herself?

God help me. She was shaking so badly she was afraid she'd collapse. She wasn't sure what was keeping her upright. Her feet didn't want to support her weight, but the wall helped, and she knew collapsing was not an option. If her strength gave out on her, she'd be dead—or maybe she'd just wish she was.

A rustle outside the cabin made her wonder if he'd gone around to the back, after all. She had no idea what he'd find—something that would keep him there, or something that would bring him back here—but she had to go now. She might never have another chance.

Sliding to the ground, she dragged herself down the hall and into the kitchen. At least she was more alert. At least the effects of the drug had mostly worn off. Full awareness brought her aches, pains and bruises to life, but it gave her hope that she could somehow outsmart him.

When she reached the front door, she didn't have to open it. He'd left it agape. She could see the gleam of his bumper but not much else.

"Madeline, you'll freeze to death out here. You know that, don't you? Tell me where you are and I'll help you back to the house."

His voice came from the forest, sounding deceptively normal. Like the Ray she'd known her whole life. But he wasn't the man she thought he was. He was evil—a creature with no soul, no concern for anyone but himself.

She just had to make it out the front door and over to someplace safe to hide, she told herself. But her coat wasn't very heavy—she didn't know how long she'd last on such a cold night. And where was safe? Ray seemed to be the only other person on the mountain. He certainly wasn't worried about being overheard.

Anyplace was preferable to being trapped in the cabin. But when she got to the porch, she saw a glimmer of moonlight shifting through the tall trees overhead and glistening off—her heart sank—*snow.* There were footsteps going every which way, but if she tried to drag herself through it, she'd be frozen before she got ten yards, and Ray would easily be able to follow her odd-looking trail.

"You'd better tell me where you are." He was shouting, his voice ricocheting through the trees. "If you don't, you'll be sorry. I can promise you that."

Using her shoulder and hip, she moved toward the steps. Shoulder, hip. Shoulder, hip. She knew that trying to cross the small clearing was insane, suicide, but she couldn't stay in the cabin. She'd rather die outside.

Then she bumped into it. The woodpile. And standing right beside it was an ax.

"Maddy, you're being stubborn for nothing," Ray said. "Where you gonna go? There's no one else around, not for miles. And it's less than thirty degrees out here. I think it's about to storm."

The wind blew snow from the branches of the trees, showering him occasionally, but the darkness bothered him most. He could see only what fell inside the narrow beam of his flashlight, which made him feel as if she was constantly evading him. He'd found one pair of footprints near the open window. He'd assumed they were hers, but they hadn't gone more than ten feet into the forest.

She would've set off, tried to put as much distance between them as possible. So which tracks were hers? And how had she gotten loose? He'd knotted those ropes damn tight.

He wouldn't underestimate her again. He'd chain her up, give her a bucket for a toilet and never let her go. But that would have to happen somewhere else. Once he found her, he was hitting the road again. They couldn't stay here. Not with that Brian Shulman snooping around.

"Maddy?" he called.

And then he paused, fairly certain he'd heard a thud in front of the cabin.

The wind had blown the door shut. The resulting bang had nearly made her cry out. Panting from fear and exertion, Madeline was trying to saw the rope off her hands by pressing it against the blade of the ax. But she was too jittery, too panicked. Ray had stopped calling out to her, and the silence was far more unnerving than hearing his voice, because now she couldn't trace him.

She wanted to hide, to hole up and pray for the best. But she knew that was foolish. He'd find her, and it would all be over. Weak, exhausted and frightened though she was, she had to use her mind and her nerve, push herself to the limits.

Keep going. She rubbed harder against the blade— back and forth, back and forth—but cutting through the rope wasn't as easy as she'd expected when she first saw the ax. The tough, scratchy fibers bit deeply into her wrists, and the blade seemed far too dull.

The adrenaline pumping through her, and the cold, were the only things in her favor. They took the edge off her pain and kept her focused, so the fuzziness in her brain didn't cloud her abilities or judgment. She had to get free, regardless of the cost. Otherwise, she had no chance.

I can do it. I can do it. She struggled to swallow with the gag in her mouth, but her throat was so dry, even that hurt. And that damn collar…

I'll get free. She wouldn't let Ray win. She'd fight back. Because he wasn't her master. Fear wasn't her master, either.

But where is he? And what's he doing?

As if in answer, she heard movement. Then the beam of a flashlight suddenly appeared.

He was here. And she wasn't ready.

25

Ray's light swept within inches of Madeline's foot. She was sure he'd seen her, but she held perfectly still. She opened her eyes as wide as she could and yet she couldn't even make out his shape. It was too dark. There was only that beam from his flashlight. And his footsteps, creaking on the wooden porch, coming closer.

Closing her eyes, she instinctively turned her face away in preparation for the worst. But his light didn't land on her. He opened the door, hesitated at the threshold, then went inside.

She had a few more seconds.

Drawing on her last reserves of strength, Madeline continued to saw at the ropes around her wrists. She might as well be trying to chew them with her teeth, for all the good that dull blade seemed to do her. But then she felt a slight give. Or was it her imagination?

Ray was still inside. She had no idea what he was doing, but she could hear him moving around and knew she didn't have much time. She worked more frantically, pulling and twisting her hands until her wrists throbbed so badly she nearly passed out from the pain. But her efforts finally paid off. Somehow she'd managed to cut the rope enough that she could, with much pain, slip one hand out. Then she merely had to shake her other hand, and she was free. Pulling the gag down, she hurried to untie her feet.

Unfortunately, the cold was no longer her ally. She was trembling violently. And her fingers were so swollen and stiff she could hardly use them. She fumbled with the knot but couldn't untie it.

Should she try to slide away from the cabin door? Around to the side, where she wouldn't feel quite so vulnerable? She longed to—but didn't dare. She was afraid the noise of her movements would draw Ray back. She was better off staying where she was and getting out of the ropes so she could sneak away more quietly. At least if he caught her at that point, she'd be able to run, kick, fight. And she'd have the ax.

A creak alerted her to the fact that Ray was at the threshold. But he wasn't using his flashlight, and he seemed to be moving stealthily. Why? Was he about to spring at her? Or did he feel that the light made his whereabouts too obvious?

Either way, his lack of light worked in her favor. Now he couldn't see anything, either. She just had to be careful not to stumble into him once she was capable of running.

She thought she heard him move again, but she couldn't tell in which direction. He was close, she knew that. He was probably standing two feet from her, listening, waiting.

After stretching her sore hands, she worked at the knot some more.

Calm down. Ignore him. Make no sound but feel the rope. Start in the right place. That's it.

Another creak sent chills down her spine. Judging

by the proximity of that noise, she could reach out and touch him. He even knocked a piece of wood off the pile above her—most likely a mistake on his part—but it nearly hit her as it tumbled to the ground.

She covered her head with her arms and remained exactly where she was. She wanted to take the ax that was behind her and swing it at him. But she had so little strength. She wasn't sure she'd be able to strike much of a blow. He'd wrest it away far too easily. And her feet were still tied.

She'd be stupid to act so soon. She could blow her only opportunity.

Patience. Swallowing hard, she opened and closed her burning hands, hoping to get the blood flowing again, and persevered with the knot. She couldn't wiggle her feet back and forth to help loosen the bands, couldn't risk any noise, which made her task harder. Ray seemed to sense that she was there. He hovered on the porch, within a few feet of her.

The tension in the ropes around her feet began to ease. Madeline was almost free. She'd slip carefully away, figure out how to find civilization and pray she didn't freeze to death first. But she must've made some sound as she started to rise because Ray's flashlight suddenly snapped on, so bright it temporarily blinded her.

She screamed as he lunged at her, then fell back, scraping herself on the wood. "No!" Her voice was unrecognizable to her own ears, but she had the presence of mind to bring her legs up and kick him as hard as she could. She knew she'd hit him in a good spot when he dropped the flashlight and sank to his knees.

Scrambling, Madeline tried to run, but she couldn't

feel her feet. She fell and whacked her knee on the porch, got up and fell again.

"I'll kill you for this," he rasped.

She'd never heard such deadly intent. Grabbing the flashlight that had now rolled closer to her than him, and the ax, she hobbled around the house—and somehow managed to keep her balance.

She could hear him trying to limp after her, still wheezing and cursing from the pain, and turned off the flashlight. He'd have to track her by sound. She wasn't going to give him a beacon to follow.

The forest stood dark and silent all around her. It was too dark to move very fast. She could turn her ankle or fall into a creek or gully. Forced to slow, she glanced behind her but couldn't see or hear anything. She longed to put some space between them, then hide and wait for morning. But she knew that wasn't a reasonable plan. Morning could be hours away—she was disoriented in her perception of time—and it was far too cold to stay outside. She didn't have boots or warm clothes, wouldn't survive even three hours. And because she didn't know the area, she had no idea which direction to take. She ran the risk of returning to the cabin without even knowing it, wandering around indefinitely, or falling off a cliff.

No, she couldn't hope to avoid Ray until she found help. She had to get inside, get warm, acquire some kind of transportation. He stood between her and all of that. Which meant her best option was to do something about it—and the sooner the better. The longer she waited, the weaker and colder she was going to get.

I can't go back into the cabin. After the pills she'd ingested, she still wasn't herself. She was so tired she could barely lift the ax. She was tempted to give up, to sit down and cry. None of this was fair; she'd done nothing to deserve it.

But if she wanted to live, she had to get him before he got her.

Ray leaned against the cabin until he was sufficiently recovered, wondering what he should do now. He couldn't go after her. He had another flashlight in his glove box, but if he used it, she'd know where he was at all times. If he didn't use it, there was no telling what he might walk into. He could chase her around the forest all night, but that would be stupid.

He had to lure her back to the cabin. And the only way he knew to do that was to make her believe he was giving up.

Climbing into his truck, he started the engine, backed up and headed toward the road. When he'd gone about a hundred yards, he parked, more enraged than ever. She had to come out of hiding eventually; she'd freeze to death if she didn't.

When Madeline heard Ray's truck, she couldn't believe it. He was leaving? Had she injured him more badly than she'd thought? She doubted it. Maybe she'd gotten lucky enough to hit him where it hurt, but she lacked the strength to do much damage.

Was he afraid she'd find help and bring the authorities down on him? That wasn't likely, either—or not in the immediate future, anyway. He knew she didn't have a clue about where she was. He'd brought her bound and gagged beneath a tarp. A person didn't get much more disoriented than that.

So what? She wasn't sure what he was doing. But she needed warmth and shelter and knew of only one place to get it. That meant he'd find her if he returned.

She needed a plan. And she needed it fast.

Dragging the ax behind her, she hurried for the cabin.

Ray waited long enough that he felt safe using the flashlight to make his way back, but he didn't need it once he started down the narrow, winding drive. Even from twenty yards, he could see that Madeline had a fire going. The flicker in the front window looked like a beacon, an invitation welcoming him home. She'd gone back inside and was hoping to get warm, poor thing.

He smiled grimly. He'd show her warm. He'd put her hand in the fire and hold it there until it was reduced to ashes. She'd probably pass out, but it'd be a nice reminder of who was boss when she woke up.

He couldn't imagine she'd fight him after that.

Stepping very quietly onto the porch, he peered through the window. Sure enough, she was sleeping in front of the fire. He could see her all bundled up in the blankets he'd used to bury her in the closet.

This would be easy.

He put his hand on the door. It was locked. But that just made him smile even wider. Because he had the key.

Madeline was finally warm. And the feeling had come back to her hands and feet, although they were still swollen. She wasn't sure how much time had passed since Ray drove off, but she hadn't heard a sound since.

Now she was almost *too* comfortable. Exhaustion weighed so heavily upon her that she could hardly keep her eyes open. She'd been battling sleep for what seemed like an eternity.

Maybe Ray had really left. Maybe he wasn't coming back.

Hang on. Stay vigilant, she told herself. But she *had* to rest.

She checked the bundle she'd arranged by the fire to make sure it looked convincing and began to slouch against the wall. But then she heard a slight creak and the doorknob near her head turned very slowly, very quietly.

Suddenly alert, she pulled her legs into her body and huddled closer to the wall. Her skin crawled as she sensed Ray peeking in the window on the other side of the door. Holding her breath, she hoped he saw her decoy—and the collar she'd tossed to the side of it. The position of that collar was her message to him. She would never allow him to control her. She'd fight and win, or she'd die trying.

Would he be fooled by the scene she'd set up? She had no idea—but guessed he was when she heard him insert the key in the lock.

The moment of truth had come. Licking her dry, cracked lips, she slid very slowly up the wall until she was standing at her full height. Then she lifted the ax over her head.

He cracked open the door and carefully pushed it inward, toward her. She could smell Ray. The scent of his clothes, his body, made nausea roil in her stomach. Briefly, she closed her eyes and offered a prayer for strength. But he wasn't coming in as decisively as she'd expected.

Move, you son of a bitch! Her plan depended on it. *I'm right in front of the fire. See that? Go for what you want....*

The door separated them. She couldn't attack him until he cleared it. But he was being so cautious!

Bending silently, she pulled the fishing line she'd found on the mantle and tied to the bottom blanket of her make-believe person. She knew he'd seen it move when she heard the quick intake of his breath. Finally, he came in, quickly and with purpose, and the other fishing line she'd strung caught him across the ankles.

He fought falling—didn't immediately topple over as she'd pictured in her mind. But her little trap sent him off balance enough that she was able to step out from behind the door and swing the ax before he even knew she was there.

He cried out when the blade slashed into what she thought was his shoulder and jerked back so hard it yanked the handle right out of her hands. Her hesitancy to actually strike someone with a weapon like that had made her weak. She felt him swipe at her in the next instant and cut her with something—a knife? It had to be. The cut wasn't deep, and was only on her forearm, but it stung and bled and the violence curdled her blood.

She wanted it to be over. But her blow didn't incapacitate him. He was screaming and cursing and stumbling around, trying to pull the ax out of his shoulder with one hand while clutching at her with the other.

When she managed to avoid his grasp, he fell to one knee and worked the ax free. She guessed he was bleeding pretty badly, but she couldn't see much in the shadowy room and was glad to be spared the visual results of her actions. He raised the ax as if he'd strike her with it, but she grabbed it at the same time. She couldn't let him have the weapon.

They wrestled for it, each grabbing and pulling, groaning and cursing. His injury was much worse than hers, however, and she could feel him losing strength and balance, fading, slowing like a wind-up toy running out of torque. He was probably losing a lot of blood. She couldn't believe he was still alive.

Eventually, she wrenched the ax away from him. When she did, he glared up at her with eyes that seemed to glow with hatred.

"You won't win," she said. "I'll destroy you, if I have to."

He gave an odd, bitter laugh. "You can't destroy me. Your father already did that."

"What did my father ever do to you?"

When he spoke, his voice was emotionless. "He made me crave my own daughter."

"No!" she said, recoiling. "He would never do that."

"He did, and more. Just ask Grace. If I know your father, he raped her. Over and over."

Madeline was shaking again. Ray was trying to gain the upper hand any way he could—wasn't he? She'd decided he was the one who'd owned that suitcase in the Cadillac. He was the one who'd confessed to her father. Her father was going to turn him in, but—

Suddenly, Grace's chalk-white face when she saw her panties on that table in the police station appeared in Madeline's mind. Grace claimed she'd never been molested. But she wouldn't have kept quiet for Ray.

She would only lie to protect her family.

Hunter had been right all along. Her father, the beloved pastor of the Purity Church of Christ, had been a pedophile, the worst of sinners. And the Montgomerys had killed him.

Ray had fallen to the floor and was clutching his shoulder, moaning.

"Who was he, really?" she asked in bewilderment.

She didn't expect an answer. He was in too much agony. But he managed one, anyway. "The most selfish man...I've ever known." He cursed, then sucked in a deep, audible breath. "He...liked 'em young. 'Bout twelve or so. But...Katie and Rose Lee were just playthings. Grace...he loved."

Madeline winced at the memory of the words her father had written in the margins of his Bible. He'd praised Grace's beauty and innocence and talked about how much he loved her. Under the circumstances, Madeline couldn't help interpreting those words differently than she ever had before. Sickened, she covered her face. She didn't want to hear any more. "Give me your keys."

He didn't respond.

"Give me your keys! I'll go for help."

The sound he emitted was part groan and part laugh. "I don't want...the kind of help you'll be bringing."

"Then you're going to die," she told him.

"That'd be...better than...prison."

She dropped the ax and pressed a hand to her own injury to stanch the bleeding. "I still need those keys."

She thought she saw the whites of his teeth as he grinned at her. "Fine. They're in...my front pocket. Feel free...to reach down there...and fish around."

She'd wait until he passed out, tie him up and then take the keys, she decided. But she didn't have to wait. The sound of a car engine drew her to the front window, where she saw headlights coming through the trees.

Standing in the open doorway, she watched dispassionately as Clay's truck came to a stop. It was over. She'd survived.

But the whole world had changed. Ray was not the upstanding citizen she'd always thought. Her father hadn't been a man of God. He hadn't been worthy of her love or respect. Her stepmother and stepsiblings weren't innocent. And she was in love with a man she'd met just a few days earlier, a man who probably wasn't ready to love her back.

She glanced behind her at the bleeding Ray. She'd done that to him, although she'd never dreamed she'd be capable of such a thing.

Even she was different now than she'd been a week ago.

"Thank God I listened to you," Clay murmured to Hunter.

Clay hung back a few steps as the investigator approached the cabin. He didn't know how Madeline would greet him, was afraid to learn what had happened before they'd been able to find her.

Madeline didn't move forward, didn't rush into his arms as Clay wished she would. Her eyes flicked toward Hunter and, for a moment, she looked as if she might crumple. But she didn't. Clay saw her stiffen and squint against the harsh glare of the headlights as she turned her attention to him.

"Madeline?" Hunter said hesitantly, gently.

"He got the worst of it." She stood there unmoving, her hair tangled and matted. Mascara ran down her face in tracks that showed the path of earlier tears, one eye was swollen, both corners of her mouth were cut, and she had an injury on one arm. She looked like she'd been through hell. And there was blood everywhere, on her clothes and arms, on the floor.

Hunter shook his head. "I knew he'd visited that site for a reason."

But if they hadn't—at Hunter's insistence—pulled off the road to use a pay phone and spoken to Brian Shulman, they never would've found it.

Hunter touched her elbow. "Where is he?"

"Inside," she said, staring directly at Clay.

Clay cleared his throat, overwhelmed by the relief he felt for her, as well as all the other emotions welling up inside him. "So you're okay?" he asked, bracing for the rejection he expected.

Tears filled her eyes and spilled down her cheeks, making fresh lines through the smudged mascara.

"Tell me you're okay," he murmured.

"Where'd you put his body?" she asked point-blank.

She was talking about her father, of course, not Ray. The moment Clay had long been expecting had finally arrived.

He glanced at Hunter, hoping for a few minutes of privacy, but he didn't have to spell that out. Hunter was already slipping past her to find Ray. A second later, Clay could hear them talking, but what he cared about was happening right here, so he didn't bother listening.

"Are you going to tell me?" she asked.

Clay had never trusted another soul with the truth

about that terrible night. Except Allie. But the truth was all he had to offer now. "Behind the barn."

She bit down on her knuckles. Clay wanted to pull her to him, to help her bear the pain and disappointment, the same way they'd dealt with other problems since they'd become family. But this time he was the source of that pain and disappointment.

"The police searched the entire yard."

"I'd already moved him."

He was grateful she didn't ask where. He knew it would be too upsetting to her. "Why'd you do it? Why not go to the police?"

"It wasn't something we planned, Maddy."

"Tell me what happened."

"It was an accident." After all the lies, he wasn't sure if she'd believe him, so he tried to explain. He couldn't shelter her from the truth, not anymore. "Mom caught him with Grace, doing—you know what he was doing, right?"

More tears filled her eyes, but she blinked them back and lifted her chin. "I know what he was doing."

Clay nodded and continued. "When she said she was going to turn him in, he got mad and started hitting her." Clay thought Madeline might argue or insist her father would never strike a woman, but she didn't.

"So you got involved," she said dully.

"Yes." The memories were still so fresh it felt like only yesterday that he was digging the grave, mopping up the blood, lying to the police. "And when he turned on me, and the violence got out of hand, Mom panicked and hit him over the head with the butcher block."

"That's it?"

He hated the agony he saw on her face but couldn't

do anything about it. "That's it. She didn't mean to kill him. Only to get him off me."

Her voice fell to a tortured whisper. "But if it was an accident, why didn't you call the police, Clay? Why would you hide something like that?"

"Do you think we should've called them up and told them their town's esteemed preacher was a pedophile, Maddy? That we got into a fight over it and accidentally killed him? Who would've believed us?"

She covered her face with her hands, but now that he'd begun, he had to tell her the whole truth.

"There was proof. He'd taken—" he struggled to break the news as gently as possible "—pictures of Grace. She told us about them afterward, and we found them in his office. But we couldn't take them to the police. They would've used them to establish a clear and powerful motive. Almost everyone in Stillwater was pressing the cops to put Mom or me in prison. And if that happened, you and Grace and Molly would've been taken into foster care. Our family would've been destroyed."

She dropped her hands. "But you lied to me. You've lied to me all these years. *Everyone* knew but me."

"We didn't want you to *have* to know."

Hunter had wrapped a blanket around Ray and was helping him to the door. "As worthless as this piece of shit is, we've got to get him to a hospital before he bleeds to death," he said. "There's no phone service here."

"You're going to do that by yourself?" Madeline asked anxiously.

"I'll tie him up. The way he's bleeding, I doubt he's

capable of giving me any trouble but I won't take any chances, okay?"

She hesitated, then stepped out of the way, her gaze trailing after the two of them. "It was me or him," she said softly.

Taking a deep breath, Clay reached out to her. "I understand."

Madeline stared at her stepbrother's outstretched palm. She felt so alone, so isolated. For two decades she'd been searching for what he and Irene, Grace and Molly had known all along.

But… *Me or him.* Her stepfamily had had to make a similar choice, hadn't they?

"I heard you…Clay," Ray taunted as he limped past. "You're going to…prison with me. She's…going to send us both…there."

Madeline drew herself up. "What are you talking about, Ray? I didn't hear Clay admit anything. Did you, Hunter?"

"Nope, not me," Hunter said. Then Madeline slipped her hand inside her stepbrother's and fell into his arms.

"I'm sorry," he murmured, his voice choked with emotion.

She closed her eyes, reveling in the inherent strength of the man who'd stood between her and what could've happened had their family been torn apart. As hard as it must have been, he'd built and guarded the fortress that had protected them all, been there for her in every way he could. Despite what her father had done and the terrible secret he carried because of it, Clay had provided her with food, shelter and love. And he'd started doing that at only sixteen years old.

"I love you," she whispered.

"Ray and I will take his truck," Hunter called, using the ropes that had bound her to bind him. "You guys come when you're ready."

Madeline pulled back, laughing a little as she dashed a hand across her wet cheeks. "Unfortunately, I love him, too," she said, speaking in a low voice so Hunter couldn't hear her as he wrangled the keys out of Ray.

Clay retained his grip on her for a second longer. "You're serious? You know that already?"

She nodded.

"He's a good man," he said thoughtfully. "One of the few who might be good enough for you."

Hunter had a new picture on his phone. Every time he used it, he saw Madeline smiling back at him. It'd been three weeks since he'd left Mississippi, but he kept opening that phone and remembering.

He'd called her once, just to make sure she was okay. She sounded as if she was recovering, adjusting as well as could be expected after her whole world had shifted off-kilter. But the conversation had been strained, with both of them wanting to say more than they did. Hunter didn't see the point of trying to maintain a long-distance relationship, so he hadn't called her again. And yet... she was present in his thoughts all the time. When he closed his eyes, he could still feel the soft skin of her neck against his lips as he'd felt it that night in her bed....

"I ran into Selena the other day," Antoinette said, joining him at the restaurant table where he'd been waiting for her to get a coffee drink.

He put his phone away. His ex-wife had had another collagen treatment. One side was slightly more swollen than the other, but she'd lined her lips perfectly with a deep-pink pencil and filled them in with shiny gloss. With her long blond hair falling in wisps around her face, and that low-cut, tight-fitting white sweater, she reminded him of Pamela Anderson.

That was probably intentional. If he knew her, she'd brought Pamela's picture to her plastic surgeon.

Hunter could tell the other men in the coffee shop were impressed. It was hard not to stare at a woman who had breasts that big. But to Hunter, Antoinette didn't look pretty—she looked plastic. A walking, talking Barbie doll. Maybe that was just because he knew what she was like under all the makeup and the trendy clothes. Anyway, she was nothing like the real, earthy woman he'd made love to in Mississippi.

"Hello?" she said, clearly annoyed when he didn't respond.

She'd mentioned Selena already. She brought up their old neighbor whenever she wanted to remind him of his shortcomings, generally right before she demanded a large concession. But it wasn't going to work today. Mississippi had changed him. He wasn't sure what had made the difference, but he was tired of apologizing for the past.

"What'd she have to say?" he asked indifferently.

"She asked about you, of course."

"What'd you tell her?"

"That you're the same cheating son of a bitch you always were."

Hunter stretched his legs out in front of him. "I cheated—once—because I was miserably unhappy."

She straightened, obviously surprised by his frankness. He'd always accepted the blame before, so this was something new. "Do you think being married to you was a picnic for me?" she retaliated.

He shrugged. "At least you wanted to be with me. I never wanted to be with you."

Her eyelashes fluttered as she blinked. "You should've thought of that before you got me pregnant!"

"*Got* you pregnant? You *wanted* to get pregnant," he said. "As far as I'm concerned, we were both at fault."

"Are you accusing me of trying to trap you?"

When her voice rose, a few people turned to stare. Hunter ignored them. "Yes."

"That's a lie!"

"Is it?" He cocked a disbelieving eyebrow, but he wasn't willing to argue about it. Antoinette would deny it to her dying day. "Regardless, it's over, Antoinette. All the extra money. All the fighting. All the games."

Her mouth sagged open. "I don't know what you mean."

"Yes, you do. You've turned me into my own worst enemy. But I'm clean and sober now, and I'm going to stay that way. I'm also going to move on with my life. No more regret for failing at a marriage I didn't want in the first place. I can't change the past."

"That's how you're going to excuse your behavior?"

"I'm not excusing anything. If this was easy for me, I would've done it a long time ago."

Appearing quite stunned, she set her drink down. "But—but what about your daughter? Are you walking away from her, too?"

"I'll never walk away from her. I'll stay in touch, be

patient and hope she eventually changes her mind about me."

"She'll never change her mind about you. Not if I can help it!"

It was a final jab, an attempt to drag him back onto the old, familiar battlefield, where she could continue to manipulate him through his love for Maria. "She's a smart girl," he said. "I trust that someday she'll figure it all out."

He took the check he'd written for next month's child support from his shirt pocket and slid it across the metal table. "Here you go," he said. Then he got up and started to leave.

"Wait!" she called.

He turned back to see her wearing an expression of panic. "What's different? Have you met someone else?"

He thought about Madeline and smiled. "Yeah, I guess I have."

Madeline sat at her computer, trying to write the most difficult article of her life. Ray had required several pints of blood and hundreds of stitches, but he was already out of the hospital and in jail. His trial hadn't started yet, but with her testimony and his confession, he'd be going to prison for pedophilia, kidnapping and attempted rape, buying and selling child pornography, incest and possibly the murder of Bubba Turk. Thanks to Hunter's insistence, they'd sent Bubba's body for an autopsy, and petechial hemorrhaging indicated that he'd been smothered. Judging by the time of death, Pontiff was now theorizing that Bubba had somehow caught Ray doing something he shouldn't, so Ray had made sure he'd never be able to tell.

Sounded logical, but no one really knew. Ray wouldn't say what had happened to Bubba. But he was more than willing to talk about anything else. He told everyone who came within ten yards of him the gruesome details of what her father had done to Katie and Rose Lee. That he and Barker had raped and tortured them both and they'd done it together. He'd laugh when others cringed and get increasingly more explicit, gaining some grotesque satisfaction from their horror and revulsion. He claimed Grace must've received similar treatment—thank God he didn't really know. He even announced the details of what he'd planned to do to her at the cabin.

But that wasn't the worst of it. Just yesterday he'd told Toby Pontiff that her father had run Katie down when she tried to get away. And he'd suggested that her father had killed her mother and covered it up by making it look like suicide.

Madeline had been up most of the night thinking about that. She'd read through Eliza's journals with an open heart this time—seeking the essence of the mother she'd lost when she was so young—and had decided she believed Ray. Her mother wouldn't have left her willingly. That was the biggest lie Lee Barker had ever told. And the only positive thing knowledge of his true character had brought her.

So now she was like Clay and Grace and Molly, without a father she would acknowledge as her own. Lee Barker had nearly destroyed them all, and she felt obliged to write his story. The citizens of Stillwater, who'd always loved and supported him, deserved the same kind of resolution she'd sought for herself. The only part she'd leave out concerned Grace and the accident at the farm. Those who didn't already know who'd killed her father would simply be left to speculate.

"Where did it all start?" she wrote. "At what moment does a man who otherwise seems sane and good, who preaches about God and the Golden Rule, choose to indulge his own darkest desires? What turns an ordinary man into a monster? That I can't tell you. But I can tell you what it was like to live with such a person—"

The telephone interrupted her. Pausing in her work, Madeline reached across her desk to answer it. "Hello?"

"Maddy?"

It was Grace. Her stepsister had stayed in frequent touch since the ordeal at the cabin. What Madeline had suffered at Ray's hands had brought her and her stepsister, who'd always been a little aloof, closer together, maybe because they were both victims of the evil spawned by her father. "Yes?"

"I have a lead on a story." Her voice was warm, cheerful.

"Really?" Grace didn't usually call her with that kind of thing, so she knew this must be good. She grabbed a pad and pen to take notes. "What kind of story?"

"A love story, actually."

Madeline frowned in confusion. "What?"

"Haven't you heard?"

"Heard?"

"Hunter Solozano just moved to town. He bought the old Dunlap place."

"What?" She hadn't received a call from Hunter in over two weeks. She thought he'd put their brief affair behind him, forgotten her already. "That can't be true."

"My source is pretty reliable."

"Who told you?" she asked, her pulse beginning to race.

"He did. I ran into him at the Piggly Wiggly."

Madeline's mouth went instantly dry. "He was grocery shopping?"

"No, he was standing in the parking lot, frowning at the sign. When I approached, he said he couldn't believe he'd be shopping there from now on."

That sounded like him. Madeline couldn't help laughing. But why hadn't he called her? "He told you he moved here? That he's staying for good?"

"That's what he said. And he told me something else."

"What?"

"He came back because of you."

The bell jingled over the door. When Madeline turned to see who'd just come in, her heart skipped a few beats. Grace was right! Hunter was in town. He was standing in her office.

"I have to go," she said numbly. "I'll call you later, okay?" She wasn't sure if Grace answered or not, but she put the phone back in its cradle.

"Hey," Hunter said, offering her a sexy smile. "Got time for lunch?"

Epilogue

Six months later

"Where do you want this to go?"

Madeline stopped digging through the box in front of her and rocked back on her heels. "What's in it?" she asked her stepbrother.

Clay's expression indicated he wasn't impressed with the contents. "Mostly yarn. And some old knitting books."

When she hesitated, he cocked an eyebrow at her. "You don't knit, Maddy."

She laughed. "I know. Mom gave me that stuff when she moved away from the farm. I thought I might learn someday."

"Someday soon?"

"Well, no."

"Then I say get rid of it."

"Fine." She saw him go out to the front yard, where Allie, Irene, Grace and Kennedy were helping her hold a yard sale, but after he left, she expected the old panic to set in. She was finally purging, letting go, moving on. But...it didn't seem to bother her nearly as much as she'd thought it would. It was time, she decided. And maybe it was easier because she had the prospect of better things to come. She'd be replacing her old junk with objects related to her life with Hunter. He'd be moving in next week, after their wedding.

"You okay?"

At the sound of Hunter's voice, Madeline turned to see him standing in the doorway of the kitchen, speckled with green paint. "Fine." She gave him a reassuring smile. "Did you hear about the baby?"

"Are you kidding? That's all your big brother can talk about. I don't think he's going to be able to wait seven more months."

She stood up to see inside the kitchen. "How's the painting coming?"

"Great. When I'm finished with it, this is going to look like a new house."

"Maybe we should sell it."

"No. You like it here too much."

She did. She wanted to raise her children in Stillwater, where she'd be close to her family. After everything they'd been through—the realization of all they could've lost because of one man's twisted obsession—they were closer than ever, united in their loyalty to each other and happy at last. But she knew Hunter worried about his daughter and the fact that he was so far away from her.

"We could go to California for a few years," she suggested. "Until Maria turns eighteen."

"I may want to revisit that idea sometime in the future, but for now I think we're fine right here."

"You really don't mind?"

"No. Especially because—" he tried to wipe some of the paint from his hand onto his tattered jeans "—she's coming to visit us this summer."

"What?" Instantly losing interest in her sorting, Madeline jumped to her feet. "She called?"

He smiled in that crooked fashion she liked so much. "Yeah. Last night while you were out shopping with Grace."

She picked her way through the boxes to throw her arms around him. She knew she was probably smearing paint all over her clothes, but she didn't care. This was wonderful news! "Why didn't you tell me when I got home?"

Lowering his head, he kissed her neck before meeting her gaze. "It was one of those things where…you just want to mull it over for a while, you know? I've been trying not to get my hopes up too high, in case she changes her mind again."

"She won't change her mind this time," Madeline said, holding his face between her hands.

"How do you know?"

"Because she's figuring it out, Hunter. She's learning that you're not what her mother's told her you are, that she's crazy to shut you out of her life."

The screen door slammed as Clay came in for another trip to the basement. "Quit making out," he teased. "We've got work to do."

But Madeline didn't care who saw them. She kissed the man who'd be her husband in another week and waved Clay out the door when he brought up the next box—without even looking through it.

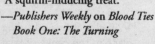

REQUEST YOUR FREE BOOKS!

2 FREE NOVELS FROM THE ROMANCE/SUSPENSE COLLECTION PLUS 2 FREE GIFTS!

YES! Please send me 2 FREE novels from the Romance/Suspense Collection and my 2 FREE gifts. After receiving them, if I don't wish to receive any more books, I can return the shipping statement marked "cancel." If I don't cancel, I will receive 4 brand-new novels every month and be billed just $5.49 per book in the U.S., or $5.99 per book in Canada, plus 25¢ shipping and handling per book plus applicable taxes, if any*. That's a savings of at least 20% off the cover price! I understand that accepting the 2 free books and gifts places me under no obligation to buy anything. I can always return a shipment and cancel at any time. Even if I never buy another book from the Reader Service, the two free books and gifts are mine to keep forever.

185 MDN EF5Y   385 MDN EF6C

Name	(PLEASE PRINT)

Address		Apt. #

City	State/Prov.	Zip/Postal Code

Signature (if under 18, a parent or guardian must sign)

Mail to The Reader Service:
IN U.S.A.: P.O. Box 1867, Buffalo, NY 14240-1867
IN CANADA: P.O. Box 609, Fort Erie, Ontario L2A 5X3

Not valid to current subscribers to the Romance Collection,
the Suspense Collection or the Romance/Suspense Collection.

Want to try two free books from another line?
Call 1-800-873-8635 or visit www.morefreebooks.com.

* Terms and prices subject to change without notice. NY residents add applicable sales tax. Canadian residents will be charged applicable provincial taxes and GST. This offer is limited to one order per household. All orders subject to approval. Credit or debit balances in a customer's account(s) may be offset by any other outstanding balance owed by or to the customer. Please allow 4 to 6 weeks for delivery.

BOB07

brenda novak

34279 DEAD GIVEAWAY	___ $6.99 U.S.	___ $8.50 CAN.
32328 DEAD SILENCE	___ $6.99 U.S.	___ $8.50 CAN.
77045 EVERY WAKING MOMENT	___ $6.99 U.S.	___ $8.50 CAN.

(limited quantities available)

TOTAL AMOUNT	$_____
POSTAGE & HANDLING	$_____
($1.00 FOR 1 BOOK, 50¢ for each additional)	
APPLICABLE TAXES*	$_____
TOTAL PAYABLE	$_____

(check or money order—please do not send cash)

To order, complete this form and send it, along with a check or money order for the total above, payable to MIRA Books, to: **In the U.S.:** 3010 Walden Avenue, P.O. Box 9077, Buffalo, NY 14269-9077; **In Canada:** P.O. Box 636, Fort Erie, Ontario, L2A 5X3.

Name: _____
Address: _____ City: _____
State/Prov.: _____ Zip/Postal Code: _____
Account Number (if applicable): _____

075 CSAS

*New York residents remit applicable sales taxes.
*Canadian residents remit applicable GST and provincial taxes.

MBN0807BL